*To the treehouse, for your shelter and for
keeping out all those pesky distractions*

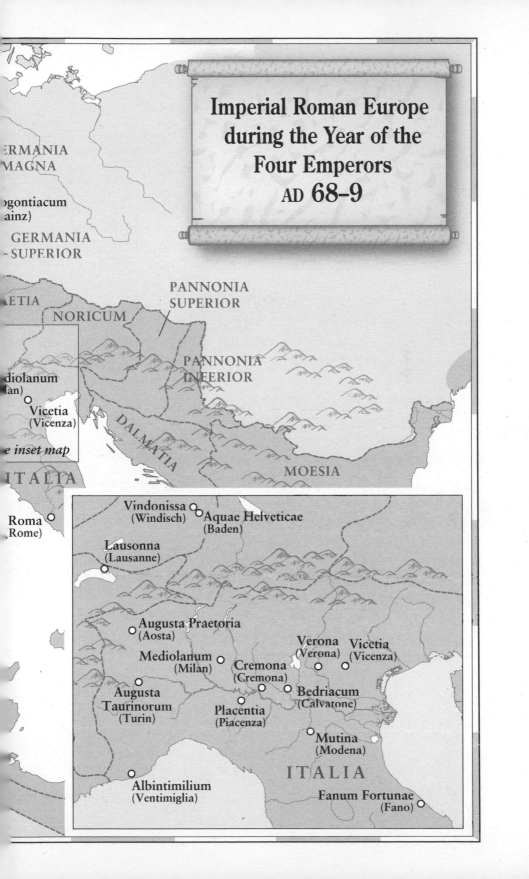

Imperial Roman Europe during the Year of the Four Emperors AD 68-9

GERMANIA
MAGNA

ogontiacum
ainz)

GERMANIA
SUPERIOR

ETIA

NORICUM

PANNONIA
SUPERIOR

PANNONIA
INFERIOR

diolanum
an)

Vicetia
(Vicenza)

DALMATIA

MOESIA

e inset map

ITALIA

Roma
Rome)

Vindonissa
(Windisch)

Aquae Helveticae
(Baden)

Lausonna
(Lausanne)

Augusta Praetoria
(Aosta)

Mediolanum
(Milan)

Cremona
(Cremona)

Verona
(Verona)

Vicetia
(Vicenza)

Bedriacum
(Calvatone)

Augusta
Taurinorum
(Turin)

Placentia
(Piacenza)

Mutina
(Modena)

ITALIA

Albintimilium
(Ventimiglia)

Fanum Fortunae
(Fano)

Dramatis Personae

Agricola, Gnaeus Julius★	Caecina Severus's oldest friend
Aulus	Caecina Severus's son
Alpinus, Julius★	Alpine rebel
Bassus, Lucilius★	Admiral of the fleet
Cerberus	Prefect of the Silian cavalry
Domitia★	Julius Agricola's wife
Galba, Servius Sulpicius★	Emperor of Rome
Galeria★	Vitellius's wife
Germanicus, Aulus Vitellius★	Governor of Lower Germania and Emperor of Rome
Laco, Cornelius★	Galba's praetorian prefect
Lugubrix	Grain merchant from Gaul
Martianus, Icelus★	Galba's freedman
Otho, Marcus Salvius★	Emperor of Rome
Pansa	Legate of the XXI Rapax
Paulinus, Suetonius★	Roman general, defeated Boudicca's rebellion
Primus, Antonius★	Legate of VII Galbiana in Pannonia
Rufus, Verginius ★	Previous governor of Lower Germania
Sabinus, Flavius★	Brother of Vespasian

9

Sabinus, Publilius★	Prefect of an auxiliary cohort
Salonina★	Caecina Severus's wife
Severus, Aulus Caecina★ (later Aulus Caecina Alienus)	Legate of the IV Macedonica and Vitellian general
Totavalas	Caecina Severus's Hibernian freedman
Tuscus, Gaius	Camp Prefect of IV Macedonica
Valens, Fabius★	Legate of the I Germanica and Vitellian general
Vespasian★	General charged with putting down the Jewish Revolt
Vindex, Julius★	Leader of the Vindex rebellion
Vindex, Quintus	Julius Vindex's son and Tribune of the IV Macedonica
Vinius, Titus★	Confidant of Galba
Vocula, Dillius★	Legate of the XXII Primigenia

★ Historical character

The dagger lies at the furthest edge of my desk. I can barely write more than a paragraph before my eyes flick towards it yet again. I have spent the last few weeks writing these memoirs of mine, but the looming presence of my old friend's dagger has lent a lightning pace to my stylus. Will the praetorians reach me before I can finish? Will anybody read these pages when I'm gone? Only the gods know these things, and they have abandoned me these last ten years. I am not an old man, but I feel it. I am forty, still in my prime. Perhaps that's why it all went wrong for me.

In the year of Nero's suicide I was twenty-nine. I'd spent half my adult life in the army and the other half in politics, but none of that could have prepared me for what was to come. I'd been drawn into that bastard Galba's conspiracy to overthrow Nero, left my comfortable post in Hispania to advise Vindex's sham of a revolt in Gaul. At least it was meant to be a sham. Instead of the handful of farm boys we had counted on to frighten Nero into exile or even suicide, Vindex had taken it into his head to rouse all of Gaul in revolt. I'd spent weeks masquerading as a Celtic tribesman among Vindex's followers, and had found myself, for the most part, with a band of brave and boisterous men. I'd even become a close friend of Vindex's son, the young Quintus. But Vindex himself had tried to get rid of me, hoping to defeat the Rhine legions that his shambolic rebellion had roused. He was outclassed. The Gauls had been crushed, annihilated. Too late Vindex realized he had overreached himself and, with a little persuasion, took his own life to preserve his family's honour.

The general who had defeated us, a harmless, kindly man called Verginius Rufus, thought he was avoiding civil war by refusing the demands of his legions to declare himself emperor. Galba even appointed me commander of one of those Rhine legions so that I could help Rufus keep the peace. But everything changed when Rufus was summoned to Rome. The men had already lost one chance to have their own general as emperor, they were not about to let another opportunity slip through their fingers. It was a daily struggle to keep the men from mutiny, especially with the scheming General Valens urging the new governor, that humongous hedonist Vitellius, to take the purple.

The final straw came when Galba himself summoned me to Rome on a charge of embezzlement. This dated from my days in Hispania, and while the accusation was true it was not something for which senators were ever prosecuted. Everyone knows that governors skim a little from each year's taxes to fund their election campaigns back in Rome. Only one man in Rome's history was hypocritical enough to prosecute his fellow senator for making the most of his time in the provinces, that parvenu Cicero. It could only mean that Galba no longer had any need of me. For better or for worse, I was shackled to an army that had just one goal: Rome.

I

The lion yawned widely, showing off his bloody fangs. He took no notice of the team of slaves trying to coax him out of the arena. One of them, the one who was brave enough to come within ten paces of the animal, was clearly the lion's keeper. The rest were plainly terrified, clutching their spears tightly, attempting to follow the keeper's directions in an effort to herd the lion through the right gate. The luckier slaves stood outside the arena, waiting to clear away what remained of the monster's meal.

One of the slaves found some courage, circled behind the lion and made a tentative jab. The brute snarled, but didn't move. The slave took a step nearer and made to jab again. In a flash the lion pounced, its jaws sinking deep into the unfortunate wretch's neck. The crowd cheered the animal's second victory.

'Talk about value for money, the beast has given us an encore!' Valens joked. A few sycophants in the box laughed.

Little Aulus tugged at my sleeve. 'Father, why is there only one lion? In Rome they have lions, tigers, sometimes elephants . . .'

I felt my face flush. These games were a celebration in Vitellius's honour. Was it my fault that this wretched northern province had only the one lion?

13

Vitellius neglected the dishes in front of him for a moment as he turned to address my son.

'Don't fret, little one, I am told the main act is still to come. Am I right, Valens?'

'Indeed, Caesar.'

Vitellius grimaced. 'If I've told you once I've told you a hundred times, I don't like it when you call me that. Call me Germanicus if you must, but I am not a Caesar.'

'It's for the men, Caesar,' Valens protested.

Vitellius said nothing, and returned to his refreshments, irritated but not protesting too much.

By this time the slaves had managed to move the lion off his backside and towards the edge of the arena. The other team had come on from the far side, still well clear of the beast, and started to pick up the body parts that lay scattered in the sand.

'Who were they?' my wife asked.

'They, Salonina?' I said.

'The men they threw to the lion.'

'Oh, the usual, I suspect: thieves, murderers, slaves that nobody could sell. Isn't that right, Valens?'

'Those sorts of people, yes. Normally it's whoever we have in the cells at the time. Apparently one of them was a Christian.'

'Really? So far north? I thought they kept themselves to Judaea and the East?' my wife asked.

'They've been in Rome for a few years now,' I said. 'Perhaps this one converted while he was in Rome.'

'Not this one,' Valens interrupted. 'He claims he was a follower of this Christ man, and on a mission from his god to spread the word here in the north. It seems the magistrates caught him early, before he could do any preaching.'

'Which god is this?' Aulus asked.

'These Christians have only one god,' I explained. 'That's why they rebel so often, like the Jews. I don't envy Vespasian.'

'Who?' my son asked.

'The man Nero sent out to deal with the latest rebellion. Men who fight for land or plunder are one thing; you try fighting against an enemy who believe they are fighting for their god. It is madness, but a madness stoked by fervour. Rome's better off without Christians and Jews.'

'Come, Severus, we are meant to be celebrating your birthday, not discussing philosophy!' Vitellius shook his finger at me in mock reproach.

It was my thirtieth birthday. A winter's day in the bitter north, but the townspeople of Colonia and many from the legions had come to the amphitheatre to celebrate Vitellius's taking of the name Germanicus. Unofficially this was my birthday celebration. I had a beautiful, pregnant wife, a clever son and the prospect of wealth and power. Even Valens, the grim man who was my rival for Vitellius's patronage, was in an affable mood. We were putting our differences aside as we planned ahead, and it was his idea to have this double celebration.

The horns trumpeted the arrival of the main event. The tunnel leading to the gladiator quarters was directly opposite our box, so we were the first to see the four men enter the arena. The master of ceremonies, who had been chatting to Vitellius, rose to speak. He drew himself up to his full height, breathing from his diaphragm so that his voice would project and echo around the amphitheatre.

'Citizens and soldiers of Colonia, your emperor is proud to present a brutal contest, the likes of which has never been seen in Rome's illustrious history. Step forward, Galba and the Three Pedagogues!'

A fearsome chorus of booing and hissing erupted as the four men stepped on to the sandy floor of the arena. Three of them were big, burly men drawn from across the gladiator styles: the *murmillo* with fish-like scales of armour covering most of his torso and armed with a simple gladius, the *retiarius*, lightly armoured and wielding a net and a trident, and finally a huge man who carried a double-handed club like mighty Ajax, the Greek hero at Troy. The three men represented the Emperor Galba's closest advisers in Rome, men Galba relied on so completely that the city mob had dubbed them 'the Pedagogues'.

Behind the three came a scrawny man, armed only with a small shield and dagger. He limped precariously, and took his place in between the two gladiators at the rear of the triangle they formed. The puny creature represented Galba himself, right down to the tell-tale limp.

'And now, representing our beloved emperor, Aulus Vitellius Germanicus, we have the champion of champions, Clothar!'

From beneath our box emerged a titan of a man, wearing the armour of a legionary, but that was the only bit of conventional kit he wore. For instead of a shield, Clothar carried a second gladius. And rather than a legionary's helmet he wore one of the German style with cheek-pieces and a nose-guard, topped with a purple plume. He turned to face Vitellius, crossed the swords in front of his chest and bowed. Vitellius smiled and twirled his fingers in acknowledgement of the salute. Then the German turned to the crowd and basked in their cheers and appreciation.

'I was trying to think how best to make a German look like a Roman emperor,' Valens said.

'So I see,' I commented. 'It doesn't bother you then that a slave is wearing the imperial purple?'

'I'm sorry, Valens, but he's right. If I'm not wearing purple, then nobody else should be.'

'But, sir, I promise it's necessary, for the men especially. Go on, tell them,' he prompted the master of ceremonies. The man stood up to address the crowd for the final time.

'This is a fight to the death. If the Pedagogues fail to protect Galba, they will be executed.' There was a murmur of excitement from the crowd. 'Or Clothar may kill each man in turn, and leave Galba defenceless. Now let the fight begin.'

A nice touch from Valens. Brutal, but clever. Even here in the provinces people knew that Galba had abandoned his pretensions of ruling with the support of the Senate and retreated behind his three loyal companions. I had met two of them almost a year ago, on that fateful night in Hispania. Titus Vinius had commanded one legion and raised another for Galba and was now a consul. The slave Icelus Martianus was the other. He was rumoured to be Galba's lover, and had been rewarded not only with his freedom but with elevation to the class of the knights, which had caused no small outrage in Rome. The third was Cornelius Laco, the praetorian prefect and the man responsible for the emperor's safety. Galba made no decision without the approval of this gang of three, and was losing popularity by the day.

All the gladiators made the customary salute to the emperor before taking up their positions for the fight. The three gladiators who represented Galba's henchmen had no choice but to defend the limping slave if they wanted to save their lives, and they drew tightly around him as Clothar advanced.

The German was a big man, towering over the others, but he wasn't too bulky to take on three highly trained gladiators. He walked obliquely, angling away from the front of the triangle, as though he hoped he could just walk round them. The three men shuffled so that the foremost, the *murmillo*, still faced Clothar directly. With a couple of quick steps, Clothar made for the gap between the *murmillo* and the club-man.

'Looks as though he's trying to take out Galba straight away and save himself a proper fight,' I remarked.

I was wrong. The *murmillo* and the club-man instinctively closed ranks to protect the scrawny slave behind them. And if you're holding a double-handed club, the last thing you want is an enemy up close, which meant the club-man had no choice but to take a swing at Clothar. The gladiators were good. As Clothar swerved to avoid the spiked club the heavily armoured *murmillo* lunged forward, hoping to catch the German off balance. Quick as lightning Clothar parried the thrust with his left, the *murmillo*'s sword rasping along the gladius safely to the side. Clothar spun away, and as he spun he scythed with his right, gashing the club-man on his arm and across the chest. Out of range, Clothar returned to his crab-like scuttle around the four men.

'A denarius says he kills the *murmillo* first. What do you say, Severus?'

I snorted. 'Stop being such a miser, Valens. Live a little; I'll wager twenty denarii.'

Valens grumbled, but didn't want to lose face. 'Done.'

'You have been,' I said quietly.

Little Aulus tugged my sleeve. 'What do you mean, Father?'

'Clothar daren't kill the *murmillo* first, otherwise he'll face two warriors with a much bigger reach.'

'But surely fighting two is easier than fighting three?'

'Normally yes,' I admitted, 'but drawn up tightly around the slave playing Galba the other two are hampered, they can't use the longer reach their weapons give them. With the *murmillo* dead the other two would have room to manoeuvre and pincer Clothar.'

A gasp from the crowd made me look up. Clothar had been circling ever further away from the iron triangle, but now he was running full pelt, straight for the *murmillo*. I stole a glance at Valens. His clenched fists were raised, urging the German on. Suddenly there was a flash of silver that darted in front of Clothar. The club-man sank to the ground, a thrown gladius embedded in his chest. The German was still running straight for the *murmillo*, who was bracing himself for the charge. But just as the imposing gladiator aimed a blow that would cleave Clothar in two, the German, who symbolized the hopes and dreams of the northern legions, stumbled. The mob groaned as one. Clothar was on his back and they sensed the inevitable.

18

Even the *retiarius* raised his trident in celebration, thankful that he had not been needed to defend the slave that stood for Galba.

But the German was a spectacular fighter. To this day, I have never seen anything to match it: he hadn't tumbled, but instead he slid along the sand feet first. The *murmillo*, encumbered with fish-like scales of armour, hardly had time to react. Too late he tried to turn his slashing cut into a downward thrust, but Clothar used his remaining sword to hack into the other man's leg beneath the knee, cutting it clean off. The gladiator teetered, blood spurting from the stump, only to crash to the ground like a felled tree, his armour clattering. All this had happened in a matter of moments, and it took all of us in the amphitheatre a few moments to comprehend what had taken place. Then the noise thundered like a storm.

'Clothar! Clothar!' they chanted. But the fight was not over yet.

The *murmillo* had fallen on top of Clothar's leg, trapping him. The *retiarius* was quick-witted enough to cast his net at the flailing pair, and there was an audible clang as one of the lead weights struck the German's helmet. The gods know what the crowd would have done if Clothar had been caught in the net. The omens for Vitellius would have been too dreadful to contemplate. And what on earth was the *retiarius* doing? Instead of going in for the kill he merely circled the entrapped pair, as though he were toying with them.

Ironically, it was the *murmillo* who saved Clothar. Writhing in pain he lashed out, and cut away a part of the net. The German squirmed his way out and rolled towards the corpse of the club-man. There was nothing the *retiarius* could do, as the wounded gladiator lay between him and Clothar. The German plucked the gladius from the dead man's chest, and the terrified slave cowered behind his last remaining champion. The scent of victory was in the air, we all felt it. So did the *retiarius*, but it was not his victory that we sensed. Two men were left standing. The classic gladiator fight was upon us: trident and net against the sword. And Clothar was a champion.

The remaining gladiator was wary of coming too close to Clothar. He had seen what had happened to the club-man. He waited at the edge of the arena, Galba's proxy in his shadow. But Clothar was too professional an entertainer to use the same trick twice. Guile had won his first victories, and we waited with baited breath to see how he would dispose of the third.

He advanced slowly, menacingly. Despite his trickery the German was a huge man who could rely on raw power alone to see him through most encounters, and as he came closer to the pair we saw how much the odds were stacked in his favour. The *retiarius*'s head probably came up to Clothar's neck, if that. But his trident was long and we had seen how his net had almost done for the bigger man. Our eyes focused on that net as the slave spun it, waiting to see which way his enemy would attack.

The tip of one sword flickered. The *retiarius* held his ground. Then he tried something very brave, or suicidal. He flung his net high into the air, and the German's head flicked up to see where it would fall. The *retiarius* used this distraction, for distraction it was, to hurl his trident like a javelin straight for the German's chest. But the throw was weak and ill-aimed, giving Clothar enough time to parry the makeshift javelin, but it still nicked his shoulder, causing the giant to flinch in pain. The net fell to the ground at the *retiarius*'s feet, and he hastily retrieved it. Clothar closed in for the kill, holding his swords aloft to deflect a throw of the net, knowing that he was safe. All the *retiarius* could do was use his net as a shield, delaying the inevitable. Clothar swung with his right; the sword bit into his enemy's arm. The crowd roared as a spurt of blood caught the giant full in the face. The smaller man's lifeless arm dropped the net but he used the momentary distraction to scamper out of range of the colossal man's gladius. 'Galba' limped out of the way as fast as he could, but Clothar knew he had all the time in the world to deal with his ultimate victim. Dropping the net, the gladiator hurled himself at the trident that lay in the sand and grabbed it with his good arm.

Clothar's face was spattered with blood, and he wiped it with his forearm as he prepared to deliver the final blow. He marched up to the weakened gladiator and knocked the trident from his trembling grasp, then swiped with both of his swords to lop off the man's head. A gush of arterial blood pumped from the poor man's neck. Little Aulus covered his eyes with the folds of his mother's dress.

The giant stood still, staring out the pathetic slave who clutched his shield close to his chest, his dagger looking like a toy next to those fearsome gladii. Clothar raised his arms to the crowd, asking for their judgement: kill or spare. But this crowd was never going to spare the wretched slave. The coward flung his weapons to the ground and fell to his knees. I could see his chest heaving, not from exhaustion but because he was sobbing, pleading for mercy. There were cries of 'Kill him!' and 'Down with Galba!' A forest of arms rose into the air, with their thumbs all pointing down. But the choice was not up to them.

Vitellius rose awkwardly from his chair, and stood with his arm outstretched and his fist clenched. Now the chant changed to a cheer. 'Vitellius!' they cried in adulation. Our emperor was clearly enjoying his moment of pure adoration. This was the son of Lucius Vitellius, three times consul and beloved of the people at a time when the ruling emperor, Claudius, was a crippled cuckold. The people and the legions of the north were behind him. Slowly, inexorably, the thumb turned towards the ground. Clothar acknowledged Vitellius's judgement with a courteous bow, then turned to face the crippled pretender.

The whole arena fell silent as we watched and waited. A few words were exchanged from one gladiator to another, and the supplicant slave gestured to his throat. The tall man nodded, and sheathed one of his swords. He held his remaining one

steady. The slave's breaths were shorter, faster, waiting for the end. A quick slash, a spurt of blood, and the dying slave slumped on to the sand.

The crowd spilled out of the stadium, eager to enjoy what remained of the public holiday. The soldiers would no doubt head straight for the taverns, and the wiser civilians would avoid those same taverns, or else risk getting caught in the inevitable brawls that night. Hot-headed fighters who have been gambling, with cheap wine coursing through their veins, do not make the safest company, I find.

'Congratulations, Caesar, they will be talking about this fight for decades. The people have taken your name into their hearts,' Valens said, more to congratulate himself than his master.

'Thank you, Valens, it was a magnificent display. Wouldn't you agree, Severus?'

'I could not have wished for a grander present, sir.'

'Come now, Severus, you don't have to "sir" me. We're all friends here.'

Good enough friends that Vitellius didn't flinch when called Caesar just now, I thought. I suppose he just didn't feel like an emperor yet, but Valens had been brilliant thus far. No one would have thought that a few months ago this man would have trembled at the very thought of challenging Galba for the throne. Now he was sitting in an imperial box and basking in the warmth of the people's affection. The free bread that we had given the crowd wouldn't hurt either.

The five of us, Vitellius, Valens, my family and I walked the streets back to the self-styled imperial palace. Really it was Vitellius's own villa as governor of Lower Germania, but it made political sense to refer to it as 'the palace'. This was my new home for the time being. Quintus Vindex, my second in command and the man who had saved me from the stupidity of his father in the middle of his ill-fated Gallic rebellion, was literally holding the fort for me back in Mogontiacum, along with the vastly experienced camp prefect, Tuscus. As Vitellius's lieutenant, theoretically I commanded both the legions encamped there: my own legion, the Fourth Macedonica, and the Twenty-Second Primigenia, not to mention the thousands of German auxiliaries. But I was needed in Colonia to plan for the coming campaign, and to keep an eye on Valens. I didn't trust him further than my son could throw him. Trust Valens to turn my birthday into his own personal triumph.

Totavalas was overseeing the filling of my bath as we entered the chambers Vitellius had set aside for my family. Technically it was a job for one of the slaves, but up in Germania we were rather short-staffed. Before I'd given him his freedom, the barbarian had been a passable body slave. Perhaps the word 'barbarian' is a little unfair. He speaks, reads and writes Latin better than most Romans, even if he does do it in a maddening, Hibernian sing-song sort of way.

'Your bath will be ready in just a moment, General.'

'Thank you, Totavalas. Have you got more water on the boil for Salonina's bath?'

'Indeed I have, sir.'

At first glance Totavalas seemed the most easy-going, carefree individual you could wish to meet. The young man was so chirpy, and so damn efficient, and when you consider he was born to the most powerful chieftain on his island I couldn't help but feel a little guilty about once owning him. But there was steel in his soul: he was fiercely proud of his lineage and had the makings of a fine warrior. He had proved his courage and loyalty on a day when my legions had threatened to run riot, and had been ready to die in defence of my family. For that I had given him his freedom.

As with many freedmen, he had decided to stay with my family, at least until he had saved enough money to pay for his passage back to his wild island in the north. So I paid him a wage to act as my chief steward and he had taken to it like a duck to water. Not that there was much for him to do in Colonia with only a couple of slaves to manage, but I didn't begrudge him the wage. At least saying thank you to him was entirely normal since he had won his freedom.

'Don't be too long, Caecina,' my wife said. 'I'll need plenty of time to get ready for the banquet tonight.'

'I'll be as long as it takes. Have fun teaching that Gallic slave girl how to use those new curling tongs!'

She playfully stuck out her tongue.

'Come on, Aulus, we don't want to distract your father from his important duties. You can help me get ready.'

Totavalas led me through to the next room where the deep copper bath waited for me, swirls of steam still streaming upwards. I began to strip as Totavalas dipped a finger in, and tut-tutted that the new body slave had forgotten to cool down the hot water to just the right temperature. He apologized and grabbed the empty pitcher, heading for the kitchens.

After a while I got bored with waiting. Thinking that the water must have cooled a bit by now, I dipped my foot into the bath. It damn near scalded me, and in the rush to get my foot out I lost my balance and landed on my back. I heard a light chuckle.

'Now that's a novel way to take a bath!' Totavalas had returned with the cold water and a towel.

'Stop your giggling and help me up.'

'As you command, General. Or should I say Admiral?' With his free hand the Hibernian hoisted me up. Once I was standing, Totavalas's eyes flicked downwards. 'And I thought it was cold water that made a man look quite so . . . small.'

I grabbed the towel from him and wrapped it round my waist. 'Very funny. And I suppose you're hung like an elephant?'

'I wouldn't say that, but certain ladies of my acquaintance are kind enough to say that they've never known anything like it.'

'I hope they charge extra for the flattery.'

★

A little while later I lay contentedly in my bath. Totavalas was massaging oil into my back, ready to scrape away the grime of the day. I could feel my muscles beginning to relax as he worked away at the knots, draining the stress and tension from my body. Tonight was the third banquet this week; Vitellius could never resist a chance to celebrate. First it was his acclamation as Germanicus by the army, then the news that the legions in Britannia had mostly sided with him, and now it was my birthday.

'On the understanding that this goes no further . . .' I began.

'Of course, General.'

I paused a moment, gently reminding him I don't care for interruptions. 'What do you think of our host?'

The Hibernian thought about his answer for all of two heart-beats.

'He's got a powerful big appetite, sir.'

'Totavalas, I like you because you've got the mind of a fox; a useless, prattling fox but a fox nonetheless. Use it!'

'Maybe if you made the question a little more specific?' he suggested.

'As a potential emperor then.'

'Potential, sir? I thought you yourself said he was the right choice for the good of the empire?'

How did he know I said those very words to Valens on the night we toasted Vitellius as emperor? I asked him, and all he did was look enigmatic and say:

'Ah well, we Celts have ways of knowing things you Romans will never understand.' I would have cuffed him, or splashed him at the least, but he had a *strigil* and was scraping my back, not a job you can do by yourself.

'Are you having second thoughts perhaps?'

'How can I have second thoughts? I'm committed now. Galba put me in this situation. He broke his word, now I'll do what I can to overthrow him.'

'So it's revenge you're after, not the golden glittering consulship the emperor has offered you?'

'I'd rather call it self-preservation. My legion wants Vitellius, Valens wants Vitellius, my wife wants Vitellius . . .'

'Surely not, sir!'

At long last, one of his jibes made me laugh. The thought of that whale and my wife together was ludicrous. Salonina was ambitious, yes, but not that ambitious!

I sighed. 'It's Valens I worry about. There's no limit to that man's greed.'

'He may worry about you, General.'

I took little comfort from that thought. He needed the support of my legions certainly, and my legions followed me. But I knew that he would do his best to discredit me in Vitellius's eyes and at the same time make himself indispensable. Totavalas finished scraping away at the oil, leaving me feeling cleansed.

'Not the most comforting of thoughts, but it will have to do. Have that slave bring me my clothes, then tell Salonina when her bath is ready, and tell her to be quick. Can't be late for my own birthday banquet, can I?'

II

The banquet was sumptuous, just as the last two had been. From a hedonist's perspective, Rome's empire was great not because of its might or its glory, but because it could cater to every possible culinary taste. And Vitellius was an expert in culinary taste. There were jellyfish from the Northern Ocean, joints of fallow deer from the German forests garnished with African dates, raisins and honey. Stuffed dormice, boiled ham drenched with fishy *garum*, figs, honeyed pastries from the East – there was anything and everything a man could desire, and all at the province's expense.

Now don't get me wrong, I love good food, and the banquet was exquisite. But after the previous two the monotony of these affairs was beginning to bore me. I found myself sitting next to the same sweaty local dignitaries, making the same dull small talk, watching Vitellius wolfing down yet another course, and nearly marinating himself with fine wines. Salonina, on the couch next to me, sensed my boredom.

'Smile, Caecina, it's your birthday!'

'Really? I'd forgotten,' I said sarcastically.

She gave me a playful shove. 'Come on, have an otter's nose.'

I didn't even deign to reply. Instead I looked idly around. On the other side of the room Valens was enjoying the attentions of one of the slave girls who served us. I put it delicately. He was slobbering, his hands were roaming, she was dutifully responding. Revolted, my eyes turned to the next couch, where Vitellius lay. Our eyes met, and he raised his goblet. A splash of wine sloshed over the rim, but then he held it steady.

'Ladies and gentlemen, a toast to General Severus! Without whom none of this would be possible,' he slurred.

'To General Severus,' the chorus echoed. I smiled politely. Hangers-on and arse-lickers every one of them, but an emperor needed his court, and in this wild corner of the empire this was the best that could be had. There were of course some officers from the province's legions, the Fifth, the Fifteenth, the Sixteenth and Valens's own, the First Germanica. One day I would have to get to know them, but I was putting off that pleasure for as long as I could. My little fame in the army was restricted to Britannia, and little further. And it would not do me much good to say that I had effectively led the Vindex rebellion that they had crushed only a few months ago. That battle had brought them together for the first time in decades, and it had given them an inkling of what they could achieve if the Rhine legions united.

Achieve is probably the wrong word. The common soldier is not concerned with affairs of state and high politics. All he wants is to fight occasionally, survive, drink, fornicate and plunder enough to ensure a comfortable retirement. And this was best attained by helping his governor become master of Rome. Not forgetting the two legions in my province, of course, or the one in the Alps and all the German auxiliaries.

I heard shouts from the corridor outside. They became steadily louder, and many necks craned to hear what was causing the commotion. Then I caught a few Gallic swear words, words that would have offended the delicate sensibilities of our guests if they had understood them.

The heavy double doors crashed open, and in strode a daunting figure, flanked by two protesting slaves. That bright shock of red hair marked him out in an instant.

'Legate Severus, would you tell these insufferable slaves to leave me alone? I forgot to bring my invitation.'

I grinned from ear to ear. Lugubrix was hardly the sort of dinner guest this crowd were used to, and he certainly didn't have an invitation. I beckoned to the doormen to let him in. He marched to the couch next to mine and stood glowering at its occupant. Unsurprisingly, the man, a local magistrate, I think, got off with barely a moment's hesitation. The Gaul clambered on to it, and demanded someone fetch him a drink.

Salonina maintained a serene smile. 'Caecina, won't you introduce me to your friend?'

'Quite right,' Lugubrix commented. 'Where are your manners, old friend?'

'Lugubrix, this is my wife, the lady Salonina. Salonina, an old friend, Lugubrix.'

The trader put on his most courteous smile and said, 'Lady, I would kiss your hand. But I won't, for fear of sullying it with my filthy Gallic skin.'

'Sir, you are the most charming Gaul I have ever met.'

'And the first, I'll bet!' Lugubrix countered.

'Lugubrix, charming my wife is my job, and no one else's.'

'Job?' he said. 'I'd consider it a pleasure. Is someone going to bring me that damn drink?'

By the smell of him he had already started, but it didn't bother me in the slightest. If the guests didn't take to him, what did I care? He was the only one in the room, my wife apart, who was actually there to celebrate my birthday.

'So how is the youngest legate in the empire?'

'It's "general" now, Lugubrix.'

'Forgive me, General!' he bowed mockingly. I had missed the rascal, and hopefully the feeling was mutual. He was sporting a

leather cuff of sorts that covered up the stump where his right
hand should have been.

'What's with the leather contraption?' I asked, gesturing at it.

'It's not a contraption, it's a fashion accessory. I put it on when
I'm going to be near squeamish folk. Not everyone wants to see
a war wound at dinner.'

'And you think we're squeamish?'

'I'll prove it to you,' he said, slipping off the cuff.

Lugubrix turned to the man on the next couch along. 'Could
you pass me that platter please?'

The man reached over, picked up the platter and held it at
arm's length.

'Thank you so much.' He leaned over as if to take the platter,
but instead dropped his stump right in the middle of the food!
The poor man dropped the platter in revulsion, shuddered, then
vomited all over the floor. Lugubrix burst out laughing.

'How's business?' I asked, forcing the subject back to a
dinner-party level. 'I'm guessing that's what brings you to
Colonia.'

'That and the chance to see how the nobs throw a party, of
course.' He winked. 'As for business, if what I hear is true you'll
be needing my grain soon, and plenty of it. Planning a raid
across the Rhine, are we?'

'If you say we are, Lugubrix, then it must be true.'

The Gaul leaned over, conspiratorially, and said in a stage
whisper: 'Of course, we both know the real reason why the
legions are mustering.'

I nodded gravely. 'Yes we do. You and I, Salonina, everyone
in this room, and perhaps half the empire knows by now that
the inevitable is going to happen.'

'So my services will still be required then?'

Gesturing at the sordid celebrations all around us, 'Mixing
business with pleasure, Lugubrix,' I said, 'what will my guests
think?'

'Like any other sensible guest they'll be drunk and won't give a damn.'

'And what should the hostess think?' my wife asked mischievously.

Lugubrix paused a moment, his eyes flitting from left to right as he searched for a suitable reply.

'She would forgive a tactless, drunken Gaul and put it down to his bad breeding.'

Salonina clapped her hands in delight. 'Caecina, why didn't you tell me the Gauls could be this charming?' I wasn't sure if she was genuinely amused or just being diplomatic. But then I suppose that is the sign of a good diplomat, isn't it?

'Because I am the exception that proves the rule,' he slurred.

'Salonina, dear, would you put your hands over your ears for a moment as I stoop to this wretched Gaul's level and talk business?'

'Or I could sit here and watch two fine minds at work. You never know, you might be glad of a woman's insight!'

'No objections from where I'm sitting,' Lugubrix said.

'It's hardly matters of state, I suppose,' I conceded. 'Are you busy tomorrow afternoon, Lugubrix?'

The Gaul fluttered his eyes at me. 'Is this a proposal, General?'

I ignored the joke. 'We're having a council of war tomorrow, with just a few select officers. I'd like you to join us.'

'Won't the others be a bit surprised to find a Gaul at their council?'

'Valens knows why I was in Gaul last year; he'll appreciate why I've invited you. So long as he and I know of your usefulness, everyone else will accept you.'

'Including your lord and master?'

'Especially my lord and master.'

'There,' Salonina interrupted, 'was that so coarse or secretive that I couldn't stay while you talked?'

'I'm sorry, Salonina. I've been so used to making decisions like these on my own, you see.'

'Well, you're not alone any more,' she said, taking my hand and squeezing it affectionately. 'I'm not just a pretty face, you know.'

'You could have fooled me,' I said.

'Do you want a present from me this year, Caecina?'

'I was only teasing!'

'I know that,' Salonina said, pecking me on the cheek. 'Now I'd better go and see if the surprise is ready.' She swung delicately off the couch and headed towards the hallway.

'You've got a special one there, my friend,' Lugubrix said.

'You've no idea how special. And yourself? Do you have anyone to keep you warm on these winter nights?'

'It depends what the madam in the town has to offer. Now Colonia, being the provincial capital, has a lot of choice. Celts, Greeks, Gyppos, the black stuff, you name it they've got it. When business takes me further afield I have to make do with what they've got. But as tonight's a special occasion, maybe I'll find some classy dancing girl to amuse me.'

Suddenly, the lights were blown out. The room was plunged into darkness. Instinctively my hand reached for my sword, but of course I was unarmed.

Valens called out: 'Silence, everyone!'

We obeyed his command, and then I heard it. The tinkling of little bells echoing around the room. The delicate, metallic sound slowly crescendoed and a glow of orange light began to illuminate the empty hall; and then they appeared. Pair after pair of the prettiest girls you ever saw, clad in soft, rustling silks of green and gold. With their graceful curves and unbound hair they looked like a gathering of Apollo's nymphs, straight from the woody glades of Greece. In no time at all there were a dozen of them, half of the girls flanking either side of the doorway. They shook their hips rhythmically, causing the bells on their leather belts to chime in unison.

Then from round the corner came a vision of exquisite beauty. She wore a long, golden *stola* that barely skimmed the floor as she glided towards us. It was Salonina. Her luscious brown hair, carefully arranged in a headdress not half an hour ago, now hung loose in curly tresses down to her shoulders. She carried a cithara, like a lyre but with eight strings across an ornately decorated sounding-board, not two. A slave hurriedly brought a stool for her, directly opposite the couch where I lay. She did not pluck the strings so much as caress them to make her music, and as the first notes floated towards the audience, the nymphs began their dance.

The tune was slow but stirring. I would like to say that I had eyes only for my wife, but these dancers had mastered the art of enflaming a man's spirits. Their graceful arms moved as one into the air.

'He is more than a hero,
he is a god in my eyes –
the man who is allowed to sit beside you.

'He who listens intimately
to the sweet murmur of your voice,
the enticing laughter that makes my own
heart beat fast.

'If I meet you suddenly,
I can't speak – my tongue is broken;
a thin flame runs under my skin.

'Seeing nothing,
hearing only my own ears drumming,
I drip with sweat.

'Trembling shakes my body
and I turn paler than dry grass.
At such times death is not far from me.'

The music stopped. The room was silent for a moment, then the audience burst into raucous applause.

Vitellius cried out: 'Superb! Superb! Play some more.'

Salonina gave a demure curtsey, and said, 'Forgive me, Caesar, but I was always told to leave the audience wanting more.'

'Salonina, it was a magnificent performance,' responded Vitellius. 'All I can hope is that my next birthday will be equally honoured. I must admit, though, I am a trifle confused. We all know who "he" is, but who is sweetly murmuring into the general's ears?'

'Why, you are, sire. This was written as a song of jealousy. You have almost stolen my husband from me, and who here will say that when a Caesar speaks it isn't sweetly?'

'I congratulate you, Severus. Your wife has a tongue of gold.'

A voice behind me said, 'Come on, Severus. Make your wife entertain us some more with her golden tongue.'

There was only one man in the room senior enough and bold enough to speak in that way to me.

'Valens, you've been honoured to witness my wife's present to me tonight. Count yourself lucky she chose to entertain anyone besides her husband!'

'Now, now, boys,' Vitellius said jovially. 'This is meant to be a party.'

He turned his attention to the dancers. 'Girls, it was an amazing performance, but I think it is time to bring in the final course.'

A slave relieved my wife of her cithara, and she returned to her couch beside me. Lugubrix was speechless.

'A little different from the tavern in Vienne?' I teased him.

The power of speech returned to my Gallic friend. 'I will

say this for our taverns. Your food may be fancier, your guests richer, your dancers classier, but the girls of Vienne will have me, warts and all. I get the feeling that if I tried anything with these girls I'd get a slap.'

I laughed. 'We'll have to show you some Roman hospitality then.' I clapped my hands, and the slave who ran Vitellius's household came scuttling over.

'Yes, master?'

'My friend here,' I said, as Lugubrix waved with his handless arm, 'could use some company. Might that be arranged?'

'Certainly, master.'

Within a little while Lugubrix was enjoying the attentions of one of Apollo's nymphs, but I had his favourite muse lying next to me.

'I think we've stayed as long as we have to. What do you say to a private performance?'

'Whatever the goddess commands,' I answered.

Totavalas was waiting for us in the antechamber that led to our wing of Vitellius's house.

'All well, Totavalas?'

'All well, General.'

'Is Aulus asleep?' Salonina asked.

'Two hours since, my lady. I was telling him a story of my people; my ancestor, if truth be told. The warrior Cú Chulainn.'

'Good story?' I asked.

'Funnily enough my family have always liked it. I was telling him how the boy Sétanta was a famous warrior even in his youth. When he was no older than Aulus he killed the famous hound that protected the hut where the king was feasting. When Sétanta saw how upset the hound's master was, he offered to take the hound's place until a new one was reared. From that day he was known as the Hound of Culann.'

'Cu . . .' I tried.

'Cú Chulainn.'

35

'And Aulus liked this story?' Salonina's face had a worried expression.

'I should say he did, my lady. He wants another story tomorrow.'

'Thank you, Totavalas,' my wife said, cutting the Hibernian short. 'We are off to bed.'

'Of course, my lady. I hope you have had a good birthday, General.'

'It isn't over yet,' I said, taking Salonina by the hand and leading her to our bedroom.

Once the door was closed, she was at me like an animal, kissing me deeply and passionately. My hands slid down her back, passing over the gauzy golden dress, down on to the gentle curves of her bottom. A grunt escaped my lips as I hoisted her up, and she instinctively wrapped her legs around my waist. Still kissing each other, I carried Salonina over towards the bed. I playfully bit at her lip before dropping her, not hard, but just enough that she bounced a little on the thick mattress, making her giggle.

With one swift motion I took off my toga, flinging it on to the floor.

'Are you ready?' I asked, leaning over her.

'What would you like me to be this time? The feisty barbarian, the demure slave?'

'I'm thinking Aphrodite.'

She laughed prettily. 'Ha! It's your birthday, not mine.'

'So I can choose what I like,' I said, grabbing her by the knees and pulling her closer to the edge of the bed. Slowly, I dropped to my knees. 'I am not worthy.'

Within moments Salonina was gasping with pleasure, opening up like a flower.

'Deeper,' she moaned, and as her humble servant I obeyed. She arched her back, then began to rub my back with her feet. It was a habit of hers, and on cue I got up from the cold flagstones and on to her warm body.

I tenderly kissed her mouth, downwards towards her neck and her breasts while with her hand she made sure I was properly attentive. I soon had her out of her dress and looked upon her beauty.

'My goddess,' I said appreciatively, before thrusting into her hard and fast. It was the best birthday I'd had for years.

III

The following afternoon I stormed through the town, the leather of my sandals loudly slapping on the road and the iron nailheads in the soles clinking against the cobbles. How dare she lecture me on how to bring up my son! Where better for a patrician boy to grow up than with the legions, and where his father was their general? The men would be falling over themselves to make a good impression on Aulus, hoping to gain favour with me.

Lugubrix was waiting outside a tavern on the way out of the city.

'Bel's ball-sack, I thought the birthday boy would look a bit happier than that.'

'Really not in the mood, Lugubrix.'

The Gaul fell into step beside me, and we marched in silence away from the town. The morning's frost lay thick on the fields and there was hardly a soul to be seen. Everyone was sheltering indoors from the German winter. Eventually he must have got bored with the silence.

'Everything not sweetness and light between the two of you?'

'I'd forgotten how much of a snob my wife could be.'

'Snob?'

'She seems to think being in Gaul is having a bad influence on our son. I don't think you're going to be invited to ours for a meal any time soon, let's put it that way.'

'Ah, I can have that effect sometimes.'

'She doesn't realize that I ate, slept and fought alongside Gauls last year. Hundreds, maybe thousands of them died under my command at Vesontio. That's not the sort of bond you can break easily.'

'And I bet the trousers aren't helping your cause either!'

'How did you guess?' I said sarcastically.

By now Colonia's fortress was directly ahead. I could make out the number of guards on duty outside the main gate. Two men flanked it on either side, and another four on the wall were watching our progress.

'Halt! Who goes there?'

'General Severus and one of my intelligence officers.'

'Advance and be recognized.'

We advanced and were duly recognized.

'What's your name, soldier?' I asked the man.

'Legionary Paetus, sir. First century, second—'

'I only wanted your name, Legionary Paetus. Are you looking forward to the march south?'

'Sir?'

'Come on, Paetus, you've heard the rumours. Galba's not going to give in without a fight, which means we're heading for Rome. How long is it since you saw her last?'

'Twelve years, sir.'

'And the rest of you?' I asked the guards.

The answers varied between four and eighteen years. These were veterans, not the downy-haired farmers' sons they had fought against in Gaul just a few months before.

'Well, cheer up,' I said. 'The emperor and I will be bringing you home soon!'

'Thank you, sir. Hail Caesar, sir.'

'Hail Caesar. Now will you let us in?'

'Of course, sir. Open the gates for the general!' Paetus called up.

The doors creaked open a few paces. The guards saluted us.

'Where are we going?' Lugubrix asked.

'The legion headquarters. Not many Gauls get to see the inside of it.'

'I can imagine. Will you have to beg forgiveness of some legion god for letting a barbarian inside?'

'Just make sure you wipe your feet outside the door and you'll be all right!'

The fort itself was even busier than the town. No one blinked an eye at Lugubrix's striking appearance. The two guards outside the principia did, though.

'May I ask where you're taking this civilian, General?'

'This is my chief intelligence officer, I can vouch for him.'

'Of course, sir. I'm afraid we have to check you for weapons. General Valens's orders.'

An understandable precaution. Galba must have heard about the rise of Vitellius, and I wouldn't have put it past the old man to send an assassin. I handed over my sword, and waited while Lugubrix fiddled with the cord that secured his sheathed dagger to his belt. The legionary stepped in to help.

'I'll manage,' Lugubrix growled. His fingers, made nimbler by years of extra work, soon had the cord undone. He handed over the dagger.

'Thank you, sirs. The council will be in General Valens's office.'

'Which office is that? This camp hasn't been used for over thirty years, there aren't any legions posted in Colonia.'

'The biggest one, sir, at the end of the corridor.'

'Of course it is.'

As we made our way inside the principia, Lugubrix asked me: 'Why are there no legions posted here?'

'A strange question from an intelligence officer,' I remarked.

'I make my money knowing about the here and now, and what might happen. History isn't going to fill my purse.'

'This place used to be the military focal point on our border with Germania. That was in the days before we organized the Rhineland into formal provinces. Colonia was our spearhead. But when Arminius routed those three legions at the Teutoburg Forest, all the plans to conquer Germania were shelved. Then when Augustus died and Tiberius became emperor the two legions here revolted, preferring another man from the imperial family, their commander Germanicus. Germanicus stayed loyal to Tiberius – much good it did him, he died soon afterwards. It was decided to split up the two legions and send the First to Bonna and the Fifth to Vetera, where they are today. Colonia became the administrative centre of the new province of Lower Germania, while this fort was left empty.'

'So why aren't all the preparations being made at one of the military towns?'

'Because this is where Vitellius is, and where the entertainment is. Our beloved emperor is fanatical about chariot races. The games too, but the races especially. Some say that's how Vitellius got this province: he and Galba's crony Titus Vinius are diehard fans of the Blues team back in Rome. To be fair to him, though, since the legions north of here will be coming south anyway, it makes sense for them to marshal around Colonia.'

I pushed open the door to Valens's office. It was empty but for one lonely figure.

'Finally I've got some company!' the man exclaimed.

'Where's everyone else?' I asked.

'Still recovering from last night, I should think. I gather it was quite a party.'

'Sorry, who is this?' Lugubrix asked.

'Lugubrix, this is Publilius Sabinus, prefect of one of the auxiliary cohorts in this province. If I'd had any say in who was coming to the banquet, Publilius, you would definitely have been invited.'

'However,' Publilius said, 'as I command a bunch of Germans, I was considered not socially acceptable for the illustrious company.'

'I made it in,' Lugubrix boasted.

Publilius looked askance. 'Gatecrasher,' I explained.

'Ah. I'm afraid I'm used to crashing town and fortress barriers, not social ones.'

Lugubrix had another question. 'Are there no more auxiliary officers coming to this council?'

I answered on Publilius's behalf. I had only known him for a fortnight or so, nevertheless I already knew he was a popular but modest man. 'The other officers have elected the worthy Publilius Sabinus their spokesman. It seems they are under the impression that he is a man of integrity and courage. Can't think why . . .'

Publilius smiled sheepishly. Just then the door opened, and in filed the rest of the council. Valens led the way, his face unshaven and eyes bleary. Then came some of the legionary legates from the province, all of whom I'd met briefly. There was one man I didn't recognize, and finally Vitellius, his frame filling the doorway.

'By Jupiter, I need a drink after that ride.'

That ride couldn't have taken long. Lugubrix and I had walked up from the town, but this was Vitellius. He must have had the mother of all hangovers. I can still remember, ten years later, the sight of the man burying his face in a double-handed goblet of wine. Valens had a clerk bring a pitcher of water. When it arrived, Vitellius didn't even wait for a cup but started drinking straight from the pitcher. One of the officers brought him the room's only chair and, pitcher emptied, Vitellius eased his mighty frame between the arms and lowered himself tentatively on to the seat. I smiled, wondering how many chairs had met their end at the hands, or rather bottom, of Vitellius.

It was only now that Valens noticed the one man in the room who wasn't encased in brightly polished armour. Someone had found (or perhaps made) a set for Vitellius that covered his great girth and gave him something of a military air.

'Why is there a civilian in this council? And a Gallic civilian at that!'

'Calm down, Valens. This is Lugubrix, my head of intelligence.'

'A Gaul, with intelligence?' one of the legates joked.

Quick as a lightning bolt, Lugubrix drew a small dagger from inside his leather cuff and threw it at the man who spoke. It flew past the man's ear and embedded itself in the door behind him, the hilt quivering with the sheer force of the throw.

'Smart enough to smuggle a weapon into the same room as your new emperor.'

The legate recovered his power of speech. 'By the gods, I'll have him strung up for trying to kill me!'

'You'll do no such thing,' I said, quietly but with a hard edge to my voice. 'Lugubrix has been invaluable to me, long before I was made legate of the Fourth Legion.'

Valens looked from me to Lugubrix, and back to me again. 'A word, Severus.'

We went into the corner of the room. Lugubrix stood where he was, looking defiant.

'You trust this man?' Valens asked.

'With my life, he saved it when one of Vindex's ruffians held me prisoner. It's thanks to him I only lost this,' I said, gesturing to the stump of the missing finger on my left hand.

'Fine, but why do we need him? You're not with the Gauls any more.'

'He's a grain merchant. Anything that happens between the River Po and the Ocean, you can be sure that Lugubrix will hear about it, quicker than most. That's how we knew that Governor Verginius Rufus was safe to approach . . .'

'What do you mean safe? I was there that night you convinced him to stand aside for Galba, no one was going to harm you.'

'Not that kind of safe. I mean we knew that we could sound him out about leaving Vindex and his Gauls alone without him running off to tell the emperor. And there's more: it was through Lugubrix that we knew how many men you took to fight Vindex at Vesontio.'

'It hardly needed a genius to work that out,' Valens scoffed.

'And if I said he was the one who told me how you and a friend murdered the governor of your own province when he refused to join you and proclaim himself emperor?'

Valens froze.

'Yes, I know your dirty secret. Vitellius might be interested to hear that particular story. I mean, once you've murdered one imperial governor out of ambition, what's to stop you from murdering another one?'

'Very well,' Valens interrupted. He turned to address the rest of the room. 'The Gaul stays.'

'Welcome to our merry band!' Vitellius said.

'Thank you . . .' Lugubrix paused, unsure of how to address Vitellius, 'Germanicus?'

'That is what my generals think it best to call me, so Germanicus it is.'

'Now that we've all been introduced,' Valens said sardonically, 'perhaps we can return to the matter in hand?' He took a rolled-up piece of vellum that rested against the wall and rolled it out across the table. It was a map of the western half of the empire, and I have included a copy of this in these memoirs of mine.

'Priscus, bring out those numbered blocks from my drawer, will you?'

One of Valens's men brought out a collection of wooden

blocks, each with different numerals carved on it. Some were cut from wood of a lighter colour.

'We have seven legions in these two provinces. Here in Lower Germania we have my legion, the First Germanica, and the Fifth, Fifteenth and Sixteenth Legions.' As he named each legion, he put the corresponding block on the map, in the towns that they garrisoned. 'In Upper Germania, the Fourth and the Twenty-Second are encamped at Mogontiacum, and the Twenty-First at the foot of the Alps in Vindonissa. Seven legions, gentlemen, totalling over thirty-five thousand men.'

'But we can't leave the Rhine border unprotected,' Vitellius observed. Everyone in the room knew that; only Vitellius felt the need to raise the point.

'Of course, sir. If I may finish?'

'Oh, please do.' The emperor missed Valens's sarcasm.

'We also have the German auxiliaries to call upon, and that gives us another twenty thousand.'

'What sort of auxiliaries do we have?' Vitellius asked.

'Mostly infantry, sir,' Publilius answered. 'Eight cohorts five hundred strong of Batavian cavalry, who also swim better than any tribe I know. The rest are a mix of German tribesmen, Lusitanians, Gauls and Britons, all fighting to gain their Roman citizenship. They make up the remaining sixteen thousand.'

'And which men do you command?'

'I'm prefect of a squadron of German cavalry, sir.'

'The other prefects have elected Publilius Sabinus their spokesman, sir. He speaks for all of them,' I said.

'And the Germans are happy to fight for me?'

'Truth be told, sir, they're spoiling for a fight. It's what the Germans do. But they do love the name Germanicus, it makes them feel like you've got their interests at heart. So long as they're paid and we give them victories, they'll follow you to Hades.'

'The question before us, then, is how many men we can afford to take south without leaving the Rhine too lightly defended.

After all, we don't know how many legions will remain loyal to Galba. We have to assume that none of them will. Galba's supporters will seek to portray us as a bunch of Germans coming to take the throne by force.'

'Then we must make our movement seem more widespread,' I said. 'If we can convince other troops to join us, the momentum will be unstoppable, and should nullify any propaganda of the sort you mention. I have two suggestions, and Lugubrix here has some information that will help us too. First, we should convince the First Italica to join us. They were sent into Gaul by Nero to help put down the Vindex rebellion, and were the last to abandon their emperor. As we're taking on the man who drove their beloved Nero to his death, it shouldn't be too difficult to convince them to join us against Galba.'

'Agreed,' Valens said. The other officers nodded their assent. 'What is your second suggestion?'

'That we divide our forces.' There was a sharp intake of breath. No right-thinking general divides his command if he can help it. Valens's man Priscus spoke.

'Why should we? Surely we'll weaken ourselves unnecessarily by splitting up? Galba will just pick us off piece by piece.'

I ignored the man, instead looking at his superior. 'Valens, would you tell your man I don't care to be questioned by a man of inferior rank, and especially not by a mere centurion. Also you can tell him that he should address me as General.' Valens held my gaze for a moment, waiting to see if I might back down. Then he glanced at Priscus and nodded.

'I apologize, General.' There was no tone of apology in his voice, but it would do for now. I had to constantly assert my authority with these men, as with the exception of Publilius I was the youngest in the room by perhaps fifteen years, and yet inferior only to Vitellius. And that was only because Valens and I had made him our superior.

'Apology accepted. I propose we divide into two forces and

take separate routes to Italia, only to meet up again on the other side of the Alps and then take on Galba's forces. One army takes the longer, easier route via Lugdunum, so they can recruit the First Italica along the way, and hopefully recruit men to replace the numbers we have taken from the Rhine. They can cross the Alps from the west.' I pointed out the route on the map, from the Rhine to the Rhône, and then the pass that Hannibal had once taken to enter Italia.

'The other army should take the short route, through the mountain passes in Raetia. They can pick up the Twenty-First at Vindonissa, and the general can send messengers to the legion commanders in Noricum and Pannonia, trying to convince them to join our cause. Then they will meet up with the other column in the north of Italia, and pincer whatever forces Galba is able to muster, that is if he has the stomach to fight our veterans.'

'Hear, hear!' Publilius said. The others made approving noises.

'This way we should also reach Italia sooner, rather than travelling as one slow, lumbering column that would need huge supplies to keep it going. If we were in enemy territory we could simply take what we needed from the locals. However, I'm not sure the Gauls along the route would take too kindly to being eaten out of house and home!'

'You command one column and I the other?' Valens asked.

'Surely I should command one of the columns?' Vitellius appealed.

'Of course, sir. This is where Lugubrix's information comes in.' I looked to my Gallic friend.

'I have been talking to friends and contacts of mine in Britannia. It seems the governor there, Trebellius, has been feuding with the legates. They complain he has left the legions in disrepair by diverting their funding straight into his pockets. I understand that those legions would be more than happy to join what looks to be a profitable campaign, and of course there is the added attraction of leaving the cold north for Italia.'

'Another three legions, gentlemen,' I said. 'Obviously we can't take all of them in case the Britons rebel again, so instead they should send detachments and make up the shortfall locally. While Valens and I head south, sir, you should also recruit as many legionaries and auxiliaries as we can afford, giving you enough men to leave the province secure and still bring perhaps another fifteen thousand reinforcements to Italia. Galba won't know what hit him!'

Despite his hangover, Vitellius beamed. 'So I am to deliver the knock-out blow?'

'Indeed you are, sir,' Valens said. 'You will ride into Rome as a conquering general, as a Caesar.'

'It doesn't bother you then that you'll be conquering your fellow Romans?' Lugubrix asked.

Vitellius shifted uncomfortably. Valens just glowered at my friend.

'We will exhaust every peaceable option before it comes to that, my friend. Let us pray that Galba will accept the inevitable. Rome deserves a worthier emperor.'

'Thank you, Caecina,' Vitellius said. I acknowledged his thanks with a bow of my head.

'Not at all, sir. We shouldn't detain you any longer, you must have more pressing duties to attend to. Valens and I will stay behind to sort out the details.'

These pressing duties would no doubt consist of a luxurious bath and an attempt to sleep off his monstrous hangover. His presence at this council was for appearances' sake only, to assuage his vanity. That done, it was time for the real soldiers to talk. The chair creaked ominously as our emperor wriggled to escape its confines. Once free, he looked each man in the eye. 'Thank you, gentlemen. As Caecina says, I have duties to attend to back in Colonia. I hope you'll forgive me for leaving you.'

We all saluted. 'Hail Caesar.' The word made him flinch again, but he did not correct us. He left the room, and I turned to Valens.

'I think your men can be dismissed, Valens. We can sort out the details between us.'

'Agreed.' While he was asking the legates to leave us, I spoke quietly to Lugubrix.

'Why did you have to ask about our fighting other Romans?'

'Because I was getting fed up with the arse-licking and the pompousness, and it felt very satisfying to bring that Valens down a peg or two.'

'I agree, but please don't do it again. A judicious amount of arse-licking and Valens and I can control Vitellius. If we didn't, he'd turn all of Rome into his banqueting hall, and all the empire his larder. The two of us can get things done.'

'So this is what they call politics, is it?' the Gaul asked, winking.

'Such as it is. I'll need you to stay here in the north to help Vitellius organize the reinforcements from Britannia, if that's all right?'

'So long as I'm paid, I'm happy. And you'll be heading south?'

'As soon as I can.'

'And Quintus?'

'I'll look after him, don't worry,' I said.

We embraced, his thatch of red hair tickling my cheek and ear.

'You'll forgive me for not showing you out?' I asked, sounding like a host at a dinner party.

'I'll survive, even if I am a Gaul in the middle of a Roman fortress. May the gods go with you, my friend.'

'You too.'

Valens watched my friend leave, and then we were alone.

'You two seem as thick as thieves,' he observed.

'We've been through a lot together.'

'Do you mind if we go for a walk? My head is crying out for fresh air.'

'Didn't you ride over?' I asked.

'I did, but you walked, and I can have a groom take my horse back into the city.'

'That's very considerate of you.'

'Don't sound so surprised. I'm not as much of a monster as you think I am.'

It was snowing gently as Valens and I walked slowly towards Colonia. The Germanic trousers were doing their job of keeping out the cold, but still we both rubbed our hands hard to try to keep them warm. Despite his years, Valens still had a thick head of hair. Unusually for a Roman he was blond, or rather he used to be; the flecks of silver among the fading yellow now lent him an air of dignity and authority. His grey eyes looked straight ahead, even when he began to speak.

'You don't trust me, do you, Severus?' he said, as though he were discussing the weather.

'What brought you to that conclusion?' I asked sarcastically.

'You don't like my ambition?'

'Ambition? That's putting it mildly. How many men have killed for their ambition?'

'Thousands,' he countered. 'Hundreds of thousands, at least. I know what I want and I take it, whether I have noble blood or not.'

'I thought I detected the slightest of chips on your shoulder. So you're not a ruthless schemer then, just a misunderstood class warrior?'

'Laugh if you like, but you've never had to work for anything in your life. I mean really work, toiling away for years for a promotion that was passed time and again to a man with better connections, to a man from "society".'

I could have flung my war record in his face, or told him that my father had died before I had even known him, but it wouldn't have made any difference. To him I was a spoiled aristocrat muscling in on his chance for glory, and nothing I did or said would change his mind.

'But then I'm not a cold-blooded killer either. I may come from a noble family, but with that comes a code of honour, of duty. My nobility doesn't define me, my actions do. As do yours. That's why I don't trust you.'

There was the trace of a smile on his lips, but only for a moment. 'Life would be a lot easier if we worked together.'

'But we're not going to be together, we're commanding separate columns.'

'Only as far as Italia,' he said. 'Once we've arrived in the Po valley we'll have to work together, and if the gods are willing, we'll be working together in Rome as well.'

'Are we not working together at the moment?' I said.

'Vitellius relies on us both equally, we each effectively run a province, have similar numbers of men under our command. It's not as though one of us is suddenly going to be out of favour. You do realize I have as much cause to hate you as you have to distrust me?'

'I don't actually.'

'You think I'm boorish, old, tight, ambitious and dangerous. I did murder Capito, you're right. I panicked, I didn't expect him to turn us down. But at least you know that I'm committed to Vitellius. You and I both knew this civil war was coming, all I needed was a governor with the balls for it. I tried with Verginius Rufus, Capito, now Vitellius, and I'll stand by him to the end. Now look at you.'

'Me?'

'You were born into a world of power and privilege. I had to earn my position, and yet you hold the same rank despite being almost twenty years younger than me. You're spoilt, arrogant, mistrustful, and your ambition is far more dangerous than mine. All this time I've been looking for a general in Germania to do this job, while you've betrayed Nero and Galba both. How do I know you won't betray Vitellius one day?'

'Because I've sworn an oath of loyalty,' I began.

'And being a patrician your word is worth far more than mine, of course. Yet you've broken it twice in one year. At least my ambition is predictable. You I'm not so sure about.'

I was silent for a time. Silent because he was right. I had been so preoccupied with despising Valens for his ambitions that I hadn't considered how other people would interpret my actions. Galba's decision to recall me to Rome on a charge of embezzlement, a crime that had been overlooked with a wink and a nod ever since Rome's reach had gone beyond the shores of Italia, was little more than a pretext. He was trying to get rid of those who had put him on the throne so that he would be beholden to no one. Well, I wasn't going to submit tamely to his will. Galba had brought this mutiny upon himself.

Salonina, Quintus, Totavalas and Lugubrix all knew that my ambition had been forced upon me. But what about the Senate, would they understand? What about my friend Julius Agricola? He would understand, I was sure, but how was he to know that it was Galba who had forced my hand by betraying me? I wish you knew, reader, how tempted I am to gloss over this conversation I had with Valens. You must believe me when I say that I write this only to record the truth, not to exonerate myself. My name has already been blackened, and these memoirs I am sure will make it no less black. But I want you to understand why I did what I did. No excuses, no apology. I will just tell you my story and hope that you understand.

IV

I was in a filthy mood when I made it back to Vitellius's palace later that afternoon. Valens and I had discussed many things on the way back to the city, talking through details of the coming campaign, then a lunch with the auxiliary officers to sound them out about the months ahead, and another few hours of bureaucracy, but it was Valens's questioning of my motives that I turned over and over in my mind. Totavalas was there to greet me at the palace gates.

'You look as sour as a Hibernian cheese, General. Anything I can do to help?'

I smiled ruefully. 'How are you at salving consciences?'

'Ah, now with my people that's a thing we tend to leave to the holy men.'

'I thought your priests made human sacrifices? Surely their consciences are guiltier than anyone's?'

'I find there's little that will stop a priest from preaching. Try being raised with the druids at Mona – I had enough religion for a lifetime.'

'And how did your druids help you when you had problems?' I asked.

'Well, druids are also interpreters of the law; as long as you haven't done anything illegal, General, your conscience should be as clear as any man's. And speaking of consciences, sir, I'd advise you to talk to your wife pretty sharpish. She's been sweetness and light since lunchtime. Seize the day, as you Romans say.'

'After this morning's pleasant chat?' I snorted. 'Vitellius's cook must have magic powers! Where's Aulus?'

'The little master is having a philosophy lesson, I think.'

'Poor boy, let's see how he's doing.'

We walked through Vitellius's marble halls, statues 'requisitioned' from the province's richest families adorning our route. I cast a glance along the wing where the palace kitchens were. It looked busier than the fortress. And why not? Yet another army of guests were expected to invade the banqueting hall that evening.

'I suppose even barbarian princes are taught some philosophy?' I mused.

'Taught would be the wrong word, I think,' Totavalas answered. 'Certainly not how Master Aulus is being taught. With my people, the sons are taken to watch their fathers, whatever their profession; blacksmiths, bards and farmers just as much as kings. I saw my first battle when I was five years old. Now that does make you think.'

I put my fingers to my lips as we approached our quarters. I could just hear muffled voices. The door was slightly ajar. I stepped nearer, close enough to hear the lesson.

'Now, Master Aulus, what was Aristotle trying to say when—'

'Please, sir, I really don't like philosophy. It's too hard!'

'I agree, that's enough sophistry for now,' I interrupted. 'Come here, my little warrior.'

Aulus ran into my arms. 'Father, can I have the rest of the day off, please? Philosophy is so boring!'

'Of course you can.'

The tutor protested. 'But, master, we have another two hours of Aristotle to cover, and then he has a test in mathematics.'

'You're going to have plenty of time to teach him in the weeks to come, Eumenes,' I reassured him. 'We're going south in a matter of days.'

'To Rome?' Aulus asked.

'You, me, your mother, Totavalas, everyone. We're all going to Rome.'

'Can I go and tell Mother?'

'Of course you can, go and tell her.' Aulus sped off to give Salonina the news, boyish excitement personified.

'Master . . .' the Greek tried again.

'You and he will be spending many weeks together on the march to Italia, and he won't be able to run off. You can teach him then. Right now I say give the boy a break.'

Aulus came in with Salonina in tow. I say in tow, for he was almost dragging her by the arm in his haste. 'Tell her, Father!'

'Tell me what?' she asked.

'We're going to Rome,' I said. It seemed to take a moment for the news to sink in, but then her deep blue eyes widened in surprise.

'We?'

'You didn't think I was going to let you rot in Germania?'

'Surely it'll be dangerous?'

I chuckled. 'Salonina, I'll be leading over twenty thousand men. I can't think of many safer places for the two of you to be.'

'Won't Galba send his own army?'

'If he can gather his troops in time, maybe. That's why we're leaving Germania as soon as possible.'

'What about Totavalas?' Aulus asked. 'Is he coming too?'

'Only if he wants to come,' I said, looking straight at the Hibernian.

'I'm surprised you have to ask, General.'

'Rome is a long way from here, Totavalas. I thought you wanted to go back to your own people?'

'That I do, but I can hardly go back home empty-handed. I'll need more than my good looks and charm if I'm to avenge my father.'

'That's settled then. The family is going to Rome.'

Winter had set in hard in Germania. My fingers were numb with cold, but I did not dare to crack my knuckles and coax some life back into my hands for fear of yet another icy glare from Salonina. Far below us, partly cloaked in mist, the Rhine flowed sluggishly, great chunks of ice and wintry debris bobbing gently in the water. The horses whinnied their displeasure, snorting tendrils of cloudy breath into the air.

'I've never known cold like this,' Salonina said.

I gave a gentle tug on the reins so that Achilles fell into step alongside my wife's horse.

'There's a spare pair of trousers in the wagon,' I suggested.

She nudged me hard in the ribs. 'Unlike you, I do have some standards. Do the German women wear these trousers?'

'I don't think so.'

'Then why should I wear them?'

'I was only joking.'

'So was I.'

We passed through a village on those heights above the river. The horses frightened a gaggle of geese and they scattered, honking. A girl was drawing some water from the well. She looked up to see what had caused the noise. She had beautiful, golden hair that danced in the wind. I smiled at her, and I swear she blushed before looking away.

'Eyes front, Caecina,' Salonina said. She was only half joking.

'Am I not allowed to admire the landscape?'

'Not when the landscape has pretty blondes in it. Not that it matters. Without your splendid horse and polished armour, I doubt she'd give you a second glance.'

'Jealousy is such an unattractive trait,' I teased.

56

Salonina sat arrow-straight in the saddle, every inch the Roman noblewoman even if her father had been a tradesman. Her hands were ash-white as she gripped the reins, and I saw that she was shivering.

'Why don't you get into the wagon with Aulus? There are plenty of furs in there to keep you warm.'

'He's having a lesson with Eumenes. Besides, someone has to keep an eye on you.'

'You can rely on me to do that, my lady, if you want to have a warmer journey,' Totavalas interrupted.

'What exceptional hearing you have, Totavalas.' Salonina's tone indicated more displeasure at being overheard than praise for the Hibernian's faculties. Totavalas took little notice, but urged his horse on so that the three of us rode abreast.

'It's not right for a Roman lady to be travelling with us smelly men and sweaty horses.'

'They are my horses,' I said, 'sweaty or otherwise, and they need the exercise. How's your nag doing?'

'He's doing grand, General. But without wishing to belittle your generosity, I'd give a month's wages to be sitting on a fine stallion from my own country.'

'Wages?' I scoffed. 'You're lucky I feed you, clothe you and lend you an expensive horse or you'd be walking bollock-naked to Mogontiacum.'

'If you two boys are going to talk about horses and your manly parts, I'll join Aulus in the warmth.' Salonina tugged hard at the reins, forcing her mare to hold up, then she turned towards the rear of our column.

'Have I done something wrong?' I murmured. Salonina was already out of earshot.

'Perhaps mentioning the word "bollock" affected her sensibilities, General?'

'Did nobody tell you, in what passed for your education, what a rhetorical question is?'

Totavalas grinned, and said in an exaggerated Hibernian brogue, 'Now why would anyone waste such a difficult term on a simple bog-trotter like me?'

He was too far away to cuff, so I sighed and shook my head. 'Why do I tolerate you, Totavalas?'

'Is that another rhetorical question?'

'You can answer it if you like.'

'Because I'm witty, charming, loyal, intelligent, almost your whole household likes me, and handsome and—'

'You forgot modest,' I pointed out.

'No I didn't. I just don't like to boast.'

I held up my hand for silence. 'Halt the column!' I shouted.

'What's wrong?' Totavalas asked.

I didn't answer, waiting instead for the horses to quieten. Afterwards there was nothing, nothing but the biting wind whistling through the pines. I cocked an ear eastwards. I thought I had heard . . .

'Voices,' Totavalas whispered. 'German voices.'

A raiding party must have crossed the Rhine. But in the depths of winter? Cursing, I wished I hadn't sent Publilius and his squadron of cavalry on ahead to warn the camp at Mogontiacum that we were close at hand. We were only a dozen men, a tutor, a woman and a boy. My hand reached for my sword, the Hibernian had already drawn his dagger. Down the foggy hillside I saw a glint of polished silver among the grey and brown.

'Totavalas, to the wagon, now! The rest of you,' I called to the bodyguards, 'form up on me.'

My heart was racing. The first figures were emerging from the mist. With my family in the wagon there was no way we could outrun the enemy. I had no idea how many there were, but maybe a sudden charge would send the raiding party packing. By now the guards had formed a line, with me in the centre. There was the rasp of swords being unsheathed. As one, we dug in our heels and made off at a canter. Down below there were cries of alarm. As we entered the forest the horses had to jink and swerve to avoid the trees, slowing us down. The cries of alarm were replaced with orders barked out.

Then someone shouted in Latin: 'Stop! Friends! We're friends!'

It was only then that I noticed the mail shirts, the long oval shields and familiar spears, and guessed that these were German auxiliaries. Too late, one of my men had careered into the German line. The horse flailed among the men who could not get out of the way fast enough and suddenly stumbled. The rider was catapulted out of the saddle.

'Halt!' I cried. The other guards had noticed too, their horses rearing at the sudden stop and the prospect of a thicket of spears.

'Who are you?' I called out.

'The Ubian Cohort,' one of them called out. 'Who are you?'

'Step forward so I can see you.'

A man broke ranks, the red plume on his helmet marking him out as the prefect in command of the cohort. Gentle blue eyes and the beginnings of a wispy beard, he was probably only a few years younger than me.

'I am General Severus, chosen by the emperor to command all units within this province. What in Hades do you think you're playing at, prefect?'

'Well, sir, we were marching along the river road to Mogontiacum, and my scouts reported a column moving along the heights heading south. I thought you might want our protection.'

'And how were we meant to know that you were *auxilia* rather than a German raiding party?' The officer had no answer, so I answered for him. 'Instead of joining us further up the road, or sending those same scouts to warn us, you marched up the hill, chatting in German, and all we could see were warriors emerging from the fog.'

I guided my mount to where my guard had fallen from his horse. The auxiliaries quickly moved out of Achilles' way.

'Fulvio, where are you?'

'Here, sir.' The man was struggling to rise. His right arm dangled limp at his side, so he rolled on to his left flank and pushed hard against the earth to lever himself up.

'You still alive, Fulvio?'

He smiled grimly. 'Pretty sure the arm's broken, but the rest of me's all right. Can't say the same for that poor sod,' he said, gesturing at the body below him.

The German's skull had caved in on one side, his face a grisly mask of blood. Fulvio's horse must have caught him full on the head when it went down, thrashing. But Fulvio was already attending to the frightened beast, calming it down.

'You're a lucky man, prefect,' I said.

'General?'

'If one of my men had died, you would have joined him. But your cohort is now a man short. You can take his place. Who's the senior centurion here?'

A voice called out from the ranks, 'Centurion Pullo, sir.'

'Congratulations, Prefect Pullo. Detail a team to bury your man, the rest of you can follow us to Mogontiacum.'

They say all roads lead to Rome. In the case of Upper Germania, all roads, tracks and muddy pathways lead to the provincial capital. The Ubian Cohort wasn't the only force that we joined on the road south. The messengers we had sent from Colonia had ridden fast and hard. We were lucky that the Germans on the far side of the Rhine had been quiet for so many years, or we wouldn't have dared to take the auxiliaries with us. Some were seconded to the provincial tax collectors, men who might need some muscle in the face of unwilling debtors. Others were in small garrisons dotted along the river, and some of them even beyond the river in strategic locations, acting not only as antennae for the mood and movement of the tribes, but as our first line of defence, holding crucial mountain passes or river crossings. Things would have been very different if the auxiliaries were conscripts, but you have to remember that they were tribesmen. They loved to fight. Joining the Roman army meant a steady salary, an alien concept to them, enemies to kill and the glittering prize of Roman citizenship at the end of their twenty-year service; added to that, Vitellius's taking the name of Germanicus had pleased the troops no end.

Mogontiacum had taken on a whole new character in the days that I had been away. It reminded me of my first day in Vienne all those months ago, the whole place seething with a sense of purpose and pride. However, there was one crucial difference. While the whole Vindex affair had reeked of amateurism and playing at soldiers, these men were the cream of the Roman army. Nothing in the world could match them. The praetorians were too few, and the legions in Dacia and Syria were too far away to play a part in the coming campaign. But even the eastern legions recognized that the men on the Rhine were the toughest in the empire. And they were mine to command.

The cohorts that had joined us peeled off to the makeshift camp where the auxiliaries were gathering. Our small convoy skirted the western side of the town, heading directly to the fort where the two legions had so nearly run riot barely a fortnight before. Totavalas had been willing to risk his life to defend my family if the troops had decided to ransack my villa, less than a mile from the main gate. The two guards on the villa door stood to attention as they recognized me.

'As you were, men. The nearest thing to an attack you'll face is a telling-off from my wife for making eyes at the slave girls.' The two of them smiled. They liked a general who commanded respect but could joke and muck in with them from time to time.

The villa was the same as when we had left it. Not that there should have been anything different, we had been gone little more than a week. Nevertheless, once she was out of the wagon Salonina was mistress of the house again, and set everyone to rights. In a matter of moments she had upbraided half the household for letting dust into the villa, the cook for not having mulled wine waiting for us by the fire, and others for the gods know what. I suspected that she was finding fault for fault's sake, just to remind them that she would not tolerate any sloppiness now that she had returned. There was much bowing and scraping, and while Salonina was in her element I had other matters to attend to.

Quintus was waiting for me in the atrium. 'General,' he began.

'Come, Quintus, I'm the same man you knew in Gaul. There's no need to call me general.' In a couple of steps I had him in a great bear hug, hitting him on the back for good measure.

'It's good to have you here again,' he said.

'I can't stop long, I'm afraid. Shall we talk while we walk?'

A slave brought the mulled wine that Salonina had insisted upon. It was a short walk to the fort, but it's always good to have something warm inside you to keep the outside warm too.

While we walked, Quintus reeled off a list of things that had happened since I'd gone north. The Vitellian messenger had arrived three days ago, and though we had known what was coming since New Year's Day, there was still much to do.

'How has Vocula reacted to all of this?' I asked. Dillius Vocula had been the senior legate who commanded the Twenty-Second Primigenia, until Galba had betrayed me, forcing me to declare for Vitellius. Now I commanded all the troops in the province.

'I think he's resigned himself to it. He wasn't exactly thrilled that you incited the rebellion without consulting him.'

'I had no idea whether I could count on him or not.'

'And you knew you could count on me?' Quintus asked.

'Of course I could, there's no man in the world I trust more.'

'I trust you, Caecina, but that doesn't mean I like what you're doing.'

I was stunned.

'But you joined your father when he rebelled against Nero,' I began.

'I was young . . .'

'Only nine months younger than you are now.'

'You think I'm not an older and wiser person after what happened at Vesontio? I watched hundreds of farm boys being slaughtered by an army, and lost a brother and a father.'

There was nothing I could say that wouldn't sound trite, so I let Quintus continue.

'Things were so much simpler back then. Nero was a tyrant, but Galba was meant to be a proper guardian for Rome. My father lost his head when Galba promised him Gaul, and I thought you were the only man who believed in the cause we were fighting for.'

'Thought?' I asked.

'Answer me truthfully, Caecina. Would you have thrown in your lot with Vitellius if Galba hadn't summoned you to Rome?'

'It's not so simple as that. The legions wanted Vitellius, Salonina wanted me to support him, so did Valens . . .'

'Valens! From what I've heard of the man, why would you use him to justify your decision?'

I grabbed him by the arm. 'Fine. You want the honest answer? Yes, I was tempted to join Vitellius. For Hades' sake, he's all but promised me the consulship now. There hasn't been a consul in my family for generations. Even before Galba tried to prosecute me, he had made it clear that he would never raise me above the post of legate, after all the sacrifices I made for him. I could have sided with Valens right at the start. We could have made Verginius Rufus emperor the very day they beat your father and his rebels, when legion upon legion was devoted to their con- quering hero. But no, I stuck by Galba because I had given my word. And after all that, Galba decides to remove me from my post on a trumped-up charge. Vitellius may be a glutton, but I'd far rather serve a glutton than an ungrateful, miserly old man!'

Quintus said nothing at first. He just looked down at the hand that still clutched his arm. I let it go at once.

'I suppose I should be grateful that you're not lying to me.'

'I'm sorry, Quintus. You're like a brother to me. I just thought that where I'd go . . .'

'I would blindly follow?'

'No, not at all. Look, I can't change what has happened, I can only say sorry.'

He sighed. 'You've made us all traitors now. Even if I didn't want to follow, I have no choice.'

We were almost within earshot of the gatehouse, I couldn't say anything more.

'Who goes there?' a voice called.

'Tribune Vindex and General Severus,' Quintus replied.

'Welcome back, General!'

'It's good to be back,' I shouted up to the man.

Quintus led me through the camp. Legionaries stopped to nudge each other and point at me. The murmur burbled from building to building: their general was back. Soon I was back on that icy parade ground where I had started a mutiny, where Quintus had saved my life yet again by giving me the sword that put an end to Strontius's troublemaking for good. And there was the principia, the headquarters of the legion, and what looked like a small welcoming party outside. There was Vocula, tall and dour, and next to him were my officers, Tuscus and Nepos. My officers saluted me, the legate remained motionless.

'Thank you, Prefect Tuscus, Centurion Nepos. I hope you've been busy in my absence?'

'Following your orders to the letter, General,' the older man, Tuscus, replied.

'Good man.'

'Shall we go inside then?' Quintus asked.

'No, this won't take long. I just want to finalize the details. As you know, I will be taking just over half the legionaries and all the auxiliaries south with me. How has the recruiting for replacements been going?'

Tuscus looked to Nepos. 'Very well, sir. We've ordered recruiting parties into all the major towns and sent word throughout the countryside for citizen recruits. Two of the auxiliary cohorts have been dispatched across the Rhine to send word to the German tribesmen.'

'Excellent. What I wanted to settle is who is to come with me to Rome and who will guard the province while I'm gone. Legate Vocula?'

The legate shifted uncomfortably. 'General?'

'I realize that I was wrong not to include you in our plans to join Vitellius, but I couldn't be sure where your loyalties lie. Whether you support Galba or Vitellius, would you defend this province against Rome's enemies?'

'I will, General.'

'Thank you, Vocula. I would like your senior tribune to command the detachment that goes south. I will leave you, Tuscus, to command the part of the Fourth Legion that remains here. Nepos and Tribune Vindex, I take it you have no objections against coming with me to Rome?'

Nepos grinned. 'None at all, sir.'

I looked at Quintus.

'You command and I shall follow, General,' he said.

'But I don't understand why you have to leave us again,' Salonina protested.

'It'll be ten days at the most,' I said, while double-checking I had everything I needed in my saddlebags.

'I thought you said that the safest place would be with you?'

'When I command the army, yes. But most of the army is still here. I need to ride to the other legion at Vindonissa and make sure everything is prepared before we cross the Alps. Quintus will look after you and Aulus while I'm gone, and as soon as the men here are ready to march, you'll march with them. Or rather ride; I can't see you marching over two hundred miles!'

'Promise me you'll be all right,' she insisted.

'Salonina, I'm just going down to make sure everything's organized. Galba will have heard of the rebellion by now, but none of his troops will be anywhere near the Alps yet.'

'Caecina, promise me.'

I still remember how she looked on that bleak day, now more than a decade ago. She wore a simple, pale blue *stola*, which elegantly disguised the bump of three months' pregnancy, as well as a warm fur cloak that reached to the ground. I even remember her bracelet. It was a wide band of silver that covered all of her wrist, embedded with lapis lazuli from Africa. I had given it to her when I came home from Britannia, when I had found not the girl I had married but a young woman, and the mother of my son. I looked into those entrancing blue eyes of hers, and in that moment I gently put my hands either side of her face and kissed her passionately.

'I promise,' I said, finally. 'Now will you let me go? I've got a hard ride ahead of me.'

Salonina smiled, and nodded her assent. The stable boy gave me a leg-up into the saddle.

'We'll be together again before you know it. Besides, what's the worst that could happen to me in Raetia?'

I had no way of knowing what havoc would unfold in the peaceful mountain pastures to the south.

V

I rode hard for hours upon end, in daytime stopping only for food and water. In two days of travelling, I slept about eight hours altogether, staying in ramshackle inns that served the road to Raetia. The monotony was broken only by halting every twenty miles at the way stations to commandeer a fresh horse. The Rhine became narrower and narrower, the floodplain began to shrink. Soon I was back in the Alpine foothills that streaked westwards for miles, even as far as Vesontio. I often found myself in little valleys that reminded me of that bloody battlefield.

It was only when I came nearer to Vindonissa that it struck me something was wrong. Granted it was the depths of winter, but there were never more than a handful of people outdoors. The road was practically empty too. On the main road from Italia to the north of the empire you would expect to find travellers and tradesmen, and yet sometimes I went for hours at a time without seeing a soul. Even the men at the way stations, normally the arteries that carried the empire's gossip just as much as they did the official correspondence, couldn't help me much.

'We sent on one of your couriers, General, not more than four days ago. A letter for the governor in Pannonia, wasn't it? But then we haven't had a messenger come north for over a week now. I know it's winter, but we've had worse here in Raetia.'

'Worse?' I asked. 'I haven't been so cold since I left Britannia.'

'I take it you've never been up the Alps before, General?'

'No, I haven't.'

'It may be snowing now, but this'll do little more than lay down a fresh white carpet. Now three winters back, that was a winter and a half, I can tell you. Snow so thick you could barely wade through it. The passes through to Italia couldn't be crossed until late spring. Not that we minded the holiday, eh lads?' The stable boys nodded as they blew on their hands to keep warm.

As I plunged deeper into Raetia the hills were turning into mountains. The remounts struggled with the altitude, and I had to rein them in for fear of blowing them. It was growing dark on the second day and snow had begun to fall when I came within sight of Vindonissa. From a crossroads on the hillside I could see over the fortress walls and into the camp itself. The place was practically deserted. I could just make out a few idle figures standing guard on the walls, but the bulk of the legion wasn't anywhere to be seen. It was then that I noticed a column of smoke away to the east. With the ever-darkening sky it was lucky that I had spotted it, but there it was, black and foreboding. I sat there, shivering, wondering which way to go. Down the mountainside and to the shelter of the camp, or a long gallop into the cold night eastwards, following the smoke? I tugged at the reins. The horse was having none of it. He had probably ridden this road before and was looking forward to the warm, cosy stables in the town. A sharp yank to the left and a kick of my heels reminded him who was master.

It wasn't long before I lost sight of the smoke against the night sky, but the smell was unmistakable. It reminded me of the stench when we set fire to Boudicca's village after we had crushed her rebellion. In the flat lands of the Iceni, the orange glow of the flames could be seen for many miles. Here in the Alps I had the merest of tinges on the eastern horizon to guide me; I had to follow my nose. But what would I find when I reached the source of the smell? The plume of smoke had been too concentrated for a freak forest fire, or the camp fires of a legion on the march. And then, after an hour ploughing through the snowstorm, I saw it.

There, guarding a high mountain pass, a wooden fortress was blazing brightly. The flames had consumed most of the walls and were licking at the high watchtowers at every corner. The base of the mountain was surrounded by what I had to assume was the Vindonissa legion, the Twenty-First Rapax. I rode hard, soon reaching the outer line of sentries.

'Where's the legate?' I demanded.

'I'll need the password first,' the sentry stated.

'I don't know the bloody password. I'm General Severus, your commanding officer. Tell me where the legate is now or I'll have you digging latrines for the rest of your career!'

The sentry hesitated for a moment then pointed me in the direction of the front line.

I passed through rank after rank of legionaries, their ring of iron stretching over a mile round the mountain. By the light of the fire I could just make out the legion's eagle, its shaft planted in the ground. Beneath it was a group of horsemen. Some wore the thin purple stripe of the junior tribune on their cloaks, but at their centre was an older man. A plume of horse-hair dyed red arced from the front of his helmet back towards his neck.

'Legate Pansa?' I shouted. The legate turned to see who had called out to him.

'Yes, and you are . . . ?'

I flicked back my cloak, revealing the silver breastplate that Totavalas had painstakingly polished. 'General Severus. I take it you knew I was coming?'

The legate looked confused. 'I knew a general was coming, but I didn't expect you to be quite so—'

'Young?' I cut him off. 'That's hardly important, Legate. What in Hades is going on here is what I want to know.'

'We're burning the fort, General,' one of the tribunes said.

I shot him a withering look. 'He's a clever one, isn't he? Legate, would you mind telling me why you are burning your own fort?'

'It's a long story, sir.'

'Well, at least we have a nice fire to sit around while you tell it,' I jibed. 'Pansa, stop bloody prevaricating and tell me what is going on.'

The legate squirmed in the saddle. 'It's the Helvetii; they're rebelling. As the emperor ordered, we gave an escort of twenty men to your messenger for the governor in Pannonia. The men in the fort captured the group and are holding them hostage in the fort. I was hoping to have this mess sorted out before the general – I mean, before you – arrived, so I laid siege to the fort and had my archers loose a few volleys of fire arrows.' Pansa gestured at the blaze.

'But it's not quite as simple as that, is it, Legate?' said a voice.

'You hold your tongue, Prefect.'

'As I see it, the general is the senior officer here, and I think he'd like to know all the facts.'

A burly man approached. Like me, he wore a pair of trousers to ward off the winter chill.

'Who are you?'

'A Helvetian, General. Gaius Torquatus, prefect of the Alpine infantry cohort. Those men up in the fort have every right to rebel. Up here in the mountains they hadn't heard that Vitellius had declared himself emperor. The legate here had given orders to collect gold from the province, and a century decided to hijack a wagon of gold that pays the salary of the auxiliaries up in the fort and for the upkeep of the fort itself.'

'I had orders to levy all provisions necessary for the campaign,' Pansa protested.

'But the gold was paid for by the local tribes, wasn't it, sir? We pay our own troops to defend Rome's borders. Can you blame those poor bastards when the army steals from them?'

Before Pansa could protest, a chorus of shouts echoed on the hillside. An army of fingers pointed up at the fort. The gates were opening.

'I knew it! They'd have to come out sooner or later,' Pansa exulted.

A group of men came running out of the gates. Something was wrong though. 'Prefect,' I called, 'how many men are stationed at the fort?'

'About two hundred, sir. Why?'

'Does that look like two hundred men to you?'

Everyone squinted to count the figures emerging from the fiery fortress.

'Looks like about twenty,' someone said.

The men were running now, running so fast from the fire that some of them lost their footing on the hillside and were sent sprawling into the snow. Soon we could hear cries of pain over the crackling of the great inferno up above us. Such was the noise of the fire that it was a while before the men were within earshot.

'Who are you?' Pansa called out.

'The escort for the imperial messenger,' a man replied.

'Address me as legate, man. Don't you know how to address an officer?'

'Do you think I give a fuck about that right now?' The man had his arms drawn tightly across his chest, as though defending himself from the cold.

'How dare you? Guards, arrest that man.'

'Ignore that order,' I shouted. 'Fetch the surgeons, now.'

'But you heard the man,' Pansa protested.

'Look at him, you fool,' I hissed.

As he stepped nearer I could make out the trails of blood down his forearms. Both his hands had been cut off.

'By all the gods,' Pansa murmured, stunned.

'They said they were cutting them off so that we could never steal from them again.'

'They? Where are they?' the legate asked.

There was no need to say anything. I nudged Pansa and pointed upwards. There on the skyline was a trail of flickering lights. The Helvetii had left the fort a long time since and were climbing further up the mountain, beyond the reach of our heavily armoured infantry.

'So much for your siege, Legate.'

The surgeon did what he could for the poor men who had been held hostage. We learned later that night that the rebels had escaped by a secret tunnel, leaving the main gate barred. The prisoners had managed to remove the hefty wooden bar by lifting it with their forearms while the building burned around them.

'Julius Alpinus, that's the man who ordered our hands to be cut off,' one of the men told us.

The auxiliary prefect nodded wearily. 'He's just the sort of man to pull a stunt like this. Hot-headed and completely lacking common sense; a dangerous mix.'

'I suppose you're the man to thank for keeping your cohort loyal,' I said.

Gaius Torquatus grimaced. 'Maybe. The fact that we knew about Vitellius and the need for gold and those bastards up on the hill didn't is probably a better reason.'

'But will your men fight with us against this Alpinus?'

'It's what we're paid to do, General.'

'Good man. Now, where is Alpinus from?' I asked.

'He's the chief of a small town to the west of here, Aquae Helveticae. He made his fortune from the healing springs on his land.'

'Then we will stop this rot before it spreads. Pansa, I want you to march the legion to the west and put this village to the sword. That'll stop anyone from joining Alpinus.'

The next morning the legion began to march slowly through the valley, following a mountain river westwards towards its source, the springs of Alpinus's town. The march was cold, but the men's boiling anger kept them going. The idea that a barbarian had mutilated some of their own fired them up; I might even have had a mutiny on my hands if I hadn't given them the chance for some retribution. I was in something of a dilemma about the Helvetian auxiliaries though. Their prefect seemed dependable, but I couldn't be sure about his men. Would they join in the punitive raid, or would they turn on us? I didn't dare send them away either, for without the legion to deter them only their commander and their sense of duty to Rome would keep them loyal, and I didn't want to put their loyalty to the test. The stench of burning pine followed us on the easterly wind, a constant reminder of the night before. The wounded men were spared the march, recovering instead in the relative warmth and comfort of a military wagon.

Pansa rode alongside me, hoping to make me forget his role in this monumental cock-up by professing his enthusiasm for the coming campaign in Italia. Thankfully I was spared his ramblings when a scout was spotted on the road ahead, galloping towards us.

'Legate Pansa,' he called. The legate raised his hand.

'You may give me your information,' I told the scout when he came close enough. 'I'm in command here.'

The scout looked questioningly at his commander, but Pansa nodded his assent.

'The whole town is out, sir. Armed with anything they could get their hands on. Picks, scythes, swords, the lot.'

'How many men do you think there are?' Pansa said.

'I'd guess about three thousand.'

'And Alpinus, is he with them?' I asked.

'I can't tell, sir.'

'All right, you may rejoin the rest of the cavalry.'

'Well, what now?' the legate asked me.

It was only now, in the daylight and with his helmet off, that I had my first proper look at Pansa. I guessed he was in his late forties. The greying hair and the not-so-taut skin made it a safe enough guess. This was a little late for a man to be made a legate, and in what was normally the most peaceful province of the empire. A younger brother of a more famous man, or a cousin perhaps, who owed his position to favour rather than merit, that's what I surmised.

'We bring peace to this province, Pansa, and quickly.'

Within a matter of hours the river we had followed had narrowed to little more than a trickle, yet the valley had broadened out a little. Nestling between the hills to the north and south lay the little town, and in front of the town stood an army. The scout was right, I guessed around three thousand men stood in one line right across the valley floor. Pansa passed my orders to his tribunes, and the legion began to form its own line. Rapidly our marching column was transformed into an immaculate wall of burnished iron and steel, with five thousand shields touching rim to rim. I took care that it was only men from the Rapax Legion in the line, and that the Helvetian cohort and its prefect were out of sight in the rear. Pansa and I were perhaps twenty paces in front of the formation.

'The legion will advance,' Pansa called. Five thousand men moved as one, each footstep sounded as one metallic clang, the metal plates of their armour jangling against each other as the men paced forward. The opposing line advanced menacingly. Pansa scanned it nervously, but my younger eyes had seen no bowmen among the townsfolk, only farmers with pitchforks, scythes and staffs. We were in no immediate danger. I could see a tremor of fear run through the peasants, like a ripple on a still pool. Some of them were edging backwards. A few men in the centre called out words of encouragement, and the line held firm again.

Just before we came within javelin range, I raised my hand for the Rapax to halt.

'Helvetians,' I shouted, 'my name is General Severus. I serve the emperor.'

'Which one?' a voice called out. There was a smattering of nervous laughter.

'The Emperor Vitellius, a man who has the interests of the Rhine-folk at heart.'

'Then why does he steal our gold?' another asked.

'There never was any intention to take the gold for the fort. Before yesterday I would have returned it gladly, but one of your own has dared to raise his hand against the soldiers of Rome, and I will burn this town as an example for all those who would join the traitor, Julius Alpinus.'

Some wailed, others screamed their protests, but I would not be deterred.

'I hear this Alpinus is a rich man. When we kill him, his fortune can go towards rebuilding your homes. Unless you give up Alpinus to me right now, your town will be burned, the men will be killed and your families will be sold into slavery.'

Deathly silence.

Then: 'Fuck off back to Rome!' the crowd roared in anger and fear, and began to charge.

Pansa and I quickly turned our horses round, and the men behind us made a gap for us to ride through. The red and silver wall closed up behind us, the men bracing themselves for the charge. I would have had the men launch a volley of javelins into the seething mass in front of us, but we would need every weapon we could muster once we crossed the Alps, so the grisly work would have to be done with swords and shields

alone. The tribesmen were fifty paces away, forty, thirty . . .
The legionaries turned their shoulders ever so slightly towards
the enemy, bracing themselves for impact. Twenty paces, ten.
There was an almighty crash as hundreds of bodies careered
into the wall. Some of the soldiers had used the impact to send
their opponents tumbling through into the ranks behind, where
hundreds of swords waited to skewer and stab them.

The first screams of pain rent the air. From my vantage point
behind the men I could see that our line was holding firm. The
nearest Helvetii with their array of knives, scythes and pitchforks were trying to catch the rim of the legionaries' shields with
their longer weapons and drag them down so that another could
lunge at the unprotected neck of his enemy. But every time one
of the tribesmen came close to succeeding, the pressure from
the eager men behind forced the man forward, within stabbing
range of the deadly gladii. The enemy were falling in their
dozens, and still they drove harder and harder against our wall.
I saw a man go down from our side, overreaching himself in a
vicious lunge. Just as his blade gutted the brute ahead of him a
scythe must have hacked into his legs, for he went down like a
mighty oak, crashing heavily to the ground. The feral tribesmen
pounced on the fallen legionary, slashing, kicking and thrusting
their blades into him when they should have made for the small
space in the line. Then it was too late, a fresh man from the rank
behind had plugged the gap.

I was watching the plight of the fallen legionary so intently
that the first I knew of the spear was when it flashed across
me, passing within spitting distance only to impale one of the
auxiliaries. So much for them being spared fighting their own
people! I saw other tribesmen at the rear of the mass were having
the same idea.

'Time to dismount, Pansa!' The legate readily agreed. We
should have dismounted long before then but we had a duty to
set an example to the men. With my feet back on the ground I

gave the signal for the bugler to call the advance. The young boy licked his lips before putting them to the cold metal. The high, harsh notes pierced the air. Up and down the line centurions heard the call and marshalled their men, readying them for the advance. By now the most eager of the Helvetii had fallen. This was the moment to send the rest of them running for the hills, where they should have gone in the first place, instead of making a suicidal stand.

With a ferocious roar, our front rank took the fight to the enemy, no longer waiting for them to charge obligingly into our thicket of swords and spears. Slowly, ponderously, we began to inch forward. The keening cries of pain from the hill-men began to fade away, not because they were gaining the upper hand but because there were fewer and fewer of them left to kill. Our crawl became a slow step. As we advanced I was soon among the dead and dying Helvetii as the men marched inexorably onwards. I didn't even draw my sword. Those who weren't dead had gaping wounds, mostly in their necks or stomachs, evidence that the months and years of sword drill had ingrained in our men the technique to kill with a single blow. The auxiliaries behind us would administer the coup de grâce. I had spared them the unpleasant task of fighting their countrymen toe to toe, but putting the wounded out of their misery would be a lesson in loyalty.

The legionaries were striding forward now, not even cheering their victory. It wasn't what they would call a victory. A full legion, not to mention the auxiliaries, against a mere three thousand poorly armed civilians. By now those same civilians were running full pelt towards the town.

'Shall we chase them, General?' Pansa asked.

'No need. All I wanted was to burn Alpinus's town and to capture him. Killing these men won't help us do either.'

'Killing a few more of his people might convince Alpinus to give himself up,' the legate ventured.

'If this were Italia would you offer me the same advice?' I asked, sneering.

'If this were Italia we wouldn't be in this situation,' Pansa shot back.

The town was empty by the time we reached it. The women and children must have fled westwards while their husbands and fathers fought us. There was nothing to loot except for the few chickens or geese that the townspeople hadn't been able to carry with them. They would provide supper for barely more than a century, but then we weren't looking to loot the place. While the auxiliaries piled up, counted and buried their countrymen, seven hundred and eighty-two of them to be exact, I had the legion collecting firewood, furniture, anything that would burn.

When we came to Boudicca's town in the miserable, flat lands of the Iceni, it hadn't taken much to burn down her hall; a few well-placed torches, then you could stand back and warm your hands on the fire. Burning an entire town was different. With the amount of firewood available the men were able to place it strategically between key buildings to lay a combustible path across the whole expanse of the settlement. They also had to take account of the wind direction; when it favoured our purpose, then and only then could they build and light the first fire. A dash of oil from the archers' supply was added to a corner of our town-shaped bonfire. A few sparks from a flint and the fire was born. Many hands thrust many torches into the fire, and each was carried to its allotted pile. Soon there were dozens of little flames that danced and flickered, steadily growing.

We stayed long enough to ensure that the whole town would catch fire before beginning our pursuit of Alpinus. Our column marched under the midday sun. Behind us Aquae Helveticae, a place of serenity and healing, was turning to ashes.

VI

Alpinus was a dead man, though he did not know it yet. With almost eight hundred dead, that left no more than two thousand who would fight with him, and after the massacre by the springs I doubted even half that number would remain loyal to their chief. Many would scatter, taking their families up into the hills where it wouldn't be worth pursuing them. But we couldn't be sure that Alpinus wouldn't draw men to him as he fled westwards. Pansa, Torquatus and I were holding a small council of war on horseback as the legion tramped through the hills and passes.

'I've known stubborn bastards in my time,' Pansa began, 'but this man caps them all. We besiege and burn his fort, attack his tribe, burn his town; I mean, any normal man would hide in the mountains somewhere and wait for us to cross the Alps. But no, this one has to rally a bunch of suicidal tribesmen and hole himself up in the strongest fastness in the entire province.'

'I did warn you, sir,' Torquatus said wearily.

'So you've said before, Prefect,' I snapped. 'Hindsight isn't going to help us now. Torquatus, you know him better than any of us. Can he be persuaded to surrender and stand trial?'

'Not a hope, General.'

'Not even to spare his people?'

'He is their chief. They're oath-sworn to fight and die for him.'

'And you're sure that he's not going to leave this fort?'

'Certain. Mount Vocetius has been our last defence ever since my people came to the Alps. He'll know by now that we've sent for the Thracian auxiliaries to block any retreat to the west. Now he'll sit on his rock and watch us throw men against his walls.'

'Then we should thank the gods that at least he didn't storm your barracks, Legate. How many men did you leave behind to defend Vindonissa?'

'Half a cohort,' Pansa mumbled.

'Two hundred and forty men to defend your own fort,' I said scathingly. 'And what if Alpinus had taken Vindonissa? You'd be court-martialled before the emperor, and Vitellius would have done what Valens and I told him to do. Let me make one thing clear, Pansa: even once my men from Germania arrive, you will be the senior officer. My senior tribune is little more than twenty and has already commanded thousands of men. One more slip-up from you and my man will take your place.'

'What would happen to me then?'

'Vitellius would decide,' I said. Pansa read the next words in my eyes.

'And the emperor would do whatever you told him to do?'

'You're learning, Pansa.'

The handful of men that Pansa had left behind were relieved to see us in Vindonissa once again, but not as grateful as our wounded were to arrive safely in the fort. Our encounter with the Helvetii had left us with thirteen dead and nearly thirty wounded, not to mention those who had been captured by Alpinus. The camp surgeon balked at the stream of men clambering out of the wagons. Some of the legionaries grabbed the men by their forearms and helped them to the ground as none of the escort had hands to grip the sides of the carts.

'This can't have happened in battle,' the surgeon said, shaking his head.

'They were prisoners, doctor,' Pansa explained.

'Whose prisoners?'

'Julius Alpinus's. He's the one who passed this way with the rabble that we defeated at Aquae Helveticae.'

'By the healing springs? Did anyone think to use the waters on these wretches' wounds?'

'They wouldn't have healed much after what the men put into them.'

'Don't tell me. Piss, shit, oil, the lot?'

'My orders were to destroy Alpinus's property, all of it.'

'It was my command, doctor,' I explained. 'I assumed it was a local superstition that Alpinus profited by. Can't you do anything for the men?'

'Of course I can, but it's often helpful to use the gifts the local gods have granted their people. I'll have to use something else on the wounds instead.'

'I never had anything special when I lost this,' I said, gesturing at what remained of my little finger. 'I just had it cauterized.'

'Who treated you?'

'A Gaul.'

'Then that tells you all you need to know. Now if you'll excuse me . . .'

The surgeon swept off with a coterie of assistants in tow, to begin sorting through the wounded to find the most serious cases.

'He does have a habit of flying off the handle, I grant you,' Pansa said, 'but he's the best surgeon north of the Rubicon, that's for sure.'

'So long as he does a good job, that's all I want from a surgeon. I just pray he won't be too busy once we cross the Rubicon.'

'So do we all, General.'

'But the fighting isn't over yet, Pansa. Would you show me your artillery?'

'Now, sir?'

'Now, Pansa. I want to put an end to this slaughter as quickly as possible. For that we'll need artillery.'

I soon saw why Pansa had been reluctant to take me straight to the siege engineers. The once-mighty siege weapons had been left almost to the point of dereliction. Onagers, ballistae, scorpions, they were all packed up in a series of crates that made the building feel more like a disused carpenter's shop than the home of Rome's most powerful war machines. I told one of the engineers to open a crate. Nervously, the man fiddled with the locks and hinges until one side of the box flapped down, releasing a cloud of dust into the air. Coughing and spluttering, we had to wait a few moments before we could see inside. We heard a mouse screech and scurry away, disturbed from its peaceful nibbling. Within the crate lay stacks of iron bars, wooden planks and a mouse's feast, four long coils of rope that had been bitten to pieces.

'I want every scrap of equipment here fully repaired and tested within two days, or I'll have each of your men flogged. Legate, I don't know if you or your idle bastards here are responsible for this, but you're on thin fucking ice.'

In hindsight I suppose I might have been too harsh on the men of the Rapax. After all, the legion had been posted to what had been the quietest province in the empire for decades and had never fought in pitched battle against the local tribes, let alone laid a siege. All my military life had been on active service. I was barely thirty years old and had fought against the Celts in the west of Britannia, Boudicca and her followers, with the Gauls against Verginius Rufus and now I commanded some of the most seasoned veterans in the entire Roman army. Raetia was almost as safe from invasion as Rome herself. If the barbarians ever mounted an assault against the empire, they would make for the Rhine or the Danube, not the freezing passes of the Alps. But the longer Alpinus was alive the more the authority of Rome and her legions was questioned, and Pansa worked his men hard to make the legion ready to march with all the supplies and equipment for a siege.

The Thracian auxiliaries were waiting for us when our column finally arrived at the foot of Mount Vocetius. Tough, hardy men who had been born in the mountains, but while the Helvetii had settled down to farm the valleys and the pastures, these men were warriors to the core. Their prefect was a young man from the south of Italia, small and olive-skinned while his men were tall and pale. But though he was young, he had laid out his defences well. His cohort had dug earthworks for the artillery to shelter behind, ditches and a palisade that stretched up the hillside to protect a little spring that would have to serve the needs of the legion, the auxiliaries and all the pack animals we had brought from Vindonissa.

'At long last, a competent officer in this blasted province!' I exclaimed, clasping the man on the shoulder. The officer's cheeks turned red, despite the cold. It was praise, but it wasn't high praise. Then I noticed what he was blushing at. Pansa, still astride his horse, was in earshot and judging from his bulging eyeballs wasn't best pleased to be criticized in front of a junior officer, even if indirectly. But what of it? Pansa knew he had disappointed me, and if he didn't like being shown up in front of a young officer without any noble blood in him, he was just going to have to put up with it.

It was dusk by now but the vanguard, with no prompting, took up their positions by the palisade. I thought of Alpinus up in his rocky fortress. To be besieged by an entire Roman legion, not once but twice. Except now we had artillery.

'It's going to be a bastard to take,' Torquatus commented.

'You're sure he can't walk away this time?' I asked. 'There aren't any secret passages out of the fort?'

The Helvetian shook his head. 'None. There's only one way into that place, and one way out. Through gates almost as thick as a man.'

'Then we will have to batter them into submission.'

'Shall I send a messenger with terms, General?' Pansa asked.

'No. No terms. Alpinus knows our demands, and those foolish enough to join him deserve what is coming to them.'

It was another four hours before the whole legion and the carts carrying the disassembled artillery arrived. The bolt-firing scorpions had been left back in the barracks; they were meant for the open battlefield where they could tear bloody great holes into massed ranks. Instead we had two catapults, huge monsters that took our pack horses the best part of two days to drag westwards towards the mountain. The engineers should have taken perhaps two hours to assemble the machines from pieces to battle readiness, but had hardly practised over the years. But when they were ready, the catapults looked impressive, and when they began to fire they would be lethal. It would be almost dawn before they were finally assembled, and I had the auxiliaries and eight of our ten cohorts steal a few hours' sleep while the engineers toiled away. After all, it wasn't as though launching the catapults required the same energy as a legionary did to charge up a mountain and storm a fort. After giving the Thracians their orders I even caught a couple of hours' sleep myself, though missing Salonina's company in bed.

With no Totavalas or slave to dress me, I took some time putting on my clothes and my armour. My fingers fumbled in the dark as I searched blindly for the clasp of my military cloak. By the time I was ready the sun had just cleared the horizon, and the men were waiting. This wasn't a day for speeches; we had a job to do and if the gods were willing we would do it well. It was snowing gently, but not enough to disrupt my plans. Pansa was waiting with Torquatus, and both men threw me a smart salute.

'General,' Pansa began, 'are you aware that the Thracian cohort left the camp last night?'

'Yes, Legate. I ordered them to.'

'Why, sir?'

'Are you questioning my orders, Legate?'

Pansa apologized hurriedly. 'Not at all, General. Where have they gone?'

'You'll soon see. But now I think it's time to begin the bombardment.'

A legionary brought Achilles to me. The man knelt down to form a makeshift mounting block. Once in the saddle I clicked my tongue loudly and the stallion began to trot. The engineers were waiting for us. The fort was high up on a shelf that had been carved into the mountain by the locals perhaps centuries ago, protected on either side by great spurs of rock. A solid wall had been built across the gap between them, and no rear wall was necessary; the cliff face behind was sheer and impossible to reach without scaling the spurs, that is if you hadn't been picked off by a slinger or bowman as soon as your head came into view. No, a full frontal assault was the only way my heavy infantry could hope to breach that place, and the ground in front would be a killing zone.

The chief engineer, with deep grey bags under his eyes, stood proudly by his machines.

'Permission to report, General?'

'Granted.'

'As you're aware, sir, we haven't the means to break down that wall with just the two onagers, but if we're lucky we might batter down the gate within a day or two. If we don't run out of ammunition that is . . .'

'But shouldn't you have unlimbered the catapults further up

the hill on our side, rather than down here on the valley floor?' Pansa asked.

'Normally we would, sir. But if we're trying to thin their numbers we need our missiles to arc high into the air and drop down into the fort. From a flatter trajectory and further away the target size would be massively reduced. If the shot was high enough to pass over the gate it would continue right into the cliff behind and not hurt a fly. Down here we can launch the shots into the sky above them and let them fall into the fort itself.'

'And you're ready to begin?'

'We're waiting for the word, General.'

'Fire away then.' The engineer nodded, then barked out a string of orders. Like a pack of hounds when the huntsman calls, his men sprang into action. Some began to wind and winch the ropes, their tension giving the onager its power. Others fetched the ammunition, clay balls filled with some noxious substance from the East, designed to burst into flames on impact. The slings were readied, the axles checked, the chief engineer had one last look to make sure the aim was right. Then he was handed a heavy-looking hammer. Taking careful aim, he knocked out the firing pin of the first catapult.

Suddenly the machine sprang into life. The ropes unravelled faster than the eye could see and the missile was flung high into the air. The onager's arm smashed into a sack of chaff secured to the axle, meant to soften the blow of the savage donkey kick which gave the machine its name. All eyes were fixed on the clay ball as it arced high into the sky until it was little more than a dark drop in a sea of blue. We saw the explosion before we heard it, a burst of flame and smoke no more than twenty paces short of the wall. Then came the noise, a burning and spitting sound like I'd never heard before.

The engineer mumbled something about the wind, but no one really heard him, and if they had they wouldn't have said anything anyway. It was testament to the man's skill that he had come so close with his first attempt. That attempt was the marker, and two men were already winching the second onager for the next shot, but with an added half-turn for extra power. The next missile went soaring upwards, and the man who had not slept as he prepared his machines through the night smiled in anticipation. This time there was no spurt of flame, but we heard the explosion and the screams from the fort. At once the legionaries cheered, five thousand men cheering themselves hoarse that first blood had been spilled.

'Congratulations, man! An excellent shot,' I complimented the officer.

"Thank you, sir. Come on, lads, we have the range now. Let's give it to 'em!'

It took a while to reload each onager, and to begin with the men cheered every hit. Hits were a rare occurrence though, and we soon began to run out of ammunition. But suddenly a flash of orange came darting across the sky that was certainly no clay ball. The Thracians were in position.

'Now we've softened them up, it's time to advance. If you would, Pansa?'

Pansa gave the signal to the trumpeter, who blew some piercing staccato notes into the chilly air. The first cohort took hold of the scaling ladders. One of the men held Achilles by the bridle as I dismounted.

'Look after him with your life, understand me?'

'Yes, General.'

The first cohort, twice the size of the other nine and thick with veterans, would lead the assault. Pansa and I walked to join the second cohort. We would march with them up the slope. The men had to see that their commander would face death with them, and each man grinned on observing that his trouser-clad general would be joining the assault. We stood, Pansa and I, a good ten paces ahead of the men.

'Nervous?' I asked.

'With respect, sir, I've been a legate longer than you've been in the army.'

I saw the man was blowing a steady stream of misty breath as he prepared himself for the battle ahead. 'I was joking, Pansa.'

'Personally, I don't think the battlefield is a place for jokes, sir.' His brown eyes bored into mine. Gone was the over-confident, dismissive legate. This was a general about to lead his men into battle, not someone who could make light of death.

'You're right, Legate. I meant no offence.' He briefly smiled his acceptance before murmuring a quick prayer. Whether it was to Mithras, a family god, it didn't matter. It is comforting to believe there might be a god or goddess up there who's watching out for us, but I didn't join him in his prayers.

When he had finished, I said quietly: 'They're your men, Pansa. It's your order to give.'

'Rapax! For the glory of Rome,' he cried.

'For the glory of Rome,' they echoed. I drew my sword and kissed the pommel for luck. Just as the engineer fired another volley, we began to march.

The fortress mocked us from its height, the grey crags looming above, waiting. We tramped forward at a steady pace, not wanting to slip on the precarious slope or wear ourselves out before the assault began. I could just make out the men on the walls; perhaps a hundred bowmen, maybe more. I counted the heartbeats in my head. It had been three hundred beats since the dart of orange in the sky. The archers waited, watching as we marched into range. The slope grew steeper, and I could hear puffs of exertion from the men behind as they climbed in their heavy armour. Pansa and I were more fortunate, our armour being lighter and more decorative, though once in the thick of battle I know which armour I would rather wear.

Four hundred heartbeats, the archers were drawing back their bowstrings ready for their first volley. A missile from the valley below smashed on to the parapet, knocking a couple of men off their perch and wounding several more. There would be no more explosions after that, for fear that we would be hit by our own catapults. The remaining archers loosed their arrows, a small cloud of them sailing into the air.

'Testudo!' Pansa called, and the two of us crouched down as the men behind rushed to protect us with their shields. The men ahead had dropped their ladders so that they could use both hands. The shafts whistled and thudded into the tortoise formation, and some cries of pain behind proved that a few had found their mark. With grim determination, the men lowered their shields and marched on. Five hundred beats. The snow-covered grass gave way to scree, and there were yelps of surprise when a man lost his footing and came tumbling down. We heard the *thwang* of bowstrings being released, and the men instinctively formed a shell of shields. But to protect Pansa and me the legionaries immediately behind us had to leave a gap between the tops of their shields and the roof of the testudo behind them, leaving themselves exposed. As an arrowhead punched through the shield, stopping within a hand's breadth of my face, there was a sickening squelch as my defender was pierced through the neck. His blood, warm enough to make you retch, spattered my cheek and shoulder. Pansa's man too was down, and the two of us automatically threaded our left arms into the now vacant arm-straps and joined the men in the front rank. There would be no gap in the formation for the next volley.

By now I had lost count of time, but we were close enough to make out the faces of those behind the parapet, and to see the elaborate carvings on the gates. The artillery fire had stopped now that the first cohort were less than forty paces from the walls. But then we heard the clattering of steel and fearsome war cries from inside the fort. The archers turned to loose their next tranche of arrows at an unseen enemy inside the fort, and the assault party took advantage of the Helvetii's distraction. They rushed to lean the ladders against the wall. Within moments there were three of them up, no, four or five. More went up with every moment. The archers were already reloading, and they were soon joined by warriors armed with swords and shields of their own. The men were climbing now, one had almost reached the top before a few men on the wall grabbed the top of the ladder and gave it a mighty heave so that it fell back on to the men beneath, the climber lost in the mass of men. Again the archers turned to fire inwards as the swordsmen dealt with the ladders.

Suddenly, the mighty gates creaked, a chink of light escaping between the two doors. Most of the first cohort were too busy either climbing the ladders or holding them in place at the bottom to stop the tribesmen from pushing them to the ground again.

'Second cohort, to the gate!' I cried. We sprinted forward, streaming past the men of the first cohort, and put our shoulders to those heavy doors. Dropping my shield, I used my free hand to push against the frosty wood. My arm slipped on the smooth surface, a couple of savage splinters driving into my forearm, but slowly the doors began to yield. The gap was soon big enough for a man to slip through, but out of nowhere a sword appeared, scything down on to the head of our foremost man. The dented helmet saved his life, but the impact sent him crumpling to the floor. The next man rammed his shield high into the gap and with his gladius stabbed beneath it, straight into the legs of his enemy. The air was rent with bellowing and wailing. I could even make out the cries of women and children.

With an almighty heave the doors gave way, and we poured into the gap. The scene was pure carnage. The Thracians were in among the enemy, not in the semblance of a battle formation but each man fighting as an individual. Up above and to the sides you could see the ropes they had used to clamber down the mountain and into the fort. Backed into a corner were dozens of women and children, screaming in fear, their husbands and fathers too busy fending us off to defend their families.

A desperate group charged straight for us; the tallest of them, seeing my silver armour and plumed helmet, launched himself at me. Raising my shield horizontally I jabbed the man in the stomach. He bent double, vomiting, so I took a quick step forward and hacked down, only for my sword to be blocked by a young boy with a spear. There was a terror and a rage in those blue eyes, but the lad had overreached himself so I struck him hard on the temple with my elbow. The boy collapsed, senseless. The older man dropped his sword at once and looked to the boy, plainly his son.

Before I could decide whether to leave them or not, I was knocked over by something heavy. Dazed, I saw it was the body of an archer, flung from the walls by one of my men. The tribesman saw me trapped beneath the corpse, and picked up the sword again. There wasn't even time to think. Desperately I tried to roll the body off me, but the man froze, sword high above his head. I watched a trickle of blood run from his mouth, then I saw the spear point that jutted out of his bruised belly. He fell to his knees, dribbling and gurgling, then the spear twisted savagely and was yanked out. The tribesman collapsed. Behind him, clutching a bloody spear, was one of my men, a giant of a man. Seeing my general's uniform, he instinctively saluted, even with all the carnage around us.

'Never mind the salute, get this damn corpse off me!' I shouted.

The soldier called to a friend to watch his back, and only then did he bend down to help roll the dead weight off me. I grasped his arm and levered myself up.

'Are you all right, General?' he asked.

'I'm alive, that's the important thing. I reckon you've just earned yourself a promotion, Legionary.'

The man grinned.

We were interrupted by a distant blast, one long calling note across the morning air. I'd recognize that sound anywhere.

'It's the legions. Quintus has brought the army.' Others heard me and took up the cry: the army from Mogontiacum was here. Any fight left in the tribesmen evaporated immediately. They flung down their arms, their spirit broken. Pansa found me, a small gash on his cheek showing that he had had a close call too.

'Still alive, Legate?' I asked.

'Still alive, sir. Though some bugger came close to taking my eye out. I took his guts out instead.'

'Well done. Now to find that bastard Alpinus.'

Thankfully he was alive, one of perhaps a hundred survivors, not counting the women and children. He stood there, proud and unbending. A centurion was busy tying his hands, and I gestured him to bring the traitor to me in the centre of the fort.

He looked at me, his gaunt face a picture of loathing.

'Just kill me quickly,' he said.

'Kill you?' I said, loud enough for all the men to hear. 'It's the emperor who will decide your fate, but first you have a debt to repay.'

'What debt?' he asked, his brow furrowed.

'You severed the hands of men who had never done you any harm. Now we're going to return the favour.' The men chuckled appreciatively. Justice had to be done.

The centurion punched Alpinus hard in the stomach, then forced him to his knees. There were any number of volunteers to do the job. The officer chose one of them, the brother of one of the wounded men I found out later, and he stepped forward, tossing his sword from one hand to the other, a grim smile on his face.

I'll say one thing for Alpinus, bastard that he was: he took his punishment well. Unprompted, he held out his arms. Down came the blade, out gushed the blood, and the men roared their approval. The centurion dragged Alpinus towards some fragment of a clay ball that still burned brightly. The stumps were forced into the flame to cauterize the wounds. The stench of burning flesh and the blood-curdling scream were enough to make my stomach turn, but then I knew something of the pain.

'The debt is paid, Alpinus,' I said, as though he had repaid the loan of a denarius. 'Now I want you to walk down to my camp, through my army, and let them see that justice has been done. There the surgeon will make sure you're fit to meet the emperor.'

The men muttered angrily, not wanting to see the traitor get away so lightly. I whispered something to the centurion as Alpinus weakly got to his feet and began to walk towards the gates; he smiled and nodded, then began to follow the traitor a few paces behind. Some of the men formed up in two lines between me and the gates, where they began to spit on the Helvetian as he walked past. I let him reach the threshold of the fort before calling out: 'One last thing, Alpinus!'

He turned wearily to face me, saying nothing.

'Did I say that it wasn't in my power to kill you?'

'You did.'

'I lied.' The centurion swiftly grabbed Alpinus, and a second man went to help him. The spirit went out of the Helvetian in an instant. 'You said you weren't going to kill me,' he cried piteously. He cursed me for promising and begged to be let go. That was his final punishment. To trick him into thinking he would live, even if it was only until he was brought before Vitellius, and then to have him killed would satisfy the men far more than the quick death he had asked for. They dragged him, kicking and screaming, until he knelt in front of me once more.

I drew my sword slowly. Alpinus was babbling now, clutching at straws.

'Caecina!' a voice called out, shrilly.

I looked up to see two horsemen, no, three. There was Quintus at the gateway, looking appalled at the bloodbath in the fort. On the other horse sat Salonina, and in front of her was Aulus. I could not back down now, not without losing face in front of the men.

'If you don't want to watch, cover your eyes,' I said.

I took a firm hold of my sword, and with a fluid, sweeping motion took Alpinus's head off his shoulders.

VII

If I close my eyes I can still see Salonina. The luscious brown hair, deep blue eyes that could rage like the sea, lips that you wanted to kiss for days and nights upon end. I remember the first years we spent together vividly, though it is some two decades ago now. I had returned, a war hero from Britannia, to a son who didn't know me and a wife I barely recognized, grown into womanhood.

It was as though we were courting. There was a bashfulness as we tried to get to know each other, first as people and then as lovers. The first time had been not so much out of love but more in the hope of fathering a son before I went to war, to make sure the family line wasn't extinguished. When I returned we grew to like each other, once I'd helped her to get rid of some of her plebeian habits. Over the years we became a loving couple, though of course we had the occasional falling-out, and Aulus was the joy of our lives. He still is mine today, even though he has gone over the sea. That is how I choose to remember my family; I have no family now.

In the days after the death of Alpinus, there were times when I caught myself thinking how blissful it had been to be back in the saddle with my wife and son out of harm's way. Aulus avoided me for days after Mount Vocetius, and Salonina explained that it was because I'd killed the traitor in front of him.

'For Hades' sake, he's only a boy. He shouldn't have to see things like that.'

'Aulus will be a man some day, and he knows his father is a soldier. Soldiers kill people, that's what we do!' I shouted back.

'Yes, but not in front of your own child,' she said, exasperated.

'Then why did you bring him up with you? You saw the catapults, you saw my men storm the fort. What did you expect to see once you passed the gates, a bloody picnic?'

'We wanted to be with you.'

'I have twenty thousand men to command, Salonina. Do you think I enjoy worrying that something may happen to the two of you on top of all that?'

Salonina pouted. 'Well, if we're such a burden to you, why don't Aulus and I go back to Mogontiacum and wait there?'

'Now you're just being ridiculous.'

'Is it ridiculous? We can't bring supplies to you, we can't build roads, we can't kill your enemies. What can we do here?'

'You can stay here and be a proper wife to me and a good mother to our son. You must remember he's not the little boy you raised in Rome. He's nine years old now, and betrothed. Aulus will get over the shock soon enough.'

'And if he doesn't?'

'He will. I grew up without a father or a brother, and I'll be damned if you're going to come between me and my only son.'

There was a delicate knock at the door. 'Who is it?' I asked.

'Quintus,' the voice answered.

'Caecina, we haven't finished talking yet.'

'There is nothing more to say, Salonina.'

'Are you going to dismiss me like one of your soldiers?' she asked coldly.

I ignored her. 'Come in, Quintus.' The door opened a fraction, Quintus took a half-step into the room.

'I can come back later,' he said.

'Don't worry, Quintus. Salonina was just leaving.'

She shot me an exasperated look before turning on her heel and storming out.

'Anything I can do to help, General?' Quintus asked.

I sighed. 'No, Quintus. My wife has to learn that she hasn't got Aulus to herself any more. She's never liked being a soldier's wife, I can understand that. But now that she's with me at last, I think she's afraid of losing Aulus to me.'

'Losing him? It's not as though he's far from her side, is it?'

'True. But then she did have Aulus to herself for nearly three years before I first set eyes on him. Maybe she just needs to get used to the idea of sharing him?'

'Who knows, General? In five months' time she might bear you another son. In the meantime, if I might suggest you don't go too hard on her, sir? After all, pregnancy does funny things to a woman. They'll argue over anything, given the chance!'

'You're a good friend, Quintus. Too good a friend to keep calling me "general". In here I'm plain old Caecina.'

'And I much prefer Quintus to Tribune Verres. I still get odd looks from the men, even from the ones who didn't fight my father at Vesontio.'

'That'll stop soon enough. You lead the men well, Quintus, that's the most important thing. Besides, there are dozens of Severi in Rome, and none of them are closer to me than second cousin. Anyway, why did you want to see me?'

'You asked to see me, Caecina.'

'Did I? Oh yes, now I remember. Can you get me twenty thousand pairs of socks?'

'Socks?'

'Yes, socks.'

'Why do you want twenty thousand pairs of socks?' he asked.

'Because I've got a mouse problem in my tent,' I said, rubbing my eyes tiredly. 'For the men, of course. We're about to march through the highest mountains in the empire, not two months after the New Year, and I don't think the men will be all that happy to make the journey in just their sandals.'

'Of course.'

'Woollen socks are the best, though I hear the locals use goat hair, and after all they live in these freezing mountains. I want every weaver in the province working night and day, understand?'

In five days we were ready to march, socks and all. After trying to organize an entire army for almost a week I had pretty much given up. Julius Agricola had a knack for logistics; I didn't. Instead I focused on one key strategic decision. Alpinus's treason meant that the message we had sent to the governor of Noricum, the province to the east, had never arrived. Noricum was only a single-legion province, but who knew whether that single legion would be needed in the fight against Galba, if indeed there was a fight. Then of course there was the original plan of taking the shortest, hardest route to Italia: Mount Poeninus, or, as the locals call it, Hannibal's Pass.

I couldn't risk Valens and his army arriving in Italia first. Galba's armies would still be mustering near Rome, giving Valens free rein across all Italia beyond the Po. He would claim all the credit with Vitellius while I would arrive second with a smaller, exhausted army. In truth, it was no choice at all. New messengers were dispatched for Noricum, and if the governor did decide to join our cause, he could march into Italia by the eastern passes and meet up with us there. If he remained loyal to Galba, then at least we hadn't wasted time and possibly risked a battle by marching through his province. After all, I had no way of knowing how Valens's march was progressing, and the Alpinus affair had put us over a week behind schedule. We had to make up for lost time.

For the first few days our route was easy. We followed the

wide valley south-west towards one of Raetia's oldest towns, Lausonna. The waters of a huge lake lay still, glistening like a great sea of glass, but with the arrival of twenty thousand men the shore road was soon teeming with fish and fishermen. Normally a small Raetian town would be lucky if it saw more than a handful of travellers a day. The army of the Alps, as we came to be known, was too big an opportunity to miss. As many men as we could squeeze in camped behind the walls of an old hill fort that the legions had built years ago, while the rest set up a makeshift camp on what little level ground there was by the lakeside.

The wind howled as Salonina and I tried to sleep, the cold and the noise of the tent flapping in the gale keeping us awake. I tenderly rubbed the bump that kept Salonina from performing her wifely duties.

'I have a feeling it will be a girl this time,' she said.

'How can you tell?'

'I just feel it will be. I don't know what this cold will do to the baby though, it can't be good for her.'

'Or him.'

'Fine, or him.'

'Don't worry, everything is being taken care of. I'm having something special made for you.'

Salonina wiggled her feet in girlish delight. 'Something for me? What is it?'

'You'll have to wait till the morning.'

'I hope you don't think I'm going to forgive you just because of a nice present,' she said playfully.

'You're not still angry with me, are you? I've got to lead twenty thousand men, Salonina, and over half of them barely know me. Executing that traitor shows the men that I'm on their side.'

'Side? Whose side are they going to be on if not yours?'

'We'll be meeting up with Valens and his army in Italia, and his army is larger.'

'Why does it always come back to Valens, Caecina? He's not as young, as handsome or as brave as you.'

'He's a wily old fox, and I can't have him stealing all the glory when we defeat Galba. Otherwise he'll become Vitellius's right-hand man and I'll be left with nothing.'

'So you'll try to reach Italia first?' she asked.

I simply nodded. There was a long silence.

'Caecina?'

'I'm trying to sleep, Salonina!'

'Imagine we do defeat Galba, and imagine you do become consul, and we become the most powerful people in Rome, after Vitellius, can you promise me one thing?'

'What?'

'You'll let me help you. You know I could never be one of those wives who stay at home and practise their needlework all day.'

'When the time comes,' I said, 'you will go to the estate in Vicetia, where all the men of my family have been born. Once the child is born, you'll be at my side, I promise.'

Salonina leaned over, her delicate perfume wafting a scent of saffron and roseships. She pecked me on the cheek. 'Thank you, Caecina,' she said before resting her head gently on my chest.

The next morning Salonina was eager to see her present. The night before I'd had some of the carpenters take the cart that she and Aulus had been travelling in and make it more fitting for a general's wife: they had made a roof for the cart and lined it with two large wolf pelts to keep the elements out and the heat in. Inside there was an array of cushions and rugs and to crown it all a thick feather mattress. I had bought it all from the merchants in Lausonna the day before and had Salonina's slaves decorate the cart as tastefully as they could. It was fit for a queen, and just as important it was barely heavier than a military wagon and practical to drag through the mountain passes.

As she was thanking me, the smallest of frowns appeared.

'But where's Aulus going to sit?'

'On his new horse, alongside me.'

Aside from Achilles I had bought two mares in Corduba. Totavalas rode one; the smaller, more docile one was for Aulus. I had been waiting for his first growth spurt to give him the horse, and now he was tall enough and hopefully old enough to ride her. Aulus himself could only mumble his thanks, and seemed less than pleased to sacrifice the warmth of the wagon for his father's company on the road. It was only when Totavalas joined us that he began to open up, but then the Hibernian had that effect on everyone.

The ascent was hard, and the road narrow. The locals had been right in that the passes were open early that year, but by open they didn't mean easy, they meant it was physically possible to cross. Little more than a fortnight earlier the passes had been blocked by snowdrifts over thirty feet deep. From Lausonna it was about ninety miles as the crow flies to Augusta Praetoria, the first town beyond Hannibal's Pass. But we were not crows. Our road wound high into the mountain tops, along treacherous slopes, over massive glaciers. You could hear the men mumbling quiet prayers to themselves; this was the nearest they would ever come to the gods in their heavens.

Two days out of Lausonna we left the great lake behind us and entered a deep defile. Torquatus told me that the river rushing down towards us from the south and into the lake was the Rhône. As our huge column trekked by the water's edge, I began to think how my life since that fateful day in Corduba had been guided by two rivers: my friend Agricola's estate by the sea, a breakneck ride towards Lugdunum and the mess that was the Vindex rebellion, then the horrors of Vesontio all within spitting distance of the Rhône. Galba had afterwards shackled me to the Rhine with the command of a legion, only for me to have my world turned upside down by the arrival of Vitellius.

And now I was riding once again by the banks of the Rhône, fated to lead another rebellion against the emperor in Rome. But this time I was fighting against the man who had set me on this path. How the gods must have laughed at the turns my life was taking; at least I could draw comfort from the fact that they were showing an interest in my fate.

We couldn't march across the breadth of the defile, the river was too wide to cross. For now we had to stay between the mountains and the eastern bank of the Rhône. Nor could our column cover all that ground; the wagons carrying our supplies, equipment and artillery had to keep to the road at all times, meaning they had to travel in single file. The men toiled through the bitter cold, their new socks pulled up almost as far as their knees. By the time twenty thousand men had tramped along the road, the white carpet had been churned into a filthy slush of compacted mud, horse shit and snow. The day that had begun with us losing sight of Lake Lausonius for good we covered perhaps twenty miles, though it was probably less. The higher we climbed, the more our rate of progress would plummet.

On the third day I sat astride Achilles at the head of the column, eyeing out the lie of the land. The vanguard that day was one of the cohorts from the Twenty-Second, the other legion that had been encamped with mine in Mogontiacum. They were busy shovelling great chunks of snow off the road and down the steep hillside.

'And to think I gave up the company of my own people for this!' a voice came up from behind me. Totavalas and Aulus were riding my mares from Corduba. The beasts trod tentatively along the narrow path, but a warming surge of pride coursed through me when I saw how confidently Aulus was riding.

'And what would you be doing back home instead of enjoying this crisp mountain air?' I asked.

'Clinging to a cool beer and a warm woman, like any sensible man would on a winter's day!' The two of us laughed. Aulus looked down towards his saddle, visibly embarrassed.

'Keep your chin up, son. If you're old enough to ride one of my horses, you're old enough to join in men's talk.'

'Yes, Father.'

'What are the women like in Hibernia?'

Totavalas gave a mischievous grin. 'The finest in the world, so they are. Some are small and dark, others have flaming red hair like the morning sun, but while making love they'll all claw at you like a wolf-bitch in heat.'

'What does Julia Agricola look like?' Aulus asked me.

I racked my brains, but I couldn't for the life of me picture the girl. 'If she takes after her mother, she'll be beautiful,' was all I could think to say.

'You don't know what she looks like, do you?' he said accusingly.

'I didn't know what your mother would be like before we were married,' I began.

'And look how well that turned out,' my son shot back.

'Aulus, you'll marry her if you like it or not. It's a fantastic match, and you couldn't marry into a nicer family. Julius Agricola will be one of Rome's great generals one day.'

'But you're Vitellius's—'

'You will call him "the emperor", Aulus,' I said sharply.

'Fine, you're the emperor's right-hand man now. What can a match with Agricola offer us? He's little better than a farmer.'

'He is my closest friend, Aulus, and I've given my word. The matter is settled.'

'While I will be a mysterious, handsome bachelor with connections to the imperial household,' Totavalas said, lightening the mood. 'Gods, the women of Rome will be queuing up to share my bed!'

I held up my hand for silence. There was a deep rumbling from up above.

'Thunder?' Aulus asked.

'With blue skies above us?' I said. The rumble soon became a roar as small rocks and stones began to skitter down the hillside, pelting the road.

'Gods, it's an avalanche!' The legionaries began to shout in terror, dropping their shovels and sprinting back down the road.

'What's an avalanche?' the Hibernian asked.

'Shut up and ride,' I shouted. There was no way we could go back, the road was clogged with fleeing men. The horses were whinnying in fear, but Aulus's mare was the first to recover. The animals' instinct to survive took over, and soon the three of us were flying down the road, searching for shelter. To our left the mountain rose ever upwards, and the first drifts of snow were falling towards us.

'Ride, ride, ride,' I screamed. There had to be some shelter somewhere. The road swung savagely round a corner; Achilles almost lost his footing on the slippery surface and for one horrible moment I thought we were going to career into the valley below. We galloped past another bend in the road, and there was a vertical cutting into the mountain where Augustus's engineers must have hacked into the cliff face to create the road. They had cut deeper at the base so there was a slight overhang about ten feet up. We didn't need words. All three of us knew we would find no better shelter in time. The first great chunks of snow and ice were already smashing into the ground all around us. I flung myself out of the saddle, and Aulus and Totavalas copied me for fear of being knocked over by the falling debris.

The noise was deafening by now. It felt as though the whole mountainside was tumbling down upon us. Achilles was yanking at the bit in fear as the snow kept on coming. I could see Aulus's knuckles were white, holding on to his reins. The snow was above our knees now. It was crashing down off the overhang and piling up around us, and fast. The youngest mare, born almost within sight of Africa, began to stamp and rear. Nothing could have prepared her for what we were going through, and as the least sheltered she was being forced ever backwards.

'Father, help!'

My heart clenched with fear. Aulus had wrapped his arm among the reins for a tighter grip, and was being dragged into the icy storm. The horse was screaming now, her mouth sopping with blood and foam as she fought against the bit. Totavalas was scrabbling with his free hands at the leather coiled around my son's arm.

'Forget the reins, hold the boy,' I shouted, reaching for my sword. Totavalas grabbed Aulus around the waist, using all his strength to hold him still. The horse was almost at the edge of the pass now. Desperately I slid my sword with my weaker left hand along Aulus's arm. The blade caught once, twice on the arm leaving angry red gashes, but I had to get the blade under all the coils. The point of the sword bit into the back of his hand and Aulus howled in pain. A hard yank and the leather coils were severed; with the weight gone, my son and Totavalas crashed back into the wall. The mare teetered for a moment before the snow sent her over the edge.

The snow was over Aulus's waist now, and up to my thighs, but the noise was slackening off. The avalanche was coming to an end. Aulus clutched his arm, blood from the gashes spattering the snow with tiny red blotches. Still keeping a firm hold on Achilles' reins with one hand, I held Aulus in a tight embrace.

'It's over now,' was all I could think to say. Aulus buried his head in the folds of my cloak, crying.

Totavalas gave the snow beyond the overhang a hefty kick or two, forcing his way out on to the unsheltered road. He peered round the corner.

'The snow's piled up at least nine, maybe ten feet high.'

'Then we'll have to wait until they dig us out,' I observed.

There was nothing else for us to do. I turned my back to Totavalas so he could cut some strips from my military cloak to use as makeshift bandages for Aulus. The blood barely showed through the deep red of the material, but the boy was careful not to spill too much blood on the fur cloak that I'd bought him for the journey. We had no way of knowing how long we stood there, two men, a boy and two horses on the lonely mountainside, but eventually we heard men's voices, cursing and shouting as they dug their way through. Achilles whinnied loudly.

'Did you hear that?' a man asked.

'Sounded like a horse, didn't it? You don't think—'

'If the two of you have finished chatting, we would like to be dug out. And bring the surgeon,' I shouted.

'We're nearly there,' the first voice called back. We could hear the shovels pitching into the snow now, and the grunts of the men who wielded them. The three of us watched the wall of snow. The force of the digging caused our side of the wall to shimmer in places, small tranches of snow falling away with every impact. At long last the barrier came crashing down. A small group of men emerged from the debris, clutching their shovels, their faces obscured by great clouds of condensation.

'Is that you, General?'

'No, I'm the ghost of Hannibal. Of course it's me. Where's the surgeon, damn it?'

For the rest of the journey Aulus travelled in the cart with Salonina. It wasn't that another horse couldn't be found for him, but if he was scared of me beforehand he was terrified of me now. We had lost around two dozen men in the avalanche. I had to send a troop of cavalry back down the pass into the valley beneath to look for the bodies amid the snow. By the time they returned the head of the column had marched into the clouds that clung closely to the mountains. Have you ever camped in the clouds? In winter? You do all you can to shut out the cold, but the moisture from your breath and the dampness of the clouds will freeze during the night. You wake up with icicles on your bedding, and the fabric of the tent is sodden. But despite all the hardships, the pain, the misery and the biting cold, one moment made up for it all.

Before we could descend into Italia, the road took us to the highest point in the pass. We had passed the treeline some hours ago and the clouds were beginning to burn off in the morning sun. Quintus and Totavalas were with me, as were Pansa and Publilius Sabinus. We all wanted to be there for that first sight of our homeland. The road arced around the mountain, heading steeply upwards. We had to shade our eyes; high above us the sun was turning the snow a dazzling white. The horses trod tentatively, even Achilles somewhat cowed by the ordeal of the march. We rode in single file and I was leading the way. No more than a hundred paces ahead the road seemed to vanish into the sky. The summit was that close.

'How about a race to the top?' Quintus joked.

'On a road as wide as a knitting needle? No thank you,' Publilius said. At least some of my officers were getting along. Pansa resented my preference for Quintus, being almost two decades older and senior in rank. But Quintus had led an army, and was like a brother to me. Pansa was just going to have to prove he was worthy of his command.

Up ahead I could make out the small pile of stones that marked the summit. I touched my heels to Achilles' side and he responded, speeding up to a rising trot. The view was breathtaking. Down below us was the icy grey lake and a way station that marked the beginning of the descent. Less snow, better roads and the start of civilization in general. Far in the distance, the white of the alpine passes began to give way to green.

'Italia,' Pansa said longingly.

'I haven't been in Italia for nearly three years now,' Publilius said.

'A day's march and we'll be in Augusta Praetoria,' I said. 'Baths, beds, good wine . . .'

'. . . and no more salted beef!' Quintus finished.

The Hibernian just sat there, gaping. I laughed. 'I've never seen you short of words, Totavalas. Haven't you got anything to compare with this in your land?'

'Nothing like this,' was all he could say.

By now the first of the infantry were arriving. They were aching, tired and cold, some of them with their hands bound to fight off the frostbite.

'Cheer up, men,' I called to them. 'Italia is waiting for you.' I gestured to the hazy, green horizon. The men thrust their spears into the air, cheering themselves hoarse.

We made our eager way down the mountain path, not daring to break into anything faster than a trot on the treacherous slopes. The lake grew larger and larger; we could make out a few sheep that were walking tentatively on its frozen surface. A man came out of a building by the lake's edge, took one look at the column of foot soldiers and the horsemen heading towards him and dashed back inside. In a moment he reappeared, now wearing a helmet. He cupped his hands around his mouth and shouted something, but we were too far away to make out what he was saying. When we came closer he tried again: 'Is General Severus with you?'

'I'm Severus,' I yelled back. Others were coming out of the house and the stables now, eager to see what the commotion was. The speaker was a young man in uniform and, stranger yet, he had the dusky colouring of a Numidian. I guessed he was a cavalryman from the long sword at his side. When the five of us reached the station the man saluted.

'Decurion Arco of the Silian cavalry, General. The prefect sent me to tell you that we have pledged to serve Vitellius Germanicus against the Emperor Otho.'

'The Emperor Otho?' Quintus asked.

'You've not heard, sir? Otho had Galba murdered over a month ago. He's the emperor now.'

108

VIII

The army was still filing past as the messenger gave us the rest of his news in the warmth of the way station. We would march to the comforts of Augusta Praetoria come what may. I was not going to send my cold and hungry men back the way they came the day we arrived in Italia.

'It was about ten days after the New Year. Word had reached Galba that Vitellius—' he began.

'You mean the emperor, soldier,' I reminded him tersely.

'Sorry, sir. That the emperor had raised his standard in Colonia. But Galba had only heard that the two legions in Mogontiacum had mutinied, not the whole army beyond the Alps. Still, it was enough for him to announce his successor. Most people thought he would choose Otho, including Otho himself. After all, he had joined Galba at the very beginning in Hispania.'

'As did I,' I remarked bitterly.

The Numidian raised his eyebrows in surprise, but continued his story. 'But Otho had also promised to marry the daughter of Galba's adviser, Titus Vinius, and had borrowed a fortune to sweeten the Praetorian Guards. And the next day Galba named his heir, a man called Calpurnius Piso. Apparently he is descended from two of the triumvirs, Crassus and Pompey.

Anyway, Galba didn't make the usual promise of gold to the praetorians on announcing the news, and he didn't pay them when he first arrived in Rome either. But Otho's been winning them over since he's been in Rome; not the officers, mind, but the men from the ranks.'

'And I'm guessing the praetorians didn't like the prospect of serving under Piso any more than Galba,' Pansa said.

'Why?' asked Quintus.

'Because he's as dour, dull and miserly as Galba was, only from a much nobler family,' Pansa answered.

'You're right, sir,' the cavalryman said. 'After all, these men were used to Nero, who always paid his guards well. Everyone knows that Nero and Otho had been as thick as thieves. Within a week, the praetorians had smuggled Otho into their camp, declared him emperor, and then they took it upon themselves to ride into the forum and murder Galba.'

'What about your man Piso?' Totavalas asked, standing by the doorway. Pansa hadn't wanted to sit at the same table as a mere freedman. 'I take it he felt he had more right to the throne than this Otho?'

'Well, when the guards came back to Otho carrying Galba's head, the story goes that Otho said it wasn't Galba's head that he wanted, but Piso's. So the troops went back into the city, found Piso, Titus Vinius and more of Galba's henchmen, and butchered them in the streets. After that, the Senate and the people didn't have much choice; they voted to confirm Otho as the new emperor.'

The five of us were stunned into silence. With Galba dead, what would we do now? Then Publilius spoke: 'So with Otho in complete control of Rome, why has your *ala* of cavalry decided to back our emperor?'

'It's simple enough, sir. The Emperor Vitellius recruited our unit when he was governing Africa eight years ago. We served him loyally then and we're ready to serve him now.'

'What land do you control?' I asked.

'The western half of all the land north of the Po, General. We cover four towns: Eporedia, Vercellae, Novaria and Mediolanum.'

'And have they chosen a side yet?' Pansa asked.

'I don't think they want to choose a side, Legate. They have no connection with the emperor or with Otho; they just want to be left in peace.'

'Thank you, decurion,' I said. 'If you go to the stables and make ready for your journey I'll have a message for your commander when you get back.'

The man nodded dutifully, his chair scraping along the flag-stones as he got up. Totavalas stepped aside to let him through the door, before catching the eye of the official who ran one of the loneliest stations in the empire.

'The general would like some privacy,' he said. The man was disappointed; I doubt he would have had as much excitement in his entire career and he would have wanted to hear the latest news straight from the horse's mouth. But we could not risk what was said between us being passed along the gossip chain as far south as Rome, losing us the element of surprise. When we were sure we were alone Publilius exhaled sharply.

'Well, a fine mess we're in!'

'How do you mean?' Pansa asked.

'Wasn't the whole point of this campaign to challenge Galba because he was unfit to be emperor? With Galba gone and a new man in his place, I don't see how we can justify taking another step southwards,' Quintus said.

'That's a bit rich coming from the son of the same Vindex who was the first to rebel against Nero, and the first to shed Roman blood,' Pansa sneered.

'Pansa, you're talking out of your arse. Quintus is not his father's son,' I said forcefully. The legate's eyes bored into mine, trying to stare me down. 'All I want from you is your professional opinion on whether the army should march south.'

'Very well. As I see it, nothing has changed. The men will fight for Vitellius whoever sits on the throne in Rome, there's no one else who can claim their loyalty. And I'll be damned if I'm marching my legion back over the Alps.'

'Publilius, what about the auxiliaries?'

'They'll fight for their Germanicus, General. He's the one with their interests at heart, not Otho. Besides, if we do retreat, you can be sure that Otho won't forgive them for mutinying. These men are fighting for their citizenship, remember, not just for plunder. What chance will they have of becoming citizens if they rebel against their emperor? I think that we all crossed our own Rubicon when we left our own provinces. I say we head south.'

'Quintus?'

'You know what I think. But what do you think, General? I'm here for my friend, not for Vitellius. Can you give me a reason why you should fight to depose Otho rather than Galba?' Trust Quintus to question my conscience, I thought. I took my time before answering him.

'We all know that Galba was miserly and ruthless, but he didn't deserve death, and especially not to be murdered by a pack of his own bodyguards in the forum. I know Otho from my time in Hispania, and I know this: if he's on the throne it will be as though Nero was never gone. He will whore himself senseless and drive Rome into the ground. I think Rome deserves better.'

'Is that what you really believe, Caecina?' my friend asked.

'Yes it is, Quintus. And you can bet your life that if it were Valens here, not me, he wouldn't bat an eyelid but would march twice as hard to catch Otho before he has time to muster an army.'

'Hear, hear.' Pansa thumped his fist on the table, oblivious to the fact that I wasn't complimenting Valens.

'We march south then. I'll leave it to you to tell your own men the news.'

112

'What about the men from Vocula's legion? Their tribune isn't here,' Quintus said.

'You'll have to tell them, Quintus.'

There was a knock at the door. Totavalas opened it a fraction. 'It's the decurion.'

'Let him in,' I said.

'Decurion, you can tell your commander that we will join him in a week's time. Publilius, I want you to take a few of the auxiliary cohorts and go ahead of us. Your men are lighter armed than the legions and can march faster. We'll need more than five hundred cavalrymen to hold the Transpadana.'

'Yes, General.'

'The rest of you, return to your men and give them the news.'

They all left, one by one, Quintus shaking his head as he went out. Only the Hibernian remained.

'Still here, Totavalas?'

'I don't have any men under my command, General.'

'Totavalas, you know I trust your opinion . . .' I began.

'You want to know whether I think you're doing the right thing?'

'I know what Pansa and Valens would do. They're career soldiers.'

'But you're wondering if Quintus is right?'

'Yes.'

'I think he has the luxury of not being in command. It's all very well to take the moral high ground when advising your superiors, but you've got twenty thousand men under your command who are prepared to risk their lives to make Vitellius their emperor. I like Quintus, I really do, but he's an aristocrat, he can't be expected to know how the rank and file think.'

'I'm an aristocrat, and your father was a king,' I countered.

'But I've also been a slave. That teaches you a thing or two about survival. You've got to think about survival of a different kind.'

'What do you mean?'

'A slave can be killed in the blink of an eye. You're a general of Rome, no one's going to kill you. But if you had decided to march back over the Alps, I reckon the men would have mutinied, put Pansa in charge and kept going south.'

'So it's civil war either way,' I concluded.

'Let's just pray it's as short as possible.'

Augusta Praetoria was a small town that nestled deep in the valley that wound its way east and then south-east towards the great towns of the Transpadana, the land north of the Po. It was the first day of Martius; two months to the day since I had led two legions into a mutiny against Galba. Now Galba was dead, the scoundrel Otho was emperor, and I was following in the footsteps of Julius Caesar and Hannibal by leading a hostile army into Italia. One was Rome's greatest enemy, the other had been made a god. I have an inkling which of the two I will be likened to in the years to come.

It was approaching sunset by the time our column reached the town. Salonina had left the comfort of her wagon to ride alongside me at the head of my army, in a crimson dress under a fur shawl to complement the scarlet of my military cloak. The gates of the town were open and a small deputation stood outside, waiting to welcome us. As more and more of the army came into view, the old men shifted nervously, whispering to each other.

'You look like a conquering hero, Caecina.'

'Thank you, but that's not exactly the image I'm after.'

'You're supposed to say how beautiful I look,' Salonina reproached me playfully.

'That too.' I smiled; my presents seemed to have been a success.

There were three men waiting for us, wearing their ceremonial togas for the occasion, the cloth as white as the snow they stood in, shivering. It was only when we came up close that I saw how old they were. The youngest of them couldn't have been under seventy; another had a face shrivelled with age and walnut-like grooves etched into his skin. The third man produced a scroll from the folds of his robe and began to read, welcoming us into their town.

'I thank you, citizens, but you must be cold. If you want to go through this rigmarole, my wife and I would be more than happy to do so indoors.' I gestured towards Salonina and the dignitaries, seeing her condition, were effusive in their apologies for keeping the noble lady out in the open for a moment more than was necessary. I signalled to the party of officers behind us, then followed the old men into the town. The youngest of the three glanced nervously at the army, and the party of horsemen following us.

'Will your *whole* army be requiring our hospitality, General?'

I chuckled. 'Your daughters and your storehouses will be safe from us, citizen. My officers would be glad of some bedding in the town, and we have enough gold to buy the supplies we need.'

Their eyes lit up at the mention of gold; we had prepared well, Germania's taxes would pay for the campaign and the sweeter we could keep the locals the easier time we would have. Living off the land means doubling the guard on forage parties, men who would be taken from the main body of the army. It looked like most of the town had gathered to see us. In front of the rustic temple the great and the good of Augusta Praetoria had assembled. Most of them would be lucky if they made a handful of gold coins a year in the frozen north, and it would be politic to pay our way.

But the dignified silence was broken. People in the crowd began to mutter and point. Some wore expressions of shock, others of disgust. I looked down at the men of the deputation to see what the matter was. The three of them were red with embarrassment, but what was there to be embarrassed about?

I noticed some of the younger men giggling at my barbarian trousers; it was still winter and we were still in the Alps, I would rise above any sniggers, but my legwear couldn't be the reason for the horrified expressions among the respectable men of the equestrian class. It was Salonina they were staring at. She looked at me quizzically, and then I saw. In the dying light of the sun, the crimson of her dress could easily have passed for purple, the colour reserved for the imperial family!

'Salonina, your dress!' I whispered.

'What about it?'

'It looks purple.'

'It's not purple, it's crimson.'

'It may be crimson, but it looks purple.'

'Well, what do you suggest I do, take the dress off and ride naked around the town?' she hissed.

I scrabbled at the gilded brooch that secured my cloak, my fingers fumbling in the cold. At last it came free, and quickly I whirled the cloak around Salonina, covering her dress. She held it together with one hand at her shoulder, the other holding tightly to her horse's reins. There were a few final titters from the crowd, who had been treated not only to a visit from a general of Rome, but also to the spectacle of a general and his wife's loss of face in front of the common citizenry.

'General,' the old man gestured towards the crowd.

'Yes?'

'Your speech of thanks,' he said expectantly.

'It's the next item on the agenda for the ceremony,' the younger one said, his dull nasal tones betraying him as the town's bureaucrat and pedant-in-chief. 'Followed by our speech of welcome, the sacrifice to the gods to read the omens for your journey, and then the feast in your honour.'

'Go on, Caecina,' Salonina said in mock seriousness. 'Give them your speech.'

She knew full well I hadn't prepared a speech, she was just

amused at seeing me put on the spot. I gently squeezed Achilles'
flanks and he took a few steps forward so that I didn't have to
shout myself hoarse to be heard by the assembled crowd.

'Good people of Augusta Praetoria,' I began, 'I would like to
thank you for a welcome as warm as the mountains have been
cold!' That brought a few appreciative smiles from the audience.

'I see before me the sons and grandsons of veterans settled
here by the Divine Augustus, the greatest of all the Caesars. But
the house of Caesar has failed, fallen; Nero had plumbed the
depths of depravity, milking the empire to pay for his art and
his vanity. Then came Galba: a sour, ruthless, heartless old man
who hoarded his wealth as if it were his son. But you, citizens,
you are the sons of the empire. You deserve an emperor who
will look after all his subjects. I lead this army in the name of
Aulus Vitellius Germanicus, a man who deserves to be emperor,
not the murderer Otho who drank and whored with Nero, and
even shared his wife with him! We will march south and present
our case in Rome, and then let the Senate and People of Rome
decide who is to be our new emperor.'

Not my best speech ever perhaps, but for one given on the spur
of the moment I was fairly pleased with it. The people before
me were of good equestrian stock, professional men and po-
faced wives who shared a strong moral code. They disapproved
of lechery and the low morals of Nero's court, and painting
Vitellius as a caring father figure for the empire was more likely
to win them over than the truth. He would probably spend an
entire province's taxes on food alone, but at least he would not
damage the empire as Nero had done. These fine citizens would
probably have warmed more readily to Galba's penny-pinching
ways, but Otho had ended Galba's rule with a bloody coup. So
the assembled townspeople rewarded my speech with a polite
round of applause. There was a ripple among the crowd as the
priest made his way forward. Behind him a boy, his son perhaps,
held a chicken under his arm. It was just as well the bird didn't

know what was coming, or else I doubt it would have been quite so docile.

The priest beckoned for the three men, clearly the senior men in that godforsaken town, to follow him into the temple. I slid easily out of the saddle and landed on the smooth surface of the stone road. The four of us climbed the steps leading to the small temple, a humble-looking structure, built not of stone or marble but largely of wood. Inside too the place was threadbare, but the gold ring on the priest's hand and his fur boots suggested that the locals were generous in their patronage. Up ahead was a pedestal, and on it stood a large stone bowl. The young boy nervously handed the chicken to the priest, who grabbed the bird by the neck and held it aloft. He raised the other hand high and called to the gods to guide his hand and to give favourable portents.

There was a sharp crack as the fowl's neck was wrung, and the body was laid in the bowl. Next the priest drew the ceremonial dagger that hung from his waist, and with a quick slash slit open the stomach. A stream of blood and guts poured out of the bird, and we all stepped forward to watch closely. The priest, who smelled like an old wineskin I should add, rummaged in among the entrails for signs from the gods.

'I see battles. Many battles. I see a general far away, a general who does not fight but will win a throne. An army crossing mountains, led by a man who rides with Nike, the goddess of victory. This man will never know defeat.'

I was stunned by the words, as were the dignitaries who would no doubt spread this marvellous prophecy round the town like a forest fire, and inevitably it would fire the imagination of the army too. However, I was less stunned when I spotted Totavalas surreptitiously giving the priest a few golden coins when he thought nobody was watching . . .

IX

The town elders had organized a huge feast in our honour. Well, it was at least officially in our honour. This feast had been planned days beforehand to celebrate the reopening of Hannibal's Pass, meaning that the trade route from Italia to eastern Gaul and Germania was open for business again, and of course to thank the gods. They just hadn't expected an army to march out of the pass, at least that's what I heard from a drunk man a couple of places down from my seat at the high table. Only the highest ranks were invited – the first-spear centurion from each cohort, the tribunes, Pansa, Quintus and the rest – but any more and we would have had to ration the diners to little more than a mouthful each.

The members of the council had honoured my family with seats at the high table, and Pansa as well since he was my second in command. The rest were evenly spread out among the townspeople in Augusta Praetoria's great hall. As you might have guessed from a region that relied upon mountain pastures for farming, mutton was the order of the day. The high table had salt and expensive luxuries to add some flavour to the meal, but underneath the meat was as tough as leather. But of course you had to smile as the chewing wore away at your jaw muscles,

119

and compliment the locals on their exquisite meal. On the other hand, at least it wasn't salted beef, the hard tack that we'd been living on since leaving Vindonissa back in the depths of winter. We were almost out of the Alps and spring was coming to meet us. We were even treated to olive oil and, more importantly, wine from the Po valley, the richest belt of land in Italia. As you know, the vital grain to feed the mob in Rome has long since come from the wider empire. Hispania, Africa and of course Egypt are the real bread baskets of Rome, but it would be a fool who ignored the revenue that the Transpadana brought into the imperial treasury.

As the night wore on, the venerable elders bored us rigid with tales of poor harvests and lessons in how to maintain a good profit margin on arable and dairy estates. Salonina turned a yawn into a cough while Aulus, who we'd treated to two cups of wine, was very red-faced and almost nodding into his food. The rest of the men were enjoying themselves though; the hall echoed with raucous laughter and drinking songs. The stuffy councillors looked almost apologetic that their younger folk were partly to blame for the racket. But the noise grew louder and louder, particularly from one direction. The songs had turned to shouting, there was the scraping of wood on the floor as benches were shoved back. My men were in among the locals, but the fight wasn't between them, they were trying to prise two figures apart. They grabbed one man in civilian clothes by the arms and held him back; some of the locals had caught the other, but he slipped from their grip and scrabbled to get at the other man. It was Quintus, arms flying before he was hauled back once more and held more firmly.

Hurriedly I apologized to the elders either side of me and got up. The murmurs of interest in the hall died down and turned to expectant silence as I strode down the hall. Quintus was panting heavily, a look of pure murder on his face. The other man had his back to me.

'Quintus,' I barked, 'explain yourself.'

'Ask him,' he said, gesturing at the other man. I turned to look into the face of Totavalas, whose nose was broken and he had a cut on his lip that dribbled blood down his chin.

'Outside,' I said. No one moved a muscle. 'Now!'

The night air was a sharp contrast to the warmth of the hall. Quintus swayed slightly like a young sapling in the wind, and while Totavalas's lip was stained with blood, Quintus's was stained with liquid of a different sort. I made sure that no one was listening; the street was empty but for a feral cat.

'What in the name of all the gods were you two doing?'

'Fighting,' said Totavalas.

'One more wisecrack from you and you'll get another kink in your nose. Why were you fighting?'

'He called my father a bastard.' This from Quintus.

'No, I called him a dopey bastard.'

'You see?' Quintus said, appealing to me.

'I wasn't calling him an actual bastard. There's a world of difference between calling your father a bastard and mocking him for being a proper idiot.'

'Why did you call him a b—? Why did you call him that?' I asked.

'Some of the locals were talking about Vindex and the rebellion, saying that was a civil war but at least they didn't get caught up in it, and now they've got an army marching through their lands, and I said that it was never a civil war. It was some dopey politician who got ideas above his station, and all of a sudden your boy here comes at me with his fists flying.'

'I'm an officer and a nobleman, and no jumped-up freedman is going to slander my father in public,' Quintus slurred.

'Would you prefer I slandered him in private?' the Hibernian shot back. Quintus swung again but hit nothing but air, Totavalas neatly side-stepping the punch. 'Let me remind you my father was High King of my homeland. If you're going to brag about your lineage, remember who you're talking to!'

'Enough, Totavalas. Go back and finish the feast.'

Totavalas smiled smugly before heading back inside, leaving Quintus and me alone in the squalid street.

'Will I be digging the latrines for a month? Or perhaps ten lashes at dawn? What is the punishment for striking a freed-man?'

'Quintus . . .'

'Oh yes, there isn't one!'

'What happened to you, Quintus? Where's the gentle man I left behind in Gaul?'

'You killed him. You, Galba, my father; when did I ever have a choice to do what I wanted to do?'

'You could have stayed behind in Germania,' I said.

'When my general commands, I must obey,' he said sarcastically. 'Do you remember that day I arrived in Mogontiacum? Of course you do, it was the day you turned a small army into a band of traitors. Did you even think for one moment that I might not have wanted to join another bloody rebellion? Did you?'

'I didn't think . . .'

'No, you didn't think. You just did it and thought I'd follow you blindly like Totavalas and the rest. You and I know the only reason you rebelled was that Vitellius could offer you more power than Galba. Where's the gallant, merciful general I knew in Gaul, eh? You can lie to yourself, pretend that Galba forced you into rebelling, but I bet you can't look into my eyes and tell me this is more than a naked grab for power.'

I looked into his eyes, and I saw nothing but indignation and contempt.

'I think you'd better get back to your billet and sleep this off, before you say anything else you'll regret.'

Quintus said nothing. He just snorted in derision before turning around and making his way, ponderously and precariously, to his bed on the other side of town. I stood there, watching him go. Had he really meant what he said? Perhaps I had taken him for granted. He had done a lot for me, it was true. But then if the campaign went as planned we would be in Rome within months, maybe even weeks. Then I would be able to reward Quintus properly for his loyalty. I decided for my friend's sake to put his insolence down to the drink. Pulling my cloak close around me, I went back in to finish the feast.

The army was in excellent spirits as we marched south. Hannibal's Pass was widening and levelling with every step we took. Granted, we had almost emptied Augusta Praetoria of its winter stores, but spring was fast approaching and we had paid good money for the supplies. It was imperative that we were seen as a disciplined imperial column, not an army of invaders from beyond the mountains. As the miles went by, the white of the high passes gave way to the green of the foothills. Trees began to adorn the hillsides, mighty firs and spruces that were taller than their north-facing cousins on the other side of the pass. One day we even had rain; a mixed blessing, for it showed that the worst of our journey was over, but it also turned much of the remaining snow into slush. The men's socks were sodden and all paths but the paved road became a mass of mud.

A few days out of Augusta Praetoria, however, the army rounded one final bend, climbed that last foothill and was greeted with a glorious sight. There before us lay Italia. The great Po valley stretched out as far as the eye could see, mile after mile of bounteous farmland that met the horizon in a golden haze. There in the distance lay the first of the Transpadana towns that the Silian cavalry had given to us, Eporedia. Looking back on that day, with hindsight I can say that it was probably the happiest moment of the entire campaign. I commanded an army composed of the finest troops in the world, our struggles through the mountains were over, and the sight of that bustling town in the distance, an island of houses and temples and taverns in a sea of plentiful countryside, reminded me of my own town of Vicetia, only two weeks' march to the east. I was home.

Like Augusta Praetoria before it, the people of Eporedia were keen to know the army's intentions. Relief washed over their faces as I told them all we required was food and shelter.

'Thank you, General. We had heard an army was coming out of the Alps, and we all prayed that we would be spared the fate of Albintimilium.'

'What do you mean? There aren't any armies in Liguria already, are there?'

'You haven't heard, my lord? Otho sent his navy to southern Gaul, hoping to stop the advance of your army in Gaul.'

'Valens's army, yes, but he can't be over the Alps yet,' I said, puzzled.

'You misunderstand, General: it was Otho's navy that attacked and plundered the town. They ransacked the town from top to bottom, even killed an old noblewoman who went out to order the men to stop.'

'Which noblewoman?' I asked, sensing the answer before it was given.

'The lady Agricola, General.'

I knew it was Julius's mother as soon as I heard that the woman had tried to shame the looters into stopping. That was just like her. When we were growing up she had never needed to raise her voice with Julius and me. She could always make us behave by saying how our fathers would be disappointed if they could see us, whether we were fighting over the same toy as children or skipping lessons to go into the raunchier parts of town when we were teenagers. Albintimilium was her favourite place, you see; like a Baiae of the north, it is a beautiful coastal resort where one goes to see and be seen by the high society of northern Italia. As the Agricola estate was in unfashionable Gaul, the resort was her one escape from rustic life into something like the life she had enjoyed in Rome before her husband's death. And now she was dead, cut down by Otho's men. Poor Julius. I wrote to him that night, letting him know how sorry I felt. There wasn't much else I could write. He had gone to Rome to stand in the elections for praetor, and I couldn't risk the letter being read by any of Otho's creatures once it reached the city. I even had to borrow the seal of one of the local landowners to send the letter. My own seal would be recognized in Rome and the letter would almost certainly be confiscated on arrival and pored over for intelligence.

But on the other hand, Otho's actions in Liguria meant that Valens's crossing of the Alps would take him longer than expected, giving me a free hand in Italia until he arrived. My ultimate destination was the key town of Placentia, one of the largest fortresses on the Po, founded in the days of Marius to protect the soft underbelly of Italia from barbarian tribes like the Cimbri and Teutones who had threatened Rome almost two centuries ago. Not only that, if you look at the map I've included in these memoirs, you'll see that it sits at the junction of the Aemilian and the Postumian Way, the two great roads of Italia. To the east were the legions of Pannonia and Dalmatia, hard-core supporters of Nero and almost certain to follow Otho. And to the south lay Rome itself.

As much as I wanted to, we couldn't make for the town on the near side of the Po, Cremona, at least not directly. We had to march from town to town, from grain store to grain store. Publilius had taken an advance party of six cohorts with him, four of infantry and two of cavalry. One of those cavalry cohorts was not for fighting, but had been broken up into much smaller squadrons and detachments to act as scouts. Some would head west towards the Maritime Alps and report to me on the progress of Valens and his army, others would head along the

Postumian Way to watch for the eastern legions while others still would head south to wait for Otho's coming.

Within a week we reached the final town of the four that the Silian cavalry, Vitellius's loyal Africans, had delivered to us. Mediolanum was the biggest city in the entire province, and it was here that the prefect of the cohort and Publilius had set up their temporary headquarters. After yet another tedious ceremony of welcome from the great and the good of the town I was free to stop being a diplomat and start being a general again. The advance force had commandeered an impressive villa in the centre of the town. A dozen men from one of the auxiliary cohorts stood guard over the house, saluting when they saw their general approach.

'As you were, men.'

A man was waiting for me in the atrium, and he escorted me to the room where the officers were laying their plans. My attendant knocked loudly on the door.

'If it's another complaint about the grain requisition, I'm not interested,' said a voice that I didn't recognize.

'It's General Severus, sir.'

'Well, show him in then!' The attendant remained hidden behind the wall while pushing the door open for me. The man who spoke must have had a fearsome temper, I thought, if his own staff didn't want to face him if they could avoid it. I was greeted by the sight of two men poring over a collection of maps. Publilius was one of them; the other was a man as black as coal.

'General Severus, I presume?'

I didn't know what to say. I had expected a Roman or at least a man from Italia to be the cohort's prefect, or else a dusky North African like his decurion. This man though was tall, built like an ox and . . .

'If my skin offends you, I'm afraid there's not much I can do except wear a longer tunic. You are General Severus, aren't you?'

'Yes I am,' I said, regaining my composure. 'And I take it you're the prefect of the Silian cavalry?'

'Prefect Cerberus, sir.'

'Cerberus, as in the giant dog that guards the entrance to the Underworld? How on earth did you get a name like that?'

'The locals gave my father that name when he settled with a group of his soldiers in the African province. He was a mercenary, sir, and a good one.'

'But that doesn't explain how a mercenary's son comes to be in command of a cohort of cavalry. You have to have a certain . . . social standing.'

'True enough, sir. I owe that to my mother. Her father was a senator. But my good looks I get from my father's side. Now, would you like to be briefed on the situation, sir?'

He didn't wait for me to answer. I suppose he had grown used to the surprise his appearance prompted and had learned to tolerate it. After all, I was in a similar position. People don't expect a general of Rome to be much under fifty, let alone thirty years old.

Publilius smiled at the exchange. 'Been having a leisurely march, General?'

'Oh, you know how it is, you're having a nice walk through the north of Italia in spring, the birds are singing, the daffodils are in flower. Some things can't be rushed.'

'Quite. Meanwhile my boys do all the work!'

'Is that a complaint or an observation?'

'Oh, I'm not complaining, it's what the auxiliaries are for, to save you infantry boys for the fighting.'

'So what have you been doing while I've been away?'

'Scouting mainly. I've got men covering all the western passes over the Alps so we know where Valens has got to.'

'And where has he got to?'

'We're not sure,' Cerberus said. 'The raid by Otho's navy delayed them, but we think he will have started crossing the mountains by now, away from the coast and out of the reach of the marines. After that he'll make for Augusta Taurinorum probably, and from there he'll be less than a week's march away.'

'So we're on our own for three, maybe four weeks?'

'It looks that way,' Publilius admitted.

'Excellent,' I said, rubbing my hands joyfully. 'And what of the enemy?'

'Once he heard that your army had appeared out of the Alps so soon, Otho sent an advance guard of about seven thousand. It's a strange mix of men, we gather,' Cerberus said. 'What's left of the legion of sailors Nero recruited but Galba then disbanded – they're now the First Adiutrix – a few praetorian cohorts, a few cavalry units and strangest of all, two thousand gladiators. We estimate around ten thousand men.'

'Gladiators? Otho must be desperate, the army hasn't used gladiators since the days of the republic!' I said.

'Can you blame him? He's only been emperor for two months and now he has nearly fifty thousand crack troops rebelling against him. Anyway, that force has been split. The legion has headed east to make sure the road from Pannonia stays open, while the praetorians and the gladiators have been sent to re-inforce Placentia, to stop us crossing the Po.'

'And how far away are the eastern legions?'

'At least a month away,' Publilius answered.

'Food, ammunition, tools, how are we off for them?'

'There's enough food in the area to keep us in the field for two months at the most, otherwise we're pretty well equipped.'

I took a moment, looking at the map in silence. Valens was in the west, several legions to the east, and to the south lay Otho and Rome, with a few paltry sailors, praetorians and gladiators in our way. I jabbed my finger at the crucial city.

'Placentia, that's where we go from here. If we can establish a foothold on the south bank of the Po we can march south long before the legions from the east could hope to arrive. Otho has what, four thousand praetorians left in Rome? And he'll no doubt recruit another legion from the city. So, four thousand men who have done little but whore in Rome and guard emperors, and a legion of raw recruits, against twenty thousand of the finest troops in the empire. I'm not going to sit here and wait for Valens to arrive. If we can take Placentia quickly we can march down the Aemilian Way and catch Otho in the open as he comes north to unite his army.'

'How soon can we be at Placentia?' Publilius asked Cerberus.

'It's fifty miles from here to Cremona, then another twenty or so across the river to Placentia. With all the siege equipment, no more than four days, I should think.'

'Can your men be ready to march tomorrow, Publilius?' I asked.

'We'll run rings around you, General!'

'Good man. Now, I don't know about you two, but I need a bath.'

'There was one last thing, sir,' Cerberus added. 'A letter arrived for you by private courier this morning. He's still in the city, waiting for your reply.'

'Who on earth sends an invading general a letter?' I asked.

'No idea, sir. The messenger didn't give his master's name.' He gestured at a cylindrical container that stood next to the table. Curious, I opened the leather tube and out fell a letter, the figure of a prancing horse pressed into the red wax that sealed it. It was the seal of my friend, Julius Agricola.

X

I waited until I was in the privacy of my own billet that evening before reading the letter from Julius. Totavalas was in the garden giving Aulus a lesson in swordplay, while Salonina was being pampered and preened in the bath by her slaves. Carefully, I picked away at the wax with my fingernails. I have this knack of tearing the vellum if I try to prise a letter open in one go, you see. Finally the wax came away:

Caecina,

Thank you for your letter. It was hard enough when your mother died only three years ago, she had been as good a parent to me as I hope my mother was to you. Mother was so proud of me when I was elected to be a praetor last year, and with your promotion to Legate of the Fourth she couldn't have been prouder of 'her boys'.

But to lose your mother to a fever was one thing, to lose mine to the swords of Otho's scum is another entirely. I admit that I cannot understand what possessed you and others to follow a man as uninspiring as Vitellius when Galba was alive, but you'll understand why I have no loyalty to Otho as emperor. He is gathering his troops to oppose you and has put our old

*general, Suetonius Paulinus, in command of the army, though
Otho intends to march with us. Paulinus has asked me to serve
as his chief of staff and I have accepted. If there is any way that
I can help you and the cause of Vitellius, write to me using the
same messenger.*

Yours in haste,
Julius

'What have you got there?' Salonina asked. Her rounded form
was delicately wrapped in a gown of expensive fabric, decorated
with swirling patterns of blue and gold.

'Read this,' I said. Her eyes flicked from left to right as she
read, her expression betraying her surprise.

'And you're going to accept his offer?' she asked.

'Why shouldn't I? It's thanks to Otho that his mother is dead;
why shouldn't he want to see him fail? But there's something
else we need to talk about.'

'And what's that?' she said suspiciously, coming to sit on the
corner of the bed.

'I would have wanted this even before I heard about Julius's
mother, but now that she's been killed I'm going to insist.'

'Spit it out, Caecina, whatever it is.'

'I want you and Aulus to wait here in Mediolanum when I
take the army south.'

'But—'

'I would have sent you home to Vicetia, but that's on the road
that Otho's reinforcements will take. You'll be safer here.'

'I thought you said there would be no safer place for me than
with your army,' Salonina said.

'When we were marching, yes. But now we're going to war.
And a proper war, not like those scraps we had in the Alps. This
will be the real thing. Thousands will die in the next few weeks,
and I don't want you among them.'

'Don't I get a say in this?'

I smiled weakly. 'You're having your say right now. As your husband I don't have to listen to it.'

'That's not funny, Caecina.'

'I know, and I'm sorry. But you can't blame me for not wanting to lose you. And it's not as though we share the same bed that much these days . . .'

'And whose fault is that?' she said, gesturing at her swollen figure.

'Yes, I realize that. But it doesn't mean I don't want to be with you.'

'So you want to be with me, but you don't want to be with me, is that it?'

'Stop twisting my words, Salonina!'

Her shoulders slumped. She looked tired. 'I'm sorry, Caecina, I didn't mean to fight with you. My mind's all over the place.'

I went and gave her a hug. 'I just want to keep you safe.'

'I know, but if you kept me any safer I might as well live in a box and only be brought out for special occasions. You know that's not the sort of wife I want to be.'

'I know. But trust me on this. One big battle and it'll all be over, then we'll be together. I promise.'

The army set out the next day. The men were spoiling for a fight. As I rode alongside them it struck me how many veterans we had in our number. You could tell the raw recruits, for they were the ones who still wore their long socks. Socks are a welcome addition when plodding slowly through the mountain passes, but in the lush plains of northern Italia we would be marching faster and harder, and that meant blisters. And blisters break. That's painful enough; more painful still is when the pus glues the wound to the sock, making every step a sore one. And then there's the agony of trying to take the wretched things off once they are stuck to you. But that was the price you paid for electing to keep your shins warm for that little bit longer, and it was a lesson once learned that was never forgotten.

As Cerberus had said, it was little more than fifty miles to the main fortress on the northern bank of the Po, Cremona. At full marching pace that should have taken two days, no more. Hampered by the siege engines I had allowed three and a half days, but what I had not accounted for was the obsequiousness and pomposity of my fellow citizens. Every tiny market town we passed sent us a deputation of dignitaries who offered us the freedom of the town, or landowners would invite the senior officers to their homes for dinner and try to ingratiate themselves with us, no doubt hoping that we would requisition grain from farms other than their own! And we could hardly ignore the overtures of our own people. Poor Totavalas probably spent more time polishing my ceremonial armour than he did in the saddle on that tiresome journey south. We ended up taking six whole days to march those fifty miles, and every day we idled meant more time for Otho's men to prepare their defences in Placentia.

The people of Cremona welcomed us with open arms. Like the citizens of Vienne and Lugdunum before them, they had a bitter rivalry with the town of Placentia.

'Just because they're on the southern side of the Po and we're not, they treat us like dirt,' one of the locals complained bitterly. 'Doesn't it matter that our town is just as old, as rich and as important? No, not to them; we're just barbarians from beyond the river!'

'I'm a Vicetian myself,' I explained. 'We may not be from the same province, but I know what it's like to be considered an inferior breed just because your home town is nearer to the Alps than it is to the decadent cities in the south.'

The man beamed at finding a kindred spirit, and the rest of the town were just as welcoming. Aside from the huge delays, my only concern now was that my officers were being over-indulged by the local hospitality as we were honoured with yet another feast, and I had to make yet another gracious speech to the citizenry. Thank the gods my scouts kept me informed of the enemy's whereabouts. That half of the advance party not in Placentia was still away to the east, keeping the Postumian Way open to the Balkan legions, while Otho and his army were still far away to the south.

Once over the Po, the raucous marching songs stopped. The men were beginning to think of the battle ahead. They knew that this would be the last campaign for some of them, and that tends to make a man rather thoughtful. But crossing the river was important. It showed we were taking the fight to Otho, and I had confidence in my men even without Valens's larger army on hand to support us.

Placentia was the biggest fortress in the north, and it grew out of the hazy western horizon at daybreak the next day. In every other direction the land met the sky in an unerringly flat line. Up in the sky, tinted a lifelike pink by the touch of a red dawn, there was a cloud that looked like a staggering boar. I don't know if it was my imagination or some omen from the gods, but it unnerved me.

Time passed, and the lump on the horizon grew and grew. At first it looked as big as the tiniest pebble on a stony beach. Then it was as large as a thumbnail. We marched on, and I could begin to make out the individual faces of each wall. To the side of the city stood a great amphitheatre, the biggest of its kind anywhere along the Po. But it was the walls, the towers and the men on the battlements that drew my attention. Soon we met another road that joined us obliquely from the south-east. This was the Aemilian Way, the road that Otho and his army would be marching along to meet his Balkan reinforcements. But if we took Placentia quickly we could leave the siege engines in the town and march at lightning pace to meet him head on, and we would outnumber him two to one. Valens would barely be in Italia and I would hand the throne to Vitellius on a plate.

Totavalas reined in alongside me. He whistled. 'That's the biggest city I ever saw.'

'Don't tell me, no big fortresses in Hibernia either!'

'We have forts, but as no one has catapults like yours, we don't need the expense of stone walls. A few ditches on a hillside, ringed by a palisade and a good bunch of men with stout shields, that's all the defence you need back home.'

'Then pray my people never invade Hibernia,' I said.

'I do, more often than you think. How long should it take for you to capture this city?'

'A day, maybe two,' I said nonchalantly.

'A day? But would you look at the size of the place?'

'You forget, we have three legions' worth of artillery with us, and my twenty thousand men face a bunch of gladiators and palace guards.'

'Doesn't the prospect of gladiators scare you a little bit?'

'They're slaves, Totavalas. They have no discipline, no stomach to defend a town that isn't their own.'

'I was a slave once,' Totavalas reminded me gently. I did not reply.

When we came within a reasonable distance of the walls I gave the order to halt.

'Have the men cook their midday meal,' I told my staff.

'In front of the city walls, sir?' Pansa queried.

'Yes, Pansa. Let the garrison see that we're so confident of taking the city that we stop to eat under their very noses. They're not going to sally out. There are too few of them, and they want to keep us sitting here while Otho's army marches to relieve them. We can spare an hour or so.'

'Do you want the men eating in any particular order, sir?' one of the staff officers asked.

'Why can't they all eat together?'

'The cooks can't feed eighteen thousand men at one sitting,

General. We have to stagger the mealtimes, dish up the food from all the cooking pots as quickly as possible, find new fuel for the fire—'

I raised a hand for silence. 'Spare me the details, man. Just get the men fed, I'll give you the honour of deciding who can eat first. Now, someone find me a white flag.'

'Sir?' one of them asked.

'You heard me, a white flag. I know it's not exactly our custom to surrender, but there must be a white flag somewhere in our column.'

An orderly scuttled off to find the flag, while Publilius opened his mouth to say something, but then thought better of it.

'You think we shouldn't parley with the enemy, Publilius?'

'Otho sent these men from Rome, General. Do you really think they're going to abandon the strongest fortress in the north?'

'No, I don't. But that doesn't mean we shouldn't try to avoid bloodshed.'

The flag was found, hiding in the depths of some baggage cart, in among the farriers' supply of spare horseshoes if you'll believe it. One of the junior tribunes offered to carry the flag and accompany me to the parley, but this was something I had to do alone.

'You can have the honour of leading the first assault on the city, if you like?' I joked.

'Thank you, sir, but I'd rather carry the flag!'

'Understood! Have someone tie the flagstaff to my saddle so I don't have to worry about holding it while I'm negotiating.'

The first cohorts were sitting down to lunch by the time my ceremonial armour was strapped on and Achilles' coat had been scrubbed clean of the dust from the road. A groom knelt down to act as a mounting block, and I bounded into the saddle. Achilles was nervous. The flagstaff hadn't been properly secured to the saddle and the strong winds from the north were making the flag flutter wildly. The groom saw this and yanked down hard on the staff to fix a tighter knot. Achilles screeched in pain and reared up high, his front legs flailing in the air as though kicking some imaginary enemy. I was flung from the saddle; there was a sickening crack as my shoulder hit the hard surface of the road.

At once there were men surrounding me, all eager to help me up.

'I can get up by myself,' I snarled. At first there was no pain, but as I attempted to rise it hit me hard. It was like the time when Quintus and Lugubrix had cauterized the stump of my severed finger with a brazier of burning coals, except that was only my finger. Now my entire shoulder was on fire, and every so often my whole arm would spasm uncontrollably as the muscles protested.

The men backed off as I staggered to my feet, leaning my body weight on my left side and using my good arm to lever myself off the ground.

'Someone go find a surgeon,' I said through gritted teeth, before turning to see what was the matter with Achilles. A stream of blood trickled gently down his flank, and my eyes travelled upwards, seeking the source. There, about a hand's span behind the saddle, was a sore-looking gash, and alongside it lay the flagstaff. Out from the staff itself jutted the end of a nail, the point red with blood. Achilles was quivering, and I stroked his neck tenderly, trying to calm him down. The groom was quivering more than the horse was, his gaze fixed on the ground.

'Look at me,' I said to the boy. The boy looked upwards, his body trembling like a hound desperate to run but too well trained to strain at the leash. As he looked into my eyes I knew he wouldn't see my fist coming. The bad hand on my good arm crashed into his jaw. The boy crumpled in an instant, out cold before he even hit the road. Behind me someone coughed gently and I spun round. It was the surgeon, with Totavalas standing beside him.

'May I look at your shoulder, General?'

Together the men gingerly extricated me from my armour to get a better look at the injury. I had no control over the arm at all, and it had to be delicately lifted and guided through the straps of the breastplate, though every movement hurt terribly. Once it was free, the arm hung limply and heavily at my side. The surgeon prodded and probed at my shoulder; sometimes it hurt, and sometimes it was excruciating.

'It looks like a simple dislocation. I can't find any evidence of broken bones,' he began. But a shrill blast interrupted him, the call of our *tubae*. But why would they be sounding while the men were having their meal? Up ahead, the city gates were opening. Out came a solitary rider who also carried a white flag. I watched him ride towards us at an easy trot to a point about halfway between us and the city walls. The surgeon was saying something to Totavalas but I wasn't paying attention. I was still watching the rider when the Hibernian slipped behind, put an arm over my good shoulder and grabbed my arm and body in a vice-like grip, leaving only my injured limb free.

'What are you doing?'

'Hold still, General, let the surgeon do his job.'

I felt a strong hand on my bicep, another perched on my shoulder. The rider sat there, watching. 'One, two, three!'

I screamed in pain and rage as the man thrust my arm back into its socket. Totavalas and the surgeon hurriedly stepped back in case they received the same treatment as the groom. Instead I took out my anger on the stiff leather of Achilles' saddle, punching it hard and hurting myself even more in the process. It was as though the fire in my arm was as fierce as Vulcan's forge, and my shoulder was the white-hot core of the furnace. I was seething, and my chest rose up and down as I tried to control my breathing. I was not going to faint in front of my men, or that solitary rider.

'Thank you,' I said to the surgeon, the words not coming easily to me.

'If you'll wait a moment I'll put that arm into a decent sling,' the man said, fumbling in his bag for some of the heavy cloth.

'No,' I said firmly. 'I don't want the men to see I'm hurt, or the man from the city.'

This time Totavalas cupped his hands and gave me a leg-up, and I made sure that Achilles was happy to have me ride him.

'If I'm not back within the hour, send a search party!' I called out, wincing as I turned in the saddle.

Achilles' hooves gently clip-clopped along the road. I deliberately had him walk steadily forward, not wanting to urge him into anything quicker after his fright, and to show the rider that I was in no hurry to meet with him. The man wore no helmet, his head covered instead with closely cropped black hair with streaks of grey at the temples. The face was stern, his posture unbending, a nobleman of the old school, I guessed. He was the one who spoke first.

'I take it you are the Legate Severus?'

I bridled at the veiled insult. 'General, actually.'

The man smiled wearily. 'I was told by the emperor to address you as "Legate". After all, that was your official rank.'

'Was?'

'Until you committed treason,' he said, as coolly as if he were discussing the weather.

'Otho was never one for subtlety. As you see, I am the general of this army, the one that stands before your city, and if these negotiations are to get anywhere I would consider it a courtesy for you to address me as such.'

'Very well, General,' he said with the air of a man indulging a small child.

'And you are?'

'My name's Spurinna. I believe we share a mutual friend.'

'Oh?'

'Tacitus, your governor in Hispania.'

'And how is the old man? Still the same world-weary soul I knew in Corduba?' I asked, smiling pleasantly despite the throbbing pain in my shoulder.

'He's back in Rome now, and much the same. But he made sure to tell me all he knew about you before I left the city.'

'All good, I hope?'

'Enough to know that there is little chance of persuading you to lay down your arms and declare your allegiance to Otho.'

I smiled. 'Very little. But don't think for one moment I want to spill any more Roman blood than is necessary. I will have Placentia, nothing can change that. But will you not join us against Otho?'

'Why should I break my oath to my emperor?'

'Because Otho, like Galba before him, is not fit to lead Rome.'

'And Vitellius is?'

'Vitellius isn't a whore-loving murderer.'

'But he is an idle, drunken layabout who will be ruled by his lieutenants,' Spurinna said pointedly.

'All emperors rely on trusted men to advise them.'

'And you would call yourself trustworthy? The man who betrayed both Nero and Galba?'

'You know as well as I do that Nero was destroying the empire, and Galba betrayed me before I even thought about supporting Vitellius.'

'Tacitus says differently,' the man shrugged.

'Well, Tacitus wasn't there,' I said forcefully. Spurinna smiled a fraction, and I cursed myself for letting this man get to me.

'So,' I continued, 'each of us is loyal to his master. But we are practical men, are we not?'

'Are we?' he said, simply.

'You know that I have nearly twenty thousand men under my command, the veterans of the Rhine, and you won't find better men in the whole empire, not even the legions in Syria. And what do you have?'

Spurinna was too old a campaigner to rise to the bait and tell me his strength, and said nothing.

'Two thousand gladiators,' I answered for him, 'some militia and a few cohorts of praetorians, men whose only military experience for the last five years has been the occasional tavern brawl. You really think your men can withstand mine?'

'I have a duty to my emperor to hold this city, and taking it will be harder than you think.'

'You wouldn't surrender for the sake of the women and children of Placentia then?' I said casually.

'What?'

'The women and children. I have no quarrel with them, but as for my men . . . We both know that our soldiers are less forgiving to the inhabitants of a fallen city than we are. If you will not surrender, will you at least allow the innocents to leave the city before we besiege it?'

Spurinna looked at me doubtfully. 'You would spare them all?'

'Why shouldn't I? It's only the presence of your garrison that puts their lives at risk. They are free to leave by the western gate, my men won't touch them.'

After a moment's pause, Spurinna smiled grimly, appreciating the cleverness of my offer. 'If I allow the families to leave, the militia won't have anything to fight for. They'll throw down their arms and surrender if your men get into the city.'

'You mean when,' I said.

'I mean if. So, with regret, I must decline your offer.' He gave a sharp tug at his reins, urging his horse to turn back towards Placentia.

'I am sorry,' I called out after him. 'Many good men will die today because of your choice.'

Spurinna looked back at me, his face full of contempt. 'I am defending Italia from an invading army. If you do take the city, killing innocent women and children, all to put an undeserving man on the throne, I hope the Furies hound you for the rest of your life.'

XI

The men looked at me expectantly as I rode back towards them. I had struggled to mask my pain from Spurinna, but now that he was heading back to the city I could try rolling my shoulder and wince as the muscles protested without losing face.

Pansa was the first to speak, which was his right as my second in command. 'What did the rider want, sir?'

'Our allegiance to Otho,' I replied. The men laughed derisively.

'I hope you told them where to go, sir.'

'Not quite. It would have made things easier if they had decided to join us, but their commander has sworn himself to Otho, and wouldn't shift. He refused to surrender, but we will take Placentia from him before the day is out!'

The officers cheered their support, while further back in the makeshift camp some of the men turned at the noise and began to cheer too, happily joining in a chorus of soldiers applauding their general.

'Publilius, where are you?' I called out.

'Here, General,' the prefect replied from among his fellow auxiliary officers.

'I want your auxiliaries to lead the assault. Take all the ladders and overwhelm them, at once, you hear?'

'Yes, General.' The man saluted sharply, smiling his enthusiasm.

'Any orders for my men, sir?' the chief engineer asked.

'Hopefully we won't have any need of your machines today. You can relax and enjoy the battle from afar!'

There was a hint of organized chaos as men scurried back and forth to pass on orders, find ladders, set the men up in formation. I had an officer take what little cavalry we had to the north-western and south-western corners of the city to keep an eye out for any men who tried to sally out of the city. Not that I expected Spurinna to do that; his garrison was already thinly stretched and I doubted he'd risk losing precious men in a surprise attack. But the whole city had to be covered, and the cavalry weren't going to be of much use in the assault on Placentia's high walls.

Soon the first auxiliaries were ready for the assault. The German tribesmen were spoiling for a fight. They had arrived too late to play any part in our assault against Alpinus in the mountains, and if any people are born to revel in the carnage of war, it is the fractious tribesmen from beyond the Rhine. Hundreds of them were already gathering around the great scaling ladders needed for the siege. Their centurions marshalled them into some semblance of order and the first of them were off in a wild charge.

Each ladder took about twenty men to carry it at a pace, with the rest of the century jogging along behind, ready to start climbing as soon as the ladders were against the walls. The groups went forward in twos and threes, all heading for the walls either side of the eastern gate. I could hear the occasional twang of bowstrings as arrows flew down from the walls, often driving into the ground but occasionally finding their mark, checking a man in mid-gallop. But each time a man fell another was there to take his place.

Soon the first ladders were against the walls and the men began to climb. Quickly the defenders tried to push the ladders back in the hope that they would tumble to the ground, but the more men who climbed upwards, the more effort it would take to dislodge them. Once the ladders were secured the handful of bowmen could fire into the seething mass on the ground, waiting their turn to climb, and these arrows were unlikely to miss. Screams began to echo off the walls and back towards us about three hundred paces away. But the first men were beginning to reach the top of the walls, only to find the deadly swords and robust shields of the praetorian guardsmen waiting for them.

I barked orders at the next wave of auxiliaries, small swarthy warriors from Lusitania. Otho had been governor of their province when Nero had exiled him from court, but these men had been serving on the Rhine before Otho had even fallen from favour; their loyalties were not in question. I told them to make for the southern and northern walls. They would be within range of the archers for longer, but by assaulting a larger area I hoped to stretch the enemy defences. Up ahead I saw two Germans halfway up their ladder struck by more arrows, so that the strength to climb deserted them and they tumbled off. Three men were higher up the ladder, but with the loss of the dead men the defenders brought their full weight to bear. The ladder teetered backwards slowly, inevitably, then tottered over with a mighty crash. I watched as one of the climbers sailed through the air, only to land head first on the hard earth.

Publilius was directing new batches of men as they arrived, his face ash-white.

'Publilius, we have to overwhelm them or your men will drop like flies.'

'They're coming as quickly as they can. Most of them were still eating when you gave the order for attack.'

'What?'

'The legionaries are ready, but most of the auxiliaries were eating or cooking. We weren't ready, General!'

Already I could see the swarms of men at the foot of the walls beginning to thin.

'Get every auxiliary that's ready to the walls now.'

The next wave lumbered forward less eagerly than the first. I counted nine ladders that still stood against Placentia's walls, but that was too few. Even when the Lusitanians had reached the more distant points for their assault, the defenders still had enough men to see off each threat.

Pansa stood by Achilles' shoulder. He looked up at me, his face grim.

'You've got to call the retreat, sir. Either that or throw even more men at the walls.'

I nodded sadly. Pansa was right. It made no sense to reinforce the failure of the first assault, so I gave the order for the auxiliaries to withdraw. Sending the legionaries in when there were so few access points to the city would have been a bloody, desperate gamble, one that I wasn't willing to take. The mournful metallic bugle sounded the recall and the men came flocking back, glad to be out of range of Placentia's marksmen.

The men on the battlements cheered as the troops ran back to the safety of our lines. A few men had managed to retrieve some of the ladders. Others clutched at arrow wounds or helped to carry their injured comrades home.

The chief engineer watched the ignominious retreat, his face a picture of resignation.

'Shall I have the artillery assembled, General?'

I didn't answer him at first. I looked out at the carnage and chaos Placentia had inflicted on my army. 'I want those bloody walls turned into rubble. Understand?'

'Yes, sir.'

★

There was a dismal, dour mood in the air that night in council. Only my inner circle were there. Quintus sat at the table, his eyes staring listlessly ahead. Pansa, Publilius and Cerberus were quietly talking together. Only Totavalas was missing. It wouldn't do to have a freedman speak in council as though he were the others' equal. I valued his advice highly, but there was no place for him in the tent. He didn't command any men, even if he did command my respect for his shrewd mind and his unswerving loyalty. The engineer stood alone at the end of the table, painfully aware that he was no more than a guest in this close circle of men, and he shuffled awkwardly from one foot to the other as I struggled to choose the right words.

'Gentlemen,' I said, bringing the meeting to order. 'I had hoped that we would be celebrating within the walls of Placentia tonight. However, my over-eagerness and a logistical error have ruled out the possibility of another frontal assault.'

I paused. My friend Agricola, the man I affectionately mocked as the glorified staff officer, would not have made the mistake I had made that day. He would have known which men were ready to fight and which were not before trying to overrun the enemy. I had never conducted a siege before. My tactical mind was suited to battles and skirmishes in the woods or open fields, using the lie of the land to help our men and hinder the enemy. What I would have given to have Julius Agricola with me that night!

'How many men did we lose today, Publilius?' I asked, already knowing the answer but wanting the number to sink in.

'Three hundred and eighty-nine dead, around one hundred and fifty who will never fight again, ninety or so lightly wounded.'

'Over five hundred men that we can't use against Otho,' Pansa observed sourly. 'We might as well have decimated a whole legion and saved ourselves the bother.'

'Pansa, when a general of Rome is man enough to admit his

mistakes to his junior officers, I suggest you treat him with the respect he deserves.'

The older man looked me full in the eyes. I could see he was tempted to make some retort, but he thought better of it. 'Apologies, General. I didn't think.'

'It's forgotten already, it has been a dispiriting day.'

Quintus, still looking dead to the world, snorted at the understatement. But he said nothing. I ignored him and looked to the engineer. 'The floor is yours, Centurion.'

'Thank you, sir.' The man smiled nervously, then began his report. 'My men have been unpacking the artillery this afternoon, and the assembly shouldn't take more than another couple of hours. We'll be ready to commence the battery by midnight, sir. We will be focusing our fire on the stretch of wall beyond the first vertex north of the gatehouse.'

'Vertex?' Cerberus queried.

'A corner of the wall, if you like, sir. Where the walls begin to turn westwards to cover the northern side of the city.'

'And why not attack the gatehouse itself?' Cerberus asked.

'Because that will be the thickest point of Placentia's wall, sir. They know the gate is vulnerable to artillery fire, so that part of the wall is reinforced with extra stone.'

'You weren't by any chance a teacher before you joined the army, Centurion?' Publilius quipped. The centurion bristled. Judging from the lines on his face the man had been raining down death and destruction on Rome's enemies while Publilius was still learning his letters.

'Thank you, Centurion,' I intervened. 'One final question: is there anything you need from us to help you?'

'There is one decision that isn't mine to make, General.'

'Go on,' I said.

'When we try to make a breach in the wall, it's likely that a great many missiles will clear the walls and hit the city beyond.'

'And?' said Pansa.

'And that city is full of Roman women and children,' a new voice said. Quintus was still staring at a fixed spot on the far side of the tent, his body motionless.

The centurion cleared his throat. 'Exactly, sir. I can have the men aim for the base of the wall, lowering the risk of our shots flying overhead, but that will mean a lot of them hitting the ground first, and then bouncing into the walls. The impact of hitting the ground will rob them of their momentum, so they won't do much damage.'

'General,' Pansa began, 'we can spend at most another two days at Placentia. Otho's army marches closer every hour we idle here, not to mention his reinforcements from the east. We can't afford to lengthen the siege any more than is necessary if we want to defeat Otho before he is reinforced.'

'But Valens and his army are coming from the west,' Cerberus reminded him. 'If they march straight to Cremona they could stop the legions from Pannonia from joining Otho's column.'

'That's a big if,' Pansa said. 'We can't afford to take the risk.'

'I'm with the legate,' Publilius said. 'We offered them the chance to surrender, it's not our fault if they refuse to take it.'

All the while Quintus had turned to look at me. My ears were focusing on my officers, but my eyes were withstanding my friend's penetrating stare. He didn't need to state his opinion, it was taken for granted. Quintus just looked at me, daring me to contradict him.

'You will aim for the base of the wall,' I said, quietly but firmly. 'These aren't barbarians we're fighting, but Roman citizens. We cannot forget that. We dare not. What if the gods decide that Otho should triumph? We will conduct this war with honour, or not at all.'

There was nothing more to say on the matter. The men dismissed themselves. Quintus was the first to leave, with not even a ghost of a smile or a nod to approve my decision. The others all stood stiffly and saluted before heading back to get some sleep, with the exception of the engineer.

'Would you like to oversee the assembly, General?'

'Thank you, but I know you don't need any help from me. Your men do their work well, I saw that the day we killed Alpinus. I'm going to get what sleep I can, but wake me when you're ready to begin firing.'

It was still a few hours before dawn when the artillery was fully assembled, aimed and primed. The legionaries stood at perfect attention by their machines as I inspected them. By the flickering light of the torches I could make out the names the men had carved on to their charges. The two from my legion had been unimaginatively called Wall-breaker and Home-wrecker, but one from the Twenty-Second Legion made me stop.

'Tell me,' I asked, 'why have you called your machine Moth?'

The soldier smiled. 'Cos she'll make some bloody great holes if she has her way, General!'

When the inspection was over, the centurion offered to let me prime and fire the opening shot, pointing at a heavy-looking metal lever on the nearest onager. The surgeon had insisted on fashioning a makeshift sling for my arm before I went to bed, but there was no way I was going to appear before my men all patched up when they had been throwing themselves against a well-defended city. My left arm was as good as ever, and I took hold of the lever with a firm grip. All I had to do was push the lever another forty degrees or so to turn the ratchet, adding the last bit of tension to the weapon.

The centurion's face fell as he realized his mistake. 'I'm sorry, sir, it takes two hands to fire the onager.'

The men were watching me now. How would it look to them if their general failed to push a simple metal lever? The muscles of my arm began to strain, I felt my face flushing red with the effort. A man moved to help me.

'Stay where you are,' I hissed. I had felt the shaft begin to move. I just had to force it down against the resistance of the ratchet, another hand's breadth would do it. A low growl escaped my lips as I pushed with all my strength. My right arm hung limply but painfully at my side, and I saw the centurion ushering the men back to their posts in case he had to step in and help me. The lever was bent almost halfway there, and I shifted my footing so that I could add my full body weight to the pushing power of my arm until at last the ratchet clicked into place. The machine was ready to fire.

I was still blowing hard with exhaustion as the engineer handed me a length of rope that released the firing pin.

'This part should be a lot easier, sir!'

I didn't have the energy to come up with a smart remark, I simply yanked the rope, hard. With the pressure on the coiled sinews gone, the onager's arm sprang into the air, thudding into the sack of straw to cushion the blow. Our eyes followed the missile's flat trajectory into the darkness. We couldn't see the impact, but we heard it, the rock smacking into the wall with a sharp crack.

'We have the right trajectory, men,' the centurion called to his underlings. 'Use this catapult as the template, jump to it.'

Soon the air was rent with the chorus of rocks smashing into the walls, but we could not tell how much damage we were doing. It would be another hour or so before the morning sun rose behind us in the east, illuminating the city with her golden glow, but nevertheless I decided to stay with the men, though my shoulder was giving me Hades.

The light of day fell upon the imposing walls, and the engineer squinted to look for signs of damage from the bombardment. There were none. The grey stone was pockmarked with dents and scratches scattered over an area perhaps two hundred paces wide, and precious few were high up. By contrast, the ground was littered with fragments of our missiles. Piles of rubble at the foot of the wall told us that the projectiles had smashed hard into the earth and shattered on hitting the wall, doing little damage that we could see. The engineer looked crestfallen.

'How much ammunition do you have left?'

The centurion looked over the carts that carried the ammunition and did a quick mental calculation, his eyes rolling skywards as he thought. 'Enough for another day, sir.'

'Will that be enough time to make a breach?'

'Hard to say, General. If our shots keep hitting the ground first it might take double the time,' he said.

I sighed heavily. 'Very well. I'll be resting in my tent, Centurion. Wake me at midday and we'll review the situation then.'

'And if we make a breach before then, sir?'

'Then by all means wake me. But the odds of making a practicable breach before then are . . . ?'

The centurion smiled tiredly. 'I'll see you at midday, General.'

Totavalas was waiting for me inside my tent; so too was a plate of bread and cheese. A bronze goblet sat on the table beside my bed.

'It's a little early in the day for wine, don't you think?' I said, inspecting the contents of the cup.

'For the rest of us, yes. For you it's more like the end of a late night. I thought it might help you sleep.'

'You're my freedman, Totavalas, not my slave. You don't need to bring me breakfast in bed any more. I have slaves to do that.'

'You do?' Totavalas looked exaggeratedly round the room. 'I can't see them.'

'You know perfectly well they're back in Mediolanum with my family.'

'Precisely. Besides, what with all your military councils and siege preparations, I thought you might have forgotten about little old me. Knowing how much you love stale army bread and mouldy cheese I thought I'd bring you some.'

One sniff of the cheese told me he wasn't joking. But what sort of general would I be if I dined on campaign as lavishly as Vitellius banqueted?

'You know how much I value your opinion, Totavalas. But you're not a soldier, at least not a Roman soldier. I doubt Publilius or Cerberus would mind you being at council, but Quintus and Pansa?' I left the rest of the thought unsaid.

'Ah, jealousy is a powerful thing.'

'If you say so. Thank you for the breakfast, Totavalas. If you could send the surgeon to me, I'd be grateful.'

The Hibernian nodded, and ducked out of the tent. My hand reached out for the hunk of bread, but it was rock hard, so instead I wolfed down the cheese. The taste was indescribable, so sour it was all I could do not to spit the stuff out. Hurriedly I drained the goblet, hoping the wine would wash away the foulness. There was a polite cough from beyond the tent flap.

'Come in,' I called, my mouth still swilling with wine as I tried to remove the spots of cheese stuck between my teeth.

I must have looked a sight, but the surgeon didn't blink. 'How is the shoulder, General?'

'On fire,' I said.

'I can give you something for the pain.' He began to fumble within his bag.

'Not if it will dull my wits, I need to keep my head focused on the siege. What can you do for the shoulder?'

'I should put it in a sling to encourage the muscles and bones to stay where they're meant to be.'

'And how long would I need that for?'

'A month? No more.'

'I can't go about in front of my men bandaged for a month!'

'It's your shoulder, General, not mine. You could always wear the sling in private, but I should warn you that without support the shoulder might dislocate again.'

'All right, all right. Out with your beloved bandages then.'

Within a quarter of an hour my arm was slinged and strapped, the forearm resting on my breastplate and fist pointing towards my good shoulder, as though beginning a salute. The surgeon guided me into bed, and I was told to lie flat on my back with a pillow for my elbow to rest on. Soon the doctor was gone and I was asleep.

XII

Galba's face loomed at me out of the darkness. 'I had such hopes, Severus. Even if you defeat my murderer, it won't even begin to repay me for saving your family from bankruptcy.'

'And what right have you got to think you can decide who should succeed Galba?' Otho chimed in. He stood up on Placentia's high walls but I could see every detail on his made-up face, the join where his wig met his scalp, even smell the perfume fairly oozing from his skin. I stood alone before the city, armed only with the Gallic sword that had once belonged to the warrior Bormo, the one that I had used to defeat the legionary Strontius, the man who almost turned my own legions against me. They were all up there, Galba, Otho, Vindex; even kindly Verginius Rufus was there. He looked down at me, disappointment creasing his face.

'So I wasn't good enough to lead my own men to Rome, but Vitellius is? Bad form, Severus.'

I glanced behind me. The army was in pristine order, rank after rank, but they stood still as statues.

'Go on then, General,' Pansa hooted, 'show us how it's done!' From among the ranks strode Valens, unkempt and panting with exhaustion but pacing forward with purpose.

'Out of the way, boy, leave this to the real men.'

But then the whole ground seemed to shake. The brilliant blue sky turned an angry black, thunder and lightning crashing and flashing in chaotic beauty. Great rocks as big as elephants began to tumble from the heavens.

'Sir, sir!' a voice called out excitedly. 'Sir!'

I sprang up. Too fast, my shoulder complained fearfully at the sudden movement. I looked around at the green of the grass, the red of the tent, the young aide poised in the gap that served as a doorway.

'Are you all right, sir? You look as pale as a Hades shade.'

'What is it, Tribune?'

'It's the walls, sir, they're beginning to fall.'

'But the centurion said he'd wake me at midday!'

'It is almost midday, General,' the aide said.

'What?' I said, astonished. 'He said it would take hours.'

'Come and have a look if you don't believe me, sir.'

Abandoning the sling, I hurried out of the tent, wiping the cold sweat from my face and neck as I jogged. I tried running but the impact of each footfall jarred my shoulder, and the aide ran impatiently ahead of me.

The siege engines were still going at it hammer and tongs, launching missile after missile at the walls. The chief engineer must have got his eye in though. A section of the battlements had crashed down on to the ground in front of us, perhaps a dozen paces wide, leaving a jagged V-shaped opening in the wall.

'Good news, General,' the centurion called to me. 'We'll soon have a full breach.'

'But how has it happened so quickly?'

'Luck, I suppose. I saw some cracks develop a few hours ago and we've been concentrating all our fire on the weak spot.'

They certainly had. I saw how the endmost machines in the line had been turned a good thirty degrees. Every piece of artillery had been realigned to focus on the point where the wall had begun to crack and crumble.

'How long until we have a breach we can attack?' The voice belonged to Pansa. I turned to face him, and he looked at me, puzzled.

'Are you all right, General? You don't look well.'

'I'll be fine. I just had some very suspect cheese, that's all.'

'So long as you're sure, sir. I don't mind taking control of the army while you recuperate,' he said earnestly.

'No need for that, Pansa. Well, you heard what he said: how long until the breach is big enough for an assault?' I asked the engineer.

'Hopefully no more than another four hours or so, General.'

'Very well, then I will sit here and wait until we are ready.'

A man was sent to bring one of the chairs from my tent while Pansa had the army prepare itself. Not wanting to be caught out by a sudden sally – after all, the machines had to be within a mere two hundred paces of the walls to be effective and we couldn't risk losing them to a suicidal enemy attack – we learned the lesson of the day before and had the men stagger their meal-times so that there was always at least a full legion ready for action.

It was mid-afternoon when I heard a clattering sound, a few cries of pain and three men were lying prone on the ground.

'Slingers!' the engineer shouted. I grabbed the helmet which had been resting beside my seat and hastily strapped it on.

'Why are they using slingers only now?' I asked, saying the words more to myself than anyone in particular.

'They've probably only just found the slings in a storeroom somewhere,' Pansa answered.

As the front two ranks weaved their way between the machines, with their shields held high to protect them, some men dragged the wounded out of harm's way. The stones, no bigger than your fist, had dented one man's helmet and knocked him unconscious. The other two had not been so lucky: their faces were a bloody mess. One was even missing some teeth.

The stones were still raining down on us as the legionaries formed a protective wall, the front rank using their shields to cover themselves while the second held theirs aloft and at a reverse angle to make a higher screen without leaving themselves exposed. The slingers' ammunition was too small to see until it was directly above you, and by then it was too late. One of the siege engineers standing next to me was suddenly plucked back, the stone catching him right on the throat. His hands clasped at his neck as he fell, gasping for breath.

We endured this barrage for an hour or more before the storm of stones began to falter, the defenders clearly running low on ammunition. We lost thirty dead and almost a hundred wounded, but the soldiers who operated the onagers if anything worked even faster, perhaps in the knowledge that once a breach was made they and their machines could retreat to the safety of our makeshift camp.

The occasional missile would fly through the gap we had battered in their wall, crashing into some unfortunate building. The only consolation was that the garrison would have moved any civilians away from the side of the city we were assaulting; the only men we killed would be soldiers. But as more and more of the wall was destroyed it reduced the size of the target for our engineers. The shots kept pounding though, and ammunition was beginning to run short. The men watched silently, waiting to be unleashed. As the sun began to sink in the west, soon to be obscured by Placentia itself, a lucky shot hit the wall low down, plumb on one of the largest cracks. Huge chunks of the wall came crashing down and to a man we craned to see the damage it had caused.

It seemed to take an age for the dust to settle, but the murky haze began to clear. At last we had a breach, wide enough for eight, maybe ten men to walk abreast. Through the dust I could make out the glint of swords and spears as the defenders massed within the gap. I turned to face the nearest cohorts.

'We have our breach, men. Only a few soft guardsmen and a bunch of slaves stand in your way. Engineers, I want you to focus the ammunition you have left on the gates, try to give our boys another way into the city. The Twenty-Second Legion will have the privilege of being the first men to cross the threshold of Placentia.' I drew my sword clumsily with my left arm and raised it to the sky. 'For Vitellius!'

'For Vitellius!' they echoed. The engineers didn't even have to cheer their own success but set to moving their lumbering machines to face the city gates. The foremost cohort of the Twenty-Second, led by their young tribune, formed a testudo to protect themselves from the archers on the walls. Once the formation was complete they shuffled forward, standing too close together to march normal-length paces for fear of making holes in the tortoise shell of curved shields.

There were two hundred paces of open ground to cross, open but for the corpses of the auxiliaries who had failed to scale or return from the walls. The second cohort was already forming up behind them, ready to reinforce the first wave; the breach was too narrow to send more than one cohort at a time into the attack. It would be suicidal to send them in close support, needlessly into range of the bowmen high up on Placentia's walls. The first cohort was nearing the walls now. I could make out the tribune in the rear rank of the testudo, the broad purple stripe on his cloak flanked by four cloaks of deep scarlet on either side. He was a brave young man to join the first attack.

The bowmen took their time, searching for chinks in the body of men beneath them. Flights of arrows thudded into the roof of shields but some of them found their fleshy targets. The cohort marched on, leaving dead and wounded men in their wake. Up ahead was a rough group of defenders, not bunched together to form an impenetrable wall, for the lumps of rubble made an organized line impossible. Most of them carried gladii, a few bore two swords, others had spears or tridents coupled with a net. They were the gladiators.

There was a loud crash, then another and another. The defenders were throwing rocks from the parapet, hefty chunks of stone too heavy to be repelled by a simple wooden shield. The cohort was at the wall now, but the breach was a good foot above ground level. It wasn't much of a height advantage, but the gladiators made it tell. The rear of the cohort was still formed up in a testudo, but the front had broken free to engage with the enemy hand to hand. The arrows and rocks just kept on coming, and I couldn't see any of our men forcing their way into the breach. How could slaves hope to fend off the cream of the Roman army?

I ordered a third cohort to prepare to join the attack. By now the first cohort was floundering, and the second was heading into the killing zone at the foot of the walls. I could just make out a flash of purple in the midst of the fighting. The rear of the testudo must have made it to the walls, but then a rock came hurtling from above, crushing the tribune's head. With the loss of their officer, the spirit of the first wave broke and they ran back towards us. The artillery was still firing shot after shot at the gates but doing no damage that I could see. Hastily I waved on the next cohort.

'Go on, don't give them time to recuperate!' But it was too late, the surviving gladiators in the front rank had rotated; now my troops faced new, fresh men.

The first of the survivors from the initial assault were making it back to our lines.

'What's wrong with you?' Pansa bawled. 'How can a few slaves send you packing?'

'They're not just any slaves, Legate,' a man answered. 'They're the best gladiators in all of Rome, used to fighting in single combat. With the rubble and the high breach we can't attack them in line.'

'I've never fought anyone like them,' another chipped in.

The sky was beginning to darken, and it was getting harder to see the impact of our attacks. I could just make out the gladiators hacking, stabbing and lunging, and a pile of bodies growing higher and higher. Soon the legionaries faced a small climb just to get within reach of the defenders' swords. The gates still stood, stubbornly refusing to cave in before the onslaught from the artillery. We needed another entry point to the city, and quickly. I grabbed the chief engineer by the arm and shouted over the noise of the mighty machines launching yet another volley.

'Can we burn the gates down?' I yelled in his ear.

'We can use naphtha, but it will make our shots less accurate.'

'Surely one hit is all we need?'

The centurion nodded, and relayed my order to his men. By now the fourth wave was preparing to join the assault; the gladiators were still holding firm. As the first fireballs were launched towards the city, Quintus caught my eye. He was the reason I hadn't sent in my own legion, the Fourth, to lead the attack on Placentia. I owed my friend so much, and he had seen too much death and tragedy for a man of his tender years. But I knew deep down that he felt our siege of the city was wrong, and I didn't trust him to lead my men into a potential death trap for a cause that wasn't his own. Thankfully it was the Twenty-Second's tribune and not my friend who had lost his life in the assault.

Most of the naphtha-infused missiles sailed way beyond the walls and into the city itself, causing huge explosions on impact. There was no way of knowing what carnage the fire was wreaking beyond the thick slabs of stone. Quintus walked away in disgust. I could have called him back but it would have served no purpose. The Fourth were far more attached to me than to the man who shared a name with the leader of a crushed Gallic rebellion. Given the right cause Quintus could have been a great leader of men, but I knew then that this was not his fight. I looked up to the heavens to issue a silent prayer to the gods that Quintus would forgive what we were doing, but then I noticed that the sky was tinged with orange. It wasn't because the sun was setting, for it had long since passed below the horizon. Placentia's majestic theatre was on fire.

The gates to the city were still intact, but the finest theatre in northern Italia was an inferno. The building must have been hit by some stray shots from our onagers, since it lay beyond the city's south-eastern corner, but on a direct line extending from our artillery towards the gatehouse. All I could see of the theatre itself were the high flames licking at the topmost parts of the timber stands for the *cavea*, where the women and plebs would have sat.

But it was the pinpricks of orange against the dark of dusk that worried me more. In retribution, no doubt, for burning their theatre, the bowmen loosed flaming arrows into the sky, hoping that a high, arcing trajectory would reach our distant lines. Immediately, nearby men moved to protect me with their shields, but through the gaps within my new layer of armour I could see that the vast majority of arrows were falling short, plummeting down early because of their heavier, flaming heads. Quickly I was ushered a good forty paces back, well beyond range. The shields were withdrawn just as another volley sailed into the night. It was like a cloud of fireflies cascading down from the heavens.

I watched as the engineers hurriedly loaded the machines. In his rush to get behind his onager, one man, using it as cover from the storm of arrows, knocked over an amphora of the foul-smelling naphtha. The soldier barely registered it, but my stomach clenched with sickening fear as I realized what might happen. The first arrows fell short, some plummeting into the earth, others skimming across it because they landed at too flat an angle. Some thudded into the wood of the machines, while a few managed to find their intended targets. They were the lucky ones, the men with searing shafts embedded in their chest or throat. My eyes were fixed on that emptying amphora. Time almost came to a halt as the inevitable arrow plunged into the dirty pool.

In horror I saw the pool ignite in an instant, the flames dancing, devouring everything in their path. They followed the trail towards a pile of amphorae neatly stacked together. The blast of the explosion knocked me back, a sudden wave of immense heat as the scene before me was transformed into a roaring, raging vision of carnage. Four of the onagers were on fire, their handlers running about wildly as their whole bodies were consumed with flames. Their cries of anguish carried over the crackling of the fire as one by one they fell to the ground and tried to smother the prancing, agonizing flames.

Before I could react, men were already hurrying forward with buckets of water, trying to put out the fires engulfing their comrades, but most of them were scorched to death long before the water arrived. They tried to put out the fires devouring the onagers but the heat was so intense that they could not get close enough to empty their buckets.

Our only hope of taking Placentia now was the breach, but many good men had already thrown their lives away on the swords and spears of the gladiators, and who knew how many more men it would need to capture the place.

'General Severus!' a voice called. 'General Severus!'

A rider was negotiating his way through the crowd of soldiers rushing forward to drag the bodies of the burned and the burning back to the line and the attentions of the medical orderlies. His dark face against the burnished metal of his helmet marked him out as one of Cerberus' men.

'Over here,' I shouted, waving my good arm. The rider

spotted me at last, urging his horse onward through the sea of moving bodies. His horse was exhausted, its chest heaving after a hard, fast journey.

'Otho's army, sir,' the rider said breathlessly, 'they're at Mutina.'

'Mutina?' I said incredulously. 'But that's only seventy miles from here!'

'They were at Mutina when I left, sir, but it didn't look as though they were stopping. They left their artillery and all the baggage that could be spared at the town, and are marching at double pace. I'd say they're just over fifty miles away by now.'

My mind whirred frantically. Only fifty miles away? At that pace, Otho and his praetorians would be at Placentia in little over a day, and my army had already taken far more casualties than I had anticipated in the assault, and the city was not yet won. Resignedly, I told a tribune to bring the senior officers to me, on the double.

'I wish I had brought better news, General,' was all the scout could say.

'You've almost killed your horse trying to bring it to me in time though. I'll ensure your commander is made aware of your efforts.'

Pansa, Publilius, Cerberus and Quintus were all found. They looked solemn and weary. Who wouldn't be after watching our pitiful attempts to take the city?

'The army will retreat in good order to Cremona,' I said.

No one spoke. They didn't know about Otho's imminent arrival and yet they all knew it would be madness to waste more men on Placentia's walls.

'Otho and his army have just passed Mutina,' I continued. 'It seems we won't be able to win this war on our own.'

'We'll make the bastards pay for the men we've lost though,' Publilius growled.

'Valens and his men can't come quickly enough,' Cerberus added.

My shoulders slumped. I had failed, and soon Valens would be there to gloat at our losses. The prospect of his sneering almost seemed worse than the sight of the charred corpses of those wretched engineers.

The army trudged forlornly back along the road towards Cremona. The defenders of Placentia had jeered as we packed up the few siege engines that had survived the explosion, dismantled our makeshift camp and headed east for the bridge over the Po. The men were silent, except for the wounded who lay in the wagons that had housed the onagers which had perished in the flames. After an hour's march you could still make out the blaze that was Placentia's theatre, a building that could seat over forty thousand people. It burned so brightly that it looked as though the sun, being contrary, had decided to rise in the west.

The bridge was up ahead. The thought struck me that we could make camp where we stood, then we could stop Otho from meeting up with his eastern reinforcements. But that would lose us the initiative. Placentia's garrison, freed from our siege, would join Otho's column. The force keeping the Postumian Way open would converge with the detachments from Pannonia and they would approach Cremona from the east, so we would be trapped between two armies. Maybe it wasn't such a good idea after all.

Totavalas rode alongside me. The officers wanted to be with their own men, trying to keep their morale up, but the Hibernian knew his place was by my side.

'Don't be too hard on yourself,' he was saying. 'The fortunes of war and all that.'

'The fortunes of war? People only say that when they can't bring themselves to admit the failure was their fault.'

'Was it really your fault that the siege weapons were destroyed?'

'No, but it was my decision to assault the city when we had only one breach. I was reckless with my men's lives.'

'But isn't it because of these men that we're rebelling in the first place? They knew that to put their man on the throne there would be blood, now they're shedding it for you and Vitellius.'

'In that order?' I asked, smiling weakly.

'Well, it is for me, but then again I haven't been spilling much blood for the cause, have I?'

'You are my rock, Totavalas, my dependable Hibernian rock.'

He laughed appreciatively. 'And what does that make Quintus?'

'Right now? He likes to think he's my conscience, but he feels more like a stone around my neck.'

There was a commotion up ahead. A man stood alone on the bridge, his horse gently nibbling at the grass on the river bank.

'I'll only say it once more, I want to talk to your general.'

'And who shall I say is asking?' one of my men replied. 'Why should we take you to him when you won't tell us your name?'

'I'm a praetor of Rome and have ridden from the emperor's column to talk to General Severus.'

'What's a praetor doing with Vitellius?'

'Vitellius? I've come from Otho's army.'

At the mention of Otho my men went to grab him, thinking that he was a messenger from the enemy. The figure drew his sword, the moonlight glinting off his blade. The onrushing men halted, watching him warily.

'I am a praetor of Rome,' the man said, simply but forcefully. 'Only the consuls and the emperor himself outrank me. The first man to lay a finger on me dies.'

I recognized the voice, the confidence and the authority.

'And what does a praetor of Rome want with a renegade general like me?'

The men lowered their weapons, hearing my casual tone.

'I want him to save the empire.'

XIII

We embraced each other in a great bear hug. Well, at least he did. I had to do the best I could with one arm in a sling.

'Gnaeus Julius Agricola, it's been too long.'

'Aulus Caecina Severus, hasn't it just?' he said, mimicking the ironic way I had used his full name. He squeezed harder.

'Not too tight,' I said, wincing.

'What happened to your arm? Some glorious wound, no doubt?' he teased.

'Shut up. I fell off my horse.'

'That'll teach you not to buy a horse you can't manage!'

We broke off the hug and looked each other full in the face. The moon illuminated my friend's wide, innocent face, the craggy jaw and noble countenance that turned the legs of Rome's maidens as weak as saplings in the wind. But even the kind light of the moon couldn't hide the bags under his eyes, or the look of a man who has been wrestling with his conscience.

'I can't begin to say how sorry I was to hear of your mother's death. Otho has a lot to answer for.'

'It's worse than that, Otho sent them north to hinder your man Valens but it seems the navy fancied turning pirate. If ever I catch their admiral I'll have him crucified.'

'Not the actual killers?'

'They're just animals. Their officers should have held them back.'

'Quite,' I said. Then I chuckled. 'I bet our mothers are laughing at us now. I don't think either of them ever expected me to be the one who would end up commanding an army. You were always the hard worker, the general in the making, while I was skipping lessons and chasing the girls down in the city.'

Julius laughed. It was good to see him smile; I had missed his company this past year. I put my hand on his back and guided him towards an empty shack where the locals housed the old ferry, for the days when the bridge was heaving with market traffic and it took more than an hour to cross. Nobody would disturb us there.

'And Salonina, and Aulus, are they well?' he asked.

'Safe and sound in Mediolanum.'

'You brought them with you?' Julius looked surprised.

'Salonina wouldn't let me leave them behind in Germania. My name is mud at the moment for keeping them in the north, out of harm's way. And what about your wife, the Venus of southern Gaul?'

'I think she's happy to be back in Rome once again. I can't stand the place, but you know what women are like. If they're more than a mile from their favourite dressmaker or haven't attended a society dinner for more than a week, life just isn't worth living. Even now I suspect she'll be charming the great and good of the city, angling for a suitor for Julia.'

I was taken aback. 'A suitor? I thought we had an agreement?'

It was Julius's turn to be shocked, shocked that the words had passed his lips. 'We do, Caecina, of course we do. You know Domitia's always had a soft spot for you.'

'Until you married her, of course. Not all of us had the option to marry for love,' I reminded him gently.

'I thought you were happy with Salonina?'

'I am, but that doesn't explain why Domitia is looking for a husband for Julia when she's already been promised to Aulus.'

'Caecina, I swear to you that my daughter and your son will marry.' Julius looked at his feet awkwardly. 'It's just that Domitia doesn't approve of the match, now that you're leading an army against Rome.'

'Not against Rome, against Otho.'

'Precisely, which is why I'm here tonight. Domitia's just going to have to put up with it.'

I relaxed. Julius and I were too close to let anything come between us, and I knew he was a man of his word.

'The perils of ambitious wives, eh?' I joked, and Julius laughed reassuringly. 'And if I'm being honest,' I continued, 'I had to convince Salonina that your family was a good enough match for our son, if we can put Vitellius on the throne.'

'You know I technically outrank you, even if you are a general?' he teased.

'For the moment,' I said.

'But to put Vitellius on the throne, you need me.'

'I do, Julius. Both of us know that Otho isn't fit to rule.'

My friend wasn't looking at me any more, but watching the army pass by, rank after rank, file by file on their way to Cremona.

'And when I find the man who killed my mother, I'll tear him apart and scatter his remains to the four winds,' he said.

I put a comforting hand on his shoulder. 'But that comes later, Julius. You know how close Otho's army is, I need to defeat him.'

'You? But what about the other column under Valens?'

'Valens is still a few days away. By my reckoning he should have reached Augusta Taurinorum by now, four or five days' march away. I need your help to break the back of Otho's army before Valens even arrives.'

'And cover yourself in glory first?' he guessed.

'You don't know Valens, you don't know what he's capable of.'

'Such as?'

I struggled for a moment. I'd never had to describe Valens's shortcomings to someone who didn't know my situation. 'Not only was he for starting a civil war months before I was dragged into it, he murdered his own governor when he decided not to take up Valens's offer to be the next emperor!'

'Murdered? The dispatches to the Senate said that Valens had executed the governor for plotting to challenge Galba.'

I snorted in derision. 'Valens killed him in case the governor decided to report the disloyalty to Galba. He's tried to get the governor on the throne, he wanted Verginius Rufus, and now at last he's got his man with Vitellius. And if Valens is the one that hands the empire on a plate to Vitellius then he'll be given the free run of the city. Do you really want a man like that unleashed upon Rome?'

'Don't worry, Caecina, I already said in my letter that I'm willing to do anything to topple Otho. Besides, it won't do any harm to have my childhood friend as the emperor's right-hand man. How can I help?'

'Good man. Our old general, Paulinus. He trusts you, doesn't he?'

'Completely. He's still shocked that the man who saved us in Britannia is leading an army against him.'

'I don't have any grudge against the old man, he just happens to be on the wrong side. I always liked him, he doesn't risk the lives of his men without good cause.'

'I agree, he's cautious but competent.'

'But I need you to help him forget his caution for just one day. Can you do that for me, Julius?'

We made our plans, Julius and I, before he rode off into the night. By then the last of my men had crossed the bridge and were bedding down in the camp we had built not four days before, outside the town of Cremona. Cerberus was waiting for me at the camp gates.

'Totavalas told me you were on your own talking with a praetor from Rome. I didn't know how long to wait before sending out a search party!'

'Totavalas needs to learn how to keep his big Hibernian mouth shut,' I said tiredly.

'Anything I should know about?'

'New information. Which means we can make one last effort to hurt the enemy before Valens arrives, then we can crush them together.'

'So you've heard then about the detachments from the Pannonian legions?'

'Yes, they've crossed the Julian Alps and are into Italia. They should be here in no more than a week.'

'As will Valens,' Cerberus said.

'So soon?'

'It seems since he heard we were attacking Placentia he's had his column march at a flying pace to make sure you don't do all the work before he arrives.'

'That was the plan,' I said bitterly. 'But cheer up, Cerberus, we'll cut the heart out of Otho's army soon enough.'

For the next few days the men licked their wounds in Cremona. Some scratched at the sores under the bandages; others scratched an itch of another kind. The camp had only been up a few days before all the whores north of the Po converged on the city, or so it seemed. Let them have their fun, that was my opinion. After all, they had toiled through the Alps and lost many of their comrades to the snow and to the defenders of Placentia, with little to show for their troubles. They could spend their coin in the town, which the army would then get back through occasional levies on the city treasury. The taxes of Germania would only stretch so far.

One night I tried Valens's trick of mooching round the barracks after the evening meal to hear the men's gossip. Most were the usual soldiers' grumbles. Lying on their bags stuffed with straw they missed their comparatively lavish bunks in the barracks on the Rhine, not to mention the well-built walls rather than the standard-issue tents that did little to keep out the chill night air. I shall record one conversation in these memoirs though, since the sentiment was echoed all around the camp.

'What chance do you reckon we've got against Otho's lot, then?'

'You sound as though you've made up your mind already.'

'What if I have?'

'Then there isn't much bloody point you asking us, is there?'

'I still want to know what you lot think.'

'All right, all right. Old Agamemnon will have one last crack at defeating Otho. He's got to, after that cock-up at Placentia.'

'Tell me about it, we've lost almost half a legion altogether. We barely outnumber Otho's men.'

'How do you know how many men Otho's got?'

'My cousin's one of the auxiliary scouts, remember?'

'All right, keep your hair on! Anyway, you said it yourself, we still outnumber Otho. And he's only got a few poxy palace guards and sailors, that new First Adiutrix Legion. Not what I'd call proper soldiers.' The others chuckled scornfully.

'But I don't see why we have to fight again so soon. Valens is bringing thirty thousand men from the west. Why can't we just wait till they show up?'

'Because by then the detachments from Pannonia will have arrived. They've been fighting Dacians for years, and I'm not going to knock a man who's survived fighting that lot. Plus we don't want any of the boys from Lower Germania sharing the spoils, do we, lads?'

'Fuck no!' they chorused.

'Look, I know you've only been with the legion less than a year, but you've got to realize that we're the famous, fighting Fourth. If the other half of the legion was here, we'd have Otho by the balls within a week!'

I smiled. These were my men; they were vicious, selfish bastards to a man, but they were my vicious bastards and no one else's. Only one thing puzzled me. Why were these illiterate soldiers calling me Agamemnon?

We had the scouts report on Otho's every move. I didn't want his column having so much as a halt for a meal without my knowing. As expected, the so-called emperor branched off the Aemilian Way long before he came close to Cremona. He knew we still outnumbered him slightly, and didn't want to risk an encounter before he was reinforced. So he crossed the Po about forty miles to the east of us, where the river began to widen so much that it was difficult to bridge without using small islands to make the building easier. In this way he managed to occupy the Postumian Way, where all he had to do was sit and wait for his reinforcements. The Pannonian legions were closest, but the men based in Moesia had a far longer march, and wouldn't be with us for over a month. If I were Otho I would have followed the example of Fabius Maximus Cunctator, the man who had saved Rome from Hannibal by scorching the earth and starving the enemy out of Italia. Even the bountiful Po valley could only sustain my army for so long.

But I knew Otho was an impetuous man, the complete opposite of my old general, Suetonius Paulinus. My information was that Otho had brought his inexperienced brother north with him to command the army, reducing Paulinus to little more than an adviser. For my plan to work though, I had to rely on Agricola to overcome the old general's instinctive caution and to egg on Otho into committing a part of his army to battle; then and only then could I spring the trap.

I had sixteen thousand men who were fit to fight. They trained for battle every day, not so hard that they would be too tired to fight, but not so little that they had enough time on their hands to dwell on the disaster at Placentia. Agricola and I had made a detailed plan for the days ahead. Valens must have had his own spies as he began to dawdle once his column came within three days' march. He must have heard that we were encamped at Cremona and Otho's army was holding his position away to the east at a town called Bedriacum. Most likely he didn't want to tire his men unnecessarily, since it would be a fool who took on an army of roughly equal size when thirty thousand reinforcements were just days away.

I had not been idle either. With some of Cerberus' riders for protection I had gone to the east to scout the way ahead. I knew most of the land already; my own estate lay but a few days' ride away. I prayed that Otho's men and the eastern detachments had left it alone in their preparations for the campaign. Less than a week after the Placentia debacle, I rode out at the head of my diminished army, confident in the knowledge that I would thin out Otho's men before Valens and I finally crushed the murderer's forces.

The eastward road ran on a causeway high above the fertile fields. The pale spring sky dominated the view, looming over mile after mile of fen-like flatness. Either side of the road tall tufts of wheat stretched upwards as though vying for the sun's attention. Great clumps of woodland littered the horizon. There might have been hundreds of peasants and slaves working in the fields that crisp morning, but we wouldn't have been able to see them, and that was my plan: an ambush.

I didn't dare risk my whole army for the encounter, my numbers were too few for that. Instead I took with me our entire force of auxiliaries under Cerberus and Publilius. We had Germans, Gauls, Britons, Lusitanians, not to mention our exotic cavalry from Africa. If everything went as planned, we would deliver a morale-shattering blow to Otho's army. Everything hinged on Agricola.

Cerberus and Publilius rode uneasily, both scanning the horizon for the enemy.

'Will the two of you relax?' I said.

'Sorry, General,' Cerberus answered. 'But in my experience if something sounds too good to be true, most of the time it is.'

'I agree with Cerberus,' Publilius said, tangling his fingers in his horse's mane. 'A spy in the enemy camp who can influence its commanders is too much to hope for.'

'Then this is the exception that proves the rule. Julius Agricola is my oldest friend. For Jupiter's sake, we grew up together. Julius would be the last man in the world to betray me.'

Up ahead, I could make out the place where we would set our trap. It was a small altar to the twin gods, Castor and Pollux, so the locals had called the place Ad Castores, to the two Castors. It struck me that Pollux must surely have been offended to be described as in effect a second Castor, in the same way that if someone had seen Agricola and me when we were growing up, and we had looked alike, I would have been hurt if they had simply called us the two Agricolae.

I gave the order to halt, and the column stopped almost as one. Seven thousand infantry and about a thousand cavalry; it was an ambush on a large scale. But the location was perfect. The men had their orders. Half the infantry clambered down from the causeway and took up their positions on the northern side, while the other half went into the fields to the south. Soon they had as good as disappeared, except for the occasional splash and curse as someone tumbled into the huge drainage ditches that separated the fields, carrying the excess rainwater away so that the farmland didn't become waterlogged.

That left the two squadrons of cavalry: the Africans and the Gauls who had come south with us from the Rhine. They were under the command of the fearsome-looking Cerberus today. Up ahead, I could just make out a small cloud of dust on the horizon. Agricola had done his work well; Otho had fallen into the trap.

'You know your orders?' I said.

Cerberus nodded. 'Just be ready to close in on them when I get back.'

He dug his heels in, and his horse took off, the two squadrons thundering as they followed the prefect towards the enemy.

'We need to get off the road, now!' Publilius and I dismounted, guiding our horses down the slope and into the fields where we hid along with the men. The unit nearest the road was a cohort of Germans, many of them a whole head taller than I was. Hiding among the wheat I could still see the last of Cerberus' men disappearing along the road, vanishing for a few moments as they entered a small grove of trees that shaded the place where the altar stood, only to re-emerge and disappear again as the causeway blocked my view. I looked around at the soldiers, and my eyes settled on one of them; a huge man, my eyes were barely level with his chin.

'You, soldier,' I said. 'How good is your Latin?'

'Quite good, General,' he said with a harsh, barbarian accent.

'All right, I want you to be my eyes. You can lean on my horse to get a better view.'

The man nodded his understanding and told the soldier next to him to give him a leg-up. The mountain of a man stepped up, then placed his forearms on the saddle and put his weight on them, the other soldier grunted something in German and another man came to support the trunk-like legs.

'Take your helmet off,' I said. 'If the sun catches it you'll give the game away.'

The German tugged at his chinstrap until it came loose, afterwards tossing the thing down to his friend to look after.

'How far can you see?' Publilius asked.

'About a quarter of a mile beyond the trees.'

We waited. There was nothing more to be said. Cerberus was riding along the road at a gentle pace as though on patrol. The plan was that he would come across Otho's cavalry on the road. They would engage, cause some damage, then make a hasty retreat. The retreat of course was a feint. The cavalry would serve their purpose in bringing the eager, unthinking men of Otho's army on to the waiting swords and spears of my auxiliaries.

The scouts had reported that the enemy cavalry was out in force, as I knew they would be. Agricola and I had agreed that they should be no more than two miles east of the twin gods' altar, and my friend had told me they were commanded by a general who was keen to prove himself to his new emperor, and so the two of us engineered his chance.

While we waited, it struck me how quiet and blissful the morning was. The Aprilis sun shone down just the same as it had done the day before, and the birds were chirping and twittering away merrily. The Germans stood in grim silence. I can even remember yanking hard at an ear of wheat then pulling it apart by its ticklish hairs, just to occupy my hands. Better that than being seen drumming my fingers nervously on the pommel of my sword.

Off in the distance there was a low rumbling.

'Thunder?' Publilius wondered. There were a few clouds in the sky, but that wasn't it. Then again, if it was what I thought it was, why had we heard it before we saw it?

'I see cavalry,' the German said.

'How many?' I asked quickly.

The soldier screwed up his eyes. 'Moving too fast to count. But there are many of them.'

I thought I saw a glimpse of movement on the horizon myself. It had to be Cerberus, I was sure of it. Soon I could make out the individual horses as they rode at breakneck speed towards the shady grove.

'They are being followed by more horses,' the German announced from his makeshift vantage point. 'More cavalry than the first group.'

I punched the air with delight, but instantly regretted it as the muscles in my arm spasmed in reproach. But the general had taken the bait.

'Pass the word down, I want our wing to wheel left towards the grove, then we can bring all our men to bear against the enemy on the causeway. Publilius, once we surprise the cavalry you take command of the men on the other side of the road.'

'Yes, General.'

Cerberus and his men were past the altar by now, not daring to ease their pace lest the enemy suspected something. Our flank was already advancing further into the fields to take up their position.

'The enemy are into the grove now,' the soldier reported.

Cerberus and his men were practically alongside us, but they couldn't stop until we had sprung the trap. I told the German to get off Achilles and rejoin his men; we would be charging within moments and I would need my horse. As the two squadrons flew past, I caught glimpses of gashed arms and riderless horses. I hoped Cerberus hadn't been too suicidal in making a convincing feint attack.

I stood by Achilles, poised to clamber into the saddle once the attack had begun. But where were the cavalry? The road to the altar was empty.

'They must still be hidden by the trees,' Publilius suggested.

I said nothing, my eyes fixed on the damned trees. Fifty heart-beats passed, and nothing happened. Still Cerberus couldn't wheel round for fear of giving the game away. What was going on? Perhaps the general had realized how close to our camp at Cremona he was, or maybe the thick clump of trees by a largely open road made him nervous of an ambush. There wasn't time to guess why, I had to act.

I mounted up, and saw the eager faces among the wheat. Drawing my sword with my left hand, I raised it to the heavens. 'Charge!'

With a shout the men dashed forward, making for the raised

causeway. Achilles was up the slope in a trice, and on seeing me the cohorts on the northern side ran to attack the stranded cavalry. A quick check over my shoulder revealed that Cerberus had seen me and was turning his squadrons round to join the fray again. The road was now awash with men who had been poised to attack as the enemy rode past. As the cavalry in the grove ahead prepared to charge the seething mass of men, they were assaulted on their left flank by the units I had sent up ahead. Down below I could see Publilius urging on his own command, sending his own wing on a flanking march so that we could attack Otho's only cavalry from three, maybe even all sides.

Achilles stayed calm among the churning crowd of soldiers eagerly sprinting forward, despite the clanging of their armour as they ran and the whinnies of pain up ahead as the first horses fell. I rode as far along the road as I dared; my weakened shoulder meant that I was unable to fight, but there was no way in Hades I would hang back while my men fought and died.

To give Otho's men credit, they kept their shape and held their nerve. As one cohort after another sprang up to encircle the enemy, the cavalrymen scythed down with their long *spatha* swords that gave them the reach they needed to fight from horseback. From down in the fields a few *pila* were hurled towards the enemy, only for most of them to stick in or ricochet off the trees that effectively shielded the cavalry's flanks.

A clatter of hooves behind told me that our own cavalry had returned.

'We took some losses, General,' Cerberus reported, 'but it looks as though we're paying them back with interest!'

I held up my hand to silence him. Beyond the crowd of spearmen and horses, I could make out more of Otho's army arriving in support. Agricola had done his work well.

'Gods, it's the Praetorian Guard!' Cerberus said. He was right, no other men wore the plumes of dyed horsehair on their helmets that in normal legions were reserved for officers only.

'Quick, Cerberus. Get your men forward now and make a screen for the infantry. The enemy will have seen some of our auxiliaries, but I want as many as possible to get down into the fields again and take up positions either side of the causeway. Let's see if we can't make this a double ambush.'

Cerberus saluted and was gone. The praetorians were marching in force; I guessed around seven thousand of them were heading into the jaws of our trap. Their cavalry were in full retreat now, the corpses of horses and men littering the road, a grisly offering at the peasants' altar. My own cavalry were hastily telling the rearmost auxiliaries to get off the road and back into their ambush positions, while the most advanced foot soldiers parted to let the horsemen through. There was little a cavalry charge on a narrow causeway could do against a mass of well-trained spearmen, but I hoped it would give the enemy cause to slow down, allowing my men to get back into their hiding place.

Soon the road was empty but for my cavalry, perhaps four or five cohorts of infantry and the column of praetorians marching ponderously forward, keeping their close formation. I made a mental note to myself to recommend to Vitellius that Agricola be made a consul for what he had achieved, after Valens and I had had our turn of course.

The enemy column came ever closer. One of the cohorts ahead, the Lusitanians, to a man grounded their arms, then drew out their slings. Lusitanians are perhaps the finest slingers in the west of the empire, and it made sense to thin the enemy numbers a bit while they were still too far away to charge. Taking stones from little pouches on their belts, they whirled their missiles rapidly round their heads before letting fly, the stones attacking the enemy like a deadly hailstorm. There was only time for two volleys before they picked up their swords and shields again, but two volleys were still better than none.

Out of the corner of my eye I sensed some movement in the

fields on our right. Probably some of the auxiliaries nervously getting into place; the column was little more than two hundred paces away. A second look showed a whole line of wheat waving wildly. As I followed the line, I saw it ran for several hundred paces. A quick glance to my left showed exactly the same on the other side of the road. The praetorians weren't alone!

'Ambush!' I cried out, and my men took that as a signal to attack. Cerberus held his men back, letting the auxiliaries charge the vanguard of the praetorian column. From either side the Britons and the Germans roared as they ran full pelt up the slope for the second time, but Otho's men had spread to occupy the whole causeway, holding the higher ground while my men toiled to battle both the soldiers and the slope.

'No, we must pull back.' Too late I saw that below me Pub- lilius had spotted the danger. Being on horseback he could see what his men could not, the glint of steel as helmets and swords flashed in the morning sun. General Paulinus's own party of ambushers were closing around my men. If we did not withdraw immediately my men would have to fight on two fronts, and they would surely be annihilated.

I caught sight of Cerberus' bugler, and forced Achilles to head towards the maelstrom. When I came close enough, I snatched the instrument from the boy's hand and blew the recall as loudly as I could. Cerberus' head snapped back at the unexpected order, but with my free hand I pointed at the oncoming danger. My co-ordinated attack was turning to chaos before my very eyes.

'He sold us out,' the black man shouted at me. 'Your friend has sold you out!'

XIV

That was the only conclusion I could reach as we beat a hasty and bloody retreat back to Cremona, with the praetorians following us nearly all the way. Thank the gods we had destroyed most of the enemy cavalry, or the retreat could have turned into a rout. Why had Agricola betrayed me?

I thought back to our conversation that moonlit night by the old ferry. He had seemed strangely nervous, but then I had put that down to his being shaken after finding himself surrounded by dozens of suspicious soldiers. The news that his wife Domitia did not approve of my son as a suitor was also a shock, but I could understand. Did my boyhood friend think the same way, or was I just being paranoid, blaming the defeat on anyone but myself? After all, my feint had worked, drawing in and obliterating the enemy cavalry, and Otho was certainly impetuous enough to throw his whole army in to repulse an ambush.

But it was the fact that the cavalry had stopped by the altar that convinced me my friend had sided with his emperor rather than his friend; or, as Agricola might have seen it, I realized, with the legitimate emperor rather than a gluttonous rebel. I had described the place to him to the last detail, explaining that my cavalry would withdraw beyond the grove and then my infantry would pounce. Agricola must have informed the cavalry commander about the altar and told him to go no further. The stationary cavalry had lured in me and my infantry, so both the cavalries had taken turns at being bait. I had hoped to destroy their cavalry and any other troops Otho was foolish enough to send my way; but my old general, my closest friend and the emperor I despised had conspired together to turn the ambushers into the ambushed, using the praetorians as a distraction while the rest of their army crept up under the cover of the high wheat fields.

'I thought he was your friend,' Publilius said.

Cerberus spat. 'Some friend.'

'He was my friend . . . I mean he *is* my friend,' I said.

'Then why would he betray you?' Cerberus replied.

'I don't know. Otho's pirates had killed his mother, I thought that was surely enough reason for Agricola to want to help us.'

'But he's a praetor, a leading member of the Senate. He's one of the establishment that stood by and did nothing when Galba was murdered. I reckon Otho bought your friend's loyalty, then he used your friendship against you,' Cerberus opined.

'He wouldn't do that to me! Julius Agricola wouldn't sell his loyalty to anyone.'

'He just did.'

'Maybe Otho has his family hostage in Rome,' Publilius suggested. 'That's as good a way as any to make sure the men on your own side stay loyal.'

'Maybe,' I conceded sullenly. But I knew in my heart of hearts that Agricola was old-fashioned enough to side with Otho simply because he was emperor, even if he had murdered his way on to the throne. For men like Agricola, the emperor is sanctioned by the gods, even if they turn out to be hateful, tyrannical bastards like Nero, Galba or Otho.

Ahead of us, the remnants of my ambush streamed along the road towards Cremona. All attempts to pursue us had now ended, so the three of us rode easily, wearily, back to camp, the two cavalry squadrons following close behind. As Cremona and our camp came into view, I was surprised to see hundreds of men tearing down the easternmost wall, the wall nearest to Otho's army. Who had given the order to break camp?

By the roadside there stood a billowing crimson tent, far bigger than even my own, except three sides of the tent were still furled. It looked more like a pavilion than a soldier's sleeping quarters. It was only when I saw a shortish figure, his blond hair regimentally cut but with flecks of grey at the temples, sitting in a solitary chair and surrounded by a court of officers, that I knew Valens had arrived.

Like a faithful hound Totavalas was there too, waiting for me. 'Dear oh dear, someone's come home with his tail between his legs!' No prizes for guessing which smug bastard greeted me with those words. Totavalas began to take my sling out of his satchel, raising his eyebrows questioningly. Did I want to wear the thing in front of Valens and his cronies? I nodded, doctor's orders and all that.

'Gentlemen, what was I thinking? We have a wounded man among us. Someone fetch him a chair.' As aides scurried to carry out Valens's orders I stood my ground.

'No need, Valens. A dislocated shoulder doesn't stop me from standing up. Besides, it doesn't do for the men to see their general on his backside when they're working.'

'As you wish,' he said, not moving. 'I'm sure it is a noble wound you took for our emperor. Some Alpine farmer did it perhaps, or one of those horrible gladiators in Placentia? I hope you took revenge on the beast that hurt you?'

The lazy smile on his odious face and the suppressed snorts from his men made it clear they knew all about my accident with Achilles. I chose to rise above his taunts.

'What are you doing here?' I asked.

'That's a nice welcome. I thought you were expecting me?'

'I meant what are you doing here when you could have joined us on the battlefield?'

'Oh, my vanguard has taken down one of the walls so that we can extend the camp. No sense building two camps for the enemy to attack.'

'And you've been here for, what, three hours?'

'Your point is?'

'Three hours ago we were fighting Otho's whole army.'

'So I heard, with a handful of spineless auxiliaries.'

Publilius and Cerberus bristled at the insult.

'We routed their entire cavalry,' the African said pointedly.

Valens got up from his chair and marched up to Cerberus, standing uncomfortably close to him. Cerberus didn't move a muscle. 'Publilius I know. Who are you?'

'This is Prefect Cerberus,' I said, 'commander of the Silian cavalry. Vitellius formed their unit when he governed Africa, and they held this land while I crossed the mountains.'

'Well, Cerberus. Your cavalry and your auxiliary infantry combined managed to rout Otho's cavalry.' He clapped his hands slowly in mock applause. Then his face hardened again. 'But at what cost?'

Cerberus had to admit that he didn't know. None of us did.

'Your infantry has been arriving at Cremona in dribs and drabs over the last hour. Their officers have reported to me losses of nearly one and a half thousand men. And that doesn't even count the maimed or the mortally wounded.' Valens still stood right next to Cerberus, but he turned to look at me. His eyes narrowed triumphantly. 'All things considered, I'd call that a defeat, wouldn't you?'

'Yes, sir,' Cerberus said.

'And the first rule of warfare is, Publilius?'

'Never reinforce defeat, General.'

'Precisely. We'll make a half-decent soldier out of you yet. I'm only sorry that you've been poorly led in our emperor's service.'

'We attacked in the belief that it would only be the cavalry, sir. The general had a contact in Otho's army who helped us set the trap.'

'And?'

'And the contact betrayed us.'

Valens snorted. 'So I'm left to mop up. Vitellius is going to have a very interesting report to read once we've defeated Otho, isn't he?'

'I'd rather be certain that we're going to beat him before you start dreaming of the scraps Vitellius will throw you. But first I'm going to see to my men. You sit here and watch your men build their walls; mine have been risking their lives for their emperor.'

And with that I swept round contemptuously, Cerberus, Publilius and Totavalas following at my heel. The three of us relieved the men who had held our horses and rode slowly towards the camp, Totavalas striding powerfully to keep up.

Cerberus was the first to speak. 'He's a confident man, that General Valens.'

'That's one way to describe him,' I said mirthlessly.

'It's hardly my place to criticize a general,' Totavalas began.

'I've a feeling you're going to anyway,' Publilius said.

'But I told him where you and the auxiliaries had gone the moment he arrived in Cremona. I said that you were going to ambush Otho and that if he got all his men together quickly he could have ended the war by nightfall. Do you know what he did?'

'What?' Cerberus said tiredly, as though indulging an irritating child.

'He had one of his men chase me off, saying that if I thought he would risk a single man to help your army, then I was a fool.'

I sighed. 'What did you expect? You're a freedman, not even a citizen. Nobody in the whole army is going to give a damn what you think.'

'Present company excepted, General?' Totavalas asked. The

question was aimed more at my officers than at me.

'Thank you for at least trying to help, Totavalas,' Publilius said. Cerberus said nothing at first. I understood his silence. Half the blood in his veins was noble, even if he had inherited the dark colouring of his African father. He wasn't obliged to tolerate another noble's freedman.

'Your master is lucky to have you,' he finally admitted. The Hibernian even gave a slight bow of the head to thank him for the compliment that Cerberus had no need to pay. I smiled; was friendship on the verge of breaking out between my advisers? I hoped so. I would need all the friends I could get if Valens was to be the favoured man; if we managed to break Otho's army, that is.

Quintus was waiting for us in the camp, his eyes red and his face pale. Either he had been crying or he had spent the night with a couple of skins for company. The discreet men I had sent to watch out for him each night had always reported the same thing: a man barely out of boyhood sat alone in a Cremonan tavern, drinking himself into a stupor. I would have to keep a closer eye on him after the final battle. Until then I was too busy to look after a drunk.

'Been having fun playing at soldiers?' he asked. Cerberus and Publilius said nothing. How could they? Quintus was technically their superior officer.

'For your sake, Quintus, I'll pretend you're still drunk from last night.'

'I wish I was drunk. So would you if you'd seen what I'd seen.'

'And what have you seen?' I said wearily.

'I'll show you.'

Quintus led us down the road that cut the camp in half, for we had constructed it right on top of the Postumian Way. After a hundred paces, past the *praesidium*, the cookhouses and the stables, I knew where we were headed. It was where we were going before we had met Quintus.

The hospital was full. So full that the lightly wounded sat on benches outside. An African with a crutch sat next to a pale-skinned Briton, an angry red scar gouged on to his face from his blind eye to the downy hair around his jaw. I dismounted slowly, not wanting to aggravate my shoulder. Quintus held the door open. The two officers and I followed, Totavalas choosing to wait outside; he didn't bear the burden of command.

At once our noses were assaulted, on one front by the dank smell of all those warm bodies in the same small room, and on the other by the pungently sweet smell of death. But it was the noise that was the worst, cries of pain and anguish that hurt your very soul. At the end of the hospital were two tables, and two surgeons worked on each table. The unfortunates clamped down hard on gags that muffled their screams as limbs were amputated and innards salvaged. Orderlies shouted at us to get out of the way as they brought in more wounded soldiers. We stepped aside mutely. They were the officers here, not us.

'General?' One of the men recognized me from my ornate breastplate. The bandages around his belly were soaked with blood.

'I'm here, lad,' I said, sitting on the edge of his cot. I tried to smile. 'You've been in the wars, haven't you?'

The soldier's face spasmed in pain. 'Sword wound from one of those praetorians, sir. Drill-master would be ashamed of me,' he gasped.

'Nonsense,' I said. 'I'm proud of you, and if I'm proud of you he must be too. You hear that, men?' I raised my voice. 'I'm proud of you all.'

'Thank you, sir,' the man mumbled.

'That accent . . . you're from Britannia?'

'Dumnonia.'

'I remember Dumnonia. Rolling hills surrounding a sea of grass, soil so rich you could feed an army off it. And in the middle, a solitary hill rising out of the levels.'

'It's a beautiful country.'

'The best,' I agreed.

'How do you know it, sir?'

'My legion was stationed at Isca Dumnoniorum.'

'You were with the Twentieth, General?'

'Am I in trouble for fighting your countrymen?' I asked half seriously.

'No, sir. I was a boy at the time. My biggest battle was steering clear of my sweetheart's older brother!'

I chuckled. 'Britannian women! We never went near them for fear of making your people riot.'

'That's my people all over, General.' The soldier winced again. I glanced up at one of the orderlies. He read my expression, then shook his head. The man gripped my hand hard as another wave of pain convulsed him.

'Am I going to die, sir?'

'Of course not! You've fought bravely for your emperor, and he's going to give you your citizenship as a reward.'

'Really?'

'Really. Now I want you to imagine going home to your family, back in the sea of grass. Think of the look on your sweetheart's face when you tell her that you, your sons and your sons' sons will be citizens of the Roman Empire, and no one can take that away from you.'

He gripped my hand still tighter, and my shoulder was in agony keeping it there but I didn't move. I couldn't. There was a smile on the Briton's face; his eyes were closed but they still shed tears.

'Dian,' he whispered. His grip loosened, and his arm fell back on to the bed.

The orderly coughed.

'I'm sorry, General, but if the man's gone then there are others who'll need his bed.'

I left Cerberus and Publilius tending to their own men. They

189

were telling them not to blame themselves, it was Valens's decision not to help that had brought them to death's door, and they had fought like lions, every one of them.

Quintus and Totavalas were waiting for me outside, but standing several paces apart. Clearly they had nothing to say to each other, but Quintus still had some hot air to blow at me.

'Are you proud of yourself?' he asked.

'Not here, Quintus,' I said forcefully, grabbing him by the elbow and walking him out of earshot of the hospital.

'Ashamed to talk to me in front of your men?' he scoffed.

'No, but it doesn't do a dying man much good if he hears a senior tribune mouthing off like a petulant child.'

'But I'm not a child any more, you put paid to that!'

'Don't you dare blame me for your own faults. You're becoming more like your father every day.'

'If I'm becoming like my father, does that mean you're going to kill me one day?'

'Your father turned a political ruse into a full-scale rebellion out of vanity and greed. If he hadn't committed suicide your family's lands would have been confiscated and you would have been exiled. I had to remind Vindex that suicide wipes the slate clean. You know that.'

'And what are you doing if not leading a rebellion? You had a choice. You've always had a choice. I couldn't disappoint my father, and what would have happened in Mogontiacum if I'd told you to stop this madness? Your men would have turned on me, the son of the traitor Vindex. I would have been strung up and you wouldn't have been able to stop it because you didn't have the courage to lead your own men.'

I slapped him hard in the face. 'Nobody calls me a coward, Tribune. You want a choice? Fine, I can relieve you of your command. You can crawl back to your estates in Gaul and nurse your precious little conscience. But I'm staying, because when we beat Otho Valens will have the rule of Rome, and I love my city too much to leave her defenceless against that scheming bastard.'

Quintus stood motionless and confused, like a puppy that's done wrong but doesn't know why he's being punished. His hand went up to feel his reddening cheek.

'You hit me,' he said quietly.

'Believe me, you've had it coming,' Totavalas chipped in.

'Let me know your decision by this evening. I'll need time to find a replacement. Come on, Totavalas, let's leave the tribune to his thoughts.'

The council met after the evening meal the following day. The cicadas were chirping relentlessly around Valens's tent. The general's body slaves had made the place as comfortable as possible. Where once there had been nothing but a table and chair with the grass as the floor, suddenly there were couches, cushions and carpet. A pretty girl served us wine from a beautiful silver jug, though perhaps the word jug does it an injustice. It was more like a chalice, with intricate patterns swirling up sides that some master craftsman must have sweated over for days.

'A little something I picked up in Vienne,' Valens called it.

'Vienne?' I asked.

'A small town near Lugdunum,' he said offhand. 'Having thirty thousand men behind me helped persuade the locals into making some charitable donations.'

'Yes, I can see how you needed fine cushions and carpets to conduct a military campaign,' I said sardonically.

'Remind me, Severus, how many battles have you won so far?'

I shifted in my seat uncomfortably. 'We defeated a rebellion by the Alpine tribes.'

'And I suppose the only spoils to be had was the deflowering of their sheep? Well, each to his own, I always say.' His men laughed as one, as if they were subordinates first and individuals second.

'I lost some good men in the mountains,' Pansa said grimly.

'How careless of you!' a centurion joked. I remembered him from the council we had held in Colonia four months earlier. This was Priscus, Valens's right-hand man.

'Now, now, Priscus. What have I told you about patronizing people?'

'That I should only do it if they deserve it.'

'Precisely, and these gallant gentlemen are the lions who conquered the goatherds of Raetia, and nearly defeated Otho's conscripts, palace guards and gladiators twice.'

'You're quite right, sir. My apologies, gentlemen!' It was like listening to a pair of bullies enthralled by their own voices, and bullies have to be stood up to.

'Remind me, Priscus, how many men did you lose against Otho's pirates in Gaul? I wouldn't ask except we ought to know our full strength before drawing up a battle plan.'

It was Valens's turn to look sour. 'We dealt with them in the end,' he said.

'After losing three entire cohorts,' I said acidly. 'And how many men was it that the general left behind to guard the province, Cerberus?'

'Three thousand, sir.'

'Thank you, Cerberus. Three thousand men, plus the two thousand you lost against some conscript sailors. Let me see, that's five thousand men we won't be able to use against Otho in battle.'

'A drop in the ocean. You've lost nearly a quarter of your whole column.'

'At least we've been trying to advance Vitellius's cause, at least we've tried to win this war by attacking Otho before the reinforcements from the east arrive,' I retorted. 'Now we hear the whole Thirteenth Legion has arrived, along with half the Fourteenth and four thousand auxiliaries. Otho's doubled his strength to nearly thirty thousand men, and you've allowed him to do it. Check with your informers tonight, they'll tell you that your men and mine all say the same thing. They wanted to unite and fight Otho without delay, but you hung back from joining us, hoping that my army would fail. Your own men blame you for the position we're in. They even wish that I was in charge of the army, and can you blame them? If I had been, we would have crushed Otho by now.'

All this time Valens's expression had hardened. Seeing his officers look down at the floor when I taunted him for his men's malcontent told him that my information was correct. My own men, rather than blaming themselves for the defeats, blamed Valens for dawdling in the west. Valens's men had immediately joined them in blaming their general to bat away the charges of cowardice.

'Instead of bickering like children, why don't we decide how we are to defeat Otho?' Valens said.

'At last,' Pansa sighed.

'Clearly we want to bring the Othonians to battle as soon as possible, but my men have been marching hard for weeks . . .'

'Not hard enough,' Publilius mumbled.

'. . . and they need another day in camp to recuperate. Are all Otho's forces encamped to the east?'

Cerberus spoke up. 'My scouts report that the garrison at Placentia, around three thousand praetorians and gladiators, are marching towards the bridge here at Cremona. They're planning to stop us making a dash south of the Po tonight and heading for Rome now that she's unprotected. Then tomorrow they will cross the river further east at Brixellum and join Otho's main army.'

'So, three thousand men who we'd rather not make it to the battlefield. If they're holding the bridge we can't assault them even with our superior numbers, and we know from experience what those gladiators are like at close quarters,' I said.

'But if we sent a legion and some auxiliary cavalry to the

river before dawn and had them start building a bridge, surely they would hold their defensive position rather than risk being chased by the cavalry as they marched east to join Otho?' Valens suggested.

It was a good idea, I thought grudgingly. Everyone agreed.

'Who out of your army are the freshest?' Valens asked me.

'Probably the detachment from my own legion, the Fourth.'

Valens smiled. 'You would have no objections to them guarding our southern flank while the army rested?'

'None at all,' I said. I didn't like the way Valens was smiling, but how could I reasonably refuse? I had used my own legion sparingly in the campaign, and we didn't expect there to be any fighting. The very act of building a makeshift bridge would scare Placentia's garrison into nailing themselves to their defensive position, depriving Otho of three thousand tried and tested fighters.

'Good. Then the day after tomorrow we will march together to Otho's camp and tear them into bloody shreds.'

'Side by side,' I said, raising my wine cup. 'For Vitellius.'

'For Vitellius,' Valens agreed.

XV

The engineers loved a challenge. So far in the campaign all I had asked them to do was to assemble their onagers, fire them, then pack them up. A good engineer has two sides to him: the destructive and the creative. His brain works out the points for assault, calculates the angles, decides how best to beat down an enemy wall. But he should also be able to find a solution to almost any problem. Now building a bridge was no great difficulty, I grant you, but it offered these men a chance to construct something rather than simply destroy.

There were shouts of alarm as we approached the bridge. Soldiers scampered back and forth in confusion as my legion emerged out of the morning mist. I could just make out groups of gladiators running to cross the bridge itself, only for them to stop halfway over in a defensive formation, perhaps ten men across and twenty deep. They watched anxiously as the legionaries made their stately progress to the river bank. These men hadn't fought at Placentia, the gladiators did not cow them!

The trusty chief engineer, now sporting a thick bandage on his forearm to cover the burns he had received that chaotic night, surveyed the river with his professional eye.

'Just to be clear, General, I'm to build a bridge that in all likelihood we won't have to use?'

'Exactly. Building a second bridge here should stop the enemy scurrying off eastwards to join Otho's main army,' I told him.

'Can I cut some corners then?'

'I'd rather you didn't, just in case we have to use your bridge. How long should it take you to build?'

'Depends what sort of bridge you want.'

'One that keeps that lot watching us until at least sunset.'

'It had better be a pontoon bridge then, but a wide and sturdy one. Otherwise we'd have it done in a matter of hours.'

'Fine.'

'Where do you want the bridge, General? Alongside this one?'

'No, I want the enemy to have to split their troops to cover the two points, but not so far apart that one section can surprise us and cross the river. I want those men nailed to the far bank.'

Much of the morning was spent with my legionaries, under the close supervision of the engineers, searching the river bank for a couple of miles either side of the bridge for the little rafts and other small craft that we needed to make our pontoon bridge. All the while Publilius and the remnants of his cavalry squadron roamed the bank, and occasionally formed up on our side of the bridge as if to charge the gladiators, just to keep them on their toes. At one point I thought I heard the low calling of horns above the gentle sounds of farmland in spring, but dismissed it out of hand. Most likely it was a noisy herd of cattle. There was nothing to be seen for miles around. Even Cremona and our camp were out of sight; nothing but the chatter of the birds, the knocking of nails into wood and the gentle gurgle of the river rolling by.

The sun was at its highest point and the bridge was nearly half built when I heard a rider fast approaching. It was odd, since Publilius had taken his squadron beyond a bend in the river to make sure none of the enemy were fording the river downstream. After all, some in that force were from Placentia and if anyone knew of a secret ford or ferry over the river, it would be them. I was doubly surprised to see that it was one of Cerberus' Africans who rode towards me, at full speed too. What in Hades was going on?

'Sir! Where can I find General Severus?' the rider panted.

'You've found him. What's the matter, man?'

'It's the army, sir, it's on the march!'

'What?'

'The whole army has moved out, sir. General Valens's legions, his auxiliaries, your own legions and the rest of my squadron; the camp will be empty by now.'

'That bloody man,' I fumed. Valens had tricked me, sending me to build a bridge with my own legion so that he could try to beat Otho on his own, but with the rest of my army. A thought struck me. 'I'm sure General Valens didn't send a man to tell me this. Who sent you?'

'Tribune Quintus Vindex, sir.'

'Quintus?' I said incredulously. 'I thought he was meant to be riding home today.'

'He was, sir, but he found me readying my horse to join my unit and ordered that you be told that the army was headed east. He's taken command of the detachment of the Twenty-Second Legion, since their tribune is dead.'

'You've done well, soldier. Remind me to have Cerberus promote you if we survive today!'

'Thank you, General,' the man beamed.

'Before you go I need you to find Prefect Publilius Sabinus and his men, they can't be more than a mile or so away.' I pointed towards the loop in the river to the west. 'Bring them here as quickly as you can.'

'At once, sir.'

Hastily I called the engineer to me, and sought out First-Spear Centurion Nepos, the legion's senior officer. He was the man who had stayed by my side in the chaos of New Year's Day, the day we had abandoned Galba in favour of Vitellius.

'Nepos, I've been rather neglecting my own legion of late. I hope you'll forgive me?'

'We do our duty, sir. Even if it means building bridges rather than a good, honest scrap with the enemy.'

'Well now, I need the two of you to stop building the bridge and prepare for battle. General Valens has left Cremona without us. For all I know the battle for the empire might already have begun!'

'I'll have the men ready to march, sir.'

'Good man.' I turned to face the engineer. 'We don't have time to pack everything away. We'll have to abandon all your tools and any other kit you don't need so that you can march at double pace. Nepos, I'm leaving you in command of the legion.'

'What about you, sir, and the tribune?'

'He's gone ahead with the Twenty-Second, and I must reach the battlefield as quickly as possible. I'll be riding with Publilius and the cavalry along the Postumian Way until we find the army.'

'Very well, sir. Good luck.'

We flew along the road, Publilius and I, at the head of two hundred cavalrymen. In under an hour we came within sight of the rearmost unit of Valens's column, thousands of legionaries marching double-time along the road, not two miles beyond the altar to the twin gods where I had suffered my first betrayal.

'You there,' I called out to the nearest soldiers, 'which legion are you?'

'The Fifteenth, sir,' they answered. They were from Valens's column.

'Where's the rest of the column?' Publilius asked.

'We're all strung out along this road, sir. We left in too much of a hurry to march in a full column, each legion marched as soon as it was ready to move off.'

So Valens had lowered his horns and charged straight for the enemy, so keen to start the battle without me that the army's march was slapdash, different units setting off in fits and starts. Without Quintus I would have been building that pointless bridge all day. So much for a shared command!

We passed cohort after cohort, hundreds upon thousands of men marching ever eastward, but with no purpose or co-ordination, simply under orders to keep on going until they found the enemy. Soon the wheat fields gave way to vineyards as we passed from one landowner's estate to another. We were not yet at the height of spring, and the infant vines offered far less cover than the tall stalks of wheat. At least we wouldn't suffer another ambush like the one General Paulinus had sprung on us just two days before.

My ears caught the sounds of clashing metal, faint over the noise of the marching men and galloping horses all around me. We had to be close to Otho's encampment at Bedriacum by now, with Cremona a good six or seven miles behind us. Rather than speeding ahead to join the battle, Publilius had his men slow down for fear of wearing out the horses. After another mile we found the battlefield.

The battle was in its infancy. I could still make out the shapes of individual units. Away on the right flank I could see a large body of men in line, four ranks deep strung out in the vine-yard. By the sheer number of them it had to be Pansa's men, the Twenty-First. It was the only full legion in the entire army. Ahead of them was another legion launching a volley of *pila* into the heavens. From the ragged timing of the volley I guessed it was the legion of conscript sailors and marines that Nero had formed, Galba had dismissed and now Otho had called upon to help him cling on to his throne.

The road was awash with praetorians, marked out by their

purple plumes, and they faced various detachments of our own legions, but everywhere else was a mess. The vines and ditches meant that the two armies had to fight in little pockets of men where the ground allowed contact between the two lines. It was impossible to tell friend from foe at this distance; you had to get near enough to see the standards to know whether to charge or support the cohorts closest to you. I was looking only for one man, and there he was, sitting haughtily on a grey horse.

'Come on,' I said to Publilius, digging my heels into Achilles' flanks.

As we rode within shouting distance, I hollered Valens's name. He turned to see who was calling, and saw me bearing down upon him. Whereas the pompous idiot Vindex had turned deathly pale at seeing the man he had tried to poison, Valens merely closed his eyes in irritation as though I were some troublesome puppy that had slipped his master's leash.

'You took my men,' I accused him.

'I'm not stopping you from joining them,' he said nonchalantly, as though he had never sent me out of the way while he took the rest of the army to fight.

'If you balls this up, we're all dead men. You know that?' I said angrily.

'What about you? Have you stopped Placentia's garrison from joining him?'

'I left the river with the cavalry as soon as I heard you'd left camp. The Fourth won't be more than an hour away by now.'

'So those three thousand men can join Otho, that's what you're saying?'

'They'll have to march the long way round to get here, far to the east then loop northwards. They won't make it.'

'Or they could just cross the bridge you've left unguarded and attack us in the rear.'

I hadn't thought of that. 'They won't,' I told Valens. 'The gladiators fight best in single combat; on open ground they won't be able to break through the Fourth's line. What do we know about the enemy's disposition?'

Valens shifted uncomfortably in the saddle. 'I can't really see with all the vines and things in the way. All we have to do is kill the enemy where we find them, then we'll win.'

'Kill the enemy where we find them? That's what I'd call a battle, Valens. What about attacks, counter-attacks, feints, artillery, cavalry charges?'

'All right, all right. I left the artillery in camp so that we could march quicker, there's nothing for them to aim at anyway. And the only place a cavalry charge would work would be on the road here, but the infantry are packed together too tightly to let even a troop of horsemen past, let alone a squadron.'

I scanned the battlefield quickly, taking in the lie of the land. He was right, the fields north of the road were criss-crossed with unseen ditches that would break the legs of unsuspecting horses and catapult their riders into the enemy. Away to the south I could see Pansa and his men engaging the other full legion.

'Look over there,' I said. 'Beyond the right flank the vines give way to water meadows. They're narrow and muddy, but it's better than having the cavalry do nothing.'

'Well then, what are you waiting for?' Valens said impatiently.

'Why, your permission, oh mighty general,' I mocked. Turning round, I called out to Publilius's squadron, 'Follow me, men!'

Our horses picked their way down the embankment that carried the road, and then we were among the vines. The gaps between them were barely wide enough for a horse and all its trappings, so we were funnelled as we rode. Publilius on my left led a file of riders, some followed me, and others still rode in separate columns. Though we were off the road, from Achilles' saddle I could just about see the Twenty-First, but more critically I could see a vast swathe of the opposing legion cutting deep into their ranks.

We closed in on them. Pansa was there on foot, shouting and chastising his men, men who had spent their entire careers high in the mountains with no one to fight. My eye lighted on the legion's eagle, high on its brass perch. It began to move frantically in the air as its bearer was jostled in the thick of the fighting. Then the standard fell for a moment before being picked up and carried towards the enemy. Only the legion wasn't advancing. The sailors had captured the eagle!

When the rearmost legionaries heard the sound of horsemen bearing down upon them, some of them turned to make a new line of shields and swords to defend themselves.

'It's me, General Severus,' I shouted, in case some of them decided to let fly with their javelins. Pansa appeared from their midst, almost unrecognizable with his face covered by the cheek-pieces of his helmet and his torso caked in mud.

'What are you doing here?' he bawled, surprised.

'We're here to help! You've lost your eagle, Pansa, I suggest you take it back if you want to keep your command.'

The legate nodded grimly, then turned to face his men.

'You heard the general, you spineless sons-of-bitches. Pass the word to the front, I want them to fan out and flatten these vines. Cut them down, crush them with your shields, whatever it takes to give us some room. I want those bastards surrounded and filleted, do you hear?'

Publilius and I were already moving towards the water meadows. It had not rained for a few days, but hundreds of hooves churned the soft earth more thoroughly than any plough. Far away on the opposite bank were the enemy troops I had supposedly been guarding. They were half marching, half jogging to reach the battle in time but still have energy left to fight. I knew that the next bridge lay on the road to Brixellum, a good hour's march away. And once they had crossed they would have to march three miles back again to join the fight.

Pansa's men were lumbering through the vines, trying to

smash their way through so that they could bring more men to
bear on the opposing line. All that lay between my cavalry and
the enemy legion was a thick hedgerow, too wide to jump. The
only way through was a narrow gap in the hedge a few hundred
paces behind the Othonian line, where there would no doubt be
a heaving mass of auxiliaries waiting in reserve.

'Do you fancy a leap into the dark, Publilius?' I asked my
friend.

'I must admit I have missed a good flanking manoeuvre!' he
joked. 'What do you say, men? Shall we put these jumped-up
sailors in their place?'

They roared their acceptance of the prefect's challenge,
thrusting their long javelins into the air.

'Before we ride, Publilius, there's one thing I'd like to know,'
I said.

'Yes, General?'

'Why Agamemnon? I don't act like a king, do I?'

Publilius smiled, then saluted me: 'Agamemnon, the great
warlord who could never quite control Achilles!'

I laughed and patted my horse's neck. 'Did you hear that,
Achilles? Apparently you're a better soldier than I am. But don't
die on me, understood?' Achilles pawed the ground eagerly, the
sound of battle ringing in his ears. The men were putting their
pila at rest, I had no spear so I drew my sword, wincing as my
fragile arm reached across my body to grasp the hilt. We were
already on the move, with no whoops, screams or sounding the
tubae to alert the enemy to our presence. We rode in a column
three men across, any wider and we would have to reorganize
ourselves to pass through the gap in the hedge and lose surprise
and momentum.

Our trot rose into a canter. The world seemed to bob wildly
up and down as Achilles ratcheted up his pace. Instinctively the
squadron wheeled away to the right, only to come round harder
to the left so that we could approach the gap head on. Our only

point of reference was the stolen eagle that was being carried back eastwards, no doubt to the safety of Otho's reserves. On either side the combination of hedge and ditch menaced us like a palisade, but through the gap there was nothing but daylight. My stomach lurched as Achilles leapt over the fearsome ditch, horse and rider airborne for a fraction of a moment that felt like eternity.

We were through. On our left Pansa's men were counter-attacking the legion of sailors who had fought their way into the bowels of the Twenty-First and taken the symbol of the men's honour. To the right a small handful of those sailors ran as fast as their legs could carry them, a triumphant soldier holding the eagle aloft. Where should we go? I made my decision in an instant. Pansa had lost his eagle, it was his duty to retrieve it, not ours. My priority was to win the battle, and charging the sailors in the rear would do more damage than pursuing the eagle or even sending a troop away from our main attack. I caught sight of Publilius and he read my thoughts exactly.

'On me!' he cried, then made straight for the unprotected rear of the enemy. We rode obliquely towards the legion's corner, the cavalrymen able to throw their javelins into the mass of men without the risk of hitting the riders in front of them. The first ranks fell with *pila* embedded deep in their backs. The men who survived were ashen-faced as they saw a horde of cavalrymen bearing down upon them. Our angled line struck the corner first, but soon the whole squadron hit the legion hard.

I hacked down at the nearest soldier. The man instinctively swerved to avoid the strike, but my sword caught him on the part of the helmet that protected his nape. The force of my blow knocked the man to the ground, but I also felt my shoulder weaken from the jarring of my halted attack. As the rider next to me dealt with the fallen man, hastily I transferred my sword to my other hand. My left arm was unused to carrying a sword, and I felt hideously unprotected. With the next few blows my

heart clenched as the sword threatened to slip from my awkward four-fingered grasp. The riders around me saw that I was
floundering and cut their way through to me. I waved them on,
fit only to finish off the men that Publilius and his comrades
didn't kill outright.

Publilius himself was fighting like a man possessed. In the
very heart of the unit the enemy legate sat astride a terrified-
looking horse. In a matter of moments Publilius snatched up a
spear that stood planted in the turf, took swift aim and let fly.
The spear struck the officer square in the chest. The man hastily grasped the shaft and tried to pull it out, but he was already
toppling from the saddle, his heart failing him. Not ten paces
beyond the dying officer I could make out the red plume of
Pansa's helmet. Our two forces had almost met, obliterating the
body of sailors.

'Publilius, I'm going to find Valens. Tell Pansa to keep on
advancing and support him with your men.'

Publilius nodded his understanding, and I had Achilles take
me out of harm's way to the safe ground behind Pansa's legion.
I had no idea how the battle was going away from the Twenty-
First. All was chaos as Roman fought Roman and auxiliary
fought auxiliary. As I rode closer to the causeway, I could see
the massed ranks of praetorians and our own men struggling
to contain them. Valens struck a solitary figure behind the
battle line, making sure he was out of range of a well-aimed
pilum.

Achilles was frothing at the mouth from exertion, but he
clambered up the embankment until he reached the road, then
stood, his chest heaving.

'The Twenty-First have lost their eagle,' I reported. 'But we
caught the marines between Pansa's men and my cavalry. When
I left, most of the enemy were dead and Pansa was going to
advance against their reserves with around two hundred horses
in support. What's happening on the left flank?'

'I'm not sure. That's where the auxiliaries are and from this distance I can't tell them apart. But the centre's where the battle will be decided. The praetorians have been massed where the ground is surest while Otho's inferior troops scuttle around in the fields. I've thrown every reserve at the road and neither side is willing to budge.'

'Most of the legionaries here must be yours. Is the detachment from my province here? The Twenty-Second?' I asked.

'Yes, they're in the thick of things,' Valens said.

'Well, instead of sitting here and enjoying the view, I think the men deserve to have their generals with them. Let's see if we can boost their morale for one last surge.'

I tugged hard at the reins and had Achilles carry me along the road to the beleaguered centre. For a moment I didn't know whether Valens would follow; after a few heartbeats he must have decided he didn't want the shame of refusing to support his younger rival.

The legionaries from Valens's province cheered when they saw me, a blood-spattered general come to egg them on, but not half as loudly as they cheered their own general who in his immaculate uniform looked lofty, even godlike. But there were still screams and yells from the front line. Somewhere there was Quintus, leading the men of a legion that was not his own.

Worryingly, Valens and I had been there barely any time at all before the rear rank had retreated almost into our horses. Otho's men were proving why they didn't deserve to be scorned as mere palace guards. Granted, some of them would have bought their position or had it given to them by influential friends, but the majority were there on merit, picked for their size, strength and ruthlessness in the field. The fact that they had turned on their own emperor, the unfortunate Galba, after Otho had mortgaged his entire estate and more to buy their loyalty, must have driven them on. The eastern reinforcements and the sailors were fighting because their emperor had summoned them. The praetorians were turncoats, they knew in their hearts they would be shown little mercy by Vitellius.

Neither Valens nor I had a clue as to what was happening on either side of the road. The fields were awash with scattered groups of men fighting equally important battles, if on a smaller scale. There were no reinforcements to be had, Valens had already thrown them in, trying to batter the enemy into submission. The line teetered ever backwards. I could see an ominous swarm of plumes bulging into the centre of our line. If they broke through, even a handful of them, the rest of their comrades would pour into the gap, bringing even more swords to bear on our line.

Then a sound as welcome as any I have heard in my life cut through the air: a series of rising staccato notes that we all recognized as the signal for the men to rally. But the call did not come from the men ahead, but from behind. My rival and I turned to see who had blown the *tubae*. The horizon shimmered gently in the day's heat, but there on the road was a thin line of red tinted with silver. A small dust cloud rose up behind them, kicked up by striding sandals. The line of colour turned into individual figures. Men carrying the red shield with a sturdy boss in the centre, a resplendent eagle towering over them, and at their head marched a solitary man, a red plume mounted across his helmet, a gladius in one hand, a long vine staff in the other: Cornelius Nepos, First-Spear Centurion of the Fourth Legion. My men, the Macedonica.

Jubilantly, I clapped Valens on the shoulder.

'Men will be reading about this day for centuries to come, Valens.'

He smiled, his face awash with relief. 'I think you're right.'

'And they'll read that Fabius Valens's arse was saved by Aulus Caecina Severus, and the men he thought he could do without.'

XVI

The arrival of reinforcements broke the spirit of the enemy. When the praetorians began to run, the rest of Otho's line rolled up like a carpet. After I left them, Publilius and Pansa had combined to trounce the auxiliaries waiting behind the legion of marines. They had not recaptured the lost eagle, but the men of the Twenty-First were so eager to blot out the shame that they fought like lions, tearing great bloody chunks out of anyone who stood in their way. Possibly the sight of the praetorians on the road struggling to contain the assault of fresh reinforcements panicked the men in the northern fields, for within an hour most of Otho's army had fled. A rump of guardsmen remained on the causeway, stubbornly refusing to surrender. It was a hard and gory fight to remove the last remnants of the elite soldiers from the road.

It was crucial for us to harry Otho's forces as long and as hard as we could. We couldn't risk the enemy regrouping; there were still thousands of men alive to fight another day. Despite my injury I insisted that I should be the one to take the freshest men in our army east towards Otho's camp at Brixellum. The Fourth had only just joined the battle in time and Publilius's cavalry squadron, despite their bloody drive into the mass of marines, were in much better shape than Valens's own cavalry. There were also volunteers from the infantry who had held out against the praetorians for so long.

'Where's Quintus?' I asked a man from the Twenty-Second. 'Where's the tribune who led you today?'

'One of them praetorians nicked him in the shoulder, General. He was taken off to see the surgeon.'

'How bad was it?' I asked anxiously.

'Don't worry, sir, he'll live, I'm sure. I've had far worse wounds myself over the years.'

Relieved, I set about co-ordinating my command. Any excess weight, unused *pila*, scabbards, anything that would slow us down was left behind. The remainder of the army would round up the hundreds of prisoners, disarm them and keep a watchful eye on them. I had cobbled together perhaps six thousand men, more than enough to deal with any stragglers fleeing the scene.

Publilius rode on ahead, overtaking the last to flee and sending them back down the road towards us. If he encountered any resistance he was to ride back to my column for support. The legionaries advanced at a gentle jog. The sun had not yet begun to set, and the highly trained men still had plenty of life left in their legs for the pursuit. As we advanced eastwards we encountered sporadic groups of men, still in full armour but without their swords. Publilius had had them drop the weapons where they stood before sending them on their way. Their faces were tired and bitter, too weary even to sling insults at the rebels who had defeated them. Instead they stepped off the road and on to the grass verge to let us pass, watching sullenly as we ran to round up more of their comrades.

Brixellum was still some way off when we caught up with Publilius and his men. I was puzzled. Surely if they had met resistance they would have ridden back as I had ordered. Why then were he and his men on the road, waiting for us? It was only when I saw the three men in brightly polished breastplates rather than the simple mail shirts of the German cavalry that I knew Publilius had captured some officers, and judging by the fact that they were on horseback, surrounded by their enemies and seemingly unperturbed, high-ranking officers at that. Then I saw the tawdry strip of white cloth tied to the shaft of a broken spear.

Riding ahead of my column, I saw Publilius was talking to the officers. Then he shouted out an order. The men of his squadron turned as one to ride back down the road towards me, leaving the four men alone.

'What's going on?' I asked one of the troopers.

'No idea, General. The prefect didn't want any of us to know what the officers had to say. He did ask that your column might halt, sir, and that you were to join him alone.'

'All right, you pass those orders on to the legionaries, I'll go on ahead.'

When I was within earshot I called out: 'You'd better have a good reason for not pursuing the enemy, Publilius. If we have to fight another battle because of this—' I stopped abruptly. The officers one by one removed their helmets. Two of them were men I had not seen for a very long time. The first was Suetonius Paulinus, his hair a peppery colour all those years ago in Britannia now as white as snow, and age had carved yet more lines on his face. The second was Verginius Rufus, the man who had refused the throne. The third was Julius Agricola.

'I'm sorry if we stopped your prefect here from carrying out his duties, Severus, but it was you that we wanted to see,' said General Paulinus. 'When your man told us that you were at the head of this column, he suggested we wait here for you to arrive.'

'And now that you've found us, I think it would be best for you to rejoin your men, Publilius.' This advice came from Rufus. Publilius tugged at the reins as he made to leave.

'Hold on,' I said. 'What can be said to me can be said in front of Publilius, surely?'

'I think these talks would proceed better with an element of discretion, Severus,' Agricola said.

'Forgive me, Praetor, but given what you did to my men at Ad Castores, you and discretion do not go together.' I wasn't about to call Agricola by his name, not for a long time yet. My old friend looked ready to argue, but Rufus intervened.

'Let it go, Agricola. We're all friends here, or we should be.'

'Shall we get to the point? I suppose you want to discuss a truce?' I said brusquely.

'No truce. We've come to offer you a full surrender,' Paulinus answered.

'A surrender? Then why all this talk of discretion?' I pointed at Publilius who had remained where he was, horse facing back towards his men but his body awkwardly turned in the saddle to watch this deputation of men, two of whom I'd served under, the other I'd grown up and fought with.

'The emperor,' Rufus began.

'You mean Otho. Vitellius is the emperor, yours and mine both,' I interrupted.

'As you wish. Otho has certain . . . requests.'

'Namely: a total amnesty for his men,' Paulinus said.

'That can be arranged. What else?'

'That Otho's family and friends will not be persecuted.'

'Hold on,' I said. 'We haven't even discussed what's going to happen to Otho himself. I know Valens will want to kill him outright, but there are other options. Exile is one, but then he's still alive for men to rally behind. Personally, I think Otho should be put on trial for the murder of Galba.'

'You don't understand,' Agricola said. 'Otho's fate has already been sealed.'

'What do you mean, sealed?'

Again old Paulinus looked uncomfortably at Publilius before answering.

'Otho told the three of us, and his brother, that if he lost the battle comprehensively he would commit suicide.'

'Suicide!' I scoffed. 'That's not Otho's style, he'll cling on to power like a limpet to a rock.'

Rufus spoke up. 'I think you'll find Otho a changed man to the one you knew in Hispania. You forget that when he took the throne he had no idea that Vitellius had had men acclaim him emperor, or that you would be bringing some of the finest men in the empire into Italia. Last night he decided that he would rather die than let thousands of others die in a war that weakens Rome and gives hope to our enemies. You know the tribes in Germania, Severus. Now that you've abandoned the Rhine, we can only thank the gods that they haven't yet invaded Gaul.'

'We haven't abandoned the Rhine, Rufus. Vitellius . . . I mean the emperor, recruited new legionaries and auxiliaries to replace the men we took south. Anyway, are you telling me that Otho is already dead?'

'Not yet. When he heard the news of the battle he decided to give himself a few more hours to say his goodbyes. Then he sent Agricola and me to find you,' Paulinus said.

'Which begs the question, what are you doing here, Rufus?'

'I'm here in case you decide not to be reasonable, Severus. I'm sure your legions would like to rip the remnants of our army into small pieces. Hopefully they will remember that I was a good general to them, and hold back if I ask them to.'

He was right. Many of my men, and those from Valens's province for that matter, had offered Rufus the throne after they had crushed Vindex's rebellion. I couldn't risk Rufus going any-where near my men, just in case they took it into their heads to offer him the throne once again, abandoning the portly Vitellius like a whore with the clap.

'How do I know that you're telling the truth? You could just be trying to stall me while Otho runs with his tail between his legs.'

'That's why he decided to send us,' Agricola said. 'Three of his most senior officers, alone and at your mercy. You could take us prisoner and parade us in front of your men, but if you want to end this war today, you can come with us and see for yourself.'

'So that I'd be alone and at your mercy? Somehow I'm not tempted.'

'Of course you can bring an escort. Bring your whole column if you like, but I'd ask that you leave the infantry out of sight of the camp and advance with this squadron. The praetorians in the camp don't know what Otho's about to do. If they did there'd be a riot. Two hundred riders won't look half as suspicious as a legion,' Paulinus suggested.

'If it ends the war, General.' Publilius looked at me expectantly.

'All right, I'll come.'

We left the infantry hidden in some woods about a mile and a half away from Otho's camp. Their officers took some convincing not to follow us into the jaws of the possible trap, but at least I would have Publilius and his men as an escort. Rufus and Paulinus flanked me as I rode. Agricola was about ten lengths ahead of me; we had nothing to say to each other.

'It's a strange thing,' Paulinus said, breaking the awkward silence since the negotiations, 'to be defeated by a man you once commanded. I suspect that you knew far more about my strategy than I did yours. Though I must say I was surprised that you made such a rash beginning to the battle, fighting before all your troops had reached the battlefield.'

'That was Valens's work,' I said. 'I was guarding the bridge at Cremona when the fight began.'

'Ah, that makes sense. Knowing your eye for land I had my reserves fill in the ditches and knock down vines so that my men could fight unimpeded while yours flapped about like a lot of wet hens.'

'Meaning that you could concentrate your best troops in the centre and try to break through our line,' I said appreciatively. 'It almost worked until I brought up the reinforcements.'

'It would have worked if Otho hadn't decided to keep back some of his praetorians in Brixellum for protection.'

'How many?' I asked.

'Four thousand.'

I shuddered. Valens had come within a hair's breadth of wasting everything my men had fought for, from the bloodstained slopes of the Alps to the costly siege of Placentia.

'And these four thousand men are still in camp?'

'Ready to fight and die for their emperor,' Rufus said dourly.

I saw some of these men milling around outside the walls of the camp, looking limp and dejected. Many were grief-stricken, while others sat in grim silence around the evening fires. The camp gates were shut.

'You don't suppose Otho's done it already?' Publilius asked quietly.

'There's no way of knowing for certain without going in.'

'And you're sure you want to do that with four thousand angry praetorians waiting for you?'

I said nothing. Paulinus and Rufus I knew were honourable men. I couldn't say the same for Agricola.

Someone on the walls must have recognized the generals, as the huge wooden gates began to open. As the stout doors parted, I could see something inside: a table, with a purple cloth covering it, its edges flapping in the breeze. On the table lay a body, dressed in a snow-white tunic. As we came closer I could make out the gash on his neck where the knife had plunged home, all the blood painstakingly washed away. Even before reaching the table I could see it was Otho, right down to his curly wig and the laurel wreath worn to hide the join. Vain to the end, that wasn't a surprise; but a noble death? That was.

This was the man who had cautioned me over a year ago not

to get my hopes up that Galba would choose me as his protégé, and maybe even his heir. As a close friend of Nero's and a popular man with the mob and the common soldiery, he had sought that position for himself, even bribing the praetorians to murder Galba and free his path to the purple. But for all that, Otho had left the world with dignity, taking the path of honour. Suicide would wash away his less than glorious deeds, and he would be remembered as a man who knew when he was beaten, a man who had ended the civil war with a short, sharp stab of his dagger. His men were watching me closely as I looked upon the body. I reached out my hand and some of them grasped the hilts of their swords. I raised my other hand innocently, then lowered it. All I did was to adjust the wig that was resting slightly askew. Let him lie like a nobleman, I thought.

I retreated a few steps then turned on my heel. The three emissaries were waiting for my answer.

'Give him his funeral tonight. Then come to us tomorrow and we will discuss the peace.'

'Thank you, Severus,' old Paulinus said.

'Come, Publilius,' I said tiredly. 'We had better give Valens the news.'

The men were jubilant as we marched back. I had seen what I needed to see, but I couldn't share their joy. It seemed as though everyone I'd touched in those chaotic months had turned to dust. From that meeting in a merchant's house in Hispania, nearly all had died. Galba, his freedman Icelus Martianus, his general Titus Vinius; and now Otho lay on a cheap wooden table with a purple tablecloth trying to lend him some majesty. Then there was Vindex, another suicide after a calamitous defeat, not to mention the thousands of brave but doomed Gauls who had thought they were fighting for a cause but had had their lives extinguished by the very legions that I had led south. And these men too had limped from one horror to the next. I thanked the gods that my friends and family had survived, now that the war was over.

Valens was waiting for me, an angry expression blotching his face so that it matched his military cloak.

'Where by all the gods have you been? You were meant to be harassing Otho's army, not going off for an afternoon stroll!'

'Save your bile, Valens. The war is over.'

'Over? What do you mean, over?'

'Tell him, Publilius.' I was too tired to explain myself to the odious man.

'We were met by a deputation of officers from Otho who had come to offer their surrender.'

'It's not the officers I want. I want Otho,' Valens said impatiently.

'I don't mean they were surrendering, they had come to surrender the whole army. Otho killed himself less than two hours ago.'

'You're sure they weren't trying to trick you?'

'We saw the body, Valens. Believe me, Otho's dead. You can talk it over with Publilius if you like, but I want to check on Quintus. Where is he?'

'He's in the field hospital. I had the surgeons come up and set up shop as soon as the battle was over. You'll find it half a mile back down the road, where the well is.'

Most of the wounded were being ferried back along the road to Cremona, where surgeries and doctors in the town were waiting for them. The field hospital was for those who could not endure the length of the journey. Quintus's wound had been slight, so I assumed that as an officer he had had his shoulder stitched up at the nearest hospital rather than join the queue of men heading back down the road, on foot or in carts.

Graves were being dug in the field for those who hadn't made it, while surviving patients lay under a canvas shade, the doctors keeping them under close observation. I stopped one of the orderlies, asking where I could find my friend.

'I don't know each man by name, General. We've had hundreds coming through here.'

'He shouldn't be difficult to remember. Senior Tribune Vindex, came here with a shoulder wound, I heard.'

'Oh him? Yes, sir, he's two tents along. And there's a man with him, a Hibernian he said.'

'Thank you. And if you can spare someone can you send a man to take a look at my arm?'

'Of course, General.'

I must have taken a wrong turn. Two tents beyond was where they were storing the dead before putting them into the ground. I called out for Totavalas. The man had told me he was with Quintus, so he must be nearby.

'I'm here, General,' a voice answered from inside a small tent. I lifted the flap, and there was the Hibernian, crouched down by Quintus. The Gaul's armour had been removed and the top of his tunic ripped open. His flesh was morbidly pale. Even the skin around the wound looked cold and grey.

'But . . . I was told it was a simple shoulder wound,' I said, not understanding. The wound was near enough to the shoulder, though any further down and I would have called it a chest wound.

'The doctors said the sword had gone deep and punctured the lung. There wasn't anything they could do,' Totavalas said.

A fly landed on Quintus's face and began to crawl across his cheek. The open eyes remained motionless. Even when the fly reached his lip he didn't stir.

'He was meant to be going home,' I began. I reached out and took Quintus by the hand. His touch was cold. Suddenly, all around me everything seemed frozen. The cries of the wounded, the sobs of the dying, the legion of buzzing flies. Totavalas's lips were moving but I could hear nothing. There was nothing else in the world but the hurt, reproachful look on Quintus's boyish face. It was almost a year to the day that his father and I had stirred up his life, and he had striven every day not to let either of us down. He had saved my life at least twice, and I had taken his unswerving loyalty for granted. But do you know what the most hurtful thing was? I couldn't cry. I couldn't even summon up one single tear. Why was that?

'We did what we could for him, I promise,' a voice said. 'But when we saw the perforated lung and the boy struggling to breathe, all we could do was reduce his pain and ease his passing.'

The doctor began to look at my arm. In an instant I had knocked him back and had my sword at his throat. 'You should have tried harder!' I roared. The doctor was confused and terrified.

'General,' Totavalas said soothingly, 'this man has other soldiers to look after. If you kill him, others will die that could still be saved.'

I was breathing hard, rage coursing through me. I struggled to control myself.

'I want another doctor. Not you. No, not you. And get me away from here.' My sword tumbled to the ground. 'Totavalas, get me out of here, please.'

XVII

The new doctor was jittery with nerves, but he set about immobilizing my arm as best he could. The fighting was all over now; for my shoulder to recover it had to be strapped into place to let it grow strong again. Then I would have to build up the muscle strength until it was back to normal. Totavalas never left my side, making sure I did nothing rash. My mind was still fixed on the pale corpse not twenty paces from me. It was Quintus who was the hero of the day, not I, and certainly not Valens. He could have easily ridden home that day, leaving us all to our fates. But instead he had taken it upon himself to warn me of Valens's treachery and to take leaderless men into battle, for a cause in which he didn't believe. It wasn't even the first time he had put another man's cause before his own. He had refused his father's orders to poison me, drugging me instead and even leaving me a horse so that I could reach Vesontio in time for the battle.

The only thought I could console myself with was that we had won. The battle was won, the war was over. Rome and a consulship beckoned, but Rome without Quintus, fearless in his honesty and unswerving in his loyalty; it just wouldn't be the same. Who could I rely on to tell me when I took a step too far, when in pursuit of my goals I forgot about the needs of those who depended on me? Totavalas? No, he and I were too alike. The Hibernian was an ambitious man – who would not be, with a kingdom over the seas waiting for his triumphant return? But Totavalas kept his desires deep beneath the surface; I didn't have his subtlety. Quintus was the first to admit that he was not a soldier at heart, but now that the battle was over and Otho had crossed the river in honour, it was Quintus on whom I had counted to help me save Vitellius from Valens's influence. That was a battle I would have to fight on my own now.

Valens was smugness personified by the time the surgeon had finished with me and I made my way to his temporary headquarters. He had had his palatial tent brought from Cremona, and he was surrounded by his officers. The mood was self-congratulatory. Pansa, Publilius and Cerberus were all there too, but they stood off to one side, not permitted to join Valens's circle. Someone had broken out the wine already. Totavalas went off to fetch me a cup.

'Still with us, Severus?' Valens joked.

'Haven't you learned that you can't get rid of me that easily, Valens?'

'Now why on earth would I want to get rid of my plucky little sidekick?'

'Sidekick?'

'Come now, you're old enough to know what a sidekick is surely? Junior partner, apprentice, errand boy; which do you like best?'

My men growled, but I stood my ground. 'Call me what you like, Valens, so long as it's to my face. I have a pretty tale about your last governor that I could whisper in Vitellius's ear if I wanted to. Then we'd see how much our new emperor really trusts you. And when I send my report of the battle, then Vitellius will know who deserves the credit for today.'

'Oh, I shouldn't count on that,' Valens said. His officers sniggered.

'And why not?'

'While you were convalescing at the hospital, I had a rider dispatched to find the emperor and give him my account of the battle. Send your own if you like, but it's mine that Vitellius will read first, and it's mine that'll be believed. If your letter contradicts mine, Vitellius will see it for what it is: a petulant upstart trying to steal credit from his elders and betters.'

'Why, you . . .' I was so angry I couldn't spit the words out. I marched up to him, only to be blocked by his man Priscus. The centurion didn't dare lay his finger on me, a general, but he could stop me from getting within striking distance of his commander.

'Sorry, sir, but I really can't be having you attacking my general.'

'Get out of my way,' I said, limbs trembling with rage. I felt a hand on my arm and I raised it to strike. It was Totavalas, his eyebrows arched with concern, his expression open, as if to say, 'What are you doing?'

I closed my eyes and took a deep breath to calm myself. A thought occurred to me as to how I might persuade Vitellius that it was Valens who nearly threw away victory, but it would have to wait until we were all in Rome. I would bide my time.

Putting on my most serene smile, I faced Valens. 'Forgive me. The pain of my shoulder, Quintus's death; I am not myself.'

I enjoyed the moment. My rival was completely taken aback by my apology. Humility always gives you the element of surprise among ego-driven military types, I find.

'Apology accepted.'

'Excellent. Do we know what the emperor's movements will be when he receives your message? You know him better than I.'

Valens considered the question. 'Most likely he'll throw a banquet in celebration on the spot, even if he's halfway up a mountain. Then he'll make his stately progress into Italia.'

'Then perhaps, as commander in the field, you should write to the Senate. You can inform them of our victory and request that they recognize Vitellius as their emperor.'

Valens looked at me long and hard, unable to understand why I was being so magnanimous.

'You're happy for me to write to the Senate?' he asked suspiciously.

'You command the larger army, it is your privilege. Of course if you don't want the honour . . .'

'No, no,' he said hastily. 'I will fulfil the duty of informing the Senate.'

I bowed my head in acknowledgement before going to join my friends. None of them could understand it.

'General, are you sure you don't want to go back to Cremona and rest? It's been a hard day,' Publilius said.

'No harder than it was for any of you,' I replied. 'Even Totavalas here has had to put up with a surly, grieving master.'

'We all fought hard today,' Pansa cut in. 'We soldiers at any rate. Why do you bow and scrape to Valens then?'

'I let him think I bowed and scraped, Pansa, which is another thing entirely. I know that the three of you fought nobly today. Even Valens's own men told me how well your men did today, Cerberus.' A corner of the African's mouth twitched upwards, as much emotion as he ever showed.

'But what good does your flattery do?' Pansa asked.

'I'm choosing my battles, Pansa. Valens doesn't know it yet, but in writing to the Senate he's about to make a big mistake. Here in the field, he may have the upper hand. Let's just see how sure his footing is on the marble floors of Rome. Now if you'll excuse me, I have a letter to write. Totavalas?'

'Yes, General.' The Hibernian followed me out of the tent so I could dictate in privacy. He said nothing as he took down my letter; he didn't know who the recipient was. But it was a day of triumph tempered with tragedy, and I had a very old score to settle. Using a lump of mud from the battlefield as makeshift wax I pressed my seal down hard, then handed the letter to a nearby aide.

'Take this to the nearest way station and have them deliver it to Corduba in Hispania Baetica, understand?'

'Yes, General. At once.' The aide looked disappointed to miss the chance of celebrating with wine in the company of his superiors, but an order is an order, and he galloped down the road to Cremona as fast as his horse would carry him. No doubt he hoped to make it back in time to help finish the last of the Falernian wine.

I had a skinful that night, but it brought me little comfort. A hangover is what it brought me. The Greeks tell a story of how their god Zeus, our Jupiter, also woke one morning with a splitting headache. The incessant banging and clanging drove him nearly mad, until at last he had the blacksmith god Hephaestus open up his skull a fraction to see what the matter was. The god did as he was told, and out jumped a fully grown Athena, clothed with a helmet and a shield too. Hubris or not, I would gladly have swapped places with Zeus that morning.

It was a miserable day. The spring rains had poured throughout the night, and many of our men had to build a new camp in the fields by the battlefield. We had perhaps two thousand of Otho's men under armed guard and they had needed shelter too. Those of the enemy who had fallen in battle wouldn't even have the shelter of a grave. If you're unlucky enough to be on the losing side in a civil war your corpse is condemned to rot where it lies, with no coins to pay the ferryman. Your spirit is forced to roam the world without rest, while your body lies in a field or clogs up a ditch. The one good thing to come of the battle was that next year the wheat would be twice as high. Gaia, or Mother Earth, clearly thrives on the flesh and bones of the dead.

Even with Otho gone, we couldn't trust our prisoners not to do something rash. They had surrendered to us, this is true, but that did not guarantee them their lives, much less an amnesty. For the unity and security of the empire, however, an amnesty was in everyone's best interests. Three emperors had come and gone within a year, and Vitellius was effectively the last man standing. The legions and auxiliaries who had fought against us at Bedriacum would be made to swear an oath of allegiance to Vitellius. They could hardly refuse. The praetorians, though, were a different matter. Many of them had been bribed by Otho to murder Galba, and those not involved were still tainted by the actions of their comrades.

Valens and I held negotiations with Suetonius Paulinus for the best part of three days. It was agreed that the old general would march his remaining men to Cremona so that we could administer the oath. There was no question of us going to Otho's camp and risking a confrontation. I also requested that Verginius Rufus be sent to prepare Rome for her new emperor. At least that was the official reason; I daren't risk the genial man meeting my own troops and being acclaimed emperor once more. No, he had to leave for Rome as soon as possible.

It was early afternoon by the time Paulinus and his men arrived at Cremona. It would hardly have been fitting to administer the oath at the battlefield with all those fallen friends lying unburied, and starting to rot. Paulinus seemed to have aged another five years over the last few days. His eyes looked sunken, his face gaunt and sombre.

'Well, here we are at last,' he said, a tired general at the head of a dejected and nervous body of men. All of the enemy's army was assembled: the remnants of the legion of marines, the reinforcements from Pannonia, the auxiliaries and the praetorians, surrounded by our victorious forces.

'There'll be no trouble from your men?' Valens said to Paulinus. It was more a statement than a question.

'Kindly address me as "General", Legate Valens. After all, that is your official rank. I have not conquered new lands for this empire to countenance disrespect from the likes of you.'

I smiled; the old warhorse had some fight left in him.

Valens muttered something that sounded like an apology.

'Let's get this over with, shall we?' I said, beckoning the priest we'd found in the town to conduct the ceremony. The old man fumbled with his accoutrements. I never could understand the intricacies of religion, too many bells, smells and interminable exhortations to the gods. The soldiers were assembled in their various units, then split up into cohorts, each cohort having to take its own oath. To let the army swear as one would give the ceremony little meaning. We had to be sure that when the oath of loyalty was made, it was meaningful for each and every man. The priest approached each cohort in turn, intoning the words of the oath one sentence at a time so that the soldiers could repeat his words. The gods were called upon to observe the oath, and then the old man would proceed to the next cohort. The whole thing would take an hour at least.

I was lost in thought, about Quintus and Otho, when Paulinus spoke.

'I hope for Rome's sake this sorry business is all over,' he said.

'It is,' Valens said flatly.

'Will you stay and dine with us, sir? Rufus and Agricola too, of course,' I offered courteously, but inwardly cursing that I had called the general 'sir'. Old habits and all that.

'Thank you, Severus, but no. We'll head south once this is over and join the rest of the Senate.'

'Then you wouldn't mind delivering this, General?' Valens said, proffering his letter.

'What is it?'

'A letter to be read out to the Senate.'

'From Vitellius, already?'

'No, I wrote this letter.' Paulinus looked surprised, but

took the letter nonetheless. He looked at me, questioningly. I had the smallest of smiles on my face. The Senate would see it as an insult that Valens had taken it upon himself to write to them. That was a job for Vitellius, to ask them to ratify him as emperor, not some provincial legate without any social connections. Thankfully, my name did not appear in that letter. One day soon enough Valens would learn the cost of ignoring the etiquette of the nobility.

As the old general rode off southwards, it was Valens's turn to look confused.

'Why did the old fool think it strange that I asked him to deliver my letter?'

'I haven't the faintest idea.'

Later that day we received a reply from our lord and master. It seemed he had heard the good news one morning in Lugdunum and, as Valens had predicted, threw a celebratory brunch within the hour. But where Valens was wrong was in assuming that our new emperor would drink and feast through the rest of Gaul while we marked time in the north of Italia, waiting for him. Instead, Vitellius wanted to start his grand tour in Italia itself, and had left his gaudy carriage for a very unfortunate horse, riding over the Alps and heading eventually for Mediolanum. We were instructed to have the mother of all banquets prepared for his arrival in three days' time. Only the senior officers were invited, of course, but Valens and I both wanted to leave a man of ours on the spot to take care of the men. The day-to-day routine would be overseen by the centurions and junior tribunes. Pansa volunteered to stay behind.

'Fancy dinners and high society isn't exactly my scene,' he explained. 'Besides, someone has to look after the men while you young bucks enjoy yourselves.'

Pansa was right; we were young bucks. Publilius, Cerberus, Totavalas and I rode north together, and at four months the wrong side of thirty I was the eldest among us. Valens and his party rode at a steady pace, but I had my own reasons for wanting to reach Mediolanum as soon as possible.

We wound our way through the streets to the large town-house where we had made our billet when we first entered the city. It was a substantial building, painted an elegant cream colour that shone like a beacon among its rather drab neighbours. Publilius and Cerberus made their way back to their own billets, leaving Totavalas and me in the street with our horses.

A knock at the door and a short wait brought Duro, my body slave, to the door.

'Welcome back, master.'

'Duro, take the horses round to the stables and make sure they're properly fed and watered. Is your mistress at home?'

'Who is it, Duro?' a voice called from beyond the door.

'The mistress is learning to play the lyre, master, and she doesn't like me to disturb her while she's practising.'

'Let's see if she minds this disturbance,' Totavalas joked.

'Tell her it's nothing, Duro. I want to surprise her.'

The slave called back, 'Just a couple of beggars, mistress.'

'Then find them a denarius and close the door,' Salonina said irritably.

Duro led the two horses round the back of the house. Totavalas closed the door behind us as we went in. I could see through the coloured gauze hangings that Salonina was at the other end of the atrium, gently plucking the strings of the lyre that rested against her pregnant frame.

'Flank attack,' I whispered, gesturing that Totavalas should distract my wife's attention while I snuck round behind her.

There was only so far down the colonnade that Totavalas could walk without Salonina spotting him. I had already veered off to the left and was watching my wife at her lyre when the Hibernian announced himself.

'Mistress Salonina?'

'Oh, Totavalas, you startled me. How long have you been standing there?'

'Not long, I didn't want to disturb you. I've come from the battlefield near Cremona.'

Salonina put her hand to her mouth. 'The battlefield?' she gasped.

I gently crept up behind her.

'And I have some good news about your husband,' Totavalas continued, looking past Salonina and into my eyes.

'He's right behind you,' I said.

She screamed, dropping the lyre on the stone floor, a couple of strings breaking with a harsh twang. Salonina threw her arms around me. 'Don't you dare do that to me again!'

My wife was in her element organizing the banquet to welcome the arrival of Vitellius. It was an immense honour to be the hostess for the inaugural banquet on Italian soil for the new emperor of Rome, and she set about it with almost military precision. Valens was a widower, so naturally Salonina was the most senior lady in all of Mediolanum's society – 'If there is such a thing,' Salonina said when I gave her the news.

Nevertheless, she soon selected the finest delicacies and most distinguished entertainment that could be found at such short notice. I often came upon her fretting that there weren't enough fresh lobsters to go round, or that a dancing girl had sprained an ankle in rehearsal. All I could think to say was that after Vitellius had been starved of refinement and culture beyond the Alps, the feast that Salonina was bringing together would be fantastic in comparison. Not the highest praise, in hindsight. Give me a general or even an emperor to placate and I can do it with the best of them; a woman complaining about the mediocre menu for a banquet and I'm as useful as a priest in a brothel.

As hard as Salonina tried to keep Time from her inexorable march, the night of the banquet came at last. We had commandeered the finest house in Mediolanum for Vitellius, and even had a hot bath ready for him when he arrived at the end of his week-long ride from Gaul. Valens and I stood either side of the main doors to the street, waiting for his arrival. Each of us had had his armour and uniform made spotless for the occasion, even if my appearance was somewhat spoiled by a sling which Salonina had fashioned out of some crimson cloth to match my military cloak.

Our ears were greeted with the sound of marching men, but something wasn't quite right. The gaps between each step were too long. Then we saw why. Around the corner strode our glorious emperor, wheezing and trying to march at a decent pace despite his slight limp. Behind him a dozen lictors, their bundles of birch rods topped with an axe-head at rest on their shoulders, walked rather than marched in step for fear of outpacing their charge. If ever an emperor of Rome has looked so unlike an emperor, despite his best efforts, I have never heard of it. An enormous length of material was needed to cover Vitellius's frame, a toga of the deepest purple looking like a glorified towel, such was its size. It was hard to ignore the patches of sweat at the armpits, staining the imperial colour. Even his gold-painted laurel wreath, which he was not yet entitled to wear, was slightly askew on his head after the exertions of his walk. He had come all of three hundred paces from his quarters and up a gentle slope to the basilica where we were holding the banquet.

'My mighty generals,' Vitellius managed in one breath. Valens and I saluted, but he insisted on embracing each of us in turn. He had been bathing not half an hour ago, but gods how he stank! The rank odour from his pits combined with the sickly smell of perfume on his neck was almost enough to make me gag.

'I cannot thank either of you enough for what you've done,' he continued.

'We did it for Rome, Caesar,' Valens said.

There was the old wince. 'Even now, Valens, I am not a Caesar. Nor will I ever let anyone call me that.'

'May we address you as "sire" then, sir?' I ventured.

Vitellius thought it over for a moment. 'Sire, eh? I like it. Why not?'

'Then, sire, we would like to welcome you to your first dinner on Italian soil as the undisputed emperor of Rome,' Valens grovelled. The two of us bowed and, as we had prepared, the great doors opened right on cue. A delicious array of smells wafted into the street and Vitellius was drawn to them like a drunkard to his drink. We followed him in, and there was Salonina, resplendent in a gown of gossamer teamed with damask, swirling patterns of flowers woven along the seams, delicately cut to help mask the bulge of her stomach. She stood, hands resting on the back of the tallest chair at the top table, waiting for the guest of honour.

'My dear,' Vitellius began, 'you are the very picture of loveliness.'

Salonina artfully blushed at the compliment. 'Your majesty is too kind.' She pulled out the chair for the big man to sit down, and all the other guests took this as their cue to sit.

Valens cleared his throat, for the two of us were still standing. The guests hastily got back to their feet. They watched and waited as the two generals took their places, I on Vitellius's left, and Valens seated to Salonina's right. As the hostess she had the honour of sitting at the emperor's right hand. And of course husband and wife do not sit next to each other at a banquet, so Valens had no choice but to sit a place away from his master. Salonina had managed it perfectly. My wife took her seat, Valens and I followed her lead. Then and only then were the guests permitted to sit. I smiled. This was going to be fun.

XVIII

The cart lurched as it hit an uneven cobble on the road. It was the cart I had given Salonina as a gift when we were crossing the Alps, and had been packed full of creature comforts. She was hardly in a position to travel on horseback to Rome. I had decided to spend the morning keeping her company instead of Aulus. He was getting some practice riding with Totavalas.

'Two months more, that's all there is left to wait,' she told me.

'Two months? You're going to get even bigger?'

'How very tactful of you, husband dear!'

'I'm sorry, this is all so new to me. Can I feel the baby kick again?' I asked.

'You felt it two miles ago.'

'I know, but I want to do it again.' No matter how many times I did it, the excitement never wore off. Salonina pulled her dress taut over her stomach and I laid my hand on top of it, waiting. Sure enough, a tiny foot made its presence felt, kicking harder this time.

'I'm sure it's another boy,' I said.

'What makes you so sure?'

'Well, a girl's not going to kick as hard as that.'

'How do you know? Just because the kicks are strong it doesn't mean it *has* to be a boy,' she argued. 'Who's to say I want a boy anyway? I might want a girl.'

This time the cart lurched to a halt. There was a knock on its side.

'Who is it?'

'It's Totavalas, General. We've arrived.'

'Just coming.' I gave Salonina a peck on the cheek, then drew back the curtains that gave us some privacy. I had a big grin on my face.

'Someone's happy,' Totavalas observed.

'It's the baby,' I said. 'He's kicking like a donkey.'

'Well, at least you're in a good mood. I doubt that lot are,' he said, pointing towards the town of Placentia. Parts of the city were on fire.

I heard later that the men had taken it upon themselves to march from Cremona to Placentia, though leaving a sizeable force to watch over the Othonians we still held prisoner, then they had set about looting the place. Their reasoning was that the town had given my column such a thrashing that the punishment was deserved, but the truth of the matter was that the men had fought hard for Vitellius but had yet to receive any reward. The belligerence of Placentia was little more than a pretext for the soldiers to rape and pillage. And to be honest, since the rigours of the battle and Quintus's death I was past caring.

Pansa didn't even have the grace to look apologetic when he recounted the events to Valens and me.

'It was your man Priscus that started it,' he told Valens. 'He was all for leaving the prisoners unguarded, but I had the men from Cerberus and Publilius's squadrons stay behind while the legions entered Placentia.' The legate braced himself for a dressing-down, but it never came.

'Very well, Pansa. The men have fought hard for little reward,' I said. 'They are overdue their spoils.'

Even Valens was surprised at my tolerance. 'You don't object?'

'Not in the slightest. If anything I'm grateful it happened while the two of us were in Mediolanum. We can discipline a few of the ringleaders, keep our own reputations intact; meanwhile the rest of the men have their fun with a city that should have welcomed us in the first place. More fool them.'

'All right,' Valens said, eager to keep the discussion going while the two of us were thinking along the same lines. 'Now we have to decide what to do with the prisoners. I think the regular legions are safe to use, providing we split them up and send them to different parts of the empire.'

'Agreed. I think we should recognize that legion of sailors, the First Adiutrix.'

Pansa was about to object, but I headed him off. 'I know they took your eagle, Pansa, but they've given it back now, and they did bloody well to take it in the first place. I'd say we should send them to Hispania to cool off. Galba stripped the place of soldiers when he marched on Rome, they'll be welcomed there.'

'Fine, but what about the praetorians?' Valens asked. 'They've sworn the oath of allegiance to Vitellius, but there's no way I want them as his guards in Rome.'

I had given this some thought on the journey south. 'We can't just ignore all those good men. Why don't we use them to fill the places of the dead in the legions that Otho used, the ones from Pannonia, and then disband the rest?'

'Disband them?' Valens queried.

'It'll be cheaper than keeping them on the strength,' I said, knowing Valens was a right skinflint at heart. The less the treasury had to pay out, the more he could skim off for himself. That was the kind of man Valens was.

'That sounds fine to me,' he hastily agreed.

'And if they don't want to be disbanded?' Pansa wondered.

'Then we can remind them that they let an emperor die on their watch,' I said. 'What is the punishment among the praetorians for failing to protect the emperor?' I asked Valens, with a shrewd idea of what the answer might be.

'I'm not sure there's a precedent. Claudius pardoned most of the guard when a bunch of them murdered Caligula. Thrown off the Tarpeian rock perhaps?'

'But certainly death?' I said.

'Oh yes, definitely,' Valens agreed.

'Well then, disbandment or death, it's their choice.'

The praetorians didn't like their choice, but there wasn't much they could do about it. There was no way we could trust them to guard Vitellius, and if they hadn't bothered to save from their exorbitant wages and bribes over the years, then it was their fault if they faced penury. They could always apply to join other legions.

We stripped them of their armour, weapons and all other military items and added them to our baggage train. They would be needed by the men we recruited to take their place in Rome. One thing I will say for Valens, he was efficient. Everything that needed to be done was done within a matter of hours and we were soon ready to continue our march south. The sailors began their march to Hispania, the detachment from the Fourteenth Legion would wait for their comrades before replacing the troops Vitellius had summoned from Britannia, but we were heading home.

I won't bore you with tedious descriptions of that journey. Needless to say Vitellius took every opportunity to gorge himself almost to the point of vomiting whenever we reached a major town, where the people were anxious to pay homage to the new emperor. At Fanum Fortunae, the city where the south-eastern Aemilian Way met our final stretch of road, leading south along the Flaminian Way, the people laid on an entire herd of wild boar for us officers and the town's dignitaries, mounted on a bed of crab meat and adorned with peacock feathers.

It took us far longer than it should have done to reach Rome.

Perhaps twelve days' hard march would have brought the army to the city gates, but we were weighed down with a baggage train, soldiers who were already beginning to lose their discipline and an emperor who put pleasure before practicality. Thus it was a whole month before we finally crossed the Apennines and caught our first sight of the seven hills and the city that sprawled over them.

The Tiber coursed its way between the Vatican fields and the Field of Mars, where crowds had already gathered to cheer the arrival of their new emperor. We halted at the Milvian Bridge, ready to begin the procession. Cerberus and Vitellius were merrily reminiscing about the times they had spent together in Africa, when I noticed something amiss. Vitellius had chosen to wear full military uniform, one that strained to contain his mighty frame but did give him an air of authority and steel that he usually lacked.

'Sire, might it be wiser to wear your imperial toga today?' I suggested.

'Why should I change my uniform? I think it suits me.'

'It certainly does, sire. But I was only thinking it might not go down too well with the people. Wearing that armour makes you look like a mighty conqueror, not the father of the nation, yet that is how the Senate will shortly acclaim you.'

Vitellius looked as though he would sulk, but he saw my reasoning. 'Very well, Severus. Make sure the army is ready to move off as soon as I've changed.'

'Your will, sire.'

The army would be led by the low-ranking officers, the centurions and the junior tribunes. All of them had to be provided with dazzling white togas that denoted their membership of the equestrian class, even if they were about to enter the city on foot. Who wants to march in a triumph, only to be dodging piles of horse droppings as you walk? Next came the thousands of auxiliaries, grouped together according to the province they came from. Germans, Gauls, Britons, Lusitanians, Africans, it seemed the entire western half of the empire was represented. Then there were the legions themselves, carrying their eagles and standards with pride. We had even stopped for a whole day before reaching Rome to give the men ample time to smarten themselves up and attend to their full ceremonial dress. Even the legions that hadn't fought at Bedriacum were represented; the detachments from the legions stationed in Britannia had sent their standards ahead while they marched along the route that Valens had taken through Gaul.

Finally, the senior tribunes and legates would march ahead of Vitellius himself, protected from any would-be assassins by his band of lictors. Valens and I would walk at his side. Salonina protested that she wasn't allowed to join me in the triumph, but it was impossible. She would have to enter with the rest of the camp-followers or sit in her carriage and sulk. At last Vitellius returned, casting his eyes enviously at me, Valens and the rest looking resplendent in our ceremonial armour, but determined that having to wear civilian clothing would not spoil his day.

'Permission to start the parade, sire?' Valens asked. The tribunes and the centurions, who normally looked so grim but in their clean white togas appeared serene and noble, were poised to march. Vitellius nodded.

'Parade, forward march!'

The men gave a rousing cheer and began to pace forward, to a man their chests swelling with pride. Vitellius waved at his soldiers, as though he had been the one who had led them through all the hardships: the snows and the precipices, the sieges, the assaults, the feints and the ambushes, and the final battle. Where had he been when my men were dying? Filling his face in Germania and Gaul – but that had always been the plan. Now Vitellius was the master of Rome, and Valens and I were masters of Vitellius.

It took almost an hour for the entire army to march by. The

auxiliaries and most of the legions had passed through the city gates before it was finally time to bring up the rear of the column. Vitellius took his place in the middle of the road. The lictors formed up in a line either side of him, senior officers in front, Valens and I a pace behind and a pace to the side of our emperor.

'Are you ready, you two?' he asked as the rear ranks of the final legion began at last to move off.

'We'll follow your lead, sire,' I said.

Vitellius took a deep breath, rolling his neck and shoulders to cover his nerves. He exhaled noisily, then cleared his throat. 'To Rome, then.'

From the Field of Mars right up to the Senate steps, the people never stopped cheering. Garlands of flowers were strewn across the road; the plebs were out in their tens of thousands to greet their new emperor. Half of Italia must have had its flowers uprooted for the occasion. Out of the corner of my eye I spotted dozens of loaves being tossed into a sea of grasping hands. I couldn't help but wonder how much quieter the people would have been had we not taken the precaution of buying up almost the entire supply of bread baked that summer morning. They had precious little else to shout about.

Vitellius though was milking every moment of the triumph. I could hear the air whistling through his nostrils as he fought to breathe evenly. I struggled to stop my grin from turning into a side-splitting laugh. Valens too had heard the odd noise, his lips quivering as he tried to control his laughter.

By the time we reached the Great Forum there was barely any space left. The whole army had congregated there to wait for their emperor, and the urban cohorts had trouble holding back the crowd. The only space in the entire market place was a path between the men, barely big enough to let the three of us through, let alone the lictors who covered our flanks. The senior man looked at the small gap nervously.

'I hardly think there's an assassin's knife waiting for me,' Vitellius reassured the burly man. 'These soldiers fought their own countrymen to make this all possible,' he continued, gesturing at the magnificent spectacle the city had put on for us.

'What are you waiting for?' Valens asked. 'Just have half your men walk ahead and the other half behind us. There's no safer place in the world for the emperor than among his men.'

On either side we were flanked by the men, their procession over but formed up in cohorts to watch their emperor claim what was his by right of conquest, even if conquest was not a word we would use where we were headed. The three of us squeezed through the mass of jubilant, sweaty men until we stepped off the brick of the forum and on to the marble steps of the Senate house, and there waiting for us was Suetonius Paulinus.

'Sire,' he said, 'it is my honour to welcome you to the Senate on the day of acclamation.'

'Thank you,' Vitellius began, before pausing uncertainly.

'Suetonius Paulinus,' I whispered.

'Suetonius Paulinus,' the emperor finished, smiling affably. 'You and the rest of the Senate will have to forgive me if I breach the imperial etiquette. This is all rather new to me!'

'If you would like to go inside then, sire?' Paulinus gestured that Vitellius should go in first. His pale and wispy eyebrows arched questioningly when Valens and I followed suit. 'These two as well, sire?'

'Where I go, they go,' Vitellius said simply.

'I am a senator of Rome too,' I reminded the old general.

'And I'm about to be made one,' Valens added. That was just the first of his rewards that day. Paulinus gently bowed his head, knowing he could hardly refuse.

The entire Senate was assembled. Indeed, the building was probably fuller than it had been for perhaps a decade. Those who had been exiled or had fled Rome in Nero's time had returned; those who had supported Galba but had hidden themselves away when Otho rose to the purple, they were there too. Vitellius didn't have an enemy in the world, so what was left of Rome's elite had felt no fear in gathering to acclaim their new emperor. As one they stood, politely applauding as Vitellius waddled towards them. Valens and I waited in the shadows either side of the Senate doors. This was Vitellius's moment, not ours.

The emperor raised his hand shyly for silence.

'Conscript fathers,' he began with the traditional words, 'I thank you for your welcome. If you had told me a year ago that I would be addressing this house as your emperor, I would have said you'd been spending too long in my cellar!'

A polite laugh rippled round the chamber.

'I say "emperor", but in truth that is for you to decide. I cannot change the fact that many men, far too many, have lost their lives to decide which man should wear the imperial purple. The past is the past. Rome and her people have suffered at the hands of three emperors unworthy of her. I am forever indebted to the army, for their belief and their faith in my ability to rule Rome wisely and justly. But you, Senators, without you Rome is nothing. My men think I should let you return to your homes while I run the empire from some lofty palace on the Palatine Hill. That is not how I wish to rule. Will you join me in the great task, to pull our beloved city out of the mire and make her great again?'

For a moment the noblemen were stunned. This wasn't the drink-sodden, gambling Vitellius, the friend of charioteers, the Vitellius they knew of old. This man spoke with purpose and humility, with vision and tact. After a brief and stunned silence they cried out: 'Caesar! Caesar!'

Vitellius called for silence once again. 'Senators, you flatter me. I am not, never have been and never will be a Caesar. That day on the Rhine I adopted a new name: Aulus Vitellius Germanicus. Call me that if you must.'

And so it was that Aulus Vitellius Germanicus was acclaimed *imperator* of the Senate and People of Rome, given the honorific 'Augustus', unanimously voted the *tribunicias potestas*, made Supreme Pontiff and granted consular power over Rome and the imperial provinces. The man of whom Galba had said, 'I do not fear a man that thinks of nothing but food,' was triumphantly acclaimed by a Senate that harboured men of more talent and more ambition. Such is Fate.

'My first act as emperor is to grant a general amnesty to all those prosecuted or exiled by my predecessors.' Cue raucous applause from sections of the assembled nobles. Nero, Galba and Otho had all made enemies, but Vitellius was proposing a clean start for all. 'And to herald this break from the past, I believe I have the privilege to appoint new consuls for the rest of the year.'

All eyes turned to the two men who wore the consular stripe on their gleaming togas. Neither showed the slightest sign of dismay at losing the most coveted rank that a man outside the imperial family could obtain; they had both been sounded out long before the decision was announced.

'And what better way,' Vitellius continued, 'to usher in this new age than by appointing two loyal and brilliant men. One is not a nobleman, but of good equestrian family. The other will be the youngest consul perhaps in all Rome's history, not counting those from the house of Caesar, given the position more often through birth than merit. These two men have served me from the very beginning, and I know they will serve Rome no less valiantly: Fabius Valens and Aulus Caecina Severus.'

The two of us advanced from the shadows, not to applause but to a babble of concerned whispering. Both of us still carried our swords and wore armour, unthinkable in the Senate house. But this moment had been delicately planned during those long weeks on the road. Behind us two men approached. Totavalas was one of them, the other a slave of Valens's. In tandem they relieved us of our swords and undressed us from our armour, leaving us both wearing the simple red toga of the legions. Over the top of these our attendants put on a second toga, white with a red stripe, the consular toga. The message was clear: together Valens and I were now both senators and consuls of Rome, but underneath we were still the emperor's loyal soldiers.

XIX

'I can't think why you chose me,' Publilius said.

'I've told you before and I'll tell you again, I chose you because you are brave, loyal and you've got something between your ears,' I said, still looking down at my papers.

'My nose?' It took me half a heartbeat to be sure he was joking.

'Valens and I were both asked to propose a man for the post of praetorian prefect, and it was between you, Cerberus and Pansa.'

'That still doesn't answer my question,' Publilius said, ignoring the slaves who were busy kitting him out in his new uniform.

I sighed. 'Do I have to spell it out? Pansa resents the fact that I'm nearly two decades younger than him and his commanding officer, let alone consul. And I don't know Cerberus well enough to trust him with this job.'

'He'd make a more menacing bodyguard than I would,' my friend pointed out.

'But you're not a bodyguard, are you? That's what the rankers are for. You have to be on constant alert, build up a network of spies to gather information, and most importantly watch that slippery bastard Priscus.'

'Valens's man?'

242

'Valens's man, exactly. You're my man.'

'Can I ask you something?'

'You just have.'

He looked at me, unamused. 'If Quintus were alive, would you still have given me this position?'

I put down my stylus. 'Quintus wasn't cut out to be a soldier, or a politician. He tried to find the good in everybody, but in some people the good is buried too deep. You're a realistic man, Publilius, and now we're in Rome you know as well as I do you can't just see everything as black or white. Quintus couldn't see the murky grey in between. The gods alone know why he fought at Bedriacum. He as good as told me I'd crossed from grey to black.'

I had said more than I meant to. Publilius was listening to me in silence. I cleared my throat. 'I don't want to talk about Quintus any more, understand? He's dead, and life must go on.'

'Yes, Consul,' Publilius replied. 'I do have one more question though.'

'What is it?'

'We now have two praetorian prefects, but no praetorians. We disbanded them all after Bedriacum.'

'That's simple enough. We'll recruit them from the Rhine legions.'

'But won't that leave the army under strength?' Publilius asked.

'Only for a few months or so,' I said. 'I suspect Otho's men will mope around for a bit before realizing that they may as well rejoin the army, even if it means lower pay and more work. Better that than farming or banditry. We'll use them to fill the spaces in the Rhine legions, them and any others from Italia that want to join up.'

There was a gentle knock. I didn't have a chance to ask who it was before Salonina popped her head round the door.

'Caecina, it's less than two hours until the guests arrive and you haven't done half the things you promised you'd do.'

'What's more important,' I said, gesturing at the sheaves of papers that littered my desk, 'tax returns from Macedonia or helping you choose which dress to wear?'

'You can play with your papers any time. I need your help now. Sorry to drag my husband away from you, Publilius, but if he doesn't come now he'll set me back at least an hour and the finest families in Rome will be waiting in the street, all because he didn't help.'

'Just a moment and I'll be with you, all right?'

'Just a moment,' Salonina repeated sternly, then closed the door behind her.

'Do you know the secret to a happy marriage, Publilius?'

'No, sir?'

'Well, if you ever find out, be sure to tell me.'

Salonina had me doing all sorts of useless chores that she could have delegated to the slaves, but she insisted on my help. She was adamant that the new and expensive additions to our household wouldn't have the first idea about which wine to serve with which course, which guests to pay particular attention to, yet every time she asked for my help or advice she was either dismissive or ungrateful.

'Caecina, the peacock feathers are meant to be *scattered*, not just littered over the floor.' Or, 'Well, if you can't be constructive in your criticism, why don't you get yourself ready for the party then help Totavalas with the entertainment.'

I didn't need telling twice. With less than an hour to go I took my time to change, figuring that I was safer in our bedroom than risking Salonina's ire by stumbling over a drape or putting the wrong dish at the wrong table; self-preservation and all that. Totavalas had had the same idea. He was in the kitchen when I found him, helping one of the cooks pour a cauldron of *garum* into little serving jugs, working with all the haste of a tortoise that had entered retirement.

'Working hard, I see!'

'Someone has to do it,' the Hibernian said.

'True enough,' I conceded, 'but can't one of the kitchen slaves do that?'

'I don't think your wife wants me anywhere near the smart part of the villa.'

'I've run away too.'

Totavalas looked up, smiling, but when he took his concentration away from what he was doing, the white sauce overfilled the jug and began to ooze on to the table. He muttered something in his phlegm-ridden language, put the cauldron down and looked about for a cloth.

'She will get used to you, you know that,' I said.

'I do. I realize I was never the conventional slave . . .'

'I wouldn't have it any other way. Salonina's always lived in this rarefied, insular world. Her father was a rich man, she grew up with everything she wanted. You're a breath of fresh air, Totavalas, with your insolent barbarian charms. I wouldn't have bought you if I didn't have the occasional longing for the soldier's life back in Britannia. Life was so much simpler then,' I mused.

'There are some compensations,' Totavalas admitted. 'I must be the first of my countrymen to see Rome. It's an amazing place, I grant you, but it's not home.'

'Then why do you stay?'

Totavalas stopped wiping at the spilled sauce, thinking. 'Curiosity. It's a grand game we've been playing this past year. I'd like to see how it ends. Besides, there's no way I'm going back to my island without a fair bit of gold. I'll go to Hibernia as High King, or not at all.'

The appointed hour approached. I managed to get out of Salonina's way for a while by claiming I'd got lost in the villa. I say villa, but palace would have been much nearer the mark. On arriving in Rome, Vitellius had decided to take the Golden Palace that Nero had built at the foot of the Esquiline Hill, adorned with a huge colossus whose face was sculpted to resemble Nero's own. Vitellius having set the precedent, Valens commandeered for himself a property on the Palatine where the noblest and richest families lived. Salonina hounded me day and night into leaving my family's not inconsiderable villa, one that had housed seven generations of the Caecina Severi, for a gaudy affair that stood at the highest point of the Palatine. The rightful owners were given promises of payment and favours to come. I was consul after all, and had the emperor's ear. In the meantime I had leased them my family's house at a good rate, filling the coffers very nicely.

Salonina had surpassed herself. Despite what had seemed like chaos everything was ready long before the guests were due. She had a new dress that flattered her heavily pregnant figure, and I told her so, though not using those exact words.

'Thank you, Caecina,' she said, squeezing my hand tenderly.

Totavalas was waiting by the door. I had given him the task of announcing the guests as they arrived. For one thing it would be a novelty to have a Hibernian accent calling out some of the most illustrious names in the world, families whose lineage could be traced back to the birth of the republic. Secondly, it would give the freedman the chance to learn the names and faces of the senators, an essential task if he wanted the position I had just offered him.

At Salonina's signal the musicians begin to play a gentle melody, loud enough to be appreciated but quiet enough that our guests would be able to make conversation. There was a loud knock at the door. The slaves picked up their platters of dainties and delicacies.

'Consul Fabius Valens,' Totavalas announced.

In walked my fellow consul, who was wearing the red-striped toga he had donned for the first time only a few days ago.

'Consul,' Salonina welcomed him. 'We are honoured to welcome you as our first guest into our new home.'

'The honour is mine, lady,' Valens said formally.

'And how smart he looks, doesn't he, dearest?'

'Very smart,' I agreed. Salonina had already gone to greet the next guest, leaving the two of us alone. 'It doesn't matter in the slightest, of course,' I continued, 'but strictly speaking one only wears the consular toga in the Senate. Socially, you'd wear something like this,' I said, gesturing at my own blue toga, spun from expensive fabrics in the east and more apt for a summer's evening in Rome than Valens's heavier clothes.

His eyes widened in embarrassment. 'Severus, you know these people better than I do. My palace is half a mile away; do I go home and change?'

'Of course not,' I said. 'It will be refreshing for some of the snobs that someone is bringing a bit of originality to these affairs.'

We were interrupted by the arrival of our lord and master. There were a good dozen or so guests by now, and all of them turned to watch the emperor's entrance. Vitellius was of course easy to recognize. The vibrant purple of his cloak clashed horribly with the deep green of his toga, but alongside the waddling whale walked a woman. This had to be the wife Vitellius had left behind in Rome, as he was too poor to take his household with him to Germania.

'Sire,' I bowed. Salonina had come to stand at my side again.

'Severus, Salonina, may I introduce you to my wife Galeria?'

I took the lady's hand and kissed it, then looked into a face that hinted at middle age. Little lines around her eyes creased as she smiled. 'My lady,' was all that needed to be said.

'Your home looks wonderful,' Galeria said. 'Especially considering you've had so little time to make it your own.' The two of us blushed, Salonina at the compliment, I because I knew that Galeria was a friend of the family who had owned the palace. Thankfully a slave broke the tension by proffering a selection of titbits to Vitellius.

'Thank you. I never could say no to a piece of salmon.' Or even two pieces, such was the speed of the emperor's hand. 'How long until the banquet proper begins, Severus?'

'Not for another half-hour, sire. We're still waiting for many guests. I hope in the meantime you find the music and the guests food for the soul instead.'

'Well put, Severus, well put. Come, Galeria, we are depriving our fellow guests of the enchanting hostess.'

Soon the atrium began to fill. All the Senate had been invited, and I expected the vast majority of them to attend. It would be a brave or unambitious man who refused the invitation of a consul, especially when it was known that the emperor would attend. However, I was waiting for two guests in particular. I could see through the doorway that a fair queue was building up in the street, and Totavalas was coping as best he could.

I was busy being gracious and charming to the senators who knew me before I had taken that fateful journey to Hispania a year and a half ago. Many were vague friends of the family, others merely wished to make themselves known to the new consul. I took particular pleasure in seeing Valens standing in a corner, with only his drink for company. He was a new man in Rome; no connections, no friends in the Senate, just a red stripe on his toga to show he was favoured by the emperor. Many fawners congratulated me for my restraint in not writing to the Senate after Bedriacum, badmouthing Valens for his presumption to write on Vitellius's behalf. I'd been right; it was for the Senate and no one else to acclaim Vitellius as emperor, and certainly not a jumped-up legate who had a mighty high opinion of himself.

Totavalas caught my eye. They were here. I excused myself and made my way to the door, the hairs on my arms rising as they felt the cool night air. There stood Julius Agricola and his achingly beautiful wife Domitia, the woman who had thought it beneath her to have her daughter marry into my family. Once upon a time that woman had been a pretty girl with lustrous blonde hair, a girl that Julius and I had fought over many times. Only he could marry for love, I had to marry for money. Our friendship had survived Domitia, only to be broken by politics, by Julius's envy of my success.

'Is there a problem, Totavalas?' I asked, loudly for all to hear.

'It's Julius Agricola and his wife, Consul. They say they've been invited.'

'I don't remember sending them an invitation,' I said. This was true enough. I had allowed word to get round that all senators and their wives were invited, but had not sent out any actual invitations.

'Come on, Caecina, if this is another of your pranks it's not funny.' Agricola's face turned redder and redder at the embarrassment. The music stopped. A small crowd had gathered, in the house and in the street, everyone listening in fascination to the exchange.

'Only my friends are permitted to call me Caecina. Our friendship ended when you betrayed me for Otho, a man who murdered his way to the throne.'

'Will the consul not be gracious and forgive his friend?' Domitia asked.

'If my son isn't good enough for your daughter, then the pair of you aren't good enough for me. And as for my "friend",' I turned to look him in the eyes, 'once your term as praetor is over, I don't want to see you in Rome again. Now go.'

Agricola took his wife by the hand and led her away, accompanied by frantic murmuring among the guests, and even laughter from some of the sycophants. Salonina appeared at my side, taking me by the hand.

'What kind of man would put someone like Otho over his childhood friend?' she said scornfully.

I said nothing, because I knew the answer. Agricola served Otho because he was a Caesar, and for him that took precedence over any friendship, even one as long as ours. I didn't like it, but at least I could understand it. Perhaps one day I might forgive him . . .

It was less than a month since we had won Vitellius his throne at Bedriacum, but the empire's administration is a slow and lumbering machine. Imperial freedmen and clerks still push pieces of paper from one room to the next. If the people of a town in Syria wish to dedicate their temple to the new emperor, such a magnanimous gesture deserves an immediate and grateful response from the imperial bureaucracy. Instead, the request may take months of consultation, discussion and ratification and if an official stamp of approval arrives in Syria a year later, the clerks pat themselves on the back for their thorough and efficient service.

Many of the imperial freedmen had been in Rome long before Vitellius, Otho or even Galba had become emperor. Most of them started their careers under the young Nero, while some had seen service under Caligula and Claudius. It was little wonder that the bureaucratic machine creaked so slowly.

The morning after the party my lictors cleared a path through the crowd outside my door. Clients, would-be clients, beggars, petitioners, all of them clamoured for my attention. The vicious axe-heads, the sturdy rods, the dagger at my waist, they all warned the throng of people not to come too close: impeding a consul carries an automatic sentence of death. I had Totavalas grab a handful of petitions before my little convoy marched down the hill to my new workplace. Not the Senate house, but the Golden Palace where Vitellius had made himself at home. The colossus of Nero smiled beatifically down at us, his arm outstretched in a pose of imperious salutation. The Hibernian was awestruck by his surroundings. So had all Rome been when Nero had begun his building spree in the wake of the Great

Fire not five years before. The Golden Palace was a hedonist's heaven, a complex of beautiful gardens, a massive bathhouse, dozens of bedrooms for Nero's guests, each assigned a pretty slave girl, or boy for that matter.

But Vitellius was a family man. Galeria had borne him a son and a daughter, and the pleasures that Vitellius sought were more gastronomic than carnal. There was talk of expanding the kitchens and doubling the palace's complement of cooks. Already the finest culinary minds from across the empire were flocking to Rome, offering their services. However, it was the west wing of the palace that was calling to me.

Valens had already found himself an office. I caught a glimpse of him hard at work through the open door; no surprise there. He had always been a material man, and it was the countless opportunities for skimming money from the treasury that appealed to him more than the flummery of the Senate. At the other end of the corridor was another office. My office. And in the anteroom was a desk.

'My desk?' Totavalas asked.

'Your desk.'

Totavalas took his seat behind the desk. He looked down at the stylus and wax tablets, waiting to be used. 'A man could get used to this!'

'Don't get too used to it, this is just your imperial office.'

'You mean there's more?'

'Your job here won't be too difficult. In the palace I want you to be my fixer, making sure the other freedmen are doing their jobs efficiently, and making the two of us a nice profit in the meantime.'

'Grand. And outside the palace?'

'Take a look in the top drawer,' I said, anticipating his reaction. The Hibernian's expression turned from puzzled to amazed when he discovered the hefty pouch. There was a metallic clunk as he dropped it on to the desk.

'Call it a signing-on bonus,' I said. 'Now look in the next drawer.'

Out came another bag of gold. 'Don't tell me, this one's a loyalty bonus!'

'Not exactly. I want you to set up a ring of spies and informers in the city. Knowledge is power, and never more so than in Rome. If there's a spice shipment that's ripe for some extra taxing, I want to know about it. If a senator is plotting something, you must be the first to hear about it. Most importantly, I want to know what Valens is up to before he knows himself.'

'Understood, Consul.'

'And you don't have to call me consul when we're alone. Call me Severus, you've earned that right.'

Totavalas smiled. 'Understood, Severus.'

There was a knock at the door. A small, furtive-looking man appeared.

'My apologies for disturbing you, Consul, but the man you sent for has arrived.'

'Thank you, Demetrios. Totavalas, meet your new secretary.'

'Secretary?' Totavalas looked worried. 'I can't afford a secretary yet.'

'Don't fret, man. Vitellius is paying. Is everything ready?' I asked the little Greek.

'Yes, Consul. I have two guards on standby, they'll be outside when you need them, and one of the palace cooks has just fired up his oven.'

'Good man. We'll probably need a slave with a mop too.'

'Very good, Consul.'

'Right, bring him in.'

The Greek left to carry out my instructions. Totavalas looked at me quizzically. 'What's going on?'

'A little unfinished business from Hispania,' I said. 'Have you had your breakfast yet?'

'Yes,' he answered.

'Then we may need two mops.' I heard footsteps along the corridor. 'I'll wait for him in my office. Send the man through, then have the guards come in when I call them.'

I left the anteroom, closing the door behind me. My office was much larger, with a fine balcony that looked out westwards over the forum. Leaning on the rails and looking upwards I could see the temple to Jupiter, Best and Greatest, looming over us all at the top of the Capitoline Hill. I prayed silently to the god, lord and master of the heavens, hoping that he would understand and forgive what I was about to do. My anger at Quintus's death had not passed with time, it had merely bubbled and boiled beneath the surface. I wanted revenge on someone, somehow, and there was a promise I had made a long time ago to the man who gave Galba the tools to strip me of my hard-earned rewards.

Behind me the door opened, and the man shuffled in.

'Consul?' he said questioningly. I didn't move, letting him see nothing more than my back.

'Your name?' I asked.

'Melander, sir.'

'Do you know why you're here, Melander?'

'I have a letter here, from the emperor himself,' the clerk said proudly. 'He even used mud from the battlefield he was so keen to write to me. But I can't think why he wrote to me of all people.'

'This is a new age for Rome. We want the best and the brightest to govern the empire. It came to my attention that you are one of the finest clerks in your province. Am I right?'

'So some have said, Consul,' Melander said bashfully.

'But talent is all very well. There is one quality I prize above all others. Do you know what that is?'

'No, Consul, but I hope I have it.'

I smiled at the irony. I had been rehearsing this moment in my mind ever since the death of my friend; all those long days as we marched to Rome, the entire empire waiting for me, my prize. Still the clerk suspected nothing.

'Loyalty,' I said, then turned to confront the greasy Hispanian. His olive skin paled, a look of horror settling on his face as he recognized me. For a moment he stood there dumbstruck. Then he saw my hand reach down towards my dagger. That got him moving. He was out through the door in a flash. There was a scream and the sound of two bodies smacking together.

The guards brought the clerk back into the room, wicked smiles on their faces, men chosen for their strength and lack of scruples. Totavalas watched from the doorway. I advanced on the clerk.

'You sold me out the moment you knew I wasn't coming back to Hispania, didn't you? I didn't see a single denarius of the money you stole for me. You've probably tucked it away safe somewhere, bought yourself a nice new villa, I'll bet. I was Galba's blue-eyed boy until you betrayed me.'

'Please, sir,' the man pleaded, 'I didn't know, I didn't think—'

'You're damn right you didn't think. You didn't think about the promise I made.' I lifted the dagger, pointed it first at his face then slowly lowered it towards his crotch. The wretched man wriggled and squirmed, but the guards had him in a vice-like grip.

'Tell these men here what I promised to do to you if you betrayed me.'

He was crying now, too petrified even to speak.

'I'm going to slice off your balls,' I said. 'That's the first thing I'll do. Then you're going to eat them. I've even had one of the emperor's cooks lined up to roast them for you. What a lucky man you are. Most of Rome would give an arm and a leg to have something prepared by an imperial chef. Hold him still, lads.'

A rummage under his toga and a vicious sawing action brought the little buggers free. A high-pitched scream pierced the air; a small patch of blood began to stain the man's toga, while more dripped steadily on to the floor.

'And for the final course,' I reminded him, staring the traitor in the face, 'a sharp stake served Parthian style, rammed so far up your arse you'll feel it tickling your throat.' The man was wailing and writhing, his severed balls lying in the palm of my hand.

'Have these delivered to the kitchens, and take this filth to his private dining room. Then finish the job.'

'Yes, sir,' a guard answered, taking the warm handful from me and dropping them into a pouch. Totavalas stepped quickly aside to let the men and their flailing captive past. He looked at the pool of blood on the flagstones, then up at me.

'Was that really necessary?' he asked.

I looked him squarely in the eyes. 'A promise is a promise.'

XX

Totavalas spent the next few days in the city itself rather than in the Golden Palace. Not, I hasten to add, because he had a weak stomach, but because he was busy making useful contacts in the lower reaches of the city. As a freedman, and a barbarian freedman at that, he could go places where I couldn't: dark alleyways and dirty buildings on the Aventine, the hill that loomed over the city docks and the place where the rougher elements of the plebs lived, or at least did their business.

I'd like to say those were happy days for me. Looking back on it, you'd think I didn't have any reasons to complain. I was the first consul in my family for three generations, married to a beautiful wife, blessed with a son, lived in one of the grandest palaces in Rome and at the beginning of a glittering career. Salonina had even floated the idea of proposing little Aulus as a match for Vitellius's daughter. It certainly wasn't a bad idea.

But Salonina, she was part of the trouble. Or to be fair to her memory, I wrongly thought she was part of the trouble. Valens was himself looking for a wife, and there were any number of ambitious women in Rome who would sacrifice a cheerful, doting husband to ally themselves with one of the emperor's trusted lieutenants. But in the meantime, my wife was the first lady in Rome, after Vitellius's wife Galeria, of course. But Galeria didn't have the flair for entertaining that Salonina did. The trouble was I felt that she was married more to her social circle than she was to me. On the occasions that I could drag myself away from the Golden Palace or the Senate house there was always some soirée, poetry reading or dinner going on at home. Then I would have to play the dutiful husband. And when we were rid of our last guests, Salonina was in no condition to fulfil her wifely duties. There were still another six weeks of pregnancy to go. It was women's politics, I understand that now. What I mistook for social climbing was actually Salonina fighting my corner but in her own way, charming and flattering the great and the good in ways that I could not. My only consolation was that in another month or so my turn to lead the business of the Senate would end and Valens would have the tedious duty. Then the pair of us would journey to my estate in Vicetia and await the birth of the child, together.

Not that Salonina ever sensed my unhappiness. She was spending all her time with the matriarchs of Rome. It was only when I was enjoying a rare moment with Aulus that it struck me how alone I really was. We were in the courtyard, playing with wooden swords that had the centre hollowed out and filled with lead to strengthen the arms and wrists.

'Do you miss Britannia, Father?'

'Why do you say that?' I asked, breathing hard. My shoulder was on the mend and I was finally free of the sling, but the arm had grown weak through lack of use.

'You don't talk much about the time you spent in Gaul, and you don't seem all that happy here.'

'Britannia's a cold, wretched, dismal island on the edge of the world. Rome has culture, civilization.'

'Or do you mean it has more theatres and bathhouses?'

'True enough. The Britons stink like animals. But if they will let their livestock sleep in the hut . . .'

'But what about your legion, Father? Did you like it there?'

'Like it? It's the only decent life for a Roman. A hard day's march, a good scrap with the tribes in the north,' I said, more to remind myself than to tell Aulus.

'Will I fight barbarians too?' The boy slashed about with his sword at imaginary enemies.

'I hope so, one day. Not for another ten years though; I wouldn't want you going north as young as eighteen. Let's sit down a while, eh? My arm's not ready to take on a little lion like you quite yet.'

A slave brought us some water and we drank it eagerly. Aulus still had more questions.

'And will I join your legion?'

'The Twentieth? I don't see why not. They sent a detachment to reinforce the emperor when we left the Rhine. They should be approaching the Po by now. It'll be good to see some friendly faces again.'

'I'd like to make some friends,' Aulus said wistfully.

'I know how you feel,' I said. 'When I was growing up, nobody wanted to know my family. An old name with no money counts for very little in Rome these days. I had Julius Agricola though. And Domitia, she had the two of us eating out of the palm of her hand!'

'I'm not going to marry Julia now, am I?' he asked.

'Their daughter? No, not now. Her father and I had an argument, you see.'

'I'd still like to meet her though. I don't have any friends in Rome; Mother hardly lets me out of the house.'

'I'm sorry, Aulus. She's been busy making new friends.'

'They're your friends too,' he said accusingly.

'No they're not,' I scoffed. 'A bunch of self-important, prattling gossips discussing the latest Parthian silks and the cost of a good house slave? Give me a bunch of legionaries any day. Their manners may not be the best, but you don't need manners in the tavern, or on the battlefield.'

'Who are your friends then, Father?'

I paused to think. Valens was no friend, nor was Vitellius, not really. 'Totavalas,' I said.

'That's one,' Aulus said.

I concentrated hard. The Agricola family no longer counted. Quintus, the friend I did not deserve, lay in a shallow grave at Bedriacum. 'Publilius, definitely. And Cerberus and Pansa.'

'Four.'

Who else was there? Most of the friends I had made in Gaul were dead too, killed by Roman swords and spears. And it had been six, no, seven years since my days in Britannia. The men I had known in my legion would be dwindling with every passing month, some lost to retirement, others to disease or a tribesman's knife.

'Can we finish our game later, Aulus? I've had a long day.'

'Come on, Father, you haven't even got to five yet!'

'Later, Aulus!' I barked. My son dropped his sword and fled. It was only then that I realized I had lifted my hand as if about to strike.

There was a gentle cough. It was one of the slaves, asking if I could return to the palace. Apparently there was a batch of papers that I had forgotten to sign, and they had to be done today or some town somewhere wouldn't be getting their tax rebate that year or some such trivia. It was late evening by the time I returned from the tavern where I occasionally took some of the underlings for a drink. It helped show them that I was a caring master, not a cold fish like Valens. Tired, hungry and swaying very gently, I was ready for a hearty supper and some time with my family. Only there was no supper, just a gaggle of stuffy, middle-aged women sitting like statues, listening to a Greek poet perform some banal ode.

There was an empty seat reserved for me at Salonina's side and I slumped into it noisily, drawing a sharp intake of breath from the ladies and a few irritated looks. I tried to listen to the poet and discover if he was reciting a well-known work or something that he had composed himself. After a good few verses I still couldn't tell.

'What is this blather?'

'This is Polycrites, Athens's finest poet for a generation. We've paid good money to hear him.'

'You mean I've paid good money,' I said darkly.

'Call it an investment, Caecina. These women are all married to powerful men in the Senate, useful friends to have, don't you think?'

'Very well. How much longer are they going to be here for?'

'Perhaps another hour.'

'An hour?' I said loudly. The women looked round, and Salonina flashed her eyes warningly.

After a quarter of an hour of tedious poetry I was in desperate need of another drink. I called for a slave to bring me some wine, prompting more dirty looks and even a shush or two.

Slowly, angrily, I got up. 'I will not be shushed in my own home.'

The poet stopped, looking quizzically at Salonina, who was hiding her face in her hands.

'This is my house, my home, and I'll do what I like in it.' There was a quiet forcefulness in my voice. 'If you don't like it, you know what you can do.'

The women exchanged a few nervous glances, then began to file out. Salonina didn't move. The slave brought me my wine as I watched the ladies soothe and praise the Greek, muttering that some people just didn't have a taste for real art or some such bilge.

It was only when the last of them went that Salonina spoke. 'I hope you're proud of yourself.'

'In actual fact I am.'

'Do you know how long it took me to get those women to accept me as one of them?'

'That's because they see you for what you are. You're a trades-man's daughter playing at being a lady.'

'Is that so?' she said, her nostrils flaring.

'I'm sorry but it's true. If you didn't go out of your way to impress those women, they'd accept you for who you are. Then you'd have some real friends, not just hangers-on who only suffer your bloody poetry sessions because you're the consul's wife!'

'So now I'm just the consul's wife?' she said, getting to her feet. 'I'm just some pretty thing you wheel out to entertain your colleagues and plough into so that she can give you children, is that it?'

'Now you're just being ridiculous,' I said, taking a gulp of wine.

Salonina's face was red with anger. 'Am I? Thanks to me, Valens can't even get a look-in to any social event in the city. The only power he has is with the army. You have soldiers of your own, a healthy son who respects you and a wife who slaves away to win you powerful friends in the Senate, and what thanks do I get?'

'A palace, a bigger wardrobe than Cleopatra ever had and the privilege of being wife to the first man in Rome, not count-ing our beloved, bloated emperor. You can even arrange your dream marriage for Aulus, now I've had to sacrifice my friends for your ambition.'

'My ambition! You're going to stand there and say you didn't want all this? This is our victory.'

I flung down the cup, which shattered on the floor, silencing Salonina. 'Not if I'd known what it would cost!' I roared. 'I've watched good men die, Salonina, and for what? Good men who didn't know they were fighting for a lost cause, and men who fought for something they didn't believe in. They did it for me, and now I'm here, Rome kissing my feet. My friends are dead or they don't want to know me, I've a son who's scared of me, a wife who loves privilege more than she loves me, and I have to battle every day to keep what I've built from crashing down. Where's the victory in that?'

I stood there, my chest heaving. Salonina stood her ground, saying nothing. All I could think to do was to get out of there. 'Fine then, enjoy your spoils, keep your palace. I'm going home,' I said, turning round and marching towards the door.

'Caecina, be reasonable. Everything I've done, I've done for you, for us!' Salonina called after me. But I was too angry to listen. She was right, of course, but I didn't think that at the time. I just wanted to be alone with my anger. I slammed the door behind me and stormed into the night.

Of course it was only when I was outside my old family home that I remembered I had rented it out to the people from whom we'd commandeered the villa, so at midnight I found myself heading once again to the Golden Palace. There were over a dozen bedrooms to spare, and I worked off my anger on the poor slave girl whose role it was to entertain the room's guest.

The next morning I found Vitellius having a late breakfast of oysters and prawns, caught less than a day ago by the fishermen of Baiae and Pompeii, then carted north in amphorae of sea water so that they could be cooked in the kitchens and served as freshly as if the emperor had haggled with the fishermen himself. In between mouthfuls he was poring over some papers that Valens held in front of him.

'I didn't expect to see you today, Severus,' the emperor said. 'It's Valens's turn to give me my morning brief.'

'I understand he made use of one of the palace rooms last night, sire,' Valens informed him, a smug smile on his face. 'Fancied a little entertainment, did we?'

'My private life is none of your concern,' I said loftily.

'Surely the emperor has a right to know who's staying in his home,' he countered.

'Calm down, boys,' Vitellius said affectionately. 'Come and have a look at these plans Valens has drawn up.'

I came over and stood behind Vitellius's shoulder. It was a plan of the Circus Maximus, with sketches of the four teams and notes scrawled underneath them.

'It's a simple enough idea, but Rome won't have seen anything like it. Chariot races, but without horses.'

'Isn't that fantastic, Severus?' Vitellius said, his eyes never leaving the plans.

'Lions, camels, tigers,' I read aloud, 'and what are the last ones? Rhinoceroi?'

'It's what the Greeks call them, it means horned nose. They're huge beasts, like oxen but with a thick black hide and two horns on their snout. Rhinoceroses in Latin.'

'Where on earth did you find them?'

'A trader from Africa had a pair of them. Apparently there's a country south of the great desert where the creatures live.'

'Is this the same land where the men have their eyes and nose on their chest?' I asked scathingly.

'Yes, the Blemmyes,' Vitellius said enthusiastically. 'I heard men talk about them when I was stationed in Africa. Do you think we could send an expedition across the desert one day?'

'It would be very hard, and very expensive, sire,' I said.

'And why should a trifling matter like expense stop the emperor of Rome from achieving his dreams?' Valens asked me.

'He's right, Severus. It was only thanks to the persuasion of you and your men that I allowed myself to become emperor in the first place. Now that I'm here I'm going to enjoy myself.'

'Of course you should, sire. If you leave it with me, I'll start preparations for an expedition right away.'

'Thank you, Valens. You know, Severus, you could learn a

thing or two from your fellow consul. Stop fretting about money, enjoy yourself! Have an oyster.'

'No thank you, sire. If you don't mind, Valens and I need to have a brief talk.'

'Anything I could help you with?'

'If you'd like to, sire,' I said. 'It's about tax evasion in Illyria.'

'On second thoughts, I'll leave you two to it.'

Valens waited until we were in his office and his secretary was out of earshot. 'What's all this guff about tax evasion then?'

'Nothing, I just didn't want to involve Vitellius in our little discussion.'

'Fine, what's so important that you want to talk to me alone? Want my advice on how to patch it up with your wife?'

'Leave my wife out of it,' I snapped. Valens smiled at the reaction he'd provoked.

'Touchy this morning, aren't we? So if it's not the shambles that is your love life, what is it?'

'Are you seriously going to waste hundreds of thousands, maybe millions of denarii on a junket across the desert, to a land no Roman has ever seen, just so that Vitellius can have a look at some oxen with horns on their snout rather than their head?'

'Of course not.'

I was confused. 'But you just promised Vitellius—'

'To keep him sweet, yes. Like this fad of his with chariot racing, except that will actually happen. Don't you understand? I keep Vitellius happy, and in return he gives me what I want.'

'What do you want that you haven't already got?' I asked.

'I don't know yet, but I'm sure I'll think of something. At the moment, I'll settle for more money than I know what to do with.'

'And all the while I'm trying to sort out the mess at the treasury, what with Nero's debts, and Otho's, and at the same time having to pay the army?'

'You can do that if you like, but you'll get no thanks from Vitellius for it. Like he said, you could learn a thing or two from me. Now if you'll excuse me, my man Priscus wants to see me about a pay rise for the new batch of praetorians we're recruiting.' He took a scroll and his copy of the imperial seal then left me, alone and in his office.

He was right, of course. I had been naive to think that Vitellius would reward me for trying to get a grip on the empire's spiralling debts, a problem that would only worsen with his outlandish and fanciful whims. I looked down dejectedly, and my eye fell on the pile of papers sitting on Valens's desk. Even upside down I could make out the letters at the top of some sort of list: PG applicants. PG . . . Praetorian Guard, it had to be. Why had Valens not told me he was shortlisting men for the new praetorian vacancies? Then the reason dawned on me. Hastily I grabbed the pile and strode out into the corridor.

I was heading towards my own office when a voice called behind me: 'Consul?'

It was Valens's secretary, yet another Greek, middle-aged and sporting an immaculately trimmed beard. An effete little man. 'Yes?' I held the pile close to my chest, hoping the man was too far away to recognize the pages.

'Did Consul Valens say where he was going?'

'He was going to speak to the praetorian prefect over at their barracks. If you run you might catch him before he leaves the palace.'

The Greek rolled his eyes at the thought of running. 'Thank you, sir,' he said, before swiftly about-turning and jogging off after his master. Relief washed over me, and I forced myself to walk slowly to my own office. A consul carrying paperwork does not run in palace corridors.

Totavalas was perched on the corner of Demetrios' desk and the two of them were in a deep discussion when I came in. 'What are you doing here?' the Hibernian asked.

'Well, hello to you too,' I said. 'Ink at the ready, men, there's work to do.'

'Shouldn't you be at home?' Totavalas asked, quickly adding the word 'sir' when he remembered that we weren't alone.

'Not when I've got the most important papers in all Rome here in my arms,' I replied. 'This is a list of all the men from the Rhine legions who've applied to join the Praetorian Guard. And the three of us are going to pick just the right men for the job.'

Later that day Vitellius was attending the theatre, and as I had no plans to go home he had asked Valens and me to join him. I was surprised that Valens had agreed, not being a natural theatre-goer, but Vitellius explained to me as he languidly signed some official papers during the interval that the man was trying to smooth away the rough edges of his reputation in the hope of finding himself a beautiful wife.

'Beauty isn't everything,' I remarked bitterly.

'Very true,' Vitellius agreed. 'I mean to say, if I weren't married, and if I weren't emperor, what right-thinking girl would choose to marry a man like me?'

'Sire, you are a man of style and substance. The lady Galeria is very fortunate in you.'

Vitellius smiled. 'Style and substance, eh? I like that. Do you mind if I use that line myself?'

'I would be honoured, sire.'

The actors were coming back on to the stage. It was some hammed-up tragedy, something about a Greek king killing his father and marrying his mother, I think, and out of boredom I found myself looking around the audience for faces I knew. A pair of eyes met mine. They were green eyes, green with the faintest hint of blue. The eyelids batted once, twice, and I thought I saw the ghost of a smile on that beautiful face. My heart convulsed. In years gone by I would have given anything for a batted eyelid from that woman, but since my marriage I had learned to bury my feelings for her. I had buried them so deep I'd forgotten I had them. Domitia was as beautiful as she'd ever been, and it was only when Vitellius tugged my sleeve that I was woken from my reverie.

'Severus, are you listening to me?'

I was back in the imperial box, mind and body, and Vitellius was looking at me earnestly.

'Sire?'

'I was saying that, what with the new men we've appointed to the Senate, and now that you and Valens have been made consuls, one of the praetors won't be able to take a province next year. I mean, there are only so many imperial provinces to go around. Unless you or Valens wants to forfeit that right? Who do you think it should be?'

'Julius Agricola is not a friend of yours, sire,' I said.

'Really? I heard he was on the wrong side at Bedriacum, but I'm told he's a very efficient man.'

'He is, but he hasn't earned the right to govern a province in your name.'

'If you say so, Severus.'

I wasn't listening any more. I was watching the beautiful woman and thinking of what might have been.

XXI

The preparations for the horseless chariot races were well under way. Vitellius never needed an excuse to go and watch his beloved Blues at the circus, but ostensibly the exotic occasion was to celebrate the unity of the empire, reinforced by the arrival of the detachments from its most far-flung province: Britannia. Three thousand men, a thousand from each legion, had marched half the length of Gaul with Vitellius while the rest of the army was doing the actual fighting against Otho. When the news of Bedriacum reached him, the emperor had ridden over the Alps to join us, leaving the legionaries to march the rest of the way alone. The logic was that after being posted in the far north of the world, few if any of the men would ever have seen a camel or a tiger, let alone one of those rhinoceros creatures.

The new arrivals would cause something of a headache though, as we had nowhere to put them. Already a part of the army, those that overflowed the temporary camp we had built on the Field of Mars had been billeted with civilians in the city. One bit of good news though was that we would soon be able to transfer some men into the praetorian camp, outside the Colline Gate. Valens was furious when he found out I'd taken his precious list.

'What the fuck do you think you're playing at?' he had shouted, storming into my office. Demetrios had scuttled off, leaving Totavalas and me to face the man's fury.

'I'm not playing at anything,' I said coolly.

'Don't get smart with me. You swiped the praetorian list from off my desk and chose thousands of your own men over mine.'

'That's a bit rich considering you were going to do exactly the same thing if I hadn't found those papers. Besides, if you check the list, of the eight thousand places that need to be filled I think you'll find that there are just as many men from your province as there are from mine.'

'Eh?'

'Give him the figures,' I told Totavalas.

'Eight thousand men,' the Hibernian explained, 'two thousand from your legions in Lower Germania, two thousand from Upper Germania, half of Pansa's legion from Raetia, and the other two thousand from the detachments from Britannia. Nice and even, at least that's what we thought.'

'Don't give me even. Pansa's men marched with you, they're loyal to you, not me.'

'Their loyalty is to the emperor, not to you or me, Valens,' I reminded him, enjoying the sight of my rival squirming with anger.

'I'll talk to Vitellius about this.'

'Why?' I asked. 'Why should he object that his guards are evenly recruited from four different provinces? You can ask him if you like, but he's already signed and sealed my recommendations.'

Valens said nothing, simply turning a shade of puce and slamming the door behind him.

'Wait till he hears that I'm something of a hero among the legions from Britannia,' I told Totavalas gleefully.

The Britannian detachments were given a muted reception from the citizens. They had had to put up and indeed put up with thousands of soldiers being billeted within the city walls. Not just the legionaries, but all the Germans, Gauls, Britons, Lusitanians and Africans had to be housed too, and it didn't go down well with their new landlords, men and women who had been born and raised in Rome. All would be forgiven, however, when the day of the chariot race arrived.

Salonina and I were still not reconciled, and I saw very little of Aulus. With a few days' notice I evicted the rich couple from my family home and began to live there. I spent long days at the Golden Palace, trying to bury myself in work. Some days I even enjoyed the tedium of the Senate, simply because it added variety to my day. All the while Vitellius threw lavish parties that Valens and I had begun to tire of, but it was only so often we could refuse an invitation from the emperor.

On a particularly sweltering summer evening Demetrios brought me a note. The message was scrawled hastily in spidery handwriting: 'Meet me at the Argosy docks in the Aventine at sunset. Wear a hooded cloak and dress down. T.'

'When did Totavalas give you this?' I asked the secretary.

'It was given to me by a street boy, Consul.'

'Then how can you be sure it comes from Totavalas?'

'He's used the boy before.' That was good to hear. It meant that the Hibernian was making good use of the gold I had given him. It was less than an hour to sunset, so I hurried off to my empty home, donned the appropriate gear and then dismissed my lictors until morning. True, I would need protection if I was to go skulking around the Aventine, but then even disguised and without their *fasces* the guards would have stuck out sorer than a Vestal Virgin.

The sun had disappeared behind the Janiculum Hill by the time I reached the docks. The last workers were unloading the barges that had come up the river from Ostia. Cargoes of marble ordered in Otho's time were still arriving from Egypt; clearly he had planned to carry on the building programme that his erstwhile friend Nero had started. This part of Rome had been one of the hardest hit by the Great Fire, which had torn huge chunks out of the city, and work was still being done to replace the lost houses; though with the treasury pouring its money into delicacies for Vitellius rather than bricks and mortar, if we weren't careful we'd soon have a housing crisis on our hands.

I was running my fingers through the grain in one of the many sacks by the wharf when someone tapped me on the shoulder. Instinctively I reached for my small dagger, only to realize it was Totavalas. He looked me up and down.

'And there was I thinking I'd seen the last of those trousers,' he said.

'No one's going to mistake me for a nobleman in these things.'

'Better hope that an auxiliary doesn't speak to you in German, or we really will be in trouble.'

'Jupiter! I didn't think of that.'

'That's what comes of living in palaces and marble halls all your life.'

'And what about the years I spent in Britannia and my spell as Vindex's nephew in Gaul?' I retorted.

'Granted, there are precious few palaces beyond the Alps, but I doubt you stopped acting like a nobleman for one moment.'

'Just you watch me then,' I said, clearing my throat noisily before spitting between his feet.

'Well done, very common. But let's get moving, eh? Two men standing by the docks, one of them a handsome man, if I do say so myself, people will think I'm a rent boy.'

'Where are we going?'

'You'll see.'

We headed deeper into the Aventine, past the huge grain silos which stored the winter reserves. During the season ships would come from all over the empire, filled to the brim with grain. Some would come from Hispania and Africa, but the bulk of our grain supply came from Egypt, which is why the Divine Augustus had turned it into a personal fiefdom of the emperor, governed by a hand-picked procurator and with the Syrian legions close at hand to secure the region if it looked like there was going to be trouble.

Totavalas led me to a tavern another couple of streets away, a regular haunt of veterans or current soldiers on leave. Not because of the bracing sea breeze, Totavalas joked darkly, but because of the entertainment the establishment offered and the 10 per cent discount for anyone with the mark of the legions on them. Inside the place stank of rotting fish, sweat and cheap wine. In classier establishments, so they tell me, they sprinkle oriental perfumes or burn scented sticks to at least try to cover up the smell. But this place had no such pretensions. It was a place for whores, gambling, drinking and catching up on army gossip.

I was chary about lowering my hood in case someone recognized me, but Totavalas assured me my legionaries were all posted on the other side of the city. Besides, it would have looked strange, a hooded man in a warm, sweaty tavern on a summer's night; out in the streets with the dusty winds from Africa, understandable, but not inside. Cautiously I lowered the hood as Totavalas ordered us some wine.

'How much do I owe you?' I asked, reaching for some coins in my trouser pocket. Totavalas kicked me under the table.

'Gods, but would you keep still? Do you want every cut-throat in this place to see where you keep your gold? I'll pay, they know me here.'

A shapely woman sauntered slowly over, bringing the wine. Standing at my side, she made a great show of putting down the two cups and leaning over the table to pour the powerfully scented wine. I say she was shapely; her breasts were so large she almost blotted out Totavalas from view.

'If you ever want anything special, love, just tip me the wink, all right?'

I was in the middle of giving a polite 'thanks, but no thanks' when she interrupted me. 'Who says I was talking to you?'

'You'll have to forgive my friend, he has an ego the size of an elephant.'

'That's all right, dear. Just so long as you know I don't shack up with any old bloke that comes through the door.'

'You're enjoying this, aren't you?' I said accusingly, once the whore had gone.

'If possible, I do like to try and mix in a little pleasure with business. Drink up, we've got a while yet before your man'll be ready.'

'What man?'

'The man we're here to talk to. But first I ought to show you something.' He fished around inside the satchel I'd given him for his papers, then brought out a wax tablet. I reached out and turned it the right way up. It was a bill of sale, a receipt for an entire shipload of grain bought by a private citizen.

'You're sure this is genuine?'

'Well, it's a genuine copy. I had the merchant transcribe this from the original.'

'Who'd want to buy an entire ship's worth of grain? The only buyers that rich are the guild of bakers or the treasury.'

'Take a look at the name of the buyer,' the Hibernian said before taking a sip of wine.

'Titus Flavius Sabinus,' I read. 'I know him.'

'Of course you know him! He's prefect of the urban cohorts. Technically, he was the most powerful man in Rome when Otho left the city and we arrived. All the praetorians had marched north, and his were the only troops left. To be fair, it is his job to organize the buying of grain for the dole, but you see he's bought it himself, not through the usual state channels.'

'So what's he doing buying up massive grain supplies?'

273

Totavalas's eyes flickered behind me. 'Here's a man who might be able to tell you.'

'Gaius, you little rogue,' a rough voice called out. 'Where's that drink you promised me?'

'Gaius?' I mouthed. Totavalas winked.

'We've had to start without you, friend. But let me get you a cup.'

A burly-looking man plonked himself down on the bench next to me. He stank fit to make even Hades retch. 'Budge up a bit, can't you?'

Sullenly I shifted along a space, then looked at our guest a little closer. Despite his size I reckoned he was barely into his twenties, and clearly he was enjoying the delights that Rome had to offer a young man. Even sitting down his frame swayed slightly, like a young oak in a storm. The wine stains on his toga were so severe that they even showed against the deep red military dye.

'On leave?' I guessed.

'Something like that,' the man said. His sluggish hand grasped the cup that Totavalas put before him. 'And taking advantage of the kindness of strangers, to boot!'

'I'm not strange!' Totavalas said.

'Ha! You're all right, Gaius, a bit small and skinny for a Roman, but you're all right.'

'I told you yesterday, I'm a Hibernian.'

'Hibernia? Where's that then?'

'It's an island . . . oh, what's the point? You'll only forget again by the time we meet tomorrow.'

'Likely as not,' the sturdy soldier agreed, downing his cup in one go, then smacking his lips appreciatively. 'Who's your silent friend?' he asked, flicking his head towards me.

'Oh, him? This is my German friend, we call him Herman.'

'Herman the German?' the soldier laughed at his own wit. The two of us played along.

'I should've guessed. You look like a German, come to think of it,' he continued. I sat bolt upright. No I did not! Totavalas saw my reaction and kicked me again.

'Tell Herman what you were telling me last night,' Totavalas said, pouring our new friend another cup of wine. I had a sip of my own, almost spitting it back into the cup, the taste was so vinegary.

'What about?'

'Your legion, of course.'

'He doesn't know?'

'You haven't told him yet. Come on, start at the beginning.'

'When you bring over another pitcher of wine, sure.'

Another pitcher duly arrived. Then and only then would the soldier begin his tale.

'I'm a Hispanian, I am. From Tarraco, or at least I was. A year ago I signed up to join a new legion, named after our governor. The Seventh Galbiana, the best legion in the whole damn world, that's us. Anyway, our Governor Galba only goes and becomes emperor.'

'Tell us something we don't know!' I exclaimed.

The young man looked at me curiously. 'You don't sound very German to me.'

'He's only half-German,' Totavalas explained. 'He's more of a Roman than I am! Go on, what's happening with your legion now.'

'All right. Well, the legion was given a new legate when the old one was put in charge of the praetorians. Antonius Primus, that's his name. Then we were shipped off to Pannonia. Horrible place, nothing but smelly tribesmen and hills you can barely scratch a living out of. When we heard the news that Vitellius was coming south, we all hoped to be involved, one way or another. But Otho didn't summon us. Maybe he thought that as Galba had recruited us we would have joined Vitellius. But it would have been nice to be asked.'

'And now someone is asking,' Totavalas said, more to me than to his drinking companion.

'Right. I was just saying to the lads before I got my . . . leave, we were saying how it was only the western legions who'd had any say in deciding who should be emperor. Now the eastern legions want their turn. After all, we can easily beat Vitellius's German lot, can't we, Gaius? Oh, no offence, Herman.'

'None taken,' I assured him.

'Good man. Now where was I?' The words were beginning to slur now. Totavalas was keen to get the rest of the story out before the man lost the thread completely.

'News from the east,' he said.

'Oh yes. Anyhow, one day we get word from the centurion that Legate Primus wants to sound out the legion about joining forces with the eastern legions. Turns out while the west has been squabbling among themselves, Nero, Galba, Otho and now Vitellius, the east looks as though it's uniting behind one man: Vespasian.'

'Vespasian? You're sure?' I asked.

'Course I'm sure. He's a good man, given the Jews a good seeing-to. He's not a murderer, he's not a miser or a glutton, and he's not a lofty nobleman like all the bastards who rule Rome. He's a man of the people, and it's about time we had one of them as emperor.'

'I'll drink to that,' Totavalas said. Once we'd all had another cupful, the Hibernian made our excuses. 'You're more than welcome to finish what's left. See you around, friend.'

'You too, Gaius.'

I couldn't wait to get out of that place and into the cool night air. We found a quiet spot where we wouldn't be overheard.

'Frankly, I think Vitellius owes me a bonus,' Totavalas said.

'Don't worry. What do you know about this man Vespasian?'

'Not much more than what the soldier told us. Nero sent him east a few years ago to deal with the Jewish rebellion, he controls

Judaea and Egypt, and has been using the legions in Syria to help him. Done a thorough job so far, from what I've heard.'

'Egypt, that's the key.'

'What about it?'

'It's the bread basket of the empire,' I told him. 'Vespasian can hold back the grain ships any time he chooses. And now we hear Sabinus is buying up the grain we have already.'

'You think Sabinus and Vespasian are linked? I know it's a bit odd Sabinus buying grain privately, but it could be a coincidence.'

'Totavalas,' I said wearily, 'Sabinus is Vespasian's older brother.'

'Ah.' There was nothing more to say.

'You've done bloody well to find this man though,' I told Totavalas. 'Now that summer's here, the trade winds will be blowing east for a couple of months at least. News can travel from here to the east, but not back again, not unless it comes overland through Pannonia, where it seems Primus and his friends aren't interested in peace. They just want another fucking war so Vespasian can give them huge bribes.'

'We don't know for certain that Vespasian's going to do anything. You know how these rumours spread. If he'd been acclaimed as emperor by his own men we'd have heard about it by now. The question is, what do we tell Vitellius?'

'Who says we tell him anything?' I asked.

'Surely we've got to tell the emperor that one of his generals might be plotting against him? It'll be good for both of us if we're the ones to give him the news.'

'I don't want Vitellius knowing yet. Or Valens. The lord of the dinner table is much more manageable when he's happy, and I'd feel safer if Valens thought everything was going swimmingly too. Meanwhile, we two keep our ears to the ground. Knowledge is power at times like these, and I'll be damned if I'm going to share my secrets with those two!'

'All right. Shall I have someone keep an eye on the soldier?'

'You know he's not really on leave, don't you?'

'He said he was,' Totavalas replied.

'The army doesn't grant leave to legionaries, especially not so soon after a war, and not to a man who only left home a year ago.'

'So he's a deserter?'

'A stupid, drink-sodden one. You're seeing him again tomorrow?'

'Yes.'

'Well then, have some men catch him on his way to the tavern. Then I want him sent to Pannonia where he'll be crucified. That should make his comrades think when they're asked if they fancy the idea of deserting their emperor.'

'I rather think it would. If you don't mind, I'll find a few men I know and give them their orders.'

'Good man. See you at the palace tomorrow then?'

We clasped arms in friendship before each heading our separate ways, Totavalas to find his hired hands, and me to my bed. I kept my hood up even once I'd reached the wealthier, safer neighbourhood where my villa was. I was hardly likely to be attacked on my own doorstep. Near the forum I was passing through the few revellers and night-walkers when I noticed a litter carried by four muscular, black slaves. It was very plain and understated, the sort of litter you'd choose for a secret tryst. If we nobles weren't naturally ostentatious I grant you it would be more discreet to travel alone, hooded and cloaked as I was. However, the leopard cannot change his spots, and a noble lady likes to travel in style and comfort, even if she doesn't wish to be seen.

The moon was high in the velvet-black sky by the time I reached my street. Ahead of me the road was empty but for my janitor, who unusually was standing outside my door.

'Anything wrong?' I called out to him.

'No, master,' the slave said. 'I was told to wait out here and deliver this message to you as soon as you returned home.'

'Another message?'

He handed me a slip of vellum. As I brought it up to my eyes to read it by torchlight, my nose caught the delicate scent of perfume. 'Meet me by the Temple of Vesta. Come alone.'

'Was it a woman who delivered this?' I asked the slave.

'It was a woman's hand that came out of the litter, master.'

'Litter?'

'A plain litter, master, carried by four Nubian slaves. They left not ten minutes ago.'

'Send word to my lictors, have them get to the forum in plain clothes. I don't want to be alone if there's trouble.'

'At once, master.'

With a tired sigh, I set off into the night once more.

XXII

The forum had emptied rapidly by now, making the supposedly unobtrusive litter stand out even more. I growled at the street urchins to get out of my way as they packed round the temple, waiting in vain for a glimpse of a Vestal Virgin. Every military instinct told me to turn round and go back home, but what was waiting for me at home? An empty bed, slaves for company and the prospect of another dreary day of administration, and now there was a mysterious summons in the night from a noblewoman, or if not that then a well-heeled merchant's wife, since litters cost a fortune. The litter-makers know that their wares are a social necessity, and can pretty much charge what they like, even for a small and restrained affair like the one that stood before me.

I came as close as I dared to the litter, my eyes darting left and right, searching the shadows for an ambush.

'Who is your mistress?' I called out to the slaves. They didn't move a muscle, but a voice answered from behind the curtains.

'If they answered you that would rather defeat the point of me hiding in here, wouldn't it?'

I relaxed, recognizing the voice. A dainty hand appeared

through the gap in the material and waved me in. Sensing no danger, I dutifully accepted the invitation.

What must I have looked like? A hooded man in a pair of barbarian trousers clambering into a lady's litter; the gossips would've wagged their tongues for a fortnight if they'd only known who we were. And there she was, in all her loveliness. Domitia lay languidly in a stunning blue dress that complimented her pale blonde hair.

'Caecina, you look a sight!'

'I could say the same to you,' I riposted.

'You could. What sort of sight am I? And don't say for sore eyes, I want something original.'

'An unexpected sight then.' She frowned at not receiving the anticipated high praise.

'And there was I going to all sorts of trouble to look nice for you,' she pouted.

'You do look fantastic, but I still didn't expect to see you.'

'After the way you cut Julius and me dead at Salonina's party.'

'Well, technically it was my party,' I said.

'But we both know it was Salonina's way of making her grand entrance into society. One day she'll learn to relax a bit more at these occasions,' she said, stretching her back as she spoke. And I dare any man in my position not to have let his eyes drop ever so slightly towards those delicate breasts that reached upwards as she stretched. Hastily I looked away.

'Why are you here, Domitia? If you've come from Julius, he knows he's dead to me. I completely understand why he came north with Otho. He was a praetor, it was his duty. But he did not have a duty to betray his friend.'

She laughed gently. 'Caecina Severus, the man who thinks he is so much cleverer than the rest of us! If I was coming on behalf of Julius, don't you think I might have just knocked on your door rather than meeting you secretly in the dead of night?'

'Why are you here then?'

'You were half right, actually.' The girlish act was coming to an end. 'I am here for Julius's sake, but he doesn't know I'm here. In fact, he mustn't.'

'Why not?' I asked suspiciously.

'I'm getting to that. Now we know that your man has been scurrying round the Aventine, poking his nose into anything and everything . . .'

'We?'

'Yes, we. You're not the only ones to have spies in the city. We know you've just met with him, so you're now a member of an exclusive little club here in Rome.'

'I don't know what you're talking about,' I said, getting ready to leave.

'Vespasian,' she said quickly. 'You've heard about Vespasian.'

I froze. I didn't like where this was headed.

'What have I heard about Vespasian?' I asked tentatively.

'Oh, don't play games with me, Caecina. You're not a brash little boy any more, and I'm not the little girl you and Julius played with all those years ago. You know as well as I do that Vespasian is considering challenging Vitellius for the throne.'

'And what's that to you, or Julius for that matter?'

'You've made it perfectly clear that Julius has no future so long as Vitellius is emperor, or rather while you are at his side. You get a feeling of satisfaction and revenge from holding Julius back, and good for you. But my interests lie with Vespasian.'

I closed my eyes, remembering. 'Of course, your mother.'

'Well done, Caecina,' Domitia said sarcastically. 'My mother was a Flavian. Vespasian and Sabinus are actually my second cousins once removed, or something like that. Not that Julius remembers these things; he was never going to be even half the politician you've become.'

The pieces were beginning to fall into place.

'I am a consul. I rule the man who rules Rome. Thousands of men have died so that I could get where I am today, good men whose feet Julius isn't worthy to kiss. And you think I would throw all of that away, just because you asked me?'

'Gods, no. Who said anything about throwing it all away? Vespasian can't take all the eastern legions to Rome. The Jews, the Egyptians, the Parthians, they'd all rise up the moment he crossed the Hellespont. Now if there was a man here in Rome that we could rely on, one with influence over the emperor and over his legions, Vespasian would make him as rich as Croesus.'

I pushed the curtain aside. 'Out of the love I once had for you, Domitia, I'm going to pretend this conversation never took place.'

I was half out of the litter when she caught me by the wrist. 'You haven't heard the other part of the reward yet,' she said.

'And what would that be?' I said tiredly.

'Me.'

I slept uneasily that night, Domitia's words turning over in my mind. I still couldn't believe that there might be another civil war within months of our victory at Bedriacum. Even if I did believe it, there was nothing I could do but sit and wait and see what the gods had in store for us. Domitia's offer had been enticing, but I pride myself I am not a slave to my passions. There was no way I was going to make war inevitable by abandoning Vitellius. Useless man that he was, he had been true to his word. I was a consul of Rome, Totavalas and Demetrios were busy making me and themselves rich. How would I profit any better by serving Vespasian?

Pushing those honeyed words to the back of my mind, the next morning I had my body slave dress me in my consular toga. I had a duty to perform in the Senate house that day. After a tedious session of listening to my clients' complaints and petitions, passing judgement and promising to look into their petty requests, I was finally free to leave the villa.

Not that it was an earth-shattering piece of legislation I had to present. It was rather amusing really, compared to the banal grievances that my clients brought to my door, anything from inheritance claims to a collection of tradesmen asking me to revoke a Gaul's licence to sell fish, on the grounds that the stench of his rotten wares was driving away customers. As I approached the Senate steps the citizens, noble and humble alike, hurriedly moved to get out of my way. I miss those days, now that I live alone, without friends and without respect. But then I am always reminded by my fellow senators that it is the office, not the man, that they admire. If I could go back and give the younger Caecina Severus one piece of advice, that would be it.

Inside the seats were already beginning to fill, since this was the last day of Senate business for over a week. Vitellius had made the next few days a public holiday to celebrate, of all things, the unity of the empire, during which time the mob would be entertained with yet more magnificent games and free bread. The nobles would watch the games too and then return to their indolent lives. After that, Valens would take the consul's chair for the month of Augustus, leaving me free for other duties.

The Father of the House, the oldest serving senator, banged his staff on the marble floor, calling the house to order. 'The Senate will hear the motion brought to us by the consul Aulus Caecina Severus.'

I rose, and the senators eyed me keenly. There were a few faces I recognized in the sea of old men in front of me. Agricola was there, of course, on the praetors' bench. So too were my erstwhile governor Verginius Rufus, General Paulinus and Vespasian's brother Sabinus. All of their eyes were fixed on me.

'Conscript fathers,' I began with the formal words, 'I have come to submit a new piece of legislation before you: a radical step that will free Rome of a band of parasites we could well do without.' There were some worried glances among those senators who had made their fortunes as money-lenders.

Commerce was certainly frowned upon among the nobles, but the days when noble blood guaranteed a seat in the Senate were long gone. The house was filled with new men, some of whom were even the sons of freedmen and grandsons of slaves. They had no such scruples.

'Our august emperor, Vitellius Germanicus, wishes you to consider his proposal to banish all soothsayers and fortune-tellers from Italia.'

Sighs of relief on all sides, and some even laughed. It was hardly the most revolutionary piece of legislation to come before the Senate, but I had a part to play, and the men sitting there had theirs too.

'For too long these men have fleeced honest citizens with their babble, supposedly messages from the gods. The peasant in the field or the simple man in the street, wishing to know what the future holds, is quite content to hand over his coins for a white chicken, or a dove, or whatever he can afford. Out comes the knife, a quick poke around the entrails, and the soothsayer gives the answer he thinks will best please his customer. And at the end of the day he probably takes the remains of the sacrificial animals to the butcher, selling a few cuts of meat and having the rest for his supper!'

The senators laughed sycophantically.

'Would anyone care to speak against the motion?' I asked.

An old-fashioned-looking man rose to his feet, wearing just a senatorial robe with no warming toga beneath, a traditionalist of the Catonian school, I guessed.

'I only ask, Consul, whether the temple priests of Italia are to be driven out as well, under the terms of this motion? Our priests and augurs help us to interpret the will of the gods. Are you suggesting they are wrong to do so?'

'Not at all, Senator. Those men are sanctioned by the state to carry out these practices. This law is aimed at the vagrants and amateurs who look into the future for a living, rather than as a calling. The emperor has no desire to offend the gods or attack our customs. He only wishes to save his citizens from swindlers and conmen abusing their faith.'

The farce was drawing to an end. In reality to pass the motion all I had to do was announce that it was the emperor's will, and the senators would fall over themselves to vote as Vitellius wanted them to. But for the sake of the republic, or at least for the sake of appearances, new laws must be put to the Senate, proposed and discussed before they can be voted on. Hence my long-winded speech on the subject, dressed up as a defence of the people's purse-strings only to make my words more enjoyable to deliver. Vitellius had only proposed the law after an encounter with one such soothsayer on his journey through Gaul, when the man had condemned Vitellius for holding a banquet on an inauspicious day!

The wizened senator put the motion to the vote, and hand upon hand went up in favour of the bill. 'Against?' No hands were raised.

'The motion is passed. Further business—'

But the old man was interrupted. There was a clattering of hoofbeats outside the doors to the Senate house and a murmur from those who stood outside, watching the proceedings. In ran an imperial courier, his shoulders slumped forward as though he had been in the saddle for many days.

'I carry a message for the Senate and People of Rome,' he announced. The men whispered among themselves.

'Read it,' I told the man. The rider took out his scroll and broke the seal. He began to read aloud, taking deep breaths when he could.

Senators,

It is my duty as Governor of Moesia to report the rebellion of the Third Gallica Legion, at the command and instigation of their legate, Dillius Aponianus. Having only recently arrived

from service in Syria, the legion has called upon their former
general, Vespasian, to contest the right of Vitellius Germanicus
to the imperial throne.
  Saturninus

There was immediate uproar in the building. Many senators
jumped to their feet to denounce the legion, while others were too
busy arguing among themselves to make a show of outrage until
their friends dragged them to their feet. All eyes were turned to
Vespasian's brother. Sabinus did his best to look shocked.

'Silence!' I shouted, the staff hitting the ground again, the
elderly man calling for order.

As the hubbub began to die down, I stood with my hands
raised, demanding to be heard.

'One legion, one single legion, has dared to mutiny, to rebel
against our emperor. They have not done this for love of the
empire, Senators, but love of power and carnage and war.
Gods, have we not decided upon an emperor who loves his city
more than himself? Did Vitellius not put aside the gaudy title
of Caesar? Are we not blessed to have an emperor who was
reluctant to serve, a man who had to be persuaded that Rome
was in need of him?'

Some of the senators murmured their agreement. Others
smiled, watching me perform a show of loyalty in the hope that
the rest would follow.

'Soldier, has the news been sent to the palace?'

'No, Consul. The governor ordered me to inform the Senate
first.'

I was puzzled. Why would a loyal governor specifically in-
struct his courier to first tell the Senate of a legion's rebellion
against their emperor, rather than the emperor himself?'

'Then with the Senate's leave,' I said, addressing them all,
'I will go to the palace and carry out the wishes of our rightful
emperor.'

The courier and I left, accompanied by a round of polite applause. I took the courier's letter, and his horse, and rode straight to the palace. Valens was in the grand hallway, waiting for me.

'Have you heard the news?' I asked immediately.

'I have, and so has Vitellius.'

'What? How?'

'I have a network of spies among all the legions from Hispania to Moesia; the benefits of a lifetime of making friends in the army. How did the Senate react?'

'As you'd expect,' I said. 'Some of them didn't know how they were meant to react at first, but I assured them it was just a one-off, a Syrian legion that had only recently transferred, that's what the governor said in his message.'

'If only it were.' Valens sighed.

'You mean there's more? Tell me, Valens. I have a right to know.'

'Calm down, boy. Saturninus has toyed with the truth a bit. I'd heard he'd reported the mutiny in a message to the Senate, but I'll bet that message doesn't mention the fact that he decided to join the rebellion the next day?'

'You guessed right,' I said darkly. 'How far has this thing spread?'

'I don't know. It's these damn trade winds, the only news we're likely to get this season will be from Moesia. There's no way of knowing what's going on in Syria, but they'll know everything that happens in Rome. Sabinus will see to that.'

'Do we arrest him?'

'And have the people say Vitellius is scared of one poxy legion?'

'You're right,' I admitted. 'We've got to show confidence. Shall we summon some cohorts and auxiliaries to help deal with the situation? We daren't leave Rome unprotected. If the mutiny spreads the Danube legions could cross the sea from Dalmatia or Greece.'

'What other troops do we have?'

'The men we left behind on the Rhine. They've been recruiting, so the remaining veterans could come south. Four thousand from my province and the same from yours? We daren't use the legion of marines though, they'd probably join the mutiny!'

'True. That bloody Vespasian. We've only been here a few weeks and now we might have another war on our hands.'

'That's probably what Otho and his men said.'

'Very funny. Now, I don't want you worrying Vitellius with any rumours about Vespasian. As far as he's concerned, it's just the one legion, even if the two of us know that there are others who might join him. The happier Vitellius is the easier our life will be, understood?'

'Of course,' I said. I saw no need to tell him of Totavalas's discovery. If the Third had started a mutiny, Galba's old legion would surely join the moment they heard the news. The tide was beginning to turn, and I had to choose a side.

I had an unenviable task to carry out that evening. It was time for Salonina to leave Rome so that she'd reach my estate in the north in time for the birth. Only I couldn't go with her, not now the news from the east had turned the world upside down. I was dreading the encounter, not least because it was the first time we had seen each other in private since our rather public quarrel. She didn't take the change of plan well.

'Salonina, be reasonable!'

'Reasonable? You promised!' she screamed, flinging another dish at me. My arm was still bleeding from where she had caught me unawares with her first missile.

'I know I promised, but that was before I knew how busy I would be as consul. With a man like Valens sharing the power, how can I leave Rome?'

'That's not what I heard,' she said accusingly.

'What do you mean?'

'I heard you were seen climbing into a woman's litter, down by the forum.'

'Who told you this?'

'So it is true!'

'Salonina, this is important. Who told you?' I demanded.

'I had you followed; I wanted to know you were safe. And all the time you were seeing someone else,' she shouted.

'Will you let me explain, woman?'

'What is there to explain? You're having an affair, and that's the end of it.'

'Listen!' I barked. 'I am not having an affair. There was a woman in the litter, yes, but she's one of my informants.'

'And I suppose you can't tell me her name?'

'Of course I can't.'

'How convenient!'

'Salonina, she told me that General Vespasian is rebelling, and there's a good chance he could unite all of the East behind him. That's why I need to be here in Rome. I can't disappear up north when I'm needed here, the future of the empire will be decided in the next few days. I can't leave now.'

'What if you're lying?' Salonina asked.

'I'm not, but I can't have people hearing I knew about the rebellion days ago. Vitellius would have my head. I'm not abandoning you, Salonina, I promise. It's just . . . bad timing.'

'If you would let me stay here . . .' she began.

'Salonina, we agreed that you would go back to Vicetia for the birth. All my family have been born at the estate, and it's a tradition I'm not about to break.'

'But you're not coming with me,' she said, her chest heaving. Gingerly I approached her and took her by the hand. She had exhausted herself chasing me round the room, and I guided her to a chair.

'Of course I'll be there, but it'll take you at least ten days to travel comfortably in your carriage. I can use the courier system and be at Vicetia in less than half the time. I will be there for you, I promise. Do you think I want to miss the birth of another child?'

'I can't tell any more,' she sobbed.

'You'll have Aulus for company on the road, and when we're back in Rome I'll throw the biggest party the city's ever seen!'

She smiled at that. 'I'll go north,' she said finally. 'But how much longer are you going to stay in the city?'

'At least another week,' I said. 'Then it will be a new month, and it will be Valens's turn in the consul's chair. Let him listen to all the old windbags for a change! Besides, now that this legion in Moesia has mutinied, I need to be in Rome for a little longer than I thought.'

'And you promise there's no other woman?'

'Salonina, you're the mother of my child. Both my children,' I said, laying my hand on her swollen stomach. 'You have always been the most important person in my life.'

'Promise?'

'Well, there was my mother,' I said. Salonina laughed, despite the tears.

'In one month all this – the mutiny, the birth – will be over. We'll come back to Rome, all four of us. We'll be a proper family. You're just going to have to trust me this last time, and then nothing will ever keep us apart.'

The next morning the wagon was prepared. There were tearful goodbyes, even from young Aulus, but that was more because he wanted to stay in Rome where all the fun was. The sound of a whip cracking echoed in the street, the wagon trundled slowly forward, an armed guard forming a protective line either side of the precious cargo. Totavalas and I were left standing in the road, watching the party head down the hill on their long journey north, Salonina and Aulus waving until they passed out of sight.

'What now?' the Hibernian asked.

'War is coming,' I said simply.

'I know that much. Which side are we on?' He looked at me, knowingly.

'The side that's going to win, Totavalas, that's always my side.'

XXIII

I could smell the place long before I saw it. Publilius guided me through the streets, clamping the edge of his cloak in front of his nose and mouth to ward off the disease. We were in the slum quarter of the city, in the depths of the Aventine, where the city was protected not by walls but by the Tiber.

'It's the southern climate, they're just not used to it,' Publilius explained. This was where we had billeted the German and Britannian auxiliaries; there was only so much room in the temporary camp we had built on the Field of Mars. We'd received reports of families abandoning their homes and staying with healthy neighbours while the soldiers were made to live together in a haphazard quarantine. Temples were filled with people praying for the sickness to pass. Those that did succumb developed a raging fever, sweating profusely, and many of them would die, shitting their guts out where they lay.

The priests and gravediggers had never been so much in demand. They had to dispose of the bodies of men from countless tribes, all with different beliefs and funeral rites. If a man was lucky enough to have a friend from the same tribe, the proper rituals could be performed. Some bodies were burned, but most were given the obligatory coins for Charon and buried.

'How many have we lost?' I asked.

'Several hundred last week.'

'And this week?'

'We passed a thousand yesterday.'

'Hades must be getting a taste for barbarians these days,' I observed.

'We can't go on losing men at this rate,' Publilius said.

'What do you want me to do about it? I'm a consul, not a bloody miracle worker.'

'We could at least move the men away from the river, that may be what's causing the sickness.'

'And I take it you don't want sick men clogging up the praetorian camp?'

'No, sir.'

'Very well, but it'll mean your men building a new camp and hospital outside the city. And before you start protesting, I know that one of the perks of joining the guard is not having to do manual labour, but we don't have much choice. They've only been under your command a fortnight or so, they can't have forgotten how to build.'

By now the plebs were coming out on to the streets to watch a consul and a praetorian prefect in their filthy part of the city. The men and women looked overwrought, the children ghostly pale and skinny. I thought of Vitellius dining on his sea-fresh prawns up in his palace.

'Come on, let's get out of here. We'll be late.'

There were cheers from all sides as imperial slaves tossed loaves of bread into the crowd. The Circus Maximus was as full as it could be; the stand at the south-eastern end was still being rebuilt after the fire in Nero's time. This race would have surprised even Nero. The animal trainers assured us that they had worked the beasts to breaking point, and that we would have a race of sorts. Two laps round the track; aiming for any more would have been optimistic to say the least, and there were no rules. How could there be rules? How by all the gods would the charioteers control the animals if something went wrong? These details meant little to Valens and Vitellius. They just wanted to watch the inevitable chaos.

We had even given instructions, Valens and I, that if at all possible Vitellius's favourite team, the Blues, should win.

'I'm afraid we can't guarantee anything in a race like this,' the organizer had told us. 'We don't have the first idea how the race is going to turn out. We can tell the other charioteers to hold back, of course, but that won't stop the beasts from attacking each other.'

The teams of slaves had real fun and games trying to make sure the four chariots were lined up straight on the starting line, and far enough apart to persuade the animals not to start fighting right from the off.

'I don't suppose you fancy a flutter, either of you?' Vitellius asked us.

Valens looked uncertain. Although profligate with the emperor's money, with his own he was as tight as an old spinster.

'I wouldn't mind a bet, sire, but I'm sure the Blues are going to win.'

'So am I, that's why I want to bet on them! What about you two?' he asked Publilius and Priscus, Valens's choice for praetorian prefect.

'If you insist, sire,' Priscus said.

'You too, Publilius?'

'How large a bet are we talking about, sire?'

'Oh, only a hundred denarii or so.' Publilius blanched. A hundred denarii was a trifle to Vitellius, and to Valens and me now that we were ruling Rome, but for the two prefects it was no small sum.

'I'll choose the Whites then, sire.'

'The camels? They're the fastest, but my Blue lions will maul them. Priscus?'

'A hundred on the Greens and their tigers.'

'And that leaves you with the Red rhinoceroi. Bad luck, Severus!' Vitellius commiserated.

Those beasts had been brought in for show, for the novelty. They looked slow, ill-tempered and entirely unsuited to racing, and faintly ridiculous with their horns painted in the team's colours.

The crowd were clamouring for the race to start. Vitellius was fidgety with excitement; there was no bigger fan of the races in all Rome, and now it was his right and privilege as emperor to begin the race. He rose ponderously from his throne, bringing out a white handkerchief with a flourish. He held it aloft, waiting for the wind to die down. He milked the crowd's anticipation for a few heartbeats, savouring the attention. The flabby hand released the delicate cloth, and the chariots were off.

The White chariot with its team of camels simply flew off the starting line, the tigers and lions in slow but steady pursuit. My chariot hadn't even budged, the driver flailing at the backsides of the two beasts with his whip, but it had no effect. The crowd were pointing and laughing. Vitellius was in tears of laughter.

'Bad luck, Severus,' he said again, feelingly.

'I must admit I'm more of a gladiator fan. Two men fighting to the death, now that's something I can bet on, with a warrior's eye.' Valens snorted with derision.

The camels had done half a lap before my chariot got under way. The crowd wanted some action; sometimes there would be up to eight teams of horses, two for each colour, doing seven laps of the circus. These animals were going a lot slower, and the people were restless.

'Valens tells me that a legion has rebelled in Moesia,' Vitellius said to me as casually as if he were discussing the weather.

Valens was smiling. 'He also tells me that you didn't want to give me the news, hoping to "keep me sweet". Was that the phrase, Valens?'

'It was, sire.'

I was taken aback. What possible gain was there to be had in telling Vitellius about the rogue legion?

'My apologies, sire. I didn't think there was any need to burden you with the news until we had assessed the situation more thoroughly.'

'I'm not going to hide the fact that I'm disappointed in you, Severus. It's up to you if you want to dismiss your wife, but you cannot dismiss me! From now on you will tell me everything I need to know. Understood?'

I could hardly say that Valens hadn't told him the whole truth, that the legion, the governor and several of the eastern legions were likely to join the rebellion. Vitellius would only flap like a wet hen, hindering Valens and me from saving his throne.

'Understood, sire.'

A gasp from the crowd drew our attention back to the race. The Whites' chariot had already lapped my Red team, giving the monstrous rhinoceroi a wide berth, but passing the other teams had proved trickier. Vitellius's lions had the inside lane, leaving only the tigers to pass. But the Whites' charioteer had misjudged his manoeuvre, and the outermost tiger leapt at the camels that were trying to overtake. There was a blood-curdling scream from the mauled camel and the entire team began to flounder. The rest of the tigers leapt on the anchored camels, and the Whites' charioteer had the good sense to abandon his race and run to safety.

Priscus triumphantly elbowed Publilius in the ribs. 'Your damn fault for choosing the camels,' he crowed. But Priscus wasn't quite so cocky when he realized that his tigers were enjoying their camel-meat far too much to think about finishing the race. Even my Red team overtook the tigers, having done only half a lap so far. Vitellius was looking smug, and why shouldn't he? His beloved Blues had already completed a whole lap. There was no way in Hades that the rhinoceroi would be able to catch up.

'Pay up, gentlemen!'

Priscus grudgingly handed over a pouch brimming with coins. Publilius turned bright red.

'I'm afraid I don't have that much money on me, sire.'

'No matter, you can owe it to me. Severus?' Vitellius held out his hand expectantly.

'Not until your team crosses the line, sire.'

Priscus and Valens scoffed. Vitellius took it on the chin. 'No, Severus is right. The Blues haven't won anything yet.'

The crowd were still cheering on the lions; they all knew which team Vitellius favoured and only the diehard Reds fans would still support the one team left standing against the emperor's favourites. The lack of pace gave us plenty of time to admire the rhinoceroi, brought from far beyond the boundaries of the empire. They were just as big as Valens had said they would be, great lumbering creatures that would probably have got up to a half-decent speed if they weren't dragging a chariot and a driver behind them.

It was now the turn of the Blues' lions to lap the rhinoceroi, and the charioteer looked to have learned from the Whites' mistake. The lions were already a good half-length ahead when the Blues' charioteer turned in too soon. His carriage swerved violently into the path of those unforgiving horns. One of the brutes butted his head against the side of the carriage, sending it off balance so that for a few heatbeats it rode on one wheel. All the spectators were on the edge of their seats, including me. Another mighty hit sent the Blue carriage crashing on to its side, and the lions were wrenched backwards in mid-stride, right into the path of the rhinoceroi. There were hideous wails and snapping bones as the huge creatures trampled the team of lions, too slow and tangled to get out of the way. I couldn't help but punch the air in delight, only to be rewarded with a dirty look from Vitellius.

The race was practically over, even though the Reds had only just completed their first lap. There was nothing to do but watch the lucky driver guide his snorting beasts to the finishing line. Wordlessly I held out my empty hand to Vitellius.

'Not yet,' he sulked. 'Your team hasn't crossed the line yet.'

Whether it was petulance or the hope that the tigers might decide to abandon their meal and win the race just for him, I don't know, but Vitellius sat, arms folded tightly across his chest. When the painted horns crossed the line, followed by the animals' bulky bodies, only then did the emperor fish out my winnings before getting up to leave.

Priscus and Publilius prepared to follow, since they were responsible for protecting Vitellius at all times. 'Don't worry, Priscus, you can owe it to me.'

Valens and I stood as a mark of respect when the emperor left, leaving the two of us alone in the box.

'That was a dirty trick,' I hissed at Valens, once Vitellius was out of earshot. 'We agreed to keep Vitellius in the dark about Moesia.'

'We did, but then I decided Vitellius had a right to know.' Valens turned to leave as well, and had gone a couple of steps away from the imperial box before saying, 'Well done, by the way.'

'For what?' I asked suspiciously.

'For winning a few coins. You've lost the emperor's trust and now his goodwill, but I'm sure it's a fair trade!' He laughed as he sauntered down the steps, leaving me standing there alone, clenching and unclenching my fists with rage.

I was still furious when I got home. I called and called for Totavalas, only to be told by one of the slaves that he was making use of the villa's baths. He was lying down on a slab in the steam room when I found him, one of my slaves rubbing oils into his back.

'When you've got a moment, Totavalas,' I said impatiently.

'Is something wrong?' he asked.

'Never mind that, I need you to deliver a message.'

The Hibernian glanced back at the slave attending to him as if to say to me, 'Now?'

'And yes, if you're wondering, I do mean now,' I said. 'You can have *my* slave scrape you clean in *my* baths later. Right now I need you to get off your arse and do something useful.'

Quickly, Totavalas grabbed a towel and wrapped it round his waist. 'What do you need me for, sir?'

'That's better. Go round to the house of Julius Agricola and wait in the street until you see his wife Domitia. I don't care how long you have to wait, stay put until you see her alone. Then say that you have a message from the consul.'

'Meaning you?'

'Yes, meaning me. But saying the word consul means she will listen to you, and the message will tell her it's from me, not Valens.'

'Right, and the message is?'

'"When can I claim my reward?"'

Totavalas looked at me hard, understanding the enormity of what I was saying.

'You sure about this? You're absolutely sure?'

'I am. It's about time I got some bloody respect in this city after all I've done for them.'

The Hibernian smiled. 'One more war, eh?'

'Unless the Hibernians decide to invade us, yes, one more war.'

The next day we started to receive reports from the provinces, but the reports were all too similar and all from the west. We still had no idea what was going on beyond the Julian Alps, where Italia gave way to Pannonia and beyond. Governor after governor replied to Vitellius's call for help, saying they wished they could, but their troops were already spread too thin or they couldn't be sure of the men's loyalty. The three legions in Hispania wouldn't help, for instance, because one was the First Adiutrix, the marines who had fought so ferociously against us at Bedriacum, and the other two were playing for time, waiting to see which would be the winning side. Britannia had already sent what they could, and there were reports from the officers we had left behind in Germania that the tribes beyond the Rhine were getting restless, especially in Batavia, and they couldn't spare a single man. And all the while Vitellius and his court had no clue what was going on in the east.

The only good news from the provinces was that the Rhine legions scraped together a small detachment and sent it towards the Po valley to meet up with the forces we would send from Rome, while in Rome itself it seemed that the worst ravages of the disease in the Aventine were coming to an end. The surviving auxiliaries were glad to move into their own camp outside the city, and happier still were the citizens whose homes they'd lived in for almost two months.

Even Vitellius took a closer interest in the running of his empire, once he'd been made aware of the threat to it. He almost fell off his chair when he saw the treasury figures. So far Rome had spent over 900 million sesterces that year, and a look at imperial expenditure for the last five years dwarfed that sum. Nero's great building programme, the decoration of the Golden Palace, his orgies and lavish theatrical productions weighed more heavily than six months of Galba's thriftiness. Otho too had spent a small fortune during his brief reign. When confronted with these figures, the very first thing Vitellius said was: 'So I suppose the Africa expedition is postponed?'

Now you know the sort of man I had to put up with.

It was made very clear to Valens and me that the budget for Vitellius's entertainment wouldn't drop, so we were ordered to find savings elsewhere. Vitellius himself even contributed.

He laid a proposal before the Senate, to levy a new tax on all freedmen. This was a sensible enough move, given that the fortunes some freedmen had made in the service of the empire dwarfed that of many senatorial families, and the new tax was greatly applauded among the nobility who resented these men's wealth. Unfortunately, this did little to improve morale in the imperial administration, which was almost entirely run by freedmen.

Totavalas complained bitterly, arguing that he had not been in Rome long enough to make much money, and yet he was still subject to the levy. I sympathized, and made an amendment to the bill exempting all those who had been given their freedom within the last year. It was no great loss financially, as it was the bureaucrats from Claudius and Nero's time who had made their millions. It also made my home a more peaceful place to live in, once Totavalas had stopped mooching about the place, as bitter as an out-of-work actor.

It was at the end of a particularly long day of assessing reports and looking at tax returns that I went back to my villa, exhausted. Totavalas was in the atrium, waiting for me, a knowing smile on his face. This alone was enough to make me suspicious.

'What are you smirking about? You look like a cat that's been fed a mouse dipped in cream.'

'It's not me who's having a grand day. Cook's prepared a rather special dinner for you, Severus.'

'Special? How special?'

'You'll see.'

He led me through to the triclinium, where there was an assortment of my favourite delicacies, and some things that I had never asked the cook to make for me. There was a whole platter of seafood, a large dish of oysters with another for the empty shells. Someone had already had a couple. There were sweatmeats and perfumed delicacies from the East that I didn't recognize, and my smartest pitcher, made entirely of silver, full to the brim with rich red wine. Quietly, elegantly, a couple of slaves came out to serve me while Totavalas took the couch opposite me, eyeing the food lustily.

'You still haven't told me what's going on,' I said.

'You'll just have to wait and see, won't you?'

'Like you waited with the oysters, you mean?' I accused him. A slave handed me a cup. I gave it an appreciative sniff before taking a gulp. It was gorgeous. Warm, full-bodied and smooth beyond belief.

'What is this?' I asked the slave.

'A Falernian, master, a thirty-year-old vintage.'

'A thirty-year-old Falernian! I don't have anything half this good in the cellar.'

'True enough. So stop asking questions and just enjoy it,' Totavalas said, taking a piece of crabmeat and a slice of avocado.

I wolfed down a few of the oysters then began on the rest of the seafood. After a quarter of an hour I was comfortably full, but there was still half of the Falernian left. I stretched, feeling my shoulder blades and back muscles after long days hunched over dull documents, before yawning tiredly.

'You don't want to be yawning for a long time yet,' Totavalas observed.

'I've got a right to feel tired, haven't I?'

'Sure you've got a right, but I'll bet all the gold I've got that sleeping is the last thing you'll be doing tonight.' He pointed towards the passage that led to my bedroom.

Just to stop the man from prattling on, I humoured him and went to investigate. As I reached the corridor I noticed the scattered rose petals on the floor, droplets of red against the cold, white marble. Turning the corner, I found the passage was lined with scented candles. At last I began to understand.

Up ahead the door to my bedroom stood slightly ajar. Excitement began to course through me as I strode purposefully forward. The door creaked gently as it opened, and my heart almost skipped a beat. There she was, kneeling expectantly on the bed. She had artfully piled the remaining petals around her so that they covered her thighs and her sex, but her curvaceous body was fully on display. Her hips, her slender waist, those beautiful breasts, a smile and a look in her eyes that screamed 'come here'.

'Julius thinks I'm visiting an old friend tonight,' Domitia said.

'And I am a very old friend, aren't I?' I said, advancing upon her. I took off my toga before it began to bulge. I had dreamed about this moment for years. Domitia knelt, motionless. I climbed on to the bed and kissed her tenderly on the mouth. She responded, her tongue darting to meet my lips. I began to enjoy the kiss even more, my hands exploring that wonderful body.

'Promise me one thing,' she murmured.

'Anything.'

'This will be our secret. Julius must never know.'

I hesitated for a moment. This was my triumph, my revenge for Julius's betrayal, putting Otho above his oldest friend. It would crush him to know what Domitia was prepared to do, even if it was to help her husband's career. But would cuckolding him be satisfying enough?

'I'll make a deal with you,' I said, nuzzling her neck. 'Make this a night to remember, and I swear to Jupiter that Julius will never hear of this from me.'

'Jupiter, the biggest fornicator in Olympus? Swear on Salonina's life. You still love her, don't you?'

'In my own way,' I said.

'Then swear it.'

How could I not, with that quivering bosom beneath me, her nipples hard with arousal, the blonde tresses framing that delicate face? I looked into her brilliant blue eyes and made my vow.

XXIV

Domitia was gone when I awoke late the next morning. But what a night it was; I had never known pleasure like it. Julius was a lucky man, but not as lucky as he was, now that I had shared in the delights his wife had to offer. I didn't have long though to bask in the memories of the previous night: there was an urgent knocking at the door.

'Master, master!' a slave called timidly.

'What is it, man?' I moaned, wanting to lie there and enjoy the memories a while longer.

'A message from the palace, master, you're needed at once.'

'What for?'

'The man wouldn't say, master, he only told me that Consul Valens had some urgent news.'

Cursing, I roused myself and began to cast about for my clothes. A quick splash of water on my face to wake myself up and I was ready to go, even if I was wearing the same clothes as yesterday. A sartorial sin, but Valens wouldn't have summoned me if it was something he could deal with by himself.

It wasn't just inside the Golden Palace that the halls were frantic with scurrying clerks and messengers, all Rome seemed buzzing. I received word that Valens was waiting for me in the throne room, along with Vitellius and a deputation from the Senate. Hurriedly tugging at my clothes to hide the worst of the creases I tried my best not to look as though I had just crawled out of bed.

It was quite a gathering: Vitellius and Valens were there, the praetorian prefects Publilius and Priscus standing either side of the emperor, the current praetors, Julius Agricola among them, and a smattering of ex-consuls, Suetonius Paulinus and Verginius Rufus included. There was also a man I did not recognize. Vitellius cleared his throat nervously. The emperor wished to speak.

'Senators, you will all have heard by now the news that the legions east of Italia have rebelled.' It may not have been news to anyone else in the hall, but it was news to me.

'Do we know precisely which legions have come out in open rebellion?' Rufus asked.

Valens had the list to hand. 'The Third Gallica, the Seventh Galbiana, the Seventh Claudiana, the Eighth Augusta—'

'Yes, yes,' Vitellius said testily, 'that's enough, Valens. In all, six legions spread across Moesia, Pannonia and Dalmatia.'

'And have they followed the example of the Third, sire?' a praetor asked. 'Have they all declared for Vespasian?'

'They have,' Valens answered.

'Treason!' some of the senators muttered, but most did it half-heartedly.

'And for that reason, I have decided to arrest the prefect of the urban cohorts, Flavius Sabinus. As Vespasian's brother, I cannot allow him to roam free, spreading lies about me and corrupting his men.'

'On what charge was he arrested?' Agricola asked. I could barely look him in the face, for fear of smiling.

Valens answered on Vitellius's behalf. 'The emperor doesn't need charges to safeguard his throne. But if he were to be tried, it would surely be for treason.'

This took the senators aback. Sabinus was an honest, decent man.

'However,' I interrupted, 'we have yet to establish whether or not he is guilty. In arresting Sabinus we stop him from spreading dissent in Rome, and I daresay we are doing him a service in protecting him from the fury of those who love our emperor.'

Valens looked at me with a puzzled expression. He did not appreciate, as I did, that Sabinus was a popular man and that trying him for treason would drive many useful men into the arms of Vespasian.

Vitellius, himself an ex-senator, saw the wisdom of my words too. 'Severus is right, it is Vespasian who has declared himself a traitor, not his brother. In the meantime, Senators, I would ask that you tell your colleagues that their emperor is assured of their loyalty. I will dispatch an army under one of the consuls to bring this mutiny to a swift end. I will, of course, keep the praetorians here to preserve the peace in Rome.'

'And the fleet, sire?' asked the man I didn't recognize.

'The eastern fleet can carry on patrolling the Dalmatian coast, Bassus. If these legions are going to invade, we will have to head them off as they cross the Julian Alps. I can't risk Rome being threatened.'

The deputation understood the significance of keeping the praetorians in Rome. Vitellius couldn't trust the supporters of Vespasian unless he had loyal troops at hand to deter some audacious move by an ambitious man, or men. But that would seriously reduce the size of the army we could send north.

'You may go now,' said Vitellius, dismissing the senators with a wave of his hand. The throne room seemed terribly deserted once they had shuffled out. The emperor and his two generals, and the praetorian prefects that his generals had chosen for him; for a moment it felt like it was only the five of us who stood in Vespasian's way.

'Well? You've all heard the news, what's to be done about all this?' Vitellius asked us.

'We'll have to send an army north to counter the invasion from Pannonia and beyond, sire,' Valens's man Priscus answered.

'I had gathered as much,' Vitellius said acidly. 'What I want is specifics. Who can we afford to send north, how many, how we can stop this revolt from spreading eastwards—'

'If it hasn't already,' Publilius muttered.

'We can't know that for sure,' Valens said. 'Our information is that the legate of the legion Galba raised in Hispania has taken charge of the rebel army, and it doesn't seem that he's all that keen to wait for reinforcements from Syria and beyond. He'll want to defeat our veterans by himself. And as we know,' he looked at me pointedly, 'such over-confidence will almost certainly backfire on him.'

'So you want to send an army large enough to defeat this legate . . .'

'Primus, sire,' I told him. 'Antonius Primus of the Seventh Galbiana.'

'. . . this legate, Primus, comprehensively.'

'Yes, sire. If we can do that, it'll convince all the other legions in the west to rally to our side, take the defeated legions out of the equation and make Vespasian realize that he's overreached himself. He can't abandon the eastern frontier to the Parthians and the rebel Jews. If we can defeat this first invasion, I can't see anyone else in the east having the stomach for another fight.'

'Severus?' Vitellius looked at me questioningly.

'I agree, sire. The only question is who should command this army.'

The emperor smiled. 'I take it you want that honour?'

That was an understatement if ever I heard one. With command of the army, I could make a present of it to Vespasian; if I wanted to, that is. I had claimed my reward from Domitia, but neither Vitellius nor Vespasian looked assured of victory yet. If I wanted to keep the position of power I held in Rome I would have to be in the north when the rebel legions emerged from the eastern passes of the Alps.

'I flatter myself I have a special bond with the men, sire. The detachments from Britannia know me from my time serving under Paulinus against Boudicca. The German auxiliaries know I respect their bravery in battle, and their winter clothing.' Valens snorted in derision. My wearing trousers in the Alps might have raised a few eyebrows among my fellow officers, but it had greatly endeared me to the Germans, costing only my sartorial reputation. 'And of course there are my own men from Upper Germania. I have commanded armies, sire, and besides, my estate lies just outside Vicetia, a few days' march from the Julian Alps. I know the land we'll be fighting in; I doubt Valens can say the same.'

'True, but at least I can say that I've never been defeated. With respect to Severus, sire, he gets along well with the troops, but this crisis calls for an experienced leader, not the men's friend. Severus almost threw away his entire army before I arrived to reinforce him; my fear is that he'll do the same again in an effort to impress you.'

'It was hardly my fault that I was betrayed,' I argued. 'Or am I to blame for thinking my oldest friend would choose Otho over me?'

'Have you forgotten Placentia, and the farce of your siege?' Valens retorted.

'What about when my legion and I saved your neck at Bedriacum? You were so keen to win the battle without me that you sent away thousands of good men on a fool's errand, and nearly lost to Otho's men, even though they had kept back thousands of praetorians in camp!'

Publilius and Priscus were edging behind their respective generals, trading insults of their own.

'Will you all be quiet!' the emperor shouted. That gave us pause. None of us had ever heard Vitellius shout before.

'Anyone would think you two were on different sides, the way you talk to each other. The matter is easily settled. Both of you are fine generals in your own right,' he said patronizingly. 'Severus, you have twice as much experience as any other man your age, and you would be just as good a choice as Valens.'

The word 'would' made my stomach lurch. I knew where this was going.

'But I need you here in Rome. You're a gifted nobleman, a man who is at ease among the senators and the mob alike. But Valens here is first and foremost a soldier. I need you, Severus, to fight the political battles instead, helping to keep sweet those who might be tempted to side with Vespasian.'

There was a look of supreme smugness on Valens's face. It is the look I see whenever I think of Valens these days. No one alive today knew him like I did: Valens the schemer, the plotter, the man who drove me into becoming the bitter, friendless wreck that writes this story. In being chosen to take the army north, while I flattered, cajoled and fawned in Rome on behalf of a man who did not deserve to be emperor, Valens had won a massive victory.

I was summarily dismissed while Valens and Vitellius sat together to draw up their plans of campaign. What was I expected to do? Dash about the city and convince the people one by one that Vespasian was a foul traitor whom the gods would strike down for thinking he could become emperor? But what had Vespasian done that hadn't already been done by Galba, Otho and now Vitellius? Nothing, except he'd had the sense to bide his time, waiting for the western legions to maul themselves to pieces so he could sweep in with the eastern veterans and knock the latest emperor off the throne. Unless of course the army we sent north could smash Primus and his legions and bring the whole rebellion to a grinding halt.

I barked angrily at the clerks to get out of my way as they scurried through the palace corridors. By the time I had made it to my office door I was fuming. The office door crashed against the wall as I kicked it open. Demetrios looked up, his face apprehensive. Totavalas was perched on the corner of the Greek's desk, and the two of them had clearly been deep in discussion until I barged in.

'Is something wrong, Consul?' Demetrios asked.

'Well guessed,' I said darkly. 'The East is up in arms, Valens has been given control of the army while I kick my heels in Rome, and on top of that I think I just broke my toe!' The biggest one was still throbbing from when I kicked the door open.

'Demetrios, can you leave us for a moment?' Totavalas asked.

'Why, sir?'

'Don't ask, just do it.'

The Greek looked confused as he headed past me. 'And close the door behind you,' Totavalas called after him.

The two of us waited in silence. With a flick of my head I gestured to Totavalas that he should check the door for eavesdroppers, then I pushed past into my own office, that much further from the corridor and hopefully out of earshot.

'All clear,' Totavalas reported. 'But I don't understand. This is good news, surely? Six legions in the east declaring for Vespasian, plus the legions in Syria and beyond. Vitellius's days are numbered, and you do your thing and all will be well.'

'My thing?' I asked.

'Well . . .' the Hibernian began, looking faintly embarrassed.

'Changing sides, is that my thing?'

'To be fair, you're a dab hand at picking the winning side, *Consul*,' he stressed, as if to make his point.

'Is that all you think I'm good at, Totavalas?' I asked.

'No, of course not,' he said hastily. 'You're a good general, a good politician, and I think you recognize that Rome deserves a decent emperor at last.'

The Hibernian's words calmed me a little. Yes, I was a good general, and a great strategist. I would hardly have become Vitellius's right-hand man if I had been neither. And if Vitellius chose not to appreciate my talent or the sacrifices I had made for him, then I was sure that Vespasian would be grateful for my services.

'But there's nothing I can do for Vespasian if I'm stuck in the city, placating the Senate,' I complained bitterly.

'So in an ideal world you'd like Valens out of the way, so you can lead the army north without him interfering?'

'Of course I would. I pray every day that Jupiter strikes down the snake with a bolt of lightning, but that doesn't mean it's going to happen.'

There was the ghost of a smile on Totavalas's face. 'And what if I could arrange that Valens wasn't around to lead the army?'

'How?'

'It's probably best I don't tell you. Then if Valens accuses you, you don't have to lie. Trust me, you'll be headed north before the week is out.'

The city was bustling as preparations were made for the army to break camp and march to meet the threat from the east. Valens was busy briefing the legates, who in turn tried to drill their men back into the semblance of an army. Too many of them had spent the summer drinking, whoring and generally letting themselves go. Gone were the battle-hardened veterans we had brought over the mountains. Valens and I inspected a legion the next day, and they looked like what they were: a bunch of drunks and layabouts in uniform. But it wasn't the men we punished. We expected them to indulge in Rome's pleasures. Instead we fined and disciplined the centurions for not looking after their men properly.

While the preparations on Vitellius's side were proceeding as well as could be expected, I decided that it would be prudent to take certain precautions. The empire still hung in the balance, and Totavalas was right about one thing at least: I was very good at picking the winning side. I held no grudge against Vitellius himself, but my position in Rome was growing weaker by the day and Valens's influence over the emperor was increasing. It would have been irresponsible of me to ignore the overtures I had received from Vespasian's side, not to mention the fact that Domitia had paid me part of my reward up front.

With my column of lictors in tow, I marched up the Esquiline Hill to find the villa of Sabinus, the man we were holding under house arrest to stop him spreading sedition and wheedling senators into giving his brother their support. You might think that it would have been better for me to try to hide the fact that I was visiting the only political prisoner in Rome, by sneaking through the shadows in a hooded cloak. On the other hand, I would have to give my name to get past the guards on the door, and then the whole city would know what I was about. Better that I go in broad daylight as though I had nothing to hide.

The soldiers either side of the door were surprised to see me.

'Are you here to see the prisoner, sir?' the centurion asked after saluting.

'What a good guess,' I said, feigning wonder. 'Actually I've come here to plot the overthrow of the emperor.'

Instantly the legionaries reached for their swords. The centurion chuckled. 'Easy, lads, this is General Severus. He's as likely to plot against the emperor as I am. Sorry, sir, these men don't know any better. They're from General Valens's legion.'

'And you're a centurion of the Twenty-First,' I said, looking at the markings on his shield.

'That's right, sir. We gave that Alpinus a good kicking.'

'So we did. Now would you let me pass? I'm here to have one last go at persuading Sabinus to tell us what he was planning, from one nobleman to another.'

'Very good, General.' The officer gestured to the men to stand aside.

A tired-looking slave was waiting for me inside. He must have heard the exchange and was ready to take me to his master.

'How is your master bearing up?' I asked him.

'Not too well, Consul. He spends a lot of time in the library.'

'Just reading?'

'And writing too.' The slave blanched as he realized what he had said. On the face of it his master was perfectly free to write in his own library, but the man's reaction betrayed that Sabinus was writing letters that somehow made their way past the guards on every door.

'Interesting. Is he in the library now?'

'Yes, Consul.' He knocked gently on the door.

'What is it?' a gruff voice called.

'Consul Severus to see you, master.'

'Ah! Show him in,' the voice said enthusiastically.

The slave pushed the door open and beat a hasty retreat.

I was greeted by the sight of rows upon rows of scrolls, entire walls of shelves heaving with valuable papyrus and vellum. The knowledge of the world lay upon those scrolls, making my paltry collection of Xenophon and Thucydides look like the weekly reading list the tutor gave Aulus in comparison. Hunched over the table, stylus in hand, sat a man with a balding head and a pair of ears that stuck out comically.

'I thought I might be having a visit from you sooner or later,' Sabinus said, still busy with his papers.

'Entertaining a consul is a better social life than none at all,' I said.

'Quite. If I had a fatted calf I'd serve it to you.'

'Some water will be sufficient.'

'Of course. Timon!' he called. The nervous slave reappeared. 'Some water for our guest. And some wine for me.'

'A bit early in the afternoon for wine,' I commented.

'But with no one to visit me I can forget these social niceties.' At last Sabinus turned in his chair to look at me. His face was

314

lined with age and worry. He was past sixty now, but his frame looked toned and full of vigour. Captivity had turned the man into a spring, biding his time and waiting until he was released. The brown eyes were tired, but inquisitive.

'Won't you sit, Consul?'

I nodded my thanks, and took the seat on the other side of the table. 'Keeping yourself busy, I see. Writing a commentary on some Greek poetry, perhaps?'

Sabinus instinctively covered the vellum with his arm. 'That's it.'

'And there was I thinking it might be a letter to one of your brother's supporters,' I said, smiling. 'Your slave isn't too bright,' I explained, seeing Sabinus's shocked expression.

'I ought to have him whipped and sent to join my wife in the country.'

'Impossible,' I said. 'Valens and I would assume he was carrying some secret message and we would regrettably be forced to torture it out of him.'

'You and Valens?'

'As the emperor's loyal servants. It could have been you in the crucifer's chamber, you know. Valens and Vitellius were all for your being tortured so that we could prise some information from you.'

'I take it I have you to thank for commuting the sentence to house arrest then?'

'More like my freedman Totavalas. It was him that told me you were buying up the grain privately, not as the urban prefect. If Valens or his spies had found out first, I doubt you'd be alive today.'

'My thanks to your Hibernian, then. I've heard a lot about him.'

'He's as insolent as a spoiled hunting hound, but he's got the cunning of a fox, I'll say that for him.'

'We all need men we can rely on,' Sabinus agreed.

'As Vespasian relies upon you?' I asked, pointedly.

'Me, and others,' he said warily. 'I hear from a certain soldier's wife that you've decided to join our merry band.' It was more of a question than a statement.

'My brother will be grateful,' he continued.

'How grateful?'

'With Valens and Vitellius out of the way, you and I will be the most influential men in Rome, until Vespasian arrives. After that, it was suggested you might replace him as commander of the eastern legions, and my brother would pay for a campaign against Parthia, if that appeals?'

It certainly did appeal. Vitellius would never allow Valens or me out of the city for his entire reign. He relied on us too heavily to risk losing one of his consuls to the golden opportunities on the Parthian front.

'I like to think that I would serve Rome best with the legions.' I left the rest of my thoughts unsaid; Sabinus understood. It was an attractive offer, but I was still torn between staying loyal to Vitellius and helping what would be my third emperor on to the throne. I say third: I had no ties to Nero or Otho.

'On the other hand,' Sabinus continued, 'I don't see how you will be in a position to help my brother if you are stuck here in Rome while Valens takes the army north.'

I chuckled. 'Don't worry about that. My Hibernian has it all in hand. You can tell your brother that once I control the army and it's far enough away from the city, then I will do what is best for Rome.'

'You mean give her an emperor who is a better man than all his predecessors put together?'

I raised my hand. 'I swear by all the gods, Vespasian is more deserving of the purple than Vitellius ever was.'

'Then we understand each other?'

'We do.'

XXV

So there I was. With the army that Totavalas would somehow provide I would march north to where the first wave of Vespasian's legions would be waiting, less than a day's ride from my own estate. Lying in bed that night I thought of Salonina. She must have reached the estate at Vicetia by now. Perhaps the baby had even been born. I prayed each night for another son, another Severus to bring honour and glory to the family.

I had given so much for men who did not deserve me. Galba's end had even come at the hand of another man he had spurned: Otho, who had supported him from the beginning. I didn't want the old man dead, gratitude was all I wanted. And now Vitellius was beginning to turn on me, after all I'd done for him. I was only thirty, I still had years and years to give in Rome's service, but Valens, Vitellius and the rest had conspired to ignore my talents. All I wanted, all any noble ever wants, was to give my sons a golden future, a future that could only have been brighter if they had been born into the imperial family itself. But Vitellius was no longer the man to provide it. True, he had made me fantastically wealthy and had appointed me consul, but my influence over him was waning every day in favour of

317

the scheming Valens. Vespasian was undoubtedly the better man, but I could only help the better man on to the throne by becoming a traitor.

But before I could lead the army north, Totavalas had to take Valens out of the equation. He was cutting it very fine; the preparations to leave were well under way, and a farewell banquet for Valens was planned for two days after my talk with Sabinus. Vitellius was supremely confident of victory, so confident in fact that he was still losing himself in the details of the vanity projects that Valens and I put before him. The expedition to Africa beyond the desert was merely postponed, not cancelled.

'And why not?' Vitellius reasoned. 'Even old Emperor Claudius travelled to Britannia with his legions.' It would have been cruel to crush his boyish enthusiasm, so tentative plans were drawn up: a great procession setting out from Alexandria, a pleasure cruise along the Nile; we even sent a message to Egypt that the emperor wished to speak to an ambassador from Nubia, the land south of the Egyptian province. Once it had been a mighty civilization but now the Nubians are reduced to sending out occasional raiding parties to steal from the scattered settlements in the disputed territory between our borders.

But while Valens and I were busy soothing the emperor's vanity, the imperial kitchens were working themselves raw. No expense was spared for the celebrations. As the banquet was in his honour, Valens was even permitted to have some say over the menu. Oysters were a particular favourite of his, which meant another cartload of amphorae filled with seawater and all manner of shellfish trundled northwards to Rome to arrive that very night. All the best people in the city were invited, of course; Salonina would have killed to be there, arranging the seating plan in order of precedence, snubbing some and ingratiating herself with others, depending on whether their wives had turned up to her pretentious poetry readings.

As I say, all the great and the good were there, even Agricola and Domitia. Barring the two of them from a private party was one thing, but this was an official state banquet. A praetor and his wife could hardly be ignored. Valens and I stood on the doors to the banqueting hall greeting the guests. Agricola bowed stiffly to his superiors, while Domitia gave the smallest of blushes when our eyes met, before her husband hustled her along to the great table.

The table was a relic from the time of the Divine Augustus. Carved from oak, it had been fashioned into the shape of a giant horseshoe to allow as many people as possible to be seated, but not so large that the table became a full circle. Augustus liked to paint himself as the *primus inter pares*, the first among equals, but his notions of equality did not stretch that far. The table itself was covered with an extravagant purple cloth, probably large enough to fit out a warship's sails, and the surface was festooned with dishes of partridge, guineafowl, pheasant – Valens preferred his white meat clearly – delicacies from across the empire, fruits of the sea and of the land. There was one thing I did not recognize: little bowls interspersed between the guests, full of nuggets of something white. I picked a piece up and smelled it cautiously, and my nostrils were assaulted with an overpowering odour. Valens laughed at my reaction.

'What are they?'

'They're the roots of a plant from my part of Italia, deep in the south. The Greeks call it glykoriza, after its sweetness. We call it liquorice. Come on,' he took one of the pieces and began to chew it, 'try some.'

Gingerly I took one of the pungent chunks and put it in my mouth. It wasn't so bad, like a chewier, sweeter version of fennel.

'See, it's not so bad. It cleans the palate and freshens the mouth. And it helps prevent colds.'

'Are we likely to catch colds at the height of summer?'

'No, but I like this root in all seasons. It only grows in the deep south and in Greece; after all that time in Germania I've been craving for a little taste of home.'

I had since swallowed the root, but the overpowering flavour still remained. 'Somehow I don't think this is going to mix too well with the Falernian wine.'

'That's part of the reason we like this stuff so much at home; our local wines need something to cover up the damned awful taste!'

A household slave struck the floor with his staff three times. The guests turned to see what was happening.

'Your Imperial Majesty, Senators, ladies: if you would all take your seats, the banquet is ready to begin.'

I was making for my seat at the right of Vitellius's wife Galeria when Totavalas caught my arm. Despite being a freedman, as my chief of staff he had been honoured with a seat at the foot of our table.

'Everything's in hand, Severus.'

'Fine, now take your hand off me and get to your seat before people begin to stare.'

All the guests took their places behind their seats, waiting for Vitellius to sit first. But he didn't sit.

'Honoured guests,' he called out, 'I don't wish to keep you from this wonderful feast that lies before us. But I would be remiss if I passed up this opportunity to say thank you and good luck to Consul Valens as he marches north tomorrow.' Vitellius's knuckles were white as his hands gripped the back of his chair, using it as a prop. No doubt he had been drinking already.

'Valens has been with me from the start. Loyal, faithful, he is a man who can make things happen. I know that when he takes my legions on to the battlefield those rebels will rue the day they rose against their emperor.' Those assembled broke into wild applause. Valens smiled graciously before turning to shake Vitellius by the hand. I made a show of clapping hard. Galeria noticed this.

'One might almost think you wanted Valens to lead the army,' she murmured.

'If your husband says that Valens is the best man for the job, then he must be,' I answered nonchalantly.

'How very magnanimous!'

Vitellius took his seat and the rest of us followed his example. I caught Totavalas's eye, far away at the foot of the table. He smiled reassuringly before tucking into some pheasant. Thankfully Valens had decided not to give a speech; he was a poor orator at the best of times, and instead opted to enjoy the comforts of civilization before the coming campaign.

I had a few mouthfuls of food before taking my first sip of wine, trying to rid my mouth of that fennel-like flavour that Valens's precious plant roots had given me. Out of the corner of my eye I spotted Valens reaching for his own bowl of oysters. Taking one, he tilted back his head and sucked at the inside of the shell. He swallowed, then grimaced uncontrollably.

'Bad oyster, Valens?' the emperor asked.

'Yes, sire.'

'Tricky things, oysters,' Vitellius commented. He knew from vast experience. 'If the next one is bad, leave the rest alone.'

The next one went down, and Valens smacked his lips appreciatively. 'Nothing wrong with that one.'

I forced myself to ignore Vitellius and Valens; it would look a bit odd if I was spotted watching every mouthful my rival ate. The hours passed, the guests' movements becoming more and more sluggish as the rich food and potent wine took effect. Even I had a few cups too many, and I had always strived to stay sober at the emperor's banquets. Eventually the meat, fish and salads were cleared away, only to be replaced by puddings and delicate fancies that turned the table into a riot of colour. The crowning glory was the cake, a great rectangular creation that was covered in red icing and sculpted to look like a cohort in the testudo formation. Someone had even added pieces of almond to represent the shield bosses and trails of yellow icing to craft the pattern on the shields of the First Germanica, Valens's own legion.

The cake itself was delicious, filled with the lightest sponge and strawberry jam, the icing flavoured with cherry to give the red its scarlet tinge, and I thought I detected the taste of figs too. The imperial slaves were emptying the cellars, judging by the speed with which they refilled our cups and goblets. Then we were treated to a performance from some dancing girls, brought, so Vitellius told me, from lands far to the east of Parthia. Some of them had tawny skin and hips so narrow it defied belief. The men watched in awe as the dancers thrust their hips rhythmically back and forth, shaking the feathers and decorations that adorned their navels. By this time many of the elderly and the married couples were beginning to drift off, Agricola and Domitia among them. But then Agricola had always been narrow-minded when it came to entertainment. He was the sort who enjoyed a good day's ploughing of his fields, followed by a simple supper and an improving story, while Domitia most likely did some embroidery in the corner.

The room was beginning to swirl and spin as violently as the dancers. A slave came to fill my cup once more, but I put my hand over it to signal that I had had enough. To my left was the sound of retching. Uncharitably I thought it might have been Vitellius trying to make room for some more pudding, but it was Valens. His cheeks were red and blotchy, flecks of vomit on his toga. By the look of disgust on Vitellius's face the mighty general had just emptied the contents of his stomach all over the emperor's feet.

With a snap of the fingers Vitellius summoned a couple of slaves who hoisted the unfortunate Valens on to his feet.

'Take him to one of the guest rooms,' he said. 'Then bring me a bowl of water and a new pair of sandals.'

'With your permission, sire, I'll take one of the spare rooms as well.'

'Of course, Severus. Looking for a bit of company, are we?' Vitellius winked knowingly.

'My dear, Consul Severus is a married man,' Galeria sniffed.

'Indeed I am,' I slurred. 'But I am also drunk, and would rather not walk across the city when there's a perfectly good bed a few moments away.'

'I'll believe you, Severus. Get to bed; let the real men enjoy the party, eh?'

'Thank you, sire. My lady,' I bowed. Soon the sounds of eager girls and revelry were but a distant echo, as I wound my way through the palace to find myself a room. Someone had thoughtfully left an empty bucket by one of the doors, and I assumed Valens was inside. Not wishing to hear Valens's supper returning, I took one of the rooms at the other end of the corridor, sending the pretty slave girl away to join the party so that I could have the double bed all to myself.

By lunchtime the next day my head had stopped spinning but the health of Vitellius's other guest had if anything got a little worse. Valens was sweating, vomiting and had spent much of the night being carried between his room and the latrine.

'It was the oysters, wasn't it?' I asked Totavalas when he came to see me.

'No, not the oysters.'

'But I saw him gag when he had one.'

'Maybe he was just unlucky. Actually it was the cake.'

'The cake? But I had some of it, so did lots of people and they must be fine, otherwise they'd be searching the kitchens for poison.'

'That's the beauty of it. I bought some information from one of Valens's household slaves, and it seems that the consul can't eat figs, ever since he was a boy. So when I took the proposed menu down to the kitchens a few days ago, I added a generous helping of figs to the cake recipe.'

'Totavalas, you're a genius.'

'I know, but it's nice to hear it from time to time.'

I smiled wearily, used by now to the Hibernian's sense of humour. 'Has Vitellius heard yet?'

'He has, but he knows he can't delay sending the army north. Primus and his legions can't be allowed to cross the Po unchallenged, so Valens has until tomorrow to recover.'

'And what if he does?'

'I doubt it. The slave told me that figs can lay the man low for almost a week.'

'And if he makes a miraculous recovery?'

'I have a reliable doctor on hand who will cut up fig skin into Valens's medicine. He won't taste the skin, but he'll react just the same.'

'Tell me again, why are you doing this? What's stopping you from selling me out and winning Vitellius's gratitude?'

He snorted. 'Do you really think Vitellius would be as good a master to me as you have been? I may not be a slave any more, but as your freedman I can work hard, put some money by and one day head home. If you fall, so do my chances of returning to my island as High King.'

I smiled at the thought. 'Totavalas, High King of Hibernia!'

'Only I wouldn't be Totavalas back home.'

'Of course; what is your name again? Your real one, I mean.'

'Tuathal,' he said. The sounds of those Celtic syllables were alien to my Roman ears.

'But here I'm Totavalas the freedman, right-hand man to a consul of Rome, and I'd like it to stay that way for at least a bit longer.'

Totavalas was right of course. He often was. Vitellius had no choice but to give me command of the army once it was clear that Valens's recovery would take more than a day or two. The gift was given grudgingly, but still Vitellius had no reason to suspect my loyalty. Nor had I given him any cause to; I was still undecided as to what I would do once I had left Rome far behind me. And it wasn't as though I was some young boy who'd been given a grown-up's job. I was thirty years old and an accomplished general, with an excellent eye for terrain though I say it myself. And choosing the right battleground can be half the battle.

Of the group of us who had ridden south together, only Pansa, Cerberus and Totavalas rode at my side the day we left the city. As praetorian prefect, Publilius had to stay behind in Rome to defend the emperor, and to defend my interests. The gods alone knew what sort of tricks Valens would get up to with me out of Rome. The other man missing was Quintus. I thought back to the days we had spent together in Gaul, training his father's army and forming the first bonds of comradeship. The other Gauls had been good men, coarse but proud men who loved their country. They lay buried on the slopes of Vesontio now, and Quintus in the rich fields of the north. They had fought for me, not for my cause. It made me uncomfortable to think where I might have ended up if it hadn't been for men like them.

We left to a fanfare of *tubae*, standards fluttering in the wind and Vitellius waving us off languidly from his imperial chariot, borrowed from his treasured Blues. His wife Galeria was there too with a chariot of her own. I heard a vicious rumour that the plan had been for them to share, but there wasn't room for them both and a second had to be found quickly for the emperor's wife.

'Long time no see,' Cerberus had said when he and Pansa found the Hibernian and me waiting at the head of the column.

'I hope you two have been enjoying yourselves in the city,' I said warmly.

'Not as much as some,' Pansa huffed. No change there then.

'You'll have to tell us what it was like to lord it over the nobles and gorge yourself at the emperor's banquets. Apparently we weren't important enough to be invited.'

'I would have gladly swapped,' I said. 'I've had my fill of banquets.'

'Oh, life is so tough,' Pansa said.

'Gentlemen,' Totavalas said courteously, 'I think the army's waiting for us to lead the way. If the emperor has to wave any more his biceps will get as big as a melon!'

Ever the diplomat, I thought. If ever he did win back his father's throne on that insignificant island of his, Hibernia would be too small for him.

'Totavalas is right. We have a rebellion to crush.' I twitched my heels against Achilles' flanks and the warhorse trotted forward. The other three rode behind me, and behind them were thirty thousand men: my army, and they would go where I led them.

Within a few days it was painfully obvious that the men were badly out of shape. Months of drinking and whoring across the taverns of Rome had softened them, gorged them, robbed them of the iron durability that had seen them through the perilous Alpine passes. I knew that, the officers knew that, but the men were convinced they were still the same legendary veterans who had defended Rome so ably from the barbarians beyond the Rhine. As for the auxiliaries, those who had survived our campaign in the north had faced the terror of plague in the Aventine. The Germans and Britons were the worst hit. We took every able-bodied man with us, but they amounted to little more than two thousand. Only two thousand out of the original twenty thousand had survived the last seven months! And we faced six legions, each five thousand strong, as well as their own auxiliaries. The only comforting thought was that like us this man Primus would have to leave men behind to guard the Danube frontier, or risk hordes of barbarians crossing the river once they heard that Rome was once again embroiled in a civil war.

It was frankly disgusting to see hardened veterans struggling after no more than a week on the march. Only when I saw one or two men collapse with exhaustion did I give the order to ease the pace. It was imperative that we reach the Po and cross it quickly if we wanted to meet the advance column of Vespasian's army in a defensible place and beat them. I had hoped to reach at least Vicetia and wait at the base of the Julian Alps for the invading army, but at the rate we were travelling we would be lucky if we beat them to the banks of the Po.

Ironically, the frostiness between Cerberus, Pansa and me began to thaw as we marched from the baking heat of Rome in summer to the cooler northern provinces. Pansa resented my success too much ever to come close to anything that resembled a friendship, and Cerberus was a dour, inscrutable character who had never quite forgiven me for the loss of practically his whole squadron of cavalry, men who had served under him and his father before him. For company I sought out the detachment from my old legion, the Twentieth Valeria Victrix, at least those who had not been recruited to join the Praetorian Guard. Some of the more grizzled veterans remembered me, and I even managed to claw back a few names from the distant past. It was almost ten years since I had led them, in a manner of speaking, to victory over Boudicca, but even the younger men had heard of my reputation.

I was reminiscing about those hard but glorious days with those who remembered them when I heard my name being called.

'General Severus? Where can I find General Severus?'

Strangely enough it was the horse I recognized, not the rider. It was a chestnut gelding from my own stables at the estate in Vicetia. But how had this rider got hold of it? I waved to grab the man's attention. The rider was red in the face; he must have been shouting my name since he reached the head of our column. But this was not a courier from Rome, but from the north.

'I'm General Severus, who are you?'

'Lucius Pollio, General. I'm one of the couriers from Vicetia.'

'Vicetia? Have Primus and his army reached the town already?'

The lad looked confused. 'I don't know about any army, sir. It's been almost a fortnight since I left home.'

'A fortnight? Changing horses it should have taken you days!'

'But I'm not with the army, General. I can't use the imperial horses for a private message.'

Now I was confused. 'But if you're not an imperial courier, who is the message from?'

'Your son, General. He lent me one of the horses from your stable, and I'm to ride it back now I've found you. Here's the message.'

He handed me a scroll from his satchel, sealed with wax but with no emblem stamped into it. The only family seal we had was the ring I wore on a chain around my neck, since my ring finger had been sliced off in Gaul.

I snatched the scroll from him and broke the seal. My eyes sped over the childish writing, then my heart clenched, the breath catching short in my body. Aulus had written because there was no one else. Salonina had died in childbirth.

XXVI

I could feel my face beginning to flush, the tears welling up inside me, but I couldn't cry, not in front of the men. Feverishly I kicked Achilles hard and dived off the road, heading for a small copse where I would be out of sight. The courier called after me but I ignored him. I had to get away from them all.

Once safely in the cover of the trees I almost fell out of the saddle, crumpling in a heap on the ground. My breath came thick and fast as I tried to take in the news. Salonina dead, and the child with her. It had been a girl, a tiny baby girl, but she had died within hours of her mother. My hands clutched at the blades of grass and I began to howl, yanking out great handfuls of the stuff in my anger and despair. I was screaming so hard that I didn't even hear the hoofbeats of the rider heading for my refuge.

In between my cries there came a voice. 'Severus, what's the matter?'

'It's Salonina,' I sobbed.

'Gods, she's not . . . ?'

I couldn't say the word, just nodded as the rest of my body shook uncontrollably.

Totavalas jumped to the ground and crouched beside me. 'Severus, I'm so sorry.'

'And I should have been there,' I moaned. 'I promised her.'

'You had to stay in the city,' he told me.

'No I didn't. I could have left Valens everything and gone home. Maybe this wouldn't have happened if I'd been there.'

'Now don't you dare blame yourself for this. These things happen, they happen all the time.'

'But why me? Why do the gods want to punish me by taking away my wife and daughter?'

'The baby died as well? You poor bastard.' The Hibernian took me in his arms and held me tight. 'How's Aulus?'

'I don't know. He wrote, but how can a boy write what he feels when his mother's just died?'

'At least he's got you, he's got his father. Both of us had to grow up without a father, remember? He's a good boy, he'll be all right.'

'On his own? I should go to him, he needs his father with him.' I broke free of Totavalas's arms and wiped away my tears.

'You're needed here, Severus,' Totavalas reminded me.

'No I'm not. Pansa and Cerberus can manage the army while I'm gone.'

'Just stop and think. Primus's army will have passed Vicetia by the time you reach the Po. How do you think you're going to sneak past a whole army?'

I stubbornly walked over to Achilles and began to check my saddlebags and make the horse ready to leave.

'You're not thinking straight. Severus, I know you're angry and upset, but you have responsibilities here. Vitellius and Vespasian, remember?'

'What have they ever done for me?' I asked, looking straight ahead at the saddle rather than the Hibernian's eyes.

'That's not the point. It's what you can do for them. You leave the army now and Vitellius will have Valens hunt you down. And you'll have nothing to show Vespasian for your efforts either. Then where will you be?'

I stood there mutely, not wanting to agree with him.

'Aulus is a strong boy, stronger than you think. He's got his father's stubbornness.'

I smiled weakly. That was true. He had his mother's eyes though, eyes that would haunt me every time I looked at them. My shoulders slumped in resignation. 'You're right, Totavalas.'

'Come on, Severus, the men will be waiting for you.'

Cerberus and Pansa were all sympathy and understanding when they heard the news. Of course they offered to look after the army for the time being if I wanted to go home, but when I told them home was Vicetia they realized that riding through enemy lines would be impossible.

If I had felt lonely before, I was even more so for the rest of that torturous march. Condolences from my fellow officers did not mean that they thought any better of me, they just treated me more carefully. I had Totavalas to confide in, but there was little more that could be said. I spent day after day riding alone at the head of the army, with no more than memories for company, and the memory that haunted me the most was that night with Domitia. I hadn't thought to ask the courier when Salonina had died, so I didn't even know if that lecherous night in Rome was before or after I had lost my wife. Not that sleeping with my friend's wife after Salonina had died would have made me feel any better about myself, but not knowing was even worse.

Every night I read and reread the letter from Aulus. Understandably he hadn't gone into any detail, only that the doctor had tried his best but had lost both the mother and the child. I didn't even know if a better doctor would have been able to prevent either of their deaths. All I knew was that my son was alone on the estate, with nobody but slaves for company.

After a few days with my thoughts, since not even Totavalas dared spend too much time with me in my black mood, my despair turned into rage. We had made a north-west turn and were heading towards the stronghold of Cremona once again, and each night Pansa had approached me with a skin bulging with wine.

'This'll help you, General. A few slugs of wine and you'll forget everything.'

I had the skinful the first night, drowning my sorrows so to speak, and regretted it in the morning. When the legate appeared outside my tent every evening for the next three days, each time with enough alcohol to make an elephant go weak at the knees, I thought of Quintus, of how he had turned to drink in an effort to numb the pain of losing his family and eventually my friendship. I had seen what the drink did to him, and I saw through Pansa's feigned friendship.

'No thank you, Pansa. I have an army to lead and I can't do that if you're pouring wine down my throat.' He wasn't going to get me out of the way that easily, however much I wanted the bloody campaign to be over so I could go home and be with my son.

The towns came and went as we marched slowly and ponderously northwards. It was only when we reached Mutina that we heard the first reports of Primus and his army. I had half expected to meet them south of the Po, but according to our information Primus had taken longer than anticipated crossing the Alps, even though it was by now late summer and the passes were clear. He had decided to bring the bolt-firing ballistae and a pair of onagers with him, and they had slowed the rebel army's progress through the narrow, twisting mountain roads. They had reached Verona, less than forty miles from Bedriacum, the place where I had seen the body of Otho with its pale skin and gash across the neck. If we marched hard we had a chance of reaching Cremona first and choosing the battleground.

Cerberus and Pansa understood their orders and had the men pick up the pace, but it was no use. The easy living in Rome had taken its toll on the army. The only thought I had to console me was the harder I marched the men, the quicker they would toughen up. On the other hand the army had to be able to fight once we found the enemy. What little loyalty I had left for Vitellius was ebbing away, but I couldn't let the men see it, or Cerberus and Pansa. The African no doubt hoped he would be rewarded with the command of a legion if we triumphed in the north, while Pansa made no attempt to hide the fact that he wanted to command the army. After all, he was a good deal older and more experienced than me, and it galled him to take orders from a jumped-up young senator, even if I had earned my position and more besides.

It was little surprise then that when at last we reached the Po we found the bridge to Cremona in enemy hands. But it wasn't another Thermopylae that was waiting for us, but a single horseman. He was in full armour and wore the cloak of a junior tribune with the tell-tale purple stripe. He also carried an olive branch, waving it high above his head to show he came in peace.

'I bring a message from General Primus,' he hollered. 'Is General Severus there?'

'Here I am,' I called back. The tribune caught sight of me and had his horse walk steadily forward. My legionaries blocked his path, but the tribune still advanced. He had a proper set of balls on him, this one, looking down at the soldiers and waiting for them to let him through. One man confronted by thirty thousand, and grudgingly the men gave way.

He clutched his olive branch tightly. 'My message is for you and your senior officers, General,' he said.

'Very well,' I said testily. Cerberus and Pansa were fetched at the double, and I led the messenger somewhere where we wouldn't be overheard. While we waited, I studied the officer's face closely. Though it was obscured by his helmet, the man looked a year or two younger than me, despite his delicately trimmed beard; young, but surely a bit old to be a junior tribune still?

'You're making a mistake, General,' Cerberus said. 'No good can come of hearing any message Primus has for us.'

'Even if it means we could save thousands of lives?' the messenger asked.

Pansa chuckled grimly. 'That's not the Primus I know. He's only sent you to try to sow seeds of doubt in our minds. He's a conniving little weasel.'

'I may have a more slender figure than you, Pansa, but I object to the other two words.' The tribune took off his helmet, and my second in command's eyes bulged.

'Primus?'

'Got it in one, Pansa. You'll forgive the deception, General, but somehow I doubt your men would have let me pass if they'd known I wasn't just a humble tribune.'

I marvelled at the courage of the man, facing an enemy army alone and disguised just to meet me and my officers.

'How do you know I'm not going to have my men put you in chains and send you to Rome on a charge of treason?' I asked him.

'Because I came here under a truce, and you're an officer and a nobleman. I'm safer in the middle of your army than I would be on, say, the Parthian front. Besides, not so long ago you three were the rebels, and I was a loyal servant of Emperor Galba.'

'He has a point,' Cerberus said reluctantly.

'And your message is that we should surrender and avoid un-necessary bloodshed?' I guessed.

'In a nutshell, yes. I wasn't at Bedriacum, but I gather it was bloody. Even if you do beat me, Vespasian is no more than two months behind me with an even larger army. He asks that you join him, for the good of Rome.'

'And suppose we decide that Rome is best served with our man as emperor?' Cerberus asked.

'Then I will have to fight you, and I shall win,' he said matter-of-factly, as though only a madman would doubt the outcome of a battle.

'Your army's no larger than ours,' Pansa said, 'and we've got the veterans from Britannia and the Rhine. What have you got?'

'Now that would be telling, wouldn't it?'

Pansa shrugged. 'It was worth a try.'

'Suppose I were to make you the same offer? Complete amnesty, you take your men back over the Alps and we go back to Rome.' It was as generous an offer as he had made to me.

'I'd say thank you, but I've already sworn my allegiance to Vespasian, and so have my men.'

'Then we have nothing more to discuss,' Cerberus said flatly.

'You're sure, General?' Primus asked me. 'I can't force you, but I would ask you one last question.'

'And that is?'

'Vespasian is a decent general, and more importantly a decent man. What makes Vitellius so special that you'd risk your men's lives for him?'

'Pansa, escort Legate Primus back to the bridge. See that he gets across it unharmed.'

Primus was surprised, but nevertheless he saluted before heading back where he came from, Pansa accompanying him.

Cerberus watched too. 'A brave man,' he observed. 'I think his message was more for the men than it was for us. If the rankers go into battle knowing they might be offered amnesty at the end of it, they won't fight half as well.'

I sighed. Not because of Cerberus' words but because I recognized something of my old self in Primus. Young, ambitious, a man who'd chanced his arm and was on the point of taking the purple with his sword. Would Primus feel as old and tired in two years' time? I asked myself.

'Have the men cross the bridge and make camp. I want to speak to them this evening.'

'Of course, General.'

'You're going to do it then?' Totavalas asked while the men were cooking their suppers.

'I think so.'

'You think so? If it was me going out in front of thousands of bloodthirsty soldiers I'd want to be pretty damn sure I knew what I was doing. Either you're for Vitellius or you're for Vespasian.'

'It's not as simple as that.'

'Gods, but it is! You've got to make a choice, and you can't do it half-arsed otherwise you'll piss off both of them and help neither.'

'Thank you, Totavalas, your cheery confidence is exactly what I need right now.'

The freedman said nothing for a while, just tut-tutting over the state I'd let my armour get into. There had been a flash storm the day before, and I hadn't bothered to dry the joints in my helmet properly, so I had to be careful of rust.

'What does your gut tell you then?'

'My gut tells me I should hate Vespasian for starting all this. We've had three emperors since Nero, three for Hades' sake, and now some low-born upstart decides to plunge us all into this madness again. Just as everything was turning out well for me.'

'And Vitellius? You've known all along there were better men for the purple. And they say this Vespasian is a competent administrator. He would be a better choice for you and for Rome.'

'And which of the two is more important to me, do you think?' I said in what I thought was a sarcastic tone.

Totavalas reddened slightly. 'Well, you do have a talent for coming out on top.'

I was taken aback. I had only been pretending that I wanted an answer, but Totavalas had as good as told me that I was an opportunist vulture who put himself before his city. The Hibernian realized his mistake.

'Severus, I'm so sorry. I didn't mean—'

'Get out,' I said, quietly and coldly.

'But—'

'Out, out, out, OUT!' I screamed, raising my hand as if to strike. Totavalas fled, leaving me alone in my tent. Dejectedly, I collapsed on to my cot. Totavalas's words still echoed in my head. If that's what my own loyal freedman thought of me, how did everyone else see me? Salonina would have comforted me, she would have said that I had always acted for the good of Rome. Betraying Nero for Galba was no crime, it had been a duty to spare Rome from the tyrant. And Galba had been no revelation either once he reached the throne. I'd had such hopes for life under Vitellius, keeping the snake Valens at bay and helping the glutton to rule his empire. But I had managed to drive away nearly everyone who had loved or cared for me. I had deceived myself into thinking that I was ambitious for Rome, rather than for myself. Salonina knew this, I think. Had I deceived others? There was only one way to find out.

I put on my helmet, stiff cheek-pieces and all, brushed the last traces of mud from my cloak, put my shoulders back and drew myself up to my full height. I had to look at my impressive best. From all over the camp the men were filing out of their tents and cookhouses. There was already a crowd packed around the makeshift platform on the parade square. Fingers pointed as the men saw me coming, others murmuring excitedly.

With two quick steps I was on the platform, surrounded on all sides by my army. There were too many men really, so that I had to turn round from time to time to let my voice carry to all corners of the crowd.

'Soldiers of Rome,' I called out, 'a few miles away stands the army of Vespasian. The first army, the advance guard.'

Cries of 'rebels' and 'traitors' were quashed as I raised my hands for silence.

'Do not call them traitors. They are ordinary men like you

and me. Two seasons ago the Senate and the armies of Galba and Otho would have branded us the same. And look at you now, the favoured soldiers of Emperor Vitellius Germanicus.'

'Germanicus, Germanicus,' they chanted.

'Today I have to make a choice,' I told them. 'A choice between you and the emperor. Valens and I led fifty thousand men from Germania to this very spot, to Cremona. You all fought like lions to win Vitellius his throne, and now the emperor is asking you to fight again. Now we are thirty thousand, softened from the pleasures of Rome. And to the east Primus and his army are waiting. They have chosen the battlefield, no doubt they've filled in the ditches on their side and dug traps on ours. They have the artillery, we had no time to bring our own. This is my choice, men. If I lead you into battle tomorrow, I am not sure we can win.'

The men's faces turned from puzzlement to dismay. No general in all Rome's history had spoken to his army this way, and maybe no general ever will again.

'I have seen many good men die over the years, from our battles against Boudicca,' I gestured at the men from Britannia to make my point, 'in the fields of Gaul against Vindex, in the Alps and here in Italia itself. And for what? To put noble after noble on the throne, that is all. Has Vitellius made your lives better? Ask yourselves, why did Vitellius not put you in the Praetorian Guard? Why do those chosen few get the rewards that you all fought for?'

'Vitellius made you consul!' a voice shouted accusingly. Many of the men muttered their agreement.

'It's true, I am a consul. Valens and I deserved nothing less for the sacrifices we made to give him his throne. But Valens is not here, he doesn't see what I see: a rebel army that has the advantages of numbers, fresh legs, artillery and open ground. It's because I care more for your lives than Vitellius's crown that I believe we should take matters into our own hands. Today we can save Rome from the horrors of another civil war, we can make peace with our comrades from the east and let Vitellius fight for the throne himself. What do you say?'

I looked at the men, my arms spread wide appealingly. I searched the crowd for friendly faces, but there were none. This was Valens's army, not mine. Most of the men I had led over the Alps were now praetorians in Rome with Publilius. A thousand were left from my own legion, the Fourth, and the men from Britannia knew me by reputation at least. But they were a drop in the ocean compared to the rest of the army. Pansa, at the head of his men, stepped forward. He at least knew I talked sense. He clambered on to the platform and stood beside me.

'Legionaries,' he cried, 'I think we've heard enough from this traitor. What say we send him back to Rome in chains?'

Before I could react, Pansa had punched me square in the jaw. I staggered, the world spinning round me. My vision was blurred but I still heard the roars of approval from the men, some of whom bounded up to join in assaulting their general. I felt the nailheads on their sandals punch into my body. Pansa stood above me. I saw the pommel of a sword scything down and I fell into darkness.

The next thing I was aware of was the sound of artillery, the roar and crackle as huge fireballs crashed into their targets. Groggily, I tried to open my eyes. One was sealed shut, dried blood caked around my eyelid, and the other was badly swollen. Then I felt the pain from my temple where someone had struck me and knocked me out. I tried to raise my hand and check the damage, but my arm wouldn't move. Instead I became aware of the cold links of iron around my body and a crushing pressure on my chest and shoulders. The chains chinked as I struggled, and my whole body began to sway. I looked down and screamed. The ground was far, far below me, more than thirty feet. I was swinging like a pendulum, suspended by a solitary chain from the walls of the camp!

I tried shouting for help, though it hurt my damaged ribs. But no one came. It was pitch dark, but flashes of orange streaked my vision. Was it dawn? Then the sound of another explosion carried across the fields. The fool Pansa must have led the army to battle as soon as I had been beaten unconscious and left to dangle so I could watch the fight.

Only the battle wasn't going well. Far away I could make out an orderly line of red, occasionally illuminated by fireballs arcing into the sky, and another line, ragged and chaotic, dashing itself like a wave upon a rock. I drifted in and out of consciousness. The pressure on my shoulders woke me sporadically, and it hurt just to move my legs in their tight chains. Pins and needles that felt more like searing hot daggers being plunged into my calves and thighs.

After a while I noticed that the onagers had ceased firing, the crashes replaced by the clattering and jangling of armour. My army was in full retreat. My one eye could just make out groups of men in the fields, scattering in all directions as Primus's army marched ominously and relentlessly forward. Some of my men were heading for the relative safety of the far bank of the river, while others ran towards Cremona. Only one small group headed back to camp, everyone else thinking that it was the first place the victors would look for survivors, and that the artillery would make short work of the wooden walls.

The group looked about the size of a century. Many of them were wounded and the unscathed men helped prop up or drag those unable to run. As they neared the camp, I heard one of the men shout:

'Look, it's the rat who wanted to sell us out!'

'Let's see how he likes a spear in the guts,' another suggested.

'Leave off, a spear won't do much against those chains.'

'I could aim for his head?' The others laughed appreciatively.

'All right, smart-arse, five sestercii says you miss.'

'You're on,' the man said. He took careful aim with his *pilum*. I was petrified; there was nothing I could do if his throw was straight and true.

There was an almighty thwack, and the soldier crumpled to his feet. Behind him, clutching his hefty vine rod, stood a centurion. 'You don't kill an officer,' he spat at his men, 'even if you think he's a traitor. Now get inside and find what you can. I want to be the other side of the river sharpish.'

The centurion kicked at the man he had felled, and the soldier slowly got to his feet.

I tried to thank the centurion for saving my life. The man looked up at me.

'You don't remember me, do you?'

I muttered something about my eye, and it being too dark to see.

'Centurion Gaius Tadius of the Twentieth Valeria Victrix, that's me. We fought together in Britannia.' It all came flooding back: an army about to break, my horse taking fright and carrying me to the heart of the battle, my legion forming up behind me in a wedge as we counter-attacked, scything through the Britons, and a young legionary who had fought at my side. We had been heroes, he and I.

'You don't deserve to die. I hope you live a long life, so you can see what you've become.' The centurion spat distastefully on to the road, then went into the camp to make sure his men were all right.

Epilogue

They're all dead now, almost everyone except me. Pansa and Cerberus died that night. Valens recovered from his daily dose of figs and led the praetorians and the remnants of my army against Primus to try to save Vitellius's throne. He was captured and had his head cut off to prove to our men that their general was dead and that resistance was futile. Rome descended into chaos and the mob turned on Vitellius, Publilius and the rest, but not before the emperor had Vespasian's brother Sabinus killed in an act of petty vengeance.

Me? Primus had his men lower me down and release me from my chains. I was treated with mock honours for making a present of my army to Vespasian, and congratulated for finding the best vantage point for the battle. Vespasian has been emperor for ten years now, ten long years of being spat at in the street and being called a traitor to my face. Vespasian revelled in being seen as a man of mercy. With his brother dead there was no one to vouch for the fact that I had changed sides long before the battle at Cremona. Nonetheless I was allowed to remain a senator, on the condition that I was given a new name: Aulus Caecina Alienus. Caecina the stranger, the outcast, the man without a friend in the world.

Totavalas lived with me in Rome. My son Aulus wanted nothing to do with me, preferring instead to stay in Vicetia and run the estate. He would visit me once a year, reciting the annual profits and losses, and that was it. I spent my days mostly whoring and drinking, a political career forever closed to me. When sober, I nursed thoughts of revenge against Vespasian for shattering my golden dreams of ruling Rome under Vitellius. I even let others in on my plotting, other malcontents with grudges against Vespasian and his court.

Agricola, on the other hand, flourished under the new emperor. I often thought of telling him that I had slept with his wife, just to see the look on his face, but I could never bring myself to do it. He married his daughter to the son of old Tacitus, the fusty man who had ridden with me across Hispania to hear Galba's plots and stratagems, over a decade ago now. Vespasian even gave Agricola the governorship of Britannia, with a full mandate to conquer the whole island. Totavalas wistfully said he would have liked to go with my old friend. After all, as the freedman of the most loathed man in Rome there were precious few opportunities for him in the city.

This afternoon I did something I haven't done in years: I paid a social call. Hooded and cloaked, I went to Agricola's house and asked the janitor to let me in. On hearing the name the slave bolted the door shut, but I pleaded with him to at least bring Agricola to the door.

'What do you want?' my old friend said tersely, looking down at me through the large peephole. Through it I could see most of my friend's face; he had hardly aged a day.

'A moment of your time, nothing more. What I have to say can't be said in the street.'

'All right, if you must,' he said.

The door was opened, and I was ushered into a spartan-looking atrium.

'How's Domitia?' I asked politely, once I was sure we were alone.

'Alienus,' he said, relishing the use of my new name, 'you didn't come here to talk about my wife.'

I smiled. Even now I wanted to tell him, but I controlled myself.

'I know what you must think of me, Agricola, I know what all Rome thinks of me. But I have a son. He's the last of his line and he's wasting the best years of his life alone on the estate.'

'What do you want me to do about it?'

'You could take him with you to Britannia.'

He snorted. 'And why would I want to do that?'

'He's a good boy. Aulus is honest, intelligent, he could be so much more than a simple farmer. No one will take him because of who his father is.'

'And you thought I might take him for old times' sake?' Agricola said sceptically.

'He was good enough to be your son-in-law once,' I reminded him.

'Not any more he isn't.'

'But it's me you don't want to be associated with, not Aulus.' I paused, convincing myself to make this one last plea. 'If you take Aulus as a tribune, I can guarantee that Vespasian will be in your debt for ever.'

'How?'

'There's a plot to assassinate him tonight. You promise to take Aulus, and I'll give you all the information I have. Names, numbers, where and when, everything.'

'And how did you get this information?'

'I'm one of the conspirators, Agricola.'

The enormity of what I was saying finally dawned upon my old friend. If he accepted and the plot was foiled, I would be executed as a traitor.

344

'My son is all I've got left. I want him to carve out a future for himself, away from Rome. Britannia can give him a fresh start.'

I was hastily shown out of the house, told to expect a package if he agreed.

The sun is beginning to set. The conspirators are moving into position. Agricola's present lies here on the desk next to these memoirs of mine: a plain, old-fashioned dagger from a plain, old-fashioned general. I have reached the final page of these memoirs, dear reader. I hope there is someone to read these memories of a lonely soldier. Totavalas will take them with him for safe keeping. Within a few months he'll be that much closer to his dream of returning to Hibernia. But my story ends here. I go to meet my friends in Hades now. I hope they'll forgive me.

Historical Note

Aulus Caecina Alienus, as I can finally call him, has taken me by the hand and guided me through one of the most fascinating and crucial periods in Rome's imperial history. Mention Rome and, for many, the first word that springs to mind is Caesar. Others may think of Romulus and Remus, Hannibal (interestingly, the names of the men who took on Carthage and won, like Fabius Maximus Cunctator and Scipio Africanus, don't have quite the same enduring appeal), mighty Cicero and the fall of the republic. However, most people's knowledge of Roman history seems to end with the death of Nero.

Much like the war fought between Julius Caesar and Pompey, or between Octavian and Mark Anthony, the civil war of AD 69 had huge repercussions for the way in which Rome was ruled. At the fall of the Republic, the House of Caesar was triumphant; but at the fall of Nero, no one knew what would follow. Nero's reign had suffocated the talents of the imperial aristocracy – those families whose stars had risen while the mighty dynasties of previous centuries had crumbled – leaving little room for the ambition of men like Caecina.

But the ascendance to the throne of four men within one year, none of whom had any blood connection to the ruling family, changed the very essence of what it meant to be a Caesar. Over the centuries, new dynasties would come and go as emperors tried to cement their families' power, but AD 69 destroyed the concept that an emperor had to be of imperial blood and set a dangerous precedent in centuries to come: able generals could try to take the throne by force.

Unlike the setting for *The Last Caesar* – the events of AD 68 – the documented evidence becomes much more detailed and wide-ranging for The Year of the Four Emperors itself, and it is these events which have driven the narrative of *The Sword and the Throne*. The inner historian in me is satisfied, but the storyteller less so. While the vast majority of characters in this novel are real historical figures, there is one liberty that I have had to take for reasons of plot. It is true that Gnaeus Julius Agricola's mother was killed in a raid by Otho's navy, but I have given him far more influence over events than is supported by the facts. As a friend of Caecina and a one-time comrade of General Paulinus, Agricola seemed to be the ideal candidate to dupe Caecina into the false ambush at Ad Castores. It is more likely, though, that Agricola stayed with the Senate in Rome, before eventually siding with Vespasian and coming to prominence through his exploits in Britain.

As for the march through the Alps, Salonina's purple dress, the use of gladiators at Placentia, Otho's defeat at Bedriacum and subsequent suicide: these are all true. The only thing we cannot know is the real motivation of Caecina to turn serial traitor. Tacitus, writing in the Flavian period, paints him as a man with 'boundless ambition', as a man with few scruples and eyes only for power. Placed as he is at the centre of the events of AD 68–9, I thought him the ideal narrator. I had no doubt, too, that by the time Vespasian's forces were nearing Italy he was a heartless, power-driven man. It was his journey I wanted to follow, watching how an intelligent, brave young warrior and aspiring politician could be corrupted. Corrupted not by others, but by the constant opportunities he was given to gain or maintain power. Aulus Caecina Severus had an extraordinary knack of being able to pick the winning side in the political and military contests of AD 68–69, but, as Tacitus remarks, in the end 'he could be loyal to no one'. He was executed when his plot to assassinate Vespasian failed in AD 79. The memoirs are safe with his fictional son Aulus and with Totavalas, who is based on the mythological prince Tuathal Techtmar. Maybe one day we shall hear their story . . .

Timeline

AD 14 – Death of Augustus. Imperator, Princeps and Pater Patriae, Augustus cloaks himself in republican imagery while establishing the dynasty that will rule Rome. He is succeeded by his stepson, Tiberius.

AD 37 – Death of Tiberius. Vilified for the rise of treason trials and unleashing the ambitious Sejanus upon Rome, he retreats to Capri, bitter that the throne he had coveted for so long has given him no enjoyment. He chooses Caligula as his heir, allegedly so that his own reign will be remembered favourably in comparison.

AD 41 – Caligula's reign is short and savage. He declares himself a god, is thought to have had an incestuous relationship with his sisters and displays a flagrant disregard for the Senate. He is assassinated by a group of officers. There are few members of the Julio-Claudian dynasty left, but the Praetorian Guard find Caligula's uncle, the limping, twitching and stammering Claudius, and declare him emperor.

AD 54 – Death of Claudius. He is succeeded by his stepson Lucius Domitius Ahenobarbus, who on his adoption as Claudius's son takes the name Nero. He ascends the throne aged seventeen. Britannicus, Claudius's only son, dies a few months later in mysterious circumstances.

AD 58 – Nero's mother, Agrippina, comes to regret helping her son to the throne. Over the course of three years he strips her of her power and honours, expels her from the imperial palace, and finally has her murdered.

AD 60–1 – Boudicca rebels against Rome. Finally defeated at the Battle of Watling Street by Suetonius Paulinus.

AD 64 – Nero 'fiddled while Rome burned'. The Great Fire of Rome: Nero blames and persecutes the Christians, then builds a new Golden Palace on the area cleared by the fire.

AD 65 – Gaius Calpurnius Piso leads a conspiracy to overthrow the emperor, because of his lack of respect for the Senate and his increasingly despotic rule. The conspiracy is betrayed and the plotters are executed, including Nero's old tutor, the philosopher Seneca.

AD 67 – Nero orders his most successful general, Domitius Corbulo, to commit suicide.

AD 68 – Aulus Caecina Severus is posted to southern Spain as the new quaestor. He is roped into the Galban conspiracy to overthrow Nero, and is dispatched to Gaul to co-ordinate the Vindex Rebellion. The rebellion ends disastrously as the legions on the Rhine crush the Gauls at the Battle of Vesontio. Caecina Severus is given command of one of these legions, the Fourth Macedonica, by Galba so that he may keep a watchful eye and defend the new emperor's interests. The Rhine legions are not happy. They want their own man as Emperor, and their hopes settle on the unlikely figure of Aulus Vitellius, their new governor.

AD 69 – New Year's Day. Ordered by Galba to relinquish his command and face charges of embezzlement in Rome, Caecina Severus incites his legions to mutiny against the emperor who has betrayed him.

Henry Venmore-Rowland was born and bred in rural Suffolk. Aside from the occasional family holiday, often to Italy, his only means of travel and adventure was through the pages of historical fiction. His fascination with military and political history, the kings and battles approach, somehow got him into Oxford to read Ancient & Modern History at St John's College. After dedicating so much time to reading grand tales of epic wars and political intrigue, he was inspired to write his first novel, the acclaimed *The Last Caesar*. He lives in London.